What the reviewers are saying...

'Well-drawn, believable characters combined with a storyline to keep you turning the page'
Woman

'The author is one to watch'
Sun

'A riveting read is just what this is in more ways than one'
Northern Echo

'Researched within an inch of its life; the novel is enjoyably entertaining. A perfect way to spend hours, wrapped up in the characters' lives'
Frost

'We're huge fans of Nancy's Shipyard Girls saga, and this is as emotional and gripping as the rest'
Take a Break

'Stirring and heartfelt storytelling'
Peterborough Evening Telegraph

'Emotional and gripping'
My Weekly

'A truly heart-warming saga of the women of the shipyard. Would definitely recommend if you love your wartime sagas!'
Stardust Book Reviews

'My series of the year! I have read all the books within the series this year and they just keep getting better and better. A superb saga series 5*'
Anne Bonny Book Blog

'Nancy Revell has created a fantastic saga that could literally have fallen from the TV. As a reader you feel like you are right there watching all the action take place'
Chellsandbooks

Christmas with the Shipyard Girls
Nancy Revell

arrow books

13 5 7 9 10 8 6 4 2

Arrow Books
20 Vauxhall Bridge Road
London SW1V 2SA

Arrow Books is part of the Penguin Random House group
of companies whose addresses can be found at
global.penguinrandomhouse.com

Penguin
Random House
UK

First published in Great Britain by Arrow Books in 2019

www.penguin.co.uk

A CIP catalogue record for this book is available
from the British Library

ISBN 9781787460850

Typeset in 10.75/13.5 pt Palatino
by Integra Software Services Pvt. Ltd, Pondicherry

Printed and bound in Great Britain by Clays Ltd, Elcograf S.p.A.

To Cassandra Di Bello, the best editor
an author could wish for.

Acknowledgements

A huge thank you to Suzanne Brown, Soroptimist International Sunderland, Lowri Bond, Project Manager at Igloo Regeneration, Kevin Johnson, Principal Landscape Architect at Sunderland City Council and Artist Rosanne Robertson, for all your determination and enthusiasm to make the commemoration to the real shipyard women a reality.

To the Sunderland Antiquarian Society, especially Linda King, Norm Kirtlan and Philip Curtis, for their help with research and for the use of the wonderful photograph on the cover of *Christmas with the Shipyard Girls*.

To Ian Mole for setting up The Official Shipyard Girls Tour, Kathleen Tuddenham for her help with research, Margaret Morgan for her transcription of taped interviews of women's experiences on the Homefront during WW2.

Thank you also to all the lovely staff at Fulwell Post Office, in particular postmaster John Wilson and Liz Skelton, Waterstones in Sunderland, researcher Meg Hartford, Jackie Caffrey, of Nostalgic Memories of Sunderland in Writing, Beverley Ann Hopper, of The Book Lovers, journalist Katy Wheeler at the *Sunderland Echo*, Stephen McCabe and all the team at Sun FM, and Lisa Shaw and her fantastic producer Jane Downs at BBC Newcastle.

Thank you 'Team Nancy' at Arrow, publishing director Emily Griffin, editor Cassandra Di Bello, my wonderful literary agent Diana Beaumont, and TV agent Leah Middleton, for all your ongoing hard work, experience and expertise.

And, of course, to my mum Audrey, dad Syd, hubby Paul, and my 'little' girl, Rosie.

Thank you all.

'And now these three remain: faith, hope and love. But the greatest of these is love.'
1 Corinthians 13:13

Prologue

Gibraltar

21 June 1942

Tommy looked up at the darkening sky. Its palette of yellow and orange mixed with an array of blues reminded him of the huge oil paintings that Arthur had taken him to see as a child in the town's museum. His grandda had told him that a person could learn a lot about the world simply by looking at these depictions of days gone by, but all Tommy had wanted to do was run out of the musty-smelling exhibition room and look up at the *real* skies and stare out at the *real* sea.

'Here you are.' A woman's soft voice drew his eyes away from the oil-painted sky. 'Let's get this around you.'

Tommy looked at the pretty face of the nurse as she bent over his stretcher and tucked a blanket tightly around his body. She nearly lost her balance a few times as the lifeboat bobbed about in the choppy waters.

'Help's on its way,' she reassured. Tommy felt her palm on his forehead. Her hands were icy cold, cooling his own hot brow.

'You're cold,' Tommy mumbled.

The nurse smiled but didn't say anything. Tommy looked at her familiar white pinafore emblazoned with the distinctive emblem of the Red Cross and he suddenly realised that he didn't know her name. Hers was the only face he had

1

seen during his spells of consciousness. He'd heard the living and the dying since he'd been hauled on board the hospital ship, but hers was the only face he'd seen, or at least remembered.

Turning his head to the side, Tommy looked out at the Atlantic Ocean, which was now covered in a layer of black oil from the ship's fractured fuel tank. He could just make out the ship itself, its white flank slowly disappearing beneath the surface.

'Here! Over here!'

Tommy felt the lifeboat sway as two dark figures got to their feet and started shouting and waving their hands. He craned his neck.

'See, I told you.' The nurse put her cold hand on his forehead again before easing a thermometer into his mouth. 'They've come to get us.' Tommy heard the Yorkshire Dales in her accent.

There was lots of movement, shouts, cries of jubilation as a ship's grey bow ploughed towards them, a sense of euphoria spreading through the packed lifeboat as salvation approached.

Tommy watched as the nurse took the thermometer out of his mouth and looked at it. Her face was sombre.

'And not a moment too soon,' she muttered, grabbing the side of the boat, unsteadied by the swell created by the approach of their rescuers.

'Come on.' She put her arm around Tommy's shoulders and helped him to sit up. 'I want you to be one of the first off.'

Tommy's body was shaking but he didn't feel at all cold.

'Listen!' a man's voice next to him suddenly shouted out.

The excitement died down.

And that's when they all heard it – an ominous drone above them.

Looking up, they saw a lone bomber thudding its way across the sky. Its target was obvious. There were no ships within sight other than the one coming to their rescue.

'Please, God, no!'

Tommy saw panic and alarm on the young nurse's face as she made the sign of the cross.

Turning his vision back to the sky's oil-painted canvas, he could just about make out the bomber's metal under-belly releasing its innards and the outline of three giant-sized bullets as they careered through the air, see-sawing awkwardly before smashing into the sea. Three white mountains of frothing, angry seawater erupted one after the other, causing Tommy's world to suddenly turn upside down. Air was replaced by water. The burning heat that had been consuming his body for weeks now, extinguished in an instant.

A familiar quietness followed. It was the sound of silence that Tommy knew well. An instinctive feeling of relief surged through him – he was where he belonged.

His body had stopped shaking and his arms and legs felt strong and fluid as they stretched out and swam back up to the surface.

Breathing in air, he looked around and saw the upturned lifeboat. Two men had managed to climb on top and were trying to pull someone out of the water. His vision blurred as another angry wave washed over him.

Blinking, he caught sight of the nurse. She was gasping for air. Tommy could see her arms were trying to keep her afloat, but her clothes, like deadweights, were dragging her under.

Tommy started swimming, punching through the surface of the sea to get to her. She disappeared under the water again, then re-emerged, coughing and gulping for air.

3

He had to get to her.

He powered through the water. His arms pulled his body forward while his legs kicked furiously.

He was nearly there.

Just a few more strokes and he'd be able to grab her.

Another wave pushed him back, but only for a second.

Coming up for air, he scanned the surface of the turbulent waters but he couldn't see her. He swung his head around, frantically treading water, but she was nowhere.

Taking a huge gulp of air, Tommy upended his body, diving underneath the waves and back into the quiet, watery underworld.

Through stinging, blurred eyes he spotted her.

You can't have her! his whole being screamed as though the sea was his foe.

Swimming, pulling water back with every ounce of energy he possessed, Tommy desperately tried to reach her.

Her eyes widened at the sight of him. Tommy saw the look of desperation as she reached out to him with splayed hands.

No!

He saw her mouth open and knew what she was about to do.

Don't breathe!

But it was too late.

Her mouth formed an oval shape, her body jerked just once before a mass of bubbles started streaming around her young, pretty face.

She was gasping silently, sucking in water instead of air, then her body began convulsing.

Please, God! No!

Tommy strained every muscle as he tried to grab her. Frantically, his arms dug deep into the darkening waters, dragging himself down after her.

But then the writhing stopped and her body became still.

Tommy saw the red cross on her white uniform fluttering like a flag in a gentle breeze.

Still he tried to reach her, but her body was now sinking. Tommy swam deeper, snatching at water, refusing to give up.

Suddenly the nurse's head tilted upwards – her brown hair swirling about her face like Medusa – her eyes dead.

It was too late.

Life had left her.

And then Tommy's own world went black.

When Tommy was hauled into the wooden lifeboat, spewing seawater and retching death from his lungs, he looked at his rescuers but the only face he could see was that of the nurse.

This would be the case for many weeks; whether in a sweat-soaked semi-consciousness or in a deep, medicated slumber, the Red Cross nurse stayed with him.

As the ship he was on rocked its way across the Atlantic, so did his mind similarly crash back and forth.

Like the pull of a strong current, he would often find himself sucked back to memories of his former life, encased in his diver's suit and twelve-bolt helmet, immersed in the murky waters of the River Wear.

Occasionally, as though elevated by strong winds and high waves, his mind's eye would surge upwards, escaping reality and catapulting itself into a future devoid of warmongering and death. It was then he would see a vision of Polly's smiling face, and he would imagine their life together. He clung to that image, but it was never long before it began to fade and in its place, like an image in a photographer's developing tray, the grey, lifeless face of the Red Cross nurse would slowly emerge.

The weeks spent crossing the Atlantic passed in a vague, dream-like haze. Tommy heard snatches of conversations. Always about either love or war. Always in a constant cloud of cigarette smoke.

He heard medics coming and going, soldiers near him either vomiting with seasickness or crying out in a delirium of agony. Occasionally someone was carried out on a stretcher and did not return.

As the ship crossed the seas, the stench of death seemed to grow increasingly odorous and might well have ended up suffocating them all had they not reached their homeland when they did.

Then the undulating wash of the Atlantic was replaced by the jarring feel of the army first-aid truck on terra firma.

On the second day of October, Tommy was stretchered out of the makeshift ambulance and into a building he guessed, by the smell of antiseptic and the blur of white coats, was a hospital.

'Have we a next of kin for this one?'

As he was wheeled along a narrow, windowless corridor, Tommy heard the polished tones of an educated man.

'I'm afraid not, Dr Parker. We don't even have a name yet.'

The front of the trolley buffeted open a pair of swing doors.

'Over here, please!' This time it was a woman's voice. She sounded old and stern.

Tommy managed to open his eyes.

'Can you tell us your name?' Dr Parker was bent over him.

As the two men manoeuvred him on to the bed, Tommy tried to speak.

Tommy! Tommy Watts! The words were as clear as day in his mind, but they seemed to lose their way before reaching his mouth.

Instead he listened as the familiar broad Scottish accent of the driver explained that any identification he might have had was now likely lying on the bottom of the Atlantic.

'We only knew to bring him here 'cos one of the lads heard him shouting in his sleep. Recognised the accent straight off.'

'Well, at least he's home.' Dr Parker's voice became distant as he moved on to the next patient.

If the doctor had turned around, he would have seen the beginnings of a smile on the face of the patient with no name.

He'd made it.

He was home.

Chapter One

The Ryhope Emergency Hospital, Ryhope Village, County Durham

Friday 16 October 1942

Tommy felt the warmth of a kiss.

Soft lips were being pressed against his own. He believed it to be a wonderful dream. One he'd be happy to remain in for eternity.

And then he felt a fluttering of whispered words in his ear.

'I love you, Tommy Watts.'

And something told him this wasn't a dream.

Wake up! Wake up!

He forced his mind to pull itself forward, to drag itself out of the dark, cloying slumber that had seemed to encase him for so long.

He forced his eyes to open for the briefest of moments.

Could it be? Please, don't let this be some cruel trick of the mind!

'Is that my Pol?'

His words were barely audible, as though part of him did not dare to ask, knowing the madness that would ensue if what he believed was not true.

'It is.'

He heard the words and the tears that were being choked back; felt a hand on his own, squeezing him gently. It took

9

all his strength to reach over and feel the hand that was holding his. It was real.

'It *is*,' he managed to say, a smile stretching across his face. 'It's my Pol!'

He managed to keep his eyes open for a few seconds, drinking in the face of the woman he loved.

'I thought I'd never see you again,' he mumbled.

'I didn't think I was going to see you again either,' the soft, lilting voice of his beloved said back to him.

He was losing the battle to stay awake.

He had to know.

'Do you still want to be my wife?'

He couldn't keep his eyes open any longer, but he felt her warm lips once again on his own.

'Of course I do.'

He felt her breath and heard her whispered words, her face gently pressing against his own.

It wasn't until just after midnight that Tommy woke again.

'Pol? Polly? Is that you?' Tommy turned his head to the side, forcing his eyes wide to see the best he could through the darkness.

For a second, he thought he saw the face of the Red Cross nurse, but then he felt a soft, warm hand take hold of his own.

He tried desperately to keep his eyes open, but it was a losing battle.

'Yes, Tommy, it's me ... I'm here,' Polly whispered, her face appearing through the darkness as she leaned forward. 'Don't you worry, I'm not going anywhere,' she reassured him, pushing a straggle of thick, curly hair behind her ear.

The ward was in darkness, save for a little night light on the nurses' station by the heavy swing doors. The matron was sitting bolt upright, her hands clasped in her lap.

You'd have thought she was wide awake, were it not for her gentle snoring.

'Polly?' Tommy's voice was croaky. 'Can yer come closer, so I can see yer properly?'

Polly got up from her chair and carefully perched herself on the side of the bed. She put the palm of her hand on his brow. It was still hot.

Feeling her touch, Tommy closed his eyes. Tears began to roll slowly down his face.

Cupping his face in both hands, Polly kissed him.

Tommy's eyes fluttered open and he kissed her back.

'I can't believe you're here,' he mumbled. 'Can't believe I'm here with you.'

He was staring at Polly, his hazel eyes still doubtful.

'It *is* you, isn't it, Pol?'

'Of course it's me,' she whispered into his ear. She could feel tears welling up in her own eyes. 'Who else would be sat here in dirty overalls, looking like they'd been dragged through a hedge backwards?'

Tommy closed his eyes again and smiled.

'That's my Pol,' he mumbled, his voice becoming slurred and sleepy. 'Building ships to win the war.' He recited the words as though he had said them many times over, which he had. He'd never tired of boasting about his sweetheart back home.

Polly kissed him gently again and looked down at the man she loved. The man she had believed was dead.

He had changed so much since she had seen him last. He'd lost weight and he looked older. Older than his twenty-six years. The stubble covering his thickset jaw was speckled grey, his fair hair now had hints of silver.

Not that any of that mattered.

Because he was alive.

And he still loved her.

Chapter Two

As Rosie started rummaging around in her handbag for her keys, she heard her neighbour's door swing open. Mrs Jenkins appeared seconds later, her hair in curlers, winceyette dressing gown wrapped tightly around her.

'Rosie! You've got a visitor!'

Rosie's heart leapt.

Peter!

As though reading her thoughts, Mrs Jenkins quickly added, 'No, sorry, pet, it's not Peter.'

She dropped her voice.

'It's a young girl. She says she's your *sister*. I hope you don't mind, but I let her in. Didn't know what else to do. She was just standing there shivering in the cold and it'd gone midnight.'

Rosie stood staring at her neighbour, not quite wanting to believe what she was hearing.

'Of course, I quizzed her,' Mrs Jenkins added quickly. 'Seemed like she was telling the truth and she was wearing a school uniform ... She didn't look like she was trying to have me on, so I let her in.' Mrs Jenkins pulled the spare key from the pocket of her dressing gown by way of explanation.

Seeing Rosie's lips purse, she asked, 'Was that all right? You *do* have a sister, don't you?'

'Yes, yes, I have a sister, Mrs Jenkins,' Rosie said through gritted teeth. 'You did the right thing.' She got her own key out as she spoke. 'It's just that she wasn't exactly expected.'

She looked at Mrs Jenkins, who was gripping the top of her dressing gown around her neck. 'Please, get yourself in, Mrs Jenkins. You'll catch your death.'

Rosie turned the key and pushed open the door.

'Thank you so much. I'm lucky to have you as my neighbour.'

Mrs Jenkins beamed. She was just opening her mouth to speak again, but Rosie had already gone in and was shutting the door.

Standing in the tiled hallway, Rosie took a deep breath. This was the last thing she needed after the night she'd just had. A meal out at the Palatine with Lily, George, Kate, Maisie and Vivian had turned into bedlam when the east end was bombed. After the all-clear, she and Maisie had run to Tatham Street, terrified that their friends and family had been buried alive in their homes. Thankfully, they'd escaped. But only just. Others living on the street hadn't been so lucky.

'Charlie!' she shouted, letting out the anger that had risen to the surface as soon as Mrs Jenkins had warned her of her unexpected visitor. Walking into the living room, she saw Charlotte curled up on the sofa, still in her school uniform. She'd already made herself at home. The fire was only just starting to dwindle and there was an empty mug and crumb-strewn plate on the coffee table.

'Rosieee …' Charlotte sang in a sleepy voice as she turned her face up to her sister, who was standing with hands on hips, glowering down at her.

'What on earth are you doing here?' Rosie spat the words out.

'I thought I'd come and see you.'

Charlotte pushed herself into a sitting position, pulling the blanket she'd taken from the airing cupboard around her shoulders.

Rosie stared at her in disbelief.

'I beg your pardon?'

Charlotte burst out laughing.

'Eee, you sounded just like Mum. "*I beg your pardon.*"' Charlotte put on her mother's voice. It was one of the few distinct memories she had.

Rosie opened her mouth, but nothing came out. She was actually speechless.

'Come, sit down next to me,' Charlotte cajoled. 'It's so cosy here. I *love* the house.'

As she spoke, she looked around. Her eyes lingered on the fire.

'Shall I put another shovel on?' She looked at Rosie. 'Do you want a cuppa?'

She looked at her sister more closely.

'Gosh, looks like you've been out picking coal yourself. Your clothes are filthy.'

Rosie looked down at her cashmere jumper and skirt and realised for the first time that she did, indeed, look a state.

'Never mind about me, Charlie.' Rosie sat down and stared at her sister. 'Explain yourself!'

Charlotte looked at her sister and knew there was no way round this.

'I'm not going back!' Charlotte declared. Her face was set. Her tone determined.

Rosie let out a bark of laughter that did not hold one iota of mirth.

'I think you'll find that you *are* going back.'

'You can't make me!' Charlotte bit back.

'I jolly well can.' Rosie laughed again. 'I'll drag you all the way back there myself if I have to.'

'Please, Rosie, don't make me go back. I want to be here. I'm *homesick.*'

Rosie looked at her sister.

'Charlotte, you're wasting your energy giving me the puppy-dog eyes. They might have worked on Mam and Dad when you were little, but I'm not them and your *poor me* act doesn't wash either.'

Charlotte straightened her back and looked her sister directly in the eyes.

'Please, Rosie, please, just let me stay a while. You won't even notice I'm here. I'll be as good as gold. Promise.'

Rosie sighed.

'I'm too tired to argue with you, Charlie. It's been a long day.' She stood up. 'You can either sleep down here or in the spare room. It's up to you.' She looked around the room and spotted Charlotte's holdall. It was bursting at the seams.

'I'm guessing you've brought a change of clothes.'

Charlotte nodded.

'Just as well,' Rosie said, disappearing into the kitchen and reappearing at the lounge doorway with a glass of water. 'If you've got an alarm clock in there – ' she nodded over to the bag ' – then set it for six. We'll need to be out the door by seven, and not a minute after.'

Before Charlotte had a chance to ask why, Rosie had turned her back on her and was making her way up the stairs.

A few moments later Charlotte heard the bedroom door shut.

Chapter Three

'You all right, Tommy?' Polly asked. She had been dozing but sensed that Tommy had woken.

'Water?' Tommy asked, his eyes looking to the bedside cabinet on the far side of the bed.

'Don't move,' Polly commanded, seeing him grimace in pain as he tried to push himself up. She hurried around the bed and put the beaker of water to his lips. Tommy took a few sips, but the effort was almost too much and he was forced to slump back down in the bed.

'What a state,' he muttered, looking at Polly, who had started to dab his dry, cracked lips with a damp flannel.

All of a sudden, he reached out and touched her face. Having felt the outline of her nose, her brows and her lips, he dropped his arm back on top of the starched white sheets.

Polly looked at Tommy, puzzled. There were so many things she wanted to ask him. What had happened to him while he'd been missing? About his time in Gibraltar – all the stories he hadn't been able to tell her in his letters.

But she knew that those questions could wait.

They had time.

Polly closed her eyes and let her mind drift to the future, imagining their life together – getting married, setting up home and having a family.

She hadn't felt so happy or relieved in her entire life.

*

When the light started to filter through the blackout blinds, Polly sat up and saw that the matron was no longer snoring.

Tommy was also stirring.

'Pol?' he asked.

'Yes?' She took his hand.

Tommy seemed to relax.

'Yer know,' he looked up at Polly, his hazel eyes sparkling, 'when I first came around, before yer got here, I thought I saw Helen.'

Polly smiled.

So, that was why he kept asking if it was really her.

'You're right. You did see Helen. She was here, just by chance.'

Tommy looked at her and furrowed his brow.

Polly's smile widened.

'I think she's friendly with one of the doctors. I think he might be *your* doctor. It was Helen who told me you were here.'

Tommy nodded. His face scrunched up in pain as he did so.

'You all right?' Polly panicked.

'I'm fine, honestly,' Tommy said.

Polly looked up to see the matron heading towards them with a steel kidney-shaped bowl and a large syringe.

'Right, young lady. I think it's time for you to leave. They'll have my guts for garters if they find out I've let you stay all night.'

Polly felt a surge of trepidation. She didn't want to leave Tommy alone.

'Go home, get some sleep,' Tommy said, trying to mask the pain that had returned now that the morphine was wearing off.

Polly bent over and kissed him.

17

'Chop-chop!' Mrs Rosendale said. 'If the rest of them see you here, getting fresh with your fiancé, there'll be a riot on.'

Polly looked around at the dozen or so beds. She could hear a few of the patients starting to wake up.

'I'll come and see you later,' Polly said, trying to keep the worry from her face as she smiled her goodbye.

Making as little noise as possible, she walked towards the swing doors, before turning to take one last look at Tommy.

Polly came face to face with a white doctor's coat as she stepped out into the corridor.

'Oh! So sorry!' She stepped back.

'Ah, Polly! You obviously managed to sweet-talk Mrs Rosendale into letting you stay the night.'

Polly looked up to see the smiling face of Dr Parker.

'How's Tommy doing?' he asked, his face now serious. 'I was just on my way to see him.' He guided Polly away from the swing doors.

'He seems all right. A little bit confused. Keeps asking if it's really me ...' Her voice trailed off.

'Come on,' Dr Parker said, cocking his head towards the canteen at the end of the corridor. 'Let me get you a nice cuppa. You look like you need one.'

Polly took a large sip of her tea and savoured it.

'Mmm, that's lovely.'

Dr Parker chuckled. 'Not a word I think I've ever heard used to describe hospital tea.'

He looked at the young woman opposite him.

'Well, it's great to finally meet you, Polly. Properly that is. Not standing in the middle of a bomb site.' His mind momentarily jumped back to the dramatic events of the previous evening, before forcing itself back to the here and now.

'So, you say Tommy's talking?' he asked.

'Yes, just a few words. He seemed a little confused, though.'

'He's been heavily sedated,' Dr Parker explained, 'and he's been in and out of consciousness since he was admitted, so it's not surprising he's a little disorientated.'

'But he's going to be all right, isn't he?' Polly asked, suddenly worried.

'All the signs are good,' Dr Parker said. 'Although it must be said, he's been through the mill. Obviously, we had no idea who he was until Helen recognised him.' Images of Helen's face as she realised the man they had named 'our poor chap' was none other than *the* Tommy Watts rushed to the fore, along with her subsequent declaration of love.

'Last night's all a bit of a blur,' Polly said, thinking of the aftermath of the air raid, 'but I remember you saying that Tommy had lost a lot of blood and needed an operation.'

'Well,' Dr Parker looked at Polly, 'Tommy is one lucky man.' He smiled. 'And not just because he has such a devoted fiancée who clearly loves him very much.'

His words were sincere. He only wished that it was *just* Polly who loved Tommy.

'Not long after he was admitted he suffered a ruptured spleen,' Dr Parker explained.

'What's that?' Polly was suddenly reminded of Helen suffering a ruptured appendix. 'Something burst?'

'Exactly.' Dr Parker nodded. 'His spleen burst, which meant he bled a lot, but we were able to operate on him before anything too catastrophic happened. He could have died. As I said, he's a lucky man in more ways than one.'

Polly didn't know whether to be elated that Tommy had survived or shocked that he had been so ill he'd nearly died. She felt tears prick her eyes again.

'I know you've had a night of it,' Dr Parker said, 'and your mind's probably all over the place. I'm also guessing you haven't slept a wink. I've been Tommy's doctor since he was admitted, so any worries or questions you've got, just come and ask me. Providing I'm not in theatre, I'll be able to see you.'

Polly gave a sigh of relief. Helen's doctor friend must have read her mind.

'Can I make a suggestion?' He smiled.

Polly looked up and nodded. A tear escaped and rolled down her cheek. She brushed it away quickly.

'I think you should go home and get your head down for a few hours at least. Tommy will need to rest, so why don't you come back this afternoon? I should be about, so you can come and grab me if needs be.'

Polly felt like hugging the man sitting opposite her. He seemed so nice. Too nice to be Helen's latest squeeze. Perhaps Bel was right and they *were* just friends.

'Actually,' Dr Parker said, seeing the familiar look of exhaustion he saw on the faces of those who'd been up all night with loved ones, 'I need some supplies picking up from the Royal in town. You could cadge a lift home if you want?'

Polly's face lit up.

'Oh yes, please. That would be great.'

The pair left the cafeteria and started walking down a long corridor towards the rear of the hospital.

'Was everyone all right after I left?' Polly asked.

'Yes, yes, all things considered.'

Dr Parker turned right and they walked down another windowless corridor.

'I sent Gloria and Martha off to the hospital to get checked over. I gave orders that they were both to be kept in for at least one night – if not more. Gloria's going to have to rest that leg of hers and make sure it doesn't get infected. And Martha took quite a bash on the back of her head. She seems all right, but best to err on the side of caution. Just in case.'

'I can't believe they made it out in one piece,' Polly said, recalling the bombed building collapsing in a cloud of brick dust.

'I know,' Dr Parker said.

'Especially Helen. She barely had a mark on her,' Polly said, walking quickly to keep up with Dr Parker's long strides.

'I know. She's one very fortunate woman,' Dr Parker agreed, thinking of Helen, her arm around Gloria; both of them standing amidst the ruins, having just escaped death by a hair's breadth.

'And very brave,' Polly added.

Dr Parker nodded his agreement as they turned down another corridor.

'You know,' Polly said, 'the only thing she was bothered about when I was helping her to the ambulance was Hope – and making sure she was all right.' Polly shook her head. 'She wouldn't rest until she saw her with her own eyes.'

Dr Parker walked on quietly for a moment before he suddenly burst out laughing.

'And that ginger moggy!'

The image of Helen sitting on the back step of the ambulance, Hope snuggled up in her lap and a marmalade-coloured tomcat weaving itself around her legs, would stay with him for ever.

'It wouldn't leave Helen alone, would it?' Polly chuckled.

'Mind you, it did well to give Gloria a wide berth. I think it might have lost the rest of its nine lives if she'd got her hands on it.'

They both walked in silence, thinking about Gloria's old friend Mrs Crabtree, who had died trying to save her beloved pet.

'The flea-bitten thing followed Helen and Hope all the way back to Gloria's.'

Dr Parker pushed open a double set of swing doors. Seeing the puzzled look on Polly's face, he explained, 'Helen's looking after Hope until Gloria's discharged.'

'Oh,' Polly said, still a little surprised. 'I just presumed Bel would have taken her back to ours. But I guess Hope *is* Helen's sister.' Polly hesitated. 'None of us realised that Helen had become so close to Hope ... and Gloria.'

Dr Parker nodded, knowing it was wise not to say any more. The dramatic events of yesterday had brought many secrets out into the open, the repercussions of which would only just be starting to be felt.

Dr Parker opened a door and the two stepped out into the backyard.

'Mr Sullivan!' he shouted over to an old man who was washing down one of the ambulances. 'Can you pick up some supplies from the Royal for me – and drop this young lady off in town while you're at it, please?'

The old man chucked the rest of the water over the bonnet and put the empty bucket down by the outdoor tap.

'You got a list for me, Doc?' the old man asked as he opened the passenger door for Polly.

'Just the usual.' Dr Parker cocked his head towards Polly.

Mr Sullivan looked momentarily perplexed before he nodded his understanding and climbed into the driver's seat.

'Thank you, Dr Parker.' Polly leant out the window.

'What for? I've not done anything.'

'Oh yes you have,' she shouted back. 'You've kept my Tommy alive!'

Dr Parker stood and waved as the ambulance drove off.

'No, my dear,' he said to the empty yard. 'It was you who kept him alive. Of that I have no doubt.'

Chapter Four

'There you are,' Helen cooed as she pulled Hope's little winter coat together at the front and started to do up the buttons.

Hope immediately objected and started pulling the coat open. 'Noo!'

'All right, all right,' Helen soothed. 'Come on then, time to go.'

Hope let out an excited laugh as Helen hoisted her onto her hip and stepped out of the flat. Shutting the door, she pocketed the front-door key and carried Hope up the stone steps.

'Shoo! Go away!' Helen waved her free hand at Mrs Crabtree's ginger cat, which was sitting halfway up the steps. 'Go on, shoo!'

The cat turned and sprang up the rest of the steps, disappearing from view.

At the top, Helen saw an old man in a shabby green cardigan standing by the grey Silver Cross pram she had hauled up the stairs a few minutes earlier.

'Can I help you?' Helen asked sharply.

'Where's Gloria?' the old man asked, his face full of worry. 'Is she all right?' As he spoke, his eyes kept flicking to Hope. 'She didn't make it to the shelter last night.'

'Ah, *Mr Brown*,' Helen said. 'You're Gloria's landlord?'

'Well, ex-landlord,' Mr Brown corrected.

'Oh.' Helen was sure Gloria had told her that the old man who lived above her owned the flats.

'*Is she all right?*' Mr Brown asked. Now it was the old man's turn to sound sharp.

'Yes, yes,' Helen reassured. 'Well, yes and no.' She moved Hope onto her other hip. She didn't feel like she had a bean of energy this morning. 'She's up at the Royal. She got trapped under a load of rubble and has a nasty gash on her leg.'

'Goodness me.' Mr Brown started to rub his hands together anxiously. 'But she's going to be all right?'

'Yes, yes,' Helen again reassured. 'I think they'll want to keep her in for another night, though.' Helen jigged Hope up and playfully touched her nose, making her giggle. 'So, I've volunteered to look after Hope until she's back.'

'Well, just give me a knock if I can help.' The old man looked at Hope and stroked her cheek with an arthritic hand.

'Do you think Gloria will be up for visitors?' he asked as Helen put Hope in the pram.

'I'm sure she'd love to see you, Mr Brown,' Helen said, taking the brake off the Silver Cross.

The old man looked at Hope, her thick black hair brushed neatly into place, and then at the young woman, her own thick black hair pulled back into a ponytail.

'If you do go to see Gloria, Mr Brown, would you please tell her I'll come and see her with Hope after work.' It was a command more than a request.

And with that Helen bumped the pram down the kerb and hurried across the road.

Turning into Tatham Street, Helen took a sharp intake of breath. It was even worse than she remembered. The devastation from last night was shocking and seemed all the more surreal in the stillness of the early morning. There was now just the one fire engine and a lone St John's ambulance, but there were still plenty of people digging about in the rubble. Helen saw one young woman near the bottom of the street crying inconsolably. She was clinging to what looked like a grey teddy bear and rocking back and forth. Another woman had her arms around her, trying, in vain, to offer comfort.

Helen looked at Hope, sitting up, alert, staring about her, her own cuddly toy clasped in her pudgy little hands.

'There but for the grace of God go I.' She mumbled the heartfelt words under her breath. Never before had she been so thankful to a God she rarely bothered with.

Stopping outside number 34, Helen was glad she didn't have to go any further down the road where lives had been taken and bodies were still buried.

She knocked on the front door.

Within a matter of seconds, the door was flung open.

'Ah, 'tis Helen, isn't it?' Agnes said.

Helen caught the Irish brogue.

'And our favourite little girl, Hope!' As soon as the words were out, Agnes felt a tug on her skirt and looked down to see Lucille's face scowling up at her.

'And this one,' she bent down and heaved her granddaughter up and onto her hip, 'is our favourite *big* girl.' She gave Helen a slightly exasperated look and tilted her head for her to follow her into the house.

Helen stood for a moment. Another surreal moment to add to the many of these past twelve hours. It was hard to believe that she was standing on the threshold of the home of the woman she had once hated. Never mind arriving with Hope.

'Just leave the pram in the hallway,' Agnes said, putting Lucille back down. The little girl immediately ran excitedly back into the kitchen.

'Come in 'n meet everyone,' Agnes said. 'Do yer want a cup of tea?'

'No, thank you, Mrs Elliot,' Helen said, getting Hope out of the pram. 'I've got to go home and change before I go into work, so I'll not stay long. You don't mind having Hope for the day, do you?'

As Helen walked into the kitchen with Hope clinging to her like a koala bear, she saw Bel coming out of the scullery.

'Of course she doesn't!' Bel put her hands out to take Hope, trying not to show her surprise at seeing Helen looking decidedly down-at-heel. She had no make-up on, her hair was scraped back into a ponytail, and she was wearing Gloria's oversized and rather frumpy brown winter coat.

As Bel gently eased Hope away from her, Helen suddenly felt loath to let the little girl go.

'I know you're in a dash,' Bel said, finally managing to pull Hope away from her big sister, 'but let me quickly introduce you to the clan.'

Bel turned to Joe, who was still wearing his Home Guard uniform.

'This is my husband, Joe.'

Helen guessed he had been out all night helping the wardens as he was filthy and looked shattered. She saw pain flash across his face as he used his walking stick to push himself up out of his chair.

'Nice to meet you, Joe,' Helen said, shaking his hand.

'Aye, you too,' Joe said. 'Bel tells me you did a brave thing last night?'

Suddenly feeling self-conscious, Helen didn't know what to say.

The sound of a loud hacking cough saved her from having to answer.

'Ahh,' Bel said. 'And this is my ma ... Pearl Hardwick.'

Helen looked round and moved aside to allow past a skinny, bottle-blonde, middle-aged woman wearing a faded pink polyester nightgown.

'Eee, it's like Clapham Junction in here this morning!' Pearl let out a cackle of laughter as she hurried towards the back door for her first smoke of the morning.

'This is Helen Crawford, Ma.'

Pearl immediately stopped in her tracks and turned around.

'So,' she scrutinised Helen, '*you're* the Havelock girl?'

Helen's shock at realising that this common-as-muck woman was, in fact, Bel's mother was immediately replaced by a feeling of unease.

'Well, Havelock granddaughter, I guess,' Helen said.

'The girl's *Jack's* lass!'

Helen turned around to see Arthur hobbling along the hallway. He was wearing his dark grey woollen suit and tartan slippers. There was a dog at either side of him.

'Lovely to see yer, pet.' Arthur took her hands in his own and squeezed them. Both dogs started sniffing at Helen's feet. Agnes looked at Tramp and Pup and then back up at Arthur.

'They'll be wanting to sleep in your room every night now, mark my words.' Agnes pursed her lips.

'Ah, the poor things were shaking like leaves when we got back last night.' Arthur bent down slowly and gave the older of the two a pat.

'I think we all were,' Agnes jibed.

Arthur straightened himself up and looked at Helen.

'Yer da will be as proud as punch to hear what yer did last night.' As he spoke, he became breathless and put his hand on the kitchen table. Agnes bustled over and guided him to his armchair by the range.

The old man let out a puff of air.

'Don't know what came over me there?' Arthur looked up at Agnes.

'Too much excitement, I reckon,' she said, pouring a cup of tea and handing it to him.

'Have you been to see Tommy yet?' Helen asked.

Everyone looked at Helen and then at Arthur.

Although they all knew that Arthur had known Helen from when she was small, having worked with her father, it still seemed strange to see their familiarity with each other.

'Not yet, pet, thought I'd wait till Polly came back. Give the two o' them a bit o' time on their own.'

Helen suddenly felt a wave of embarrassment as she had a flash recall of the previous evening when she had declared her undying love to Tommy. She must have come across as some love-struck imbecile. *God knows what John must have thought.*

'Well,' Helen said, quickly scratching the scene from her mind, 'you couldn't ask for him to be in better hands. He's got a brilliant doctor looking after him. Dr Parker. Just ask to see him when you do go up there and he'll tell you everything you need to know.'

As she spoke, Helen felt her heart lift. She resolved to call John as soon as she got to work.

'Well, I'd better get going.' Helen leant towards Hope, who was now balanced on Bel's hip. She had been surprisingly quiet during the introductions.

'You be good.' She put her hands around Hope's face and kissed her nose.

''Eeeelen!' Hope suddenly started to cry. She reached out for her big sister.

Helen looked at Bel and Agnes.

'She'll be fine.' Agnes guided Helen out of the kitchen and into the hallway. 'It'll do her good to be with the other children today. Keep to her routine.'

Helen nodded. 'Yes, you're right, Mrs Elliot.'

'Did she sleep all right last night?' Agnes asked as she went to open the door.

'Actually, she did. Soundly.' Helen smiled. 'But she *was* totally exhausted.'

'Well, 'tis a good sign. Especially after what happened, and with her mam being gone 'n all that. When something like this happens – ' Agnes stepped out onto the pavement and looked at the bomb site further down the street ' – it's good to keep some semblance of normality. As much as possible anyways.'

'Well, thank you for looking after her, Mrs Elliot. I'll come and pick her up after work. It'll be around six. Is that all right?'

'Course it is, hinny.' Agnes looked at the dark rings under Helen's eyes. 'And you watch yerself today. It's not just the bairn who's had a bit of a shock.'

When Helen reached the top of Tatham Street she turned left and walked back along Borough Road. As she passed the flat, she saw Mrs Crabtree's cat back in its original spot on the middle step.

'You might have survived last night,' Helen said out loud, 'but I don't rate your chances if Gloria finds you here when she gets back.'

As she rounded the corner onto Fawcett Street, Helen saw the cordoned-off bomb site where the town's most salubrious department store had once stood. Her home town was slowly but surely being razed to the ground.

She had heard mutterings that there had been at least twelve killed.

She just counted her blessings that Gloria and Hope weren't part of that death toll.

As soon as she got home, Helen went straight upstairs to her room. It had already gone seven. If she hurried, she mightn't be too late for work.

Passing her mother's bedroom, she heard her snoring and knew that she would have probably spent last night's air raid in the basement of the Grand with her friend Amelia and the latest from the Admiralty to be billeted at the hotel. She'd have returned home before midnight and had a nightcap, chased down with a couple of her sleeping pills. Helen could probably stand outside her door banging on a drum right now and her mother wouldn't stir.

Once in her own room, Helen quickly changed out of her dirty red dress, which amazingly had survived the previous evening's drama without suffering a nick. Having bathed at Gloria's last night, she stepped straight into a black dress that had been made to measure by the young woman at the Maison Nouvelle.

She felt wearing black would be appropriate, knowing the town would be in unofficial mourning as the full extent of the air raid became public knowledge.

Sitting down at her dressing table and seeing her reflection, Helen baulked.

She looked dreadful.

She reached for her Max Factor Pan-Cake foundation and got to work.

Five minutes later the face looking back at her in the mirror was transformed.

After pinning her hair back into victory rolls, she packed a few essentials for another night at Gloria's, then hurried back downstairs and out the front door.

There was no need to leave her mother a message to tell her she wouldn't be back this evening. She'd clearly not noticed she hadn't been back last night, despite the fact there'd been an air raid. At least she was spared the hassle of having to lie. God, she could just imagine the look on her mother's face if she knew where she'd really been – and, moreover, with whom.

Chapter Five

When Rosie arrived at the gates of Thompson's with Charlotte in tow, Alfie couldn't help but stare. The yard had a few lads who looked around the girl's age, but they were usually apprentices, brought into the yard by their dads or older brothers. Working in the shipyards was a family affair. A *male* family affair.

It looked like it was now also a family affair for the fairer sex.

'Do you want me to put a good word in for you with Kate?'

The question threw Alfie, as did the sternness of Rosie's manner. She was usually friendly. Amicable.

'Erm ... Well ... Yes, please,' Alfie stuttered. He had a huge crush on Kate, which everyone, apart from Kate herself, seemed to know about.

'Well then, you'll give me a yard pass, no questions asked.'

It took Alfie a moment to work out that Rosie needed the pass for the young girl who was with her, and another to realise the girl's presence at the yard had not been authorised.

'Yes, of course,' Alfie said. He would probably have done just about anything to help win over Kate.

A few minutes later Rosie and Charlotte were walking over the threshold of one of the biggest shipyards along the Wear.

'Wow!' Charlotte looked about her at the mass of metal and machinery – huge coils of chains, stacked-up sheets of steel, mammoth overhanging cranes – before her eyes found the overbearing hull of a half-finished frigate in the dry dock.

'"Wow"?' Rosie repeated. 'Is that what you get after spending a small fortune on the best education money can buy? A simple "wow"?'

Charlotte threw her sister a look and wrapped her grey mackintosh around her. It was cold and the wind was getting up. Rosie had been like this since the moment they'd woken up. Not that it had bothered Charlotte too much. Enduring the wrath of her sister was preferable by far to being hauled to the railway station and shoved onto a train back to Harrogate.

'Well, I could say something in French or Latin—' Charlotte stopped on seeing the glowering look her sister was giving her.

Taking in her surroundings, Charlotte saw young boys about her own age dressed in dirty overalls, joking around, smoking rolled-up cigarettes and rubbing their hands over a brazier. They were standing in front of a huge building, the inside of which was piled high with sheets of metal.

'It's like a medieval metal city,' Charlotte said, her eyes still scanning her new terrain.

As another gust of wind caused her mac to flap open, she wished she'd worn something warmer.

Rosie looked at her little sister, now realising that she was not so little. She had shot up this past year and the two of them were almost the same height.

'Follow me,' Rosie commanded.

She had purposely got to the yard early, partly because she wanted Charlotte to experience the punishing hours that were demanded of those who worked there, and partly because, at this time of the day, it was relatively quiet and she would be able to give her a tour before the flood of workers descended at the start of the shift.

For the next half an hour Rosie showed Charlotte just about every part of the shipyard, from the dry docks to the drawing office, from the platers' shed to the frame benders' building. She took her through the basics of how a ship was built, from the design to the laying of the keel, right through to the launch and the final fitting-out stage.

Rosie ended her talk at her squad's work area. Out of her team of five, it would probably only be Dorothy and Angie who turned up for work today.

She guessed that Gloria's leg would keep her off work for at least a week.

Martha, she reckoned, would be back on Monday. She'd lay money on the group's gentle giant convincing the doctors – and her parents – that she was fine.

And as for Polly, she'd probably been up all night with Tommy and would be in no fit state to do anything other than sleep.

'So, you all have your own helmets?' Charlotte said, picking up a welding mask with the name 'Martha' emblazoned on it. It occurred to Charlotte that she hadn't really asked her sister much about her workmates.

'Yes.' Rosie's answer was curt.

'So,' Charlotte began tentatively, 'when you were ill that time, with ... what was it you called it ... "arch eye"?'

'*Arc* eye,' Rosie corrected. She could feel herself tense.

'So,' Charlotte said again, 'when you suffered this "arc eye" and you got all those burns and nearly blinded yourself, how did that happen?'

Rosie looked at Charlotte. At the time, Charlotte had only been twelve and she'd told her it was an accident at work. She wanted one day to tell her the truth about what had really happened that day two years ago, but not now.

'Here they are!' Rosie raised her hand and waved over to two women who were linking arms as they walked across the yard.

Charlotte guessed they were around twenty. They were wearing men's boots and overalls, their hair was up and in turbans, and they were marching across the yard as if they owned the place. She was instantly intrigued.

'Oh. My. God!' Dorothy shouted out as soon as she clapped eyes on Charlotte. She let go of Angie's arm and strode over.

'Would I be right in saying that you are the infamous Charlotte?' Dorothy inspected the young girl in front of her, arms akimbo.

'You would be,' Rosie butted in, giving Dorothy a look that told her to tread carefully.

'What yer deeing here?' Angie was staring at Charlotte. 'Yer big sister never allowed yer to come back here.' Angie looked at Rosie. 'Did yer, miss?'

'No, I certainly didn't,' Rosie confirmed.

Charlotte was looking slightly gobsmacked, her eyes flitting from Dorothy to Angie, and then to her sister, who she couldn't believe had just been called 'miss'.

'But now that she's here,' Rosie gave her sister another schoolmarmish glower, 'I thought she might as well see how she finds working in a shipyard.'

Charlotte gave her sister a slightly apprehensive look. She had never said anything about *working* at Thompson's.

'Ha!' Dorothy laughed. 'So, you'll be heading back to Harrogate tomorrow then?'

Charlotte didn't say anything to the pretty, dark-haired young woman, but shook her head.

'Well, dinnit be giving yer big sister any hassle!' Angie ordered. The look she was giving Charlotte spoke volumes.

'Come on then, Charlie. Let's go and find Miss Crawford. See if she's prepared to take you on.' Turning her attention back to Dorothy and Angie, Rosie looked up at the frigate docked in the dry basin.

'As there's just the three of us today, I think we'll team up with Terry's lot.'

'Aye, miss, we'll see yer up there,' Angie said solemnly.

'Yes, Rosie, we'll tell Terry you'll be joining us a little later.'

'They seem a right pair.'

Charlotte finally found her voice as she and Rosie walked across the yard, passing groups of workers, flat caps on their heads, fags hanging from their mouths.

'Bloody hard workers, the pair of them,' Rosie said. 'And they didn't exactly pick the soft option when it came to doing war work.'

'Why did they?' Charlotte asked, genuinely interested. Neither women looked well built. In fact, they both looked more suited to waitressing or working in a shop than welding ships.

'You'll have to ask them that yourself,' Rosie said.

Charlotte was just about to ask another question when the klaxon blared out the start of the working day. She jumped, startled by the horn for the first time. Rosie had to suppress a chuckle.

As they neared the admin offices, Charlotte tugged Rosie's arm. She shouted, but not loud enough for Rosie to hear.

Rosie leant towards her sister and put her hand to her ear.

'Toilet?' Charlotte shouted again.

Rosie nodded, turned away from the admin offices and walked over to a row of prefab buildings to the right.

Pointing at the outdoor lavatory, she watched as her sister carefully opened the door to look inside. The women's washroom was dark and cold, consisting of two toilets and a single wash basin. Charlotte gave Rosie a look of uncertainty. Rosie stabbed a finger at an imaginary watch on her wrist and as Charlotte went in, Rosie banged hard on the corrugated-iron frontage.

Like most of the female workers who used the facilities, Charlotte didn't hang about and was out within minutes, shaking her hands dry.

When they reached the admin building and the door closed behind them, making conversation possible, Charlotte asked, 'Why did you bang on the toilet when I went in?'

'To get rid of any unwanted visitors,' Rosie said, leading the way up the stairs to the first floor.

It took a few moments for the penny to drop.

'Like mice?' Charlotte asked.

Rosie laughed as she reached the top of the stairs and turned to look at her sister.

'I wish!'

Charlotte paled.

As they walked into the main office they were hit by a blanket of warmth. Charlotte undid her mac and visibly relaxed. At least she was out of the wind and the cold. She had forgotten how raw the weather in the north-east was.

Bel and Marie-Anne were sitting at their desks near the window. On seeing Rosie, they both jumped out of their chairs and hurried over.

'Is this who I think it is?' Bel asked, her voice soft and maternal.

'I'm afraid it is.' Rosie turned to her sister. 'Charlie, this is Mrs Elliot, the administrative assistant, and this is Miss

McCarthy, head of department and secretary to Miss Crawford, the yard manager.'

'Hello, Mrs Elliot, Miss McCarthy.'

'You look as white as a sheet, Charlotte. Do you want a nice cup of tea?' Bel asked.

'She's fine,' Rosie jumped in, before her sister had a chance to open her mouth. 'That's kind of you to offer, Mrs Elliot, but we've come to see Miss Crawford.' She looked over Bel's shoulder to the yard manager's office.

It had gone through Rosie's mind that Helen might have taken the day off after last night, but she'd immediately dismissed the idea. Helen had only been off sick once in all the years she'd been working at the yard and that was because she'd been rushed to hospital with a burst appendix.

'Miss Crawford has just arrived,' Anne-Marie said, falling into the role play. She couldn't wait to have a good gossip with Bel. *What a turn-up for the books!*

Rosie looked around and saw a chair on its own by the window.

'Charlie, you sit there quietly while I go and have a word with Miss Crawford.'

Charlotte did as she was told, while Bel and Marie-Anne forced themselves to keep straight faces and went back to their own desks.

'Helen. I guessed you'd be in.' Rosie stood in the office doorway. 'How you feeling?'

'Come in, come in.' Helen beckoned her over.

Rosie shut the door behind her. She'd normally have left it open, but this was one conversation she did not want anyone earwigging in on.

'You all right, after last night?' Rosie asked, taking a seat in the chair in front of Helen's desk.

'Fine. Remarkably fine,' Helen said.

Rosie looked at Helen. She reckoned if she scraped off all the make-up Helen had piled on today, one very exhausted woman would be revealed. Mind you, she felt shattered herself. She too had hardly slept a wink, but for very different reasons.

'And Hope was all right when you got her back to Gloria's? No kind of delayed reaction?'

'No, thank goodness,' Helen said, getting up and pouring them both a cup of tea from the tray Marie-Anne had brought in. 'She slept like a log and I couldn't find any cuts or bruises on her, which I think is not far off a miracle.' To be sure, though, Helen had moved Hope's cot next to her own bed and had sat up most of the night watching her.

'It has to be said ...' Rosie smiled her thanks as Helen put a cup of tea down on the desk for her ' ... if it wasn't for you and Martha, Gloria and Hope wouldn't be alive.'

Helen waved her hand, shooing Rosie's words away.

'Don't. I can't bear to even think about it. Makes me feel ill.' She took a drink of her tea, pulled out a cigarette from her packet of Pall Malls and lit it. 'I take it Gloria and Martha got to the Royal all right?'

'Yes, although it was pretty mad up there. Lots of casualties being brought in.'

'I'm going to visit them both this evening. Take Hope up to see Gloria,' Helen said.

'Actually,' Rosie said, looking out a large window at the open-plan office beyond and seeing that Charlotte was, thankfully, sitting and behaving herself, 'I've got a favour to ask you.'

'Oh, yes?' Helen blew out smoke.

'Well, can you see the young girl in the grey mac sitting in the chair next to the window?'

Helen turned her head and blinked.

'Dear me, where did she spring from? I didn't see her come in.'

Probably, Helen realised, because she'd been on the phone to John. She'd caught him before he went into theatre and they'd chatted for a good while about last night. She'd only just hung up seconds before Rosie had come to see her.

'Well, the young girl presently looking like butter wouldn't melt is my very naughty and wayward little sister, Charlotte.'

Now Helen really was intrigued.

'Really?' she said, keeping her eyes fixed on the fresh-faced teenager who was now taking off her coat. 'I'll be honest, Rosie. I had no idea you had a sister.'

'I guess there's no reason you would have known,' Rosie said. 'Especially as – until midnight last night – she didn't live with me. Nor did she even live in the north-east.'

Helen's eyes widened. 'Gosh, go on.'

She looked at Charlotte, who was starting to wiggle about in her seat whilst carrying out an inspection of everything in her immediate vicinity.

'Well,' Rosie sighed, taking another sip of her tea. 'You know that my parents died years ago?'

Helen nodded.

'Well, fortunately,' Rosie continued, 'my mam and dad left enough for Charlie to go to a boarding school in Harrogate.'

'Not the Runcorn School for Girls?' Helen suddenly asked.

'That's the one. Do you know it?'

Helen let out a laugh that Rosie thought sounded a little bitter.

'Oh, yes, my dear mother tried to force me to go there. Said it was "the best education money could buy". In reality, I think it had more to do with getting shot of me.'

It hurt Rosie to hear that someone like Miriam had said the same words she herself had said to Charlie.

'Let me guess,' Helen said, recalling her one and only visit to the school, which was miles away from anywhere, 'Charlie's decided she doesn't want to be at the school any more.'

'Exactly,' Rosie said, 'and her timing couldn't have been any worse. Her train was delayed due to the air raid, so she only just got home before I did, at midnight.'

'When it rains it pours,' Helen said, stubbing out her cigarette. 'So, I'm guessing she just up and left – got on a train on her lonesome and came up here?'

Rosie nodded.

Helen let out a burst of laughter.

'She's got bottle! I'm surprised they've not sent out a search party for her.' Helen looked up at the clock on the wall above the door. It had gone eight o'clock. 'They'll have realised she's not in her bed by now.'

'She left them a letter,' Rosie sighed, 'telling them that as it was half-term, she had returned home.'

'Ah… so, tell me, where do I come into it all?' Helen asked.

Rosie took a deep breath. She'd spent until the early hours of the morning working out what she was going to do.

'I was hoping Charlie could work at the yard for the next week. You wouldn't have to pay her. My theory is, if I make her realise how hard and mundane working for a living can be – especially unskilled or labouring work – she'll feel she's jumped from the frying pan right into the fire.'

'And might then want to jump back into the frying pan?' Helen couldn't keep the scepticism out of her voice. If Charlie had packed her bags, made good her escape, walked the two miles she knew it was to the local railway station, got a train to York, then another up to Sunderland, only to arrive at her sister's house at midnight, knowing she would get an earbashing at the very least, then Rosie was kidding herself if she believed her little sister would choose to return to the school of her own accord.

'I thought if you could put her to work in admin and then we go from there. Perhaps get her out in the yard doing some sweeping up ...' Rosie let her voice trail off.

'Tough work, but keep her away from anything that might be too dangerous?' Helen asked.

'Exactly!' Rosie said, relieved. 'The only other favour I have to ask,' she added, 'is that I don't want her being mollycoddled, if you know what I mean? Perhaps if she could see the Helen we've always known?'

Helen laughed again – loudly.

'You want me to be a total bitch?'

'Yes, please.'

This time they both burst out laughing.

Chapter Six

'Thanks so much.' Polly clambered out of the ambulance and shut the door.

'Yer welcome, pet,' the old man said, looking at the young woman in her dirty overalls, her long curly hair all over the shop and her face in need of a good wash.

He knew exactly why Dr Parker had wanted him to bring her back into town. It wasn't just her appearance that was in a bit of a state; the girl was clearly not entirely with it.

As Polly made her way up the front entrance of the Royal and along the corridor to casualty, she felt as though she knew the true meaning of being in seventh heaven.

Pushing open the swing doors of the short-stay ward, she looked to her left and then to her right. And that's when she saw them. In beds next to each other. Both sitting up with a cup of tea in their hands.

'It's not visiting time!'

Polly looked down to see the stern face of the ward nurse looking up at her.

'Oh, I'm so sorry.' Polly's eyes darted back to her two workmates, who, having just spotted her, were waving frantically, demanding she come over.

The nurse swivelled round to see what had caught the overall-clad woman's attention. Realising it was two of the survivors from last night's air raid, she turned back to Polly.

'You've got twenty minutes. Not a second over.'

'Oh, thank you!' Polly felt like hugging her, but she restrained herself, hurrying over to her two friends and hugging them instead.

'How are you both?' She looked at Gloria, who appeared remarkably well and relaxed. Martha also looked well, although not as laid-back.

'Good! All good!' they answered in unison.

'But we're dying to know about Tommy,' Gloria said.

'Get that chair and sit down and tell us everything!' Martha demanded.

Polly chuckled. 'You sound like Dorothy!'

The three women suppressed their laughter, aware that the nurse was keeping a sharp eye on them.

Polly grabbed the chair and sat down.

'I still can't quite believe it.' She looked from Gloria to Martha. 'When I saw him, I thought I was dreaming. Honestly, I think it's taken me all night to convince myself that this is real.'

'Eee, Pol, we're made up for yer, we really are, aren't we?' Gloria said.

Martha nodded vigorously.

'I thought he was a goner.'

'I think we all did,' Gloria admitted.

Tears started to trickle down Polly's face.

'I did too,' she confessed.

Gloria leant forward and squeezed Polly's hand.

'So come on, we want a blow-by-blow account before Mrs Mardy over there chucks you out.' She cast a look over at the nurse, who was checking a patient's chart.

Polly relayed the events of last night, how, after leaving them all at the bomb site, she and Maisie had practically run all the way to Lily's, before George had taken her to the Ryhope in his red MG. 'When I got to the ward, I saw him there, lying in his bed, fast asleep.'

'Did yer wake him up?' Gloria asked.

'No, I just sat there for ages, looking at him. I think I was in some kind of a trance. What with everything that had happened before.'

She looked at Martha and then Gloria. It wasn't only Tommy who was lucky to still be in the land of the living.

'Eventually I gave him a kiss and he woke up.'

'Like Sleeping Beauty,' Martha said.

Polly and Gloria laughed.

'It was, come to think of it. I don't think he was entirely sure it was me. He kept asking if it was *really* me.'

Polly paused.

'Then he asked me if I still wanted to marry him.'

Martha and Gloria 'aahed' in unison.

'Well, I hope yer said yer would!' Gloria chuckled.

'We both agreed we'd waited long enough,' Polly said.

'You've been sad for so long,' Gloria said, 'it's lovely to see yer so happy, isn't it?'

Martha nodded, a big smile on her face.

'I don't think I've *ever* felt this happy,' Polly admitted. 'Not even after Tommy proposed, although that was different, I was happy but sad—'

'Because he'd just signed up?' Martha said.

Polly nodded.

'This time, though,' she beamed, 'I've got him for keeps. He's home now – for good. There's no way they'll send him back out there.'

Her face clouded over momentarily.

'Dr Parker said he's lucky to be alive. Still has a long way to go before he'll be anywhere near back to normal.'

Looking up at the clock, she realised her twenty minutes was nearly up.

'But enough about me and Tommy. How are you two?'

46

'Well, Gloria here's happy as a dog with two tails,' Martha grouched. 'Thanks to all the painkillers she's been given. *And* she's slept like a baby.'

She gave Gloria a sidelong look.

'She snores, you know?'

Polly chuckled while Gloria pulled a face of disbelief.

'Martha's only in a one 'cos they won't give her anything because of her head injury. They woke her up every few hours during the night to check she was all right.'

'Let's have a quick look,' Polly said, getting up from her chair.

Martha obliged and turned her head.

'Urgh,' Polly said, seeing a neat row of stitches and a black crust of dried blood where Martha's hair had been shaved.

'Looks worse than it is,' Martha said. 'I should be allowed out later today.'

Just then they heard the nurse coughing and turned to see her pointing up at the clock.

'And Hope?' Polly asked Gloria quickly. 'Dr Parker said Helen was looking after her?'

'Helen said she wanted to look after her while I was in here,' Gloria explained. 'And you know Helen, there's no arguing with her once she makes her mind up.'

Polly was on the verge of quizzing Gloria about how she and Helen had become so close when the nurse coughed loudly again. Her time was up.

'Go on, get yourself home. Get some sleep,' Gloria said. 'You look like yer need it!'

'I'll be back to work on Monday. See you then!' Martha added as Polly gave them another hug and hurried out the ward.

After Polly's departure, Gloria put her tea down on the bedside cabinet and turned to Martha.

'Yer know, Martha, I don't think I'll ever be able to thank yer enough for what yer did last night.' Gloria's words were still slightly slurred from the painkillers she'd been given shortly before Polly had turned up. 'I don't think I'll ever forget opening my eyes and seeing you slapping me around the chops, trying to bring me round.'

Martha chuckled. Gloria had repeated this story a few times since they had been admitted last night.

'And then looking up and seeing Helen standing there, with Hope clinging to her like a little monkey. I don't think I've ever felt so relieved in my whole life.'

Gloria's eyes closed for a moment as she reran the film that seemed to be on a continuous loop in her head: Helen giving Hope over to Martha, Gloria and Helen yelling at Martha to get Hope out of the house before it collapsed, then seeing the bloody gash on the back of Martha's head as she'd made her way down what was left of Mrs Crabtree's hallway.

When Gloria opened her eyes again, her vision was blurred. She was crying. Again. She didn't seem to be able to stop the tears. But she didn't care. Nothing mattered except that her little girl was alive and well.

Gloria stretched over to Martha and grabbed her friend's hand.

'And when Hope's old enough to understand, I'm gonna tell her about what happened. I'm gonna tell her that she didn't have a guardian angel looking after her that night, but her brave aunty Martha.'

Martha squeezed Gloria's hand back.

She didn't say anything as she too was choking back tears, thinking how close they had been to losing the woman and child they all loved so much.

When Polly jumped off the bus at the top of Tatham Street, she realised why she hadn't seen many trams. The tracks all the way down her street were buckled and bent and the tram that had been derailed last night was still there, covered in debris, all its windows shattered.

She walked slowly, taking in the devastation. Further down the road she could see there was now just the one fire engine and a lone St John's ambulance on site, but there were still people digging around in the ruins of those who had lived in numbers 2, 4 and 6. The Education Architect's Offices, which had once stood opposite those houses, was no longer there either. There was a small mountain of red bricks in its place.

As Polly reached her own front door, she realised just how near to death they had all been. If the bomb had landed a hundred yards further up the street, it would have been their home that was now in ruins. And if that had been the case, every one of them would have perished, without a shadow of a doubt.

'Watch yerself, hinny!'

Polly jumped back to stop herself colliding with Pearl coming out the front door.

'Yer fella all right then?'

'Yes, yes, he is.' Polly was taken aback. She and Bel's ma rarely spoke to each other, even though they'd lived under the same roof for more than a year. 'You off to the Tatham?' she asked, watching Pearl spark up a fag as she stepped onto the pavement.

'Aye, yer knar what they say, "Keep calm 'n carry on!"' She puffed on her cigarette. 'Can't disappoint the regulars. Bombs or no bombs.'

Polly watched as Pearl crossed the road, coughing as she went.

Walking into the house, Polly could smell one of her ma's favourites – rabbit, black pudding and dumpling stew – cooking in the range. The house felt warm and homely.

'I'm back!' she hollered down the hallway.

Within seconds Agnes had appeared at the kitchen doorway, drying her hands on her pinny, the two dogs by her side. She threw her arms open to give her daughter a hug.

'Look at the state of yer! Is Tommy all right?'

Polly nodded. Tears pooled in her eyes. She didn't trust herself to speak.

Agnes made the sign of the cross, cast her eyes up to the ceiling and mumbled a quick 'Thanks be to God.'

She bustled over to Arthur who was snoozing in his chair by the range.

'Arthur, Arthur, wake up.' She gently shook the old man's arm. 'It's Polly,' she told him. 'She's back.'

'Ah, Pol.' Arthur sat up in his chair. 'How's our Tom?'

Polly crouched down, wrapped her arms around the old man, squeezed him hard and started sobbing. It was as though the floodgates to her emotions had just burst open and all the happiness, sadness, worry, dread and heart-break of the past year just came rampaging out.

Again she tried to speak but couldn't.

'There, there, pet.' Arthur patted her head with his bony hand as she knelt by his chair and clung to him, the sound of her crying muffled by his jacket. After a while, Polly became aware that Tramp and Pup were by her side and were trying to push their heads under her arm, needing reassurance that she was all right. Polly let out a laugh as the dogs tried to lick the salty tears from her face.

'Come and have a cuppa.' Agnes beckoned her daughter over to the kitchen table.

Polly stood up and dried her eyes on the back of her overall sleeve.

'Where's everyone?' she asked, sitting down at the table while her ma poured her a steaming cup of tea.

'Joe's round at Major Black's.' Agnes added milk and a good heap of sugar. 'Bel's at work and Hope and Lucille are next door at Beryl's. Now drink yer tea 'n tell us all about it.'

More tears rolled down Polly's face.

'I don't know why I'm crying.' She smiled at Arthur. 'Tommy's alive and he's going to be all right.' She took a deep, juddering breath. 'That's what his doctor said. Dr Parker's his name. He said Tommy's been through the mill. Said he was on a Red Cross ship that got bombed, but he was rescued and brought back in a cargo vessel with a load of other injured soldiers.'

Arthur had shuffled forward on his chair and was patting Pup, although his eyes were trained on Polly.

'He said he had something called a "ruptured spleen",' she went on, 'lost a lot of blood and had an operation. He's only just regained consciousness, but the doctor seems to think he'll be all right.'

'That's fantastic news, pet,' Arthur said, smiling at Polly. 'Sounds like he's in the right hands. And he's back home. Which is the main thing.'

Polly nodded and smiled through the tears. 'Yes, he's home.' She laughed. 'He says he wants to set a date for our wedding.'

'He's definitely all right, then,' Arthur said, looking across at Agnes, who returned his look of relief.

'He does look a bit rough,' Polly added. 'I think he'll need to be in hospital for a good while.'

Arthur nodded his understanding.

'Right, then,' he said, pushing himself out of his chair. 'I better get up there.'

Polly noticed that Arthur had on his best shoes and suit. He'd clearly been waiting for her to come back before he went to visit.

'Tell him I'll be up later,' she said.

'I will, pet. Now you do as yer ma tells you. Have something to eat, get yerself cleaned up, 'n put yer head down for a few hours.'

Polly gave the old man another hug.

'I still can't quite believe it,' she said.

'Aye,' Arthur agreed. 'Neither can I.'

Chapter Seven

The horn sounded out the end of the shift, starting the mass exodus from the yard.

Charlotte was obeying orders and waiting for Rosie outside the main admin offices. She was shuffling about from one foot to the other. Being out in the cold had made her need the loo even more than before. She was determined to hold it in until she got home, though. She had used the outdoor lav at lunchtime, but it had been daylight then. She had banged so hard on the corrugated iron she'd hurt her knuckles. She'd been in and out in record-breaking speed.

'*There she is!*'

Charlotte looked up to see Dorothy marching towards her. She was flanked by her scary friend, Angie, and a stern-looking Rosie.

'How was it?' Dorothy asked.

'Fine, fine,' Charlotte nodded.

'Yer behaved yerself?' Angie demanded.

Charlotte nodded again, nervously tapping her time card against the side of her mac.

'That yer board?' Angie asked, pointing down at the whitewashed card.

Charlotte looked puzzled.

'Yer board – yer time card?'

'Ah, yes, Miss McCarthy just gave it to me. Apparently, I have to give it in at the end of every day.'

'Well, remember yer number,' Angie ordered.

Charlotte looked at the card, which had '445' printed on it.

'We're like cattle here, aren't we, Dor?' Angie looked at her friend. 'They don't brand us, but we're all just numbers.'

'Come on then,' Rosie said, forcing herself to keep a straight face. 'Let's get out of here.'

Charlotte hurried to join her sister. It was the lesser of two evils.

As they reached the small cabin at the yard's entrance, Rosie turned to Charlotte.

'Alfie's the timekeeper. You give him your board at the end of the shift and he makes a note of the hours you've worked. When you come in Monday morning, you'll shout out your number and he'll give you your board back.'

Charlotte duly handed her time card to Alfie, followed by Rosie.

'You won't forget about our deal?' Alfie leant out of the hatch so as not to have to shout.

'What deal was that, Alfie?' Rosie said, her face deadpan.

Alfie looked crestfallen, but was wise enough not to argue the point.

Charlotte looked at her sister. She had never seen this side to her before.

'So, I'm working here – properly?' Charlotte asked as they strode down to the ferry landing.

'It's either that or Harrogate,' Rosie said. 'The choice is yours.'

'Rosie! Rosie!'

Charlotte looked ahead to see a petite, dark-haired girl waving across at them. Next to her was a young lad with a thick mop of short blond hair. He was sporting round, black-rimmed spectacles.

'Is this who I think it is?' Hannah looked wide-eyed at Rosie and then at Charlotte.

'It certainly is,' Rosie said. 'Hannah, this is my sister Charlie ... Charlie, this is Hannah, who, I might add, is one of the most talented trainee draughtsmen – or I should really say *draughtswomen* – at Thompson's.'

Hannah blushed.

'So, Charlie,' she said, reaching out and taking her hand, 'it's lovely to meet you. We've all heard so much about you.'

Charlotte looked at Rosie. She doubted her sister had been singing her praises.

'Oh, and coincidentally,' Rosie turned to her sister, 'Hannah *also* ran away from where she was living.' She glanced at the group's 'little bird' and smiled sadly. 'Only Hannah here had good reason to.'

Charlotte looked at the young woman in front of her. Taking in her dark eyes, olive skin and bobbed jet-black hair, she guessed she was Jewish.

'Where are you from?' Charlotte asked.

'Prague, Czechoslovakia,' Hannah said proudly. 'But don't ask me about it,' she added, 'otherwise I might cry.'

She looked at Rosie.

'I'm feeling so ... what is the word?' She thought for a moment. 'That's it – I feel so *weepy* after last night.'

They were all quiet.

'We went to see Martha and Gloria during lunchtime,' Hannah said, breaking the silence. 'Took them some of Aunty Rina's *rugelach* she'd made for the Sabbath.'

'*Pastries*,' Dorothy whispered in Charlotte's ear. 'Made with raisins, nuts and jam. Totally delicious.'

'We gave one to the matron,' Olly chuckled, pushing his glasses back up the bridge of his nose, 'and she let us stay a little longer.'

'Were they both all reet?' Angie asked.

'Yes, they were in good spirits. Some good news for a change. *Díky Bohu.*'

'"Thanks be to God",' Olly informed.

'They said Polly had popped in this morning.'

'Really?!' Dorothy and Angie exclaimed in unison.

'They said she was "floating on a cloud",' Hannah relayed with a big smile.

'Ahh,' the women chorused, just as the *W.F. Vint* gently bumped the front of the ferry landing.

'Yer learning Czech now?' Angie asked Olly as they all lined up to board.

Olly nodded nervously. Charlotte clocked the interaction and was glad she wasn't the only one to feel intimidated by Angie.

'We have a lot to be thankful for, don't we?' Hannah said after they had each paid their penny fare and made their way to the front of the boat.

Rosie, Dorothy and Angie all nodded solemnly.

'Were you two all right after we left you?' Hannah's question was directed at Dorothy and Angie.

'We needed a good bath!' Dorothy half laughed.

'And the water was nearly as black as when my dad gets out the tub!' Angie hooted.

'Angie's dad's a miner,' Dorothy explained to Charlotte.

Charlotte nodded her understanding. She liked Dorothy.

'So, are you staying long, Charlotte?' Hannah asked.

Charlotte gave her sister a defiant look.

'Yes, I'm going to be working at the yard.'

'Well, if that's the case,' Hannah said, clapping her hands together, 'let's have lunch together in the canteen soon, and you can tell me all about the subjects you've been studying at school. Rosie says you're learning Latin?'

Charlotte nodded.

'I do miss school,' Hannah said wistfully. 'I was going to go to university, you know? To study Classics.'

Charlotte noticed Olly, who had been standing quietly next to Hannah, take her hand and give it a gentle squeeze.

As they reached the south docks, there was no chance for any further chit-chat. As soon as they disembarked, they were buffeted onto the landing, before being carried up Low Street by the swell of workers all eager to get to the pub or back home for their tea.

'Are we getting the bus home?' Charlotte asked. They were heading into town, having said goodbye to everyone. She was desperate to get back to Brookside Gardens as she wasn't sure how much longer her bladder could hold out.

'We're just going to nip in to say a quick hello to Kate,' Rosie said. She got out her little electric torch and switched it on.

'Come here.' She linked her arm with Charlotte's, knowing she wasn't used to the blackout. They walked down Little Villiers Street, along Borough Road, past Gloria's flat and the municipal museum, and on to Holmeside.

'Here we are,' she said. 'The Maison Nouvelle.'

'The "new home",' Charlotte translated.

Rosie felt a flourish of pride.

As they walked into the boutique, the brass bell above the door jangled, causing Kate to jump with nerves. Seeing it was Rosie – and that Charlotte was behind her – she jumped again. Only this time for joy.

'Charlie!' Kate hurried across the shop floor and flung her skinny arms around her friend's little sister. 'I often wondered if I'd recognise you, but I needn't have worried.'

Kate looked at Rosie.

'She's the spit of your mam, isn't she?'

Rosie nodded. It was true. Even more so this past year, as she had changed from a girl into a young woman.

'Shame she hasn't also inherited her calm and sensible nature,' Rosie said, shutting the door and taking off her overcoat. Kate always kept the boutique lovely and warm.

She claimed it was because she wanted customers to feel relaxed, but Rosie thought it had more to do with the fact that, after all the years spent living on the streets, Kate was determined never to be cold again.

'Rosie, I think you might be looking back on the past with slightly rose-tinted glasses.' Kate laughed as she turned the sign on the door from 'Open' to 'Closed' and ushered them through the shop and into the back room. 'Your mam was a lovely woman, but I don't remember her being that calm or sensible.'

Charlotte looked at Rosie, only just managing to keep a look of triumph from spreading across her face.

'She was so full of life,' Kate recalled, going over to her little stove and putting the kettle on. 'Whenever she used to come around ours, my mam would say, "Poor David, he's got his hands full there!"'

Seeing Rosie's and Charlotte's faces as they savoured every word she spoke about their beloved mother, Kate smiled. 'Mam thought it was great, you know, that Eloise was so free-spirited.' She chuckled. 'And that your dad was so easy-going.'

'That's the way I remember her,' Charlotte said. 'Always chatting and laughing.'

Kate busied herself with making the tea.

Charlotte started shifting about uncomfortably on her chair.

'Kate, would I be able to use your toilet, please?'

'Of course, you can,' Kate said. 'Go through the door and it's just on your right. It's a bit of a squeeze, but at least it's indoors.'

Rosie had to stifle a chuckle at the obvious relief on Charlotte's face.

'Maybe bang on the door, just in case,' Rosie said, suppressing a smile.

Charlotte looked at her sister and caught the laughter in her eyes.

As soon as Charlotte had left the room, Kate sat down at the table. She leant towards Rosie.

'So, tell me, what on earth is Charlotte doing here?' she whispered.

'She's bloody well run away from school!' Rosie whispered back. 'Turned up last night while I was up the hospital with Gloria and Martha. Came back to find an excited-looking Mrs Jenkins peering round her front door, telling me some young girl "claiming" to be my sister had turned up and was it all right that she had let her in with the spare key Peter had given her?'

'Oh my goodness! Bet you were livid.' Kate's eyes were trained on her friend.

'Was? I still am!' Rosie said. 'I was up all night trying to work out what to do.'

'And?' Kate was staring at Rosie. She looked worn out.

Charlotte came back into the kitchen before Rosie had a chance to answer.

Kate got up and poured out their tea. Charlotte sat down quickly and started to sip hers, relishing it. She hadn't drunk anything since lunchtime.

'Isn't it wonderful news about Tommy?' Kate perked up. 'You should have seen Polly's face last night when she turned up with Maisie. I think she was in shock. She hardly said a word. George took her up to the hospital and said she practically flew through the front doors.'

'Sounds like she's still flying high.' Rosie chuckled. 'Apparently she popped into the Royal to see Gloria and Martha this morning. Seems like she'd been by Tommy's bedside all night.'

Kate's face suddenly lit up.

'My guess is they'll be wanting to get married soon?'

Rosie laughed.

'I think Tommy will have to get better first! But don't worry, Kate, there'll be another wedding dress to be made in the not too distant future.'

Rosie finished the dregs of her tea.

'Come on, drink up.' She looked at Charlotte. 'Home time.'

Rosie stood up.

'And Kate, would you mind telling Lily that I won't be able to come and do her books this evening, please?'

'Yes, of course,' Kate said.

'Who's Lily?' Charlotte asked, taking a final swig of her tea.

'I do her bookkeeping on an evening and she's Kate's landlady.'

'I've never heard you mention her before?' Charlotte said.

'Perhaps,' Rosie said sternly, 'if I wasn't having to deal with the repercussions of all your shenanigans at school, we might have had more time to chat about life in general.'

Charlotte knew when to keep quiet. She stood up and put her mac back on.

Rosie ushered Charlotte towards the front door.

'Tell Lily I'll try and get in tomorrow for a few hours, probably early evening.'

'I'll tell her,' Kate said, following them. 'I'm sure she'll be *very* excited to hear that Charlotte's in town.'

'So, what happened to Kate after her mum died?' Charlotte asked as they walked up Holmeside and on to Vine Place. Now that her bladder was empty, she was more than happy to walk home. Even if it was a bit nippy.

'Well, she ended up in Nazareth House.'

'With the nuns?' Charlotte asked.

'Yes, with the nuns,' Rosie added, taking her sister's arm as they crossed over to Tunstall Road. 'Where they had their own peculiar idea of caring for those who no longer had a mam and dad.'

Charlotte caught her sister's profile in the darkness. She saw anger.

'What do you mean?' she asked.

'Well, put it this way,' Rosie said, 'by the time she was fourteen, Kate had decided life on the streets was preferable to staying another night with the Sisters.'

They walked on in silence.

Charlotte couldn't help but draw parallels. Kate had been orphaned when she was ten. Her own parents had died when she was eight. But where Kate had been taken in by the nuns at Nazareth House, she had been taken on as a border at Runcorn.

There was no arguing that Kate had drawn the short straw.

Both of them, however, had decided that they'd had enough of where they were and done a bunk when they were fourteen.

As they approached Brookside Gardens, Charlotte counted her blessings.

'So, how did Kate end up with the Maison Nouvelle?' Charlotte asked.

Rosie noticed how well her sister pronounced the name of Kate's boutique.

'It's a long story,' Rosie said, 'but Kate ended up going to live with Lily, who encouraged her to do what she was clearly born to do.'

'Make gorgeous clothes,' Charlotte added, having seen the beautiful pastel pink wedding dress displayed in the front window.

'Yes,' Rosie smiled, 'make gorgeous clothes.'

She turned to Charlotte as she opened the small five-bar gate at the end of Brookside Gardens.

'Now, not a word. And quiet as a mouse until we get indoors.'

Charlotte agreed, although she had no idea why they were having to be so silent.

They stole along the gravelled private road and Rosie's heart felt heavy as she thought of Lily. There was no way Charlotte could know the truth about her 'other life' at the bordello. That was one thing she knew for certain. When Charlotte was older, perhaps, but definitely not now. She was still far too young.

As they made it through the front door, Rosie shut it softly behind them, breathed a sigh of relief and shook off her coat.

'Right, first things first.' She turned to Charlotte. 'As you are such a dab hand at building fires, get one going in the lounge. I'll make us some sandwiches and a pot of tea.'

Charlotte felt like dancing down the hallway and into the lounge. She hadn't felt so happy in a long, long time.

Chapter Eight

Helen sat down on the only free seat left on the tram.

'Oh, isn't she gorgeous!' the old woman she'd sat next to exclaimed. 'Incredible eyes.' She looked at Helen. 'She's obviously got them from her mammy.'

Brushing Hope's mop of black hair to the side, Helen smiled at the old woman, who smelled heavily of lavender. She couldn't, of course, correct her and explain that this gorgeous little girl on her lap was, in fact, her sister. That the bonny little girl was her father's love child – a child he'd had to a woman she was just on her way to see.

Helen was glad when the old woman struck up a conversation with the passenger on her other side. She wanted to be left to her own thoughts. Hope also seemed happy to sit and simply look around her.

The day, Helen reflected, had passed in a haze, ending with the slightly bizarre conversation with Rosie in which she had reassured her that she had been a cow of a boss to Charlotte.

She had seemed satisfied, but Helen thought Rosie was delusional if she thought she was going to scare her sister back to Harrogate simply by making her work.

Whenever she looked out to check on Charlotte – or *Charlie*, as she'd heard her telling people to call her – she seemed happy as Larry, hurrying around the office, making tea, sorting out the post, tidying up. And, of course, Marie-Anne and Bel had fussed over her, even though they were under strict instructions to give her a hard time.

Helen had told Rosie that she'd put Charlotte on the payroll as a temporary worker and that she'd be given a very basic wage, which, she'd said, might be a good way of showing her how little she would earn if she were *not* to go back to school; although something told Helen that it wasn't so much that Charlotte was averse to going to school, but more that she didn't want to go back to the one she was at.

As the tram trundled up Holmeside, Helen's mind started to mull over a slightly throwaway comment Rosie had made explaining how Charlotte was able to go to such an expensive boarding school.

What was it she'd said?

Helen's thoughts were broken momentarily by the old man opposite her who had fallen asleep and had started to half snore.

That was it. She'd said her parents had left enough money in their will.

But why, Helen wondered, hadn't they done the same for Rosie?

As the tram squealed to a stop on Vine Place, Helen thought about all the secrets and lies her mother's investigator had unearthed: Dorothy's bigamous mum, Angie's mam's bit on the side, Martha's evil birth mother, Hannah's aunt's financial troubles ...

The only blot on *Rosie's* copybook was that she had fallen in love with a man almost twice her age.

Something told her that her mother's private eye hadn't dug deep enough.

The blinds of the tram were pulled down in line with blackout regulations, and as there was little light, Helen allowed herself to rest her tired eyes, which still felt dry and scratchy from all the brick dust last night.

Likewise, Hope curled up in her big sister's arms and started sucking her thumb.

For a little while, Helen allowed herself the indulgence of imagining that Hope really was her child. The one she had lost when she'd been four months gone.

Since the miscarriage, she had wanted to ask John whether or not the baby she had been carrying was a girl. He must know. After all, he had operated on her.

But she had never asked him – and he had never told her.

Perhaps it was best if she never knew.

Wanting, yet not wanting to know.

It was like having a scab and itching to pick it, but knowing that if you did, it would hurt, there would be blood and it would take even longer to heal.

Chapter Nine

'How you feeling?'

Polly sat down by the side of Tommy's bed. It was evening visiting hours and there was a low murmur of chatter in the ward. Anyone who got too raucous received a scathing look from matron.

'All the better for seeing you.' Tommy turned his head towards Polly, his hazel eyes drinking in the sight of the woman he loved.

'What time is it?' he asked.

'It's just gone seven,' Polly said.

'I must have slept most of the afternoon after you and Arthur left.'

Tommy's voice sounded croaky and Polly automatically reached over to the bedside cabinet for a glass of water. Tommy pushed himself up so that he was half sitting. It seemed to take every bit of energy he had to do so.

'Here.' Polly went to put the tumbler to his lips, but he stopped her and took the glass himself.

'Thanks, Pol,' he said, taking a few sips. 'Was Arthur all right when he got back?' he asked. 'He looked tired.'

'He was fine,' Polly said, 'although he's slowing down a bit now. He's cut down on the hours he spends at Albert's allotment. He's had to admit it's getting too much for him, especially now winter's just around the corner.' Polly looked at Tommy. 'You probably noticed a difference in your grandda since you saw him last?'

Tommy smiled sadly and nodded.

'He looks a lot older.' He paused and took Polly's hand. 'You, however, look even more beautiful than I remember, if that's at all possible.'

Polly blushed and squeezed his hand.

'It won't be long before I'm back to the way I was,' Tommy said, aware of how different he must look from when Polly had last seen him. From the man she'd waved off at the train station almost two years ago.

'I love you just the way you are, Tommy Watts,' Polly said. 'You're alive, and you're here, and we've got our whole lives ahead of us. That's all that matters.'

Tommy looked at Polly for a moment before pulling her gently towards him so that he could kiss her.

'I'll love you until the day I die, Polly Elliot,' he whispered.

Catching a sadness in his tone, Polly looked at him.

'Do you remember much? From your time on the hospital ship?'

Tommy was hit by the image of the young Red Cross nurse as she'd taken her fatal gasp.

'No,' he lied, his voice distant, as though he himself were sinking back down to the bottom of the Atlantic along with the nurse.

'From before then?' Polly asked gently.

'From before then?' Tommy repeated.

'Yes,' Polly said, looking at him with concern now. He had turned even paler than he already was. 'Before you ended up on the hospital ship.'

Tommy closed his eyes briefly. His mind's eye flickered back to that day in June. He could almost feel the intense North African sun beating down on his face as he put on his diving suit, the heat made only just bearable by the cool sea breeze.

'Not really. It's all a bit of a blur,' he lied.

67

His memory of that day was, in fact, vivid – the adrenaline coursing through his body as he swam down to the bottom of the ship's hull, how he'd spotted the limpet mine more or less straight away, worked hard to get it loose, knowing it could go off at any moment. He remembered well the relief on freeing it, the sight of it slowly floating down towards the seabed. He'd swum away from it as quickly as he could. The new diver's gear he was wearing allowing him more freedom and, therefore, more speed.

If he'd been wearing his normal cumbersome canvas suit, lead shoes and twelve-bolt copper helmet, he would, quite simply, not be here now.

'There was an explosion underwater,' Tommy volunteered, knowing he had to say something.

The force of the explosion had knocked him senseless, his body feeling like a feather caught in the eye of a tornado.

'What happened?' Polly asked in earnest.

'I just remember being pushed through the water.' Tommy paused. 'Then everything went black. After that I can't remember much.'

This was true. The force of the explosion had knocked Tommy unconscious.

'I vaguely remember being hauled aboard the hospital ship, but that's about it,' he said, hoping this would satisfy Polly.

Polly was filled with such anger for a country she had not even been able to pinpoint on a map before this damned war. North Africa had stolen the life of one of her brothers, maimed the other, and very nearly taken the man she loved.

'I don't think I'll ever stop counting my blessings that you made it back here alive,' she said, tears beginning to fill her eyes.

Tommy looked at Polly. It hurt him to see her upset. And even more that he was the cause.

'Tell me more about last night,' Tommy asked, wanting to change the subject. 'Arthur told me bits and bobs.'

Polly sat back and sighed. 'Oh, Tommy, it was awful.'

Tommy held her hand as she relayed how they had all been at home when the sirens started up. They'd been getting ready to go to the shelter when they'd heard two huge explosions, one after the other.

'Then there was this banging on the front door,' Polly said. 'Like someone was trying to batter the door down. It was Pearl, looking the most worried I think I've ever seen her.'

Tommy had never met Pearl but had read all about her in Polly's letters.

'She told us one of the bombs had landed in Tavistock Place, where we normally go, which was obviously why she was so worried. Bill was with her and he told us to take refuge in the pub cellar.'

Tommy was listening intently.

'We could see when we went across to the Tatham that the other bomb had obliterated the bottom end of the street, where Gloria had told us she was visiting an old friend – *with Hope*.' Polly took a breath. 'As soon as the all-clear sounded out, Bel and I rushed to see if she was all right. And that's when Dorothy and Angie told us they were still in the house. Or rather, what was left of the house. Martha and Helen were in there as well.'

'So, they'd gone in there to save Gloria and Hope?' Tommy asked, pushing himself up in the bed.

Polly nodded.

'So, there we all were, staring at this building that looked like a house of cards on the verge of collapse.' Polly laughed a little. 'And then Rosie just said, ever so matter-of-factly,

"Well, we better go in there and get them," and so we all started clambering over bricks and mortar to get to the house. But before we got there, Martha appeared, carrying Hope.'

'Blimey,' Tommy said, enthralled.

'Poor Martha,' Polly said. 'She put Hope down and then she just went down like a bag of hammers.'

'What? She just keeled over?'

Polly nodded, her eyes wide.

'Then there was this awful cracking noise and we looked up and what remained of the house came down in one fell swoop.' Polly breathed out. 'Dr Parker was there with us and we all stood there, waiting and praying. And then through all the dust and dirt we saw them. It was the strangest sight. Helen was holding Gloria up and they were both just stood there – like statues.'

'Blimey,' Tommy said again. 'Talk about lucky.'

'I know,' Polly agreed. 'Then when everyone was over at the St John's ambulance, Helen suddenly blurted out that you were alive – and you were here!'

Tommy looked at Polly's face, her eyes sparkling with happiness. He listened as she chatted on, telling him how she and Maisie had raced over to Ashbrooke, and how Rosie's friend, George, a war veteran, had brought her to the hospital.

Polly had just got to the part where she'd walked through the swing doors of the ward and seen him, when the matron rang her little bell to tell them all that visiting time was over.

After Polly left, Tommy closed his eyes.

Images of the Red Cross nurse overlapped those of the Tatham Street bombing. He railed inwardly, realising how easily the air raid could have claimed the life of the woman he loved. The woman who had given him the will and the

70

strength to survive. He thought about the compassion and care of the nurse whose name he didn't even know. And the bravery of Helen and Martha, risking their own lives to save Gloria and her little girl.

And the more he thought, the angrier he became.

It wasn't just those fighting overseas who were dying in their droves, innocent women and children were being killed on their own doorsteps.

There was no escaping the danger, death and destruction that walked hand in hand with Hitler and his fellow warmongers.

This madman and his crazed cohorts had to be stopped.

'Eee, Bel, I feel like I'm floating on a cloud. I really do. I've never felt like this – ever before.'

Bel smiled. It was so lovely to see her sister-in-law glowing with such happiness, love and gratitude. Especially after what had happened last night. She had just heard that the death toll had gone up to fourteen – and that seven of those had been children.

When Beryl had told her, she'd burst into tears. She hadn't been able to stop them. Seeing Polly now, so happy and in love, full of expectations for the future, was a much-needed respite.

'Did Helen's doctor friend say how long it'll take for Tommy to get better?' Bel asked.

Polly shook her head as she bit into one of her ma's homemade oatmeal biscuits. Whenever anything really bad or really good happened, her mother went into a cooking and cleaning frenzy. As there had been both good and bad events in the past twenty-four hours, she'd gone into overdrive.

'He said we just had to take it day by day,' she said, wiping crumbs from her mouth. 'And that the main thing was for him to rest and for his body to get its strength back.'

'And was Arthur all right?' Bel asked. She was sitting in the old man's armchair by the range. Tramp and Pup were by her feet. 'Only, when I told him last night that Tommy was alive and that you'd gone to the Ryhope to see him, he just stood there. Didn't move a muscle. It was as though he'd been struck by lightning. Agnes had to sit him down at the table and give him a cup of sweet tea. He just looked at the cup and then up at Agnes and tears started trickling down his face.'

Bel paused.

'Then he just put his head in his hands and sobbed his heart out.'

Bel looked at Polly. Her eyes had started to fill with tears.

'It was like all the pent-up emotions from the months of waiting and wondering and thinking Tommy was dead just came pouring out of him.'

Polly nodded her understanding.

'I have to admit,' Bel said, 'me and your ma were struggling not to cry too. When he finally stopped, he stood up and hugged Agnes like she had been the one to bring Tommy back from the dead all by herself. Then he gave me a big hug and took himself off to bed.'

Polly listened intently. Arthur had been such a pillar of strength to her ever since Tommy had left for war.

When she'd gone up to the hospital earlier, she'd walked into the ward and seen Arthur half snoozing in a winged chair she'd guessed the matron must have got him. Tommy had been out for the count, but he had his hand over Arthur's. They'd looked so close. And Arthur had looked so peaceful.

The two women drank their tea in silence.

Suddenly Bel put her finger to her lips. 'I think I can hear him talking in his sleep?' she said, cocking her ear to the hallway.

'He's probably shattered,' Polly said. 'I could tell he was tired coming back on the bus.'

'Mmm. It's not a five-minute journey, is it? The sooner we get Tommy back here the better, eh?'

Polly nodded.

She took another sip of her tea.

'Bel, I feel I've been given my life back. I'm the luckiest woman alive.'

'You should have seen our lad, pet.'

Arthur was lying on his back in his bed, hands clasped together as if in prayer. His eyes were closed. He didn't need them open to see his Flo.

'White as a sheet. And skinny as a rake he was. But he's alive.'

He yawned.

'I knew you'd pull some strings up there 'n bring him back safe 'n sound.'

Arthur chuckled.

'And seeing Polly 'n how happy she is – ah, it's just wonderful, pet. Really wonderful.'

Arthur yawned again.

He'd never felt so happy himself – nor so tired.

Within a few minutes he had fallen asleep in the middle of his chat to Flo.

Not that she minded.

Chapter Ten

The following day

Sunday 18 October

'So, just remind me,' Charlotte said as she hurried to keep up with her sister's brisk pace as they walked along Burdon Road. 'We're going to meet Polly and her family who live in the east end?'

'That's right,' Rosie said.

'And Polly is one of your squad. A welder. And she's the one who's over the moon because her fiancé, who everyone thought was dead, is alive?'

'Yes,' Rosie confirmed.

'And ...' Charlotte hesitated for a moment. She had met so many people yesterday. 'Polly lives with Mrs Elliot who works in admin?'

'Yes, they're sisters-in-law. Mrs Elliot is married to Polly's brother Joe, who was medically discharged after he got caught by a landmine out in North Africa.'

'Gosh, that sounds awful,' Charlotte said. 'I'm guessing he's all right now?'

'He's got a bad limp. He had a load of shrapnel in his leg. Sometimes it's a job to get it all out. Walks with a stick, but he still manages to do quite a bit with the Home Guard.'

Charlotte didn't say anything. She'd never met a real soldier before.

'Let's cut through the park,' Rosie suggested.

As soon as they'd got through the gate, Charlotte gasped in horror.

'Oh my goodness.' She stood stock-still and stared at the forty-foot-wide crater.

Rosie didn't say anything, but instead turned back to the gate they'd just walked through.

'I forgot I wanted to show you something,' she said.

Charlotte followed, her eyes still trained on the crater.

'Can you remember Binns?' Rosie cast a look at her sister.

'Of course I can,' Charlotte said. 'Mam used to take us there every Christmas to see the window display.'

'That's right,' Rosie said, noticing that Charlotte was now referring to their mother as 'Mam' and not 'Mum'. It had been 'Mammy' when their mother was alive.

'Well, that's what it looks like now.' Rosie pointed over to a cordoned-off bomb site on the corner of Fawcett Street. They'd actually passed it last night on their way to see Kate, but it had been too dark to see properly. Rosie had also purposely not pointed it out then as she had wanted Charlotte to see the town in the clear light of day.

'When did that happen?' Charlotte asked.

'April last year,' Rosie said. 'It was gutted by a load of incendiary devices and they had to pull it down.'

'Why didn't you tell me?' she asked as Rosie started walking along Borough Road.

'Why would I?' Rosie replied.

Charlotte was just about to tell her sister exactly *why* she should have told her, when she stopped in her tracks.

'Is that ... *was* that the Victoria Hall?' she asked, her eyes glued to a mountain of debris where the music hall had once stood.

Rosie nodded solemnly.

'That happened just a week after Binns was bombed.'

Rosie started walking again.

Charlotte followed.

A few minutes later they came to another bomb site.

'This is Tavistock Place, where one of the bombs dropped the other night,' Rosie said.

She stopped at the top of the road and pointed to yet another mountain of bricks and mortar.

'That was a food warehouse.'

Rosie turned right and the two sisters walked down the long line of terraced houses that made up Laura Street. At the junction with Murton Street there was another massive crater. It looked as though someone had hit the cobbles with a gigantic hammer.

'You'd probably have just been getting on the train at York when that one landed, but fortunately it didn't explode.'

It took them another minute or so to walk down Murton Street before turning right into Tatham Street.

Charlotte stared at the devastation at the end of the road. It looked as if the houses at the bottom had been stomped on. She'd never seen anything like it. There was upended furniture, half-buried sofas, a crushed tricycle. About half a dozen people were wandering around the bomb site. Some were salvaging goods. Others were simply looking. She recalled the snippets of conversation she'd caught yesterday amongst the women in the office. It was one thing hearing it discussed, quite another seeing it first-hand.

'More than a dozen killed,' Rosie said.

She looked at Charlotte who was still staring at the ruins.

'Sixteen others were badly injured,' she added.

They stood and looked.

'Gloria and her little girl Hope nearly died when number two came down.' Rosie pointed to a mound at the bottom right-hand side of the street. 'And Martha and Miss Crawford nearly died saving them.'

Rosie turned to her sister and gently placed her hands on her shoulders.

'Now do you understand why I don't want you to live here?' She looked in earnest at her sister. 'At least in Harrogate I know you're safe. Safe from all this.' Rosie turned her head to look at the devastation just a hundred yards from where they were standing.

'Families are evacuating their children out to the country, not the other way around,' she added, with more than a hint of exasperation in her voice.

Charlotte had to bite her tongue.

She wanted to say that Rosie wasn't her mother – and that at fourteen she was no longer a child.

More than anything, she wanted to tell her the real reason she didn't want to go back to Harrogate, but she knew she couldn't.

'Come on,' Rosie said. 'Let's go and meet the Elliots.'

'I thought Charlie was a lad's name?' Pearl came bustling down the stairs, fag, as usual, scissored between her fingers ready to spark up. She'd heard Rosie introducing her sister to everyone and knew there'd be a cuppa begging, as well as a few biscuits. Agnes was in a baking mood and Pearl was determined to make the most of it.

'It's short for Charlotte, Ma, as you well know,' Bel rolled her eyes theatrically to the ceiling before continuing to pour out everyone's tea.

'Well, *Charlotte*,' Pearl said, balancing two pieces of shortbread on the saucer of her cup of tea. 'I think yer far too bonny fer a boy's name. It's like my Isabelle here, she *will* insist on being called Bel – like something yer bloody well ring!'

'Ma, out the back and smoke your fag,' Bel ordered, before Pearl could say anything else. 'And don't drop your biscuits, 'cos that's your lot!'

Charlotte couldn't believe this coarse, mutton-dressed-as-lamb woman was Bel's mother. She stared as Pearl hurried out into the backyard.

'I'm afraid I'm gonna leave yer all to it,' Joe said, pushing himself up from his chair. 'The Major's expecting me in ten.'

Charlotte looked at Bel's husband and thought he was totally gorgeous. Especially in his uniform. The spit of Errol Flynn.

'Nice to meet you, Charlie.' He put out his hand.

Charlotte could feel herself go bright red as she shook it.

'You too, Mr Elliot.'

Joe laughed loudly.

'Please, call me Joe. Mr Elliot makes me sound like an old man!'

Agnes quickly wrapped half a dozen biscuits in a sheet of greaseproof paper and tied it with string into a neat little parcel.

'For you and the Major.'

As Joe left, Arthur came into the kitchen and was introduced to Charlotte. He was reminded of his own daughter when she was that age, but didn't say so. Even now he still found it hard to talk about Tommy's mam, who had taken her own life after losing her husband in the First War.

'Well, I can't hang around idly gossiping!'

Pearl had reappeared from the backyard.

'Bill's asked me to gan in early to help open up. It'll be busy today. Always is after an air raid,' she informed everyone as she left the kitchen.

For the next half-hour, Agnes, Polly, Arthur and their two guests chatted, drank tea and ate home-made biscuits.

The bombing was, naturally, the main topic of conversation – as was Tommy's return.

Rosie had to stop her own thoughts straying to Peter, wondering about him in France. What kind of covert operations was he involved with? How dangerous were they? She prayed that he was keeping himself safe.

On hearing that Charlotte was working at Thompson's, Agnes showed her disapproval with a loud tut and shake of the head.

'If Rosie's little sister wants to work in the yards, she should be able to,' Polly said, giving Charlotte a wink. 'I'd have given anything to start work at Thompson's when I was that age.'

Charlotte appreciated the show of solidarity but felt like a bit of a fraud. It hadn't exactly been her choice to start working there – although she would probably have agreed to work down the mines if it meant not going back to Harrogate.

When Rosie mentioned the fact that she had shown Charlotte what was left of Binns, as well as the once magnificent Victoria Hall, Agnes proceeded to give Charlotte a rundown of just about all the other air raids in other parts of town that had killed, maimed and mangled over the past two years. She knew Rosie's intention today was to show Charlotte the devastating reality of war, and how different it was to living in Harrogate, which, from what Charlotte had told them, had suffered just the one air raid with no one hurt. They had all laughed loudly when Charlotte had told them that part of the bomb was currently being displayed in a shop window.

What Agnes didn't realise, though, was that there was another reason why Rosie had brought Charlotte to the east end, and that it was something Rosie had wanted to do since the horrendous night two years ago when she had nearly died at the hands of her uncle. She wanted her to meet the woman to whom she would be eternally grateful

– a woman who had stayed up with her all night, nursing her through the hell of arc eye, tending her wounds and facial burns and not once asking any questions or making any judgements.

One day Rosie would tell Charlotte why Agnes was such a special person.

When it was time to go, Charlotte felt loath to leave the cosy kitchen-cum-living-room.

'Don't forget,' Polly said, 'if you have any problems at work, either go and see Bel or just come and see us lot out in the yard.'

'Charlie might be working out in the yard soon,' Rosie said, shrugging on her grey mac, which oddly enough matched her little sister's. 'I think Miss Crawford's going to have her doing all sorts. Give her a good grounding in all things shipbuilding,' she added, walking down the hallway.

Agnes tutted even more loudly than last time. She was no fool, though. She knew what Rosie was doing and certainly didn't blame her. The way Charlotte had blushed in front of Joe showed she was still very innocent. If she found out that her older sister, the one stable presence in her life since her parents' death, had worked as a call girl in a brothel she now part-owned, it would not bode well.

'Well, you just take care in them yards, pet.' Agnes wrapped her arms around Charlotte and gave her a hug. She felt her stiffen in her embrace and realised the girl wasn't used to physical affection. She let her go but took hold of her hand.

'Yer one of the family now, yer know?' She looked at Charlotte and then up at Rosie. 'No matter whether yer here or back in Harrogate.'

'Aye,' Arthur said, standing up and ruffling her hair, 'never feel like yer on yer own.'

Charlotte suddenly felt the urge to cry. She told herself not to be stupid and to 'buck up'.

'See you tomorrow,' Rosie shouted back to Polly and Bel.

Polly had told her that she'd be back at work tomorrow. Her plan was to work a full shift, but to pass up any overtime and go up to the Ryhope on an evening to see Tommy.

Rosie was glad. It would mean she'd have her squad back. All apart from Gloria. She knew Helen would also be pleased. She might have joked the night of the air raid about continuing to be a pain when it came to hitting the new tonnage record, but Rosie knew part of her was deadly serious.

And if Rosie was honest, she too wanted to see the yard break the thirty-six-year production record. With more women working in the yards it would prove her point that the women were as good as the men – that they were just as hard-working and productive, if not more so.

'I have to go out and work this evening,' Rosie told Charlotte after they'd had their pie and pea supper. It had always been Charlotte's favourite when they were small, and by the look of the plate scraped clean, it still was.

'At Lily's?' Charlotte asked as she gathered up the dirty dishes and started washing up. It hadn't escaped Rosie's notice that Charlotte was endeavouring to be the perfect house guest.

'Yes,' Rosie said, wanting to keep any talk about Lily's down to a minimum. 'But before I go, we need to sit down and talk properly.'

Charlotte felt her heart sink. She shouldn't have been surprised. She'd thought Rosie was going to have 'the talk' with her last night, after they'd had their supper. But she hadn't said a dicky bird.

'So,' Rosie said, taking a sip of her tea and looking at her sister across the small kitchen table. 'Why has being at Runcorn become a fate worse than death?'

Rosie gave what she hoped was a sympathetic smile. She hadn't quite given up on the idea that she could get to the bottom of whatever it was that was making Charlotte unhappy at school. She could then sort it out. Get Charlotte back there. Everything could return to normal and there'd be no more stress over her sister finding out about what really went on at Lily's.

Charlotte took a deep breath. She had to make this convincing. She thought about some techniques she had been taught in her drama class. Her teacher had told them that acting was really an expert form of lying, and the main way to master the skill was to believe what you were saying yourself.

'I'm just really, really homesick,' Charlotte said.

This was true.

'I miss *you*. I miss being where I belong.'

Again, this was true.

'And is there anything else, apart from feeling homesick, that has made you want to leave school?' asked Rosie, being as empathetic as possible.

Charlotte shook her head. 'No.'

'Are you sure?' Rosie asked. 'What about all the hoo-ha at the start of term? That awful fight with that girl? It seems like a bit of a coincidence ...'

Charlotte shook her head again and pasted a look of puzzlement on her face, as though she couldn't quite understand why the two might be related.

'Perhaps,' she perked up, 'that happened because I was so homesick.'

Charlotte felt like patting herself on the back. The school debating club had come in useful for something.

'Mmm.' Rosie took another sip of her tea. 'Well, if that's all that's really the matter ...' She stopped. 'Not that I'm belittling the fact you feel homesick. But if that really *is* the problem, then I have a solution.'

She took a deep breath.

'I think the ideal situation would be for you to go back to school, but to come back here during half-term and holidays. Weekends if you're really feeling homesick.'

Charlotte's heart sank for the second time. She tried to make her eyes tear up, but they stayed dry as a bone.

'But Rosie, I want to be here *all the time*. I want to *live* here. Not just visit during the holidays.' She knew her voice was sounding whiny, which was never good, but she couldn't help it. So much for her drama lessons.

Rosie sat back and looked at her sister.

She then looked at her watch.

'Think about it, Charlie. *Really* think about it. Remember, Harrogate has been your home for the past six years. You may well miss it if you just up and leave and never go back.'

Charlotte had to clamp her mouth shut.

'Just give it some thought, eh?' Rosie said, getting up and grabbing her boxed gas mask and handbag. She kissed her sister on the head.

'And try and get an early night. You'll be up early tomorrow for work, don't forget.'

Chapter Eleven

'*Mon Dieu!*' Lily said, making no attempt to conceal her exasperation.

'The girl's fourteen years old now! She's old enough to go out and get a job. I really, *really* do not understand you, Rosie! Why on earth can't you just tell her about this place?' She gestured at the rather beautifully decorated front reception room that was now Rosie's office.

At that moment George walked in.

When he saw the look on his future wife's face, as well as the one on the young woman he thought of as his own flesh and blood, he wished he could rewind the last thirty seconds and carry on walking down the hallway to the back parlour.

'Thank Gawd for that,' Lily said, ushering her fiancé into the room. 'Perhaps you can talk some sense into this obstinate *enfant*, George!'

Rosie opened her mouth in outrage.

George immediately stepped forward so that he was strategically placed between the two women. It was never good to hear Lily swing between faux French and natural-born cockney in the space of a breath.

'Well, I think we should start by calming down,' George said, firmly. He had automatically put his two hands out and was suddenly reminded of a referee standing in the middle of a boxing ring, warning the two opponents to stay apart.

'I'm guessing,' he said, 'that this has to do with Charlotte.'

'Bloomin' too right it does,' said Lily.

'Rosie,' said George, 'would you mind pouring me a cognac, please?' He turned to Lily. 'And darling, can you sit yourself down on the chaise longue?'

Lily looked at George, ignored his request and stomped over to Rosie's desk. She snatched up her packet of Gauloises, pulled out a cigarette and lit it before walking over to the fireplace with the ashtray, all the while glowering at Rosie, who was standing with her hands on her hips.

As no one seemed willing to do what he'd asked, George poured his own brandy and sat down in the leather chesterfield armchair that had been placed in front of the desk for clients who came to settle their bill.

'Tell me from the start,' he said directly to Rosie. 'What's happened with Charlotte?'

'George, you know exactly what's "happened with Charlotte",' Lily butted in before Rosie had a chance to answer. 'The girl's run away from that posh school of hers and is now here – back in her home town.'

She took a deep draw on her cigarette.

'Of course, as per the norm, we were the last to know. And *as per the norm*, we got to know second-hand through Kate. After everyone else.'

Another deep draw.

'Charlotte had even started at the yard! Everyone at Thompson's knew before us.'

'God, Lily,' Rosie huffed, 'I'll never understand this obsession you have with being told everything first.'

'We were even the last to know you'd got married!' Lily said, ignoring Rosie and glaring across at George for support but seeing only the bottom of his brandy glass. 'Every Tom, Dick and Harry knew you'd tied the knot with your detective sergeant before we did.'

'Lily, I told you as soon as I could,' Rosie defended herself.

'No, you didn't. You could have rung us from Guildford.'

Rosie looked at Lily and George and realised for the first time that they had been hurt. She *could* have called them from the hotel. She just hadn't thought to.

'Let's keep on track,' George said. 'Kate told us that Charlotte turned up late on Friday night after that awful air raid. And that you had her working at Thompson's yesterday.'

He smiled at Rosie.

'So, tell me, what's happened?'

Seeing Lily about to butt in again, George threw her a warning look.

'Well,' Rosie sighed. 'Charlie's claiming to be homesick. Seems to be adamant that she wants to come back and live here.'

'"Claiming?"' George said. 'Sounds like you're not totally convinced.'

'I'm not,' Rosie said. 'Well, I do think there's an element of truth in it. I think she *is* probably homesick.'

'Probably been homesick the whole time she's been there,' Lily mumbled under her breath to George.

'But I think there's more to it,' Rosie said. 'Only, for whatever reason, she's not saying.'

'What I don't understand,' Lily said, 'is why obsess about what is making her want to come back? The girl's clearly unhappy where she is, and at fourteen she knows her own mind enough to be able to choose *where* she lives.'

'Lily, she may well be fourteen, but she's still young for her age. She's been cosseted.'

'Which is exactly why it's time she started living in the real world.' Lily stubbed her cigarette out and marched over to pour herself a brandy.

'Which is exactly why I'm doing what I'm doing at the moment,' Rosie countered, 'and getting her to work at Thompson's.'

'Pah!'

Lily coughed as the brandy caught the back of her throat in her eagerness to get her words out.

'What you are doing, Rosie, *ma chère*, is actually the opposite. You are putting her to work in that dirty, noisy shipyard in an attempt to make her feel that the real world is so bleedin' awful she'd rather go running back to Harrogate.

'I'm surprised you think she'll take the soft option. I might not ever have been *allowed* to meet Charlotte, but I think I know her a damn sight better than you do. I would bet the total cost of my wedding, which is substantial – '

George muttered his agreement.

' – that your little sister would rather slum it in the yard, earning a pittance, than go back to that school she clearly hates so much.'

'Have you thought any more about the Sunderland Church High School up the road?' George ventured.

'I have,' Rosie said, sitting back down in her chair. Lily's words had hit a nerve. 'But that doesn't get around the main issue.'

She sighed.

'If she lives here permanently, it is inevitable that she will find out about this place and that I used to work here – still do.'

'And that you own half the business!' Lily added vehemently.

There was a pause.

'Does Charlotte know about the school up the road?' Lily asked.

'No,' Rosie said quickly. 'And there's no way I want her to find out about it, otherwise she'll start a campaign to go there.'

'It would be cheaper,' George suggested tentatively.

Lily walked over and sat on the arm of George's chair.

'And she'd still be getting a top-notch education,' Lily added.

'And it does sound like Charlotte is genuinely homesick,' George said.

Lily put her hand on his shoulder.

Rosie looked at the pair. She loved them both dearly. They were the most non-judgemental, freethinking people she had ever come across. Which was why they couldn't understand just how devastating it would be for Charlotte to find out that the sister she looked up to had sold her body for money.

'Charlotte's going to have to find out one day,' Lily said, reading her thoughts. 'And more importantly, she needs to know the reason for you coming here to work. She needs to know that everything you have done, you have done for her. And it's only because of what you've done that you've been able to give her the best possible start in life.'

As if on cue there was a rap on the door and Maisie appeared, closely followed by Vivian. Rosie suspected the pair had been eavesdropping.

'What's up with you two?' Lily asked, staring at them whilst dabbing her neck with a handkerchief she had just pulled from her ample cleavage. She didn't know what was wrong with her these days. She was either piping hot or freezing cold. 'You both look full of *joie de vivre*?' she said with a puzzled expression.

'Well,' Maisie said, patting down her hair, 'we have two Admiralty in this evening. They've just been billeted at the Grand.'

'Gawd, I hope there's not too many staying there when we're celebrating our nuptials.' Lily cast a look at George and winked.

'They want two escorts for a night on the town,' Maisie said.

'And naturally,' Vivian stepped forward, 'they chose us.'

'Mmm,' Lily said, knowing the other girls wouldn't have got a look in and that it would have been a case of Maisie and Vivian choosing the two naval officers rather than the other way round. There was a reason these two young women standing in front of her now were her top earners. They had a nose for money – and more importantly, for those willing to spend it.

'All right,' Lily said, going to the mirror above the mantelpiece and fluffing up her bird's nest of orange hair and wrestling her bosom into position. She still looked a little red, but at least she'd stopped sweating. 'Let me go and introduce myself and then I'll send them in to you, Rosie.'

Everyone made their way out of the office.

Lily was the last to go and turned before she left.

'Charge them double,' she said. Her face was now all business. 'More if they want an overnight. Dinner is to be included. A private car to bring them back here and a time. I want to know *when* they'll be back. Officers don't always mean gentlemen.'

Rosie nodded. Lily was always a little on edge whenever any of her girls had to leave the safety of the bordello to do a job. But she also knew that tonight Lily wouldn't be overly worried. Out of all her girls, if there were any two who were more than capable of looking after themselves, it was Maisie and Vivian.

Later on, as Rosie made her way back to Brookside Gardens, she mulled over her head-to-head with Lily. Even George had shown her which side he was on this evening. Something he'd refrained from doing previously.

Lily was right. Everything she'd done, she'd done for Charlotte. But that was why it was imperative that her sister *didn't* find out about Lily's.

How would that make Charlotte feel, knowing the money Rosie had made from sleeping with strangers had funded her education?

There was no other option. Charlie was going back to Harrogate, by hook or by crook. Or by force, if Rosie had to.

Chapter Twelve

When Polly walked through the swing doors of the post-operative ward, she stopped in her tracks on seeing two of the other patients by the side of Tommy's bed. They had a wheelchair and were helping Tommy to manoeuvre himself into it.

When one of the injured soldiers, who was called Percival, looked up and saw her approaching, he put his finger to his lips and pointed to the bottom of the ward where the matron was standing with her back to them. She was listening to the laments of another injured soldier called Shorty, who, strangely enough, was anything but short.

Walking on tiptoes over to Tommy and his two accomplices, Polly whispered, 'What are you all doing?'

'We're springing him from this joint,' Percival whispered back with a convincing American accent.

'Got to get a bit of fresh air,' Tommy said, giving Polly a wink.

Polly looked at the matron, who was still standing with her back to them, and then down at Tommy, grimacing in pain as he hauled himself off the bed and into the wheelchair.

As soon as he'd done so, Percival started pushing the wheelchair around the bed.

'Give it here,' Polly whispered, grabbing both handles.

As the two young lovers made their escape, Percival shoved some pillows under the covers of Tommy's empty bed and drew the curtain, just in time to see the matron turning away from Shorty.

'Tommy wanted a bit of privacy,' Percival said, nodding over to the curtained-off bed. He hobbled on his plastered leg back to his own bed, which was now devoid of pillows.

Matron was just heading over to check on Tommy when one of the other lads, who had one of his legs resting in the harness of a pulley, called her over.

She couldn't help thinking they all seemed very demanding this evening.

'Honestly, I can push myself.' Tommy looked up at Polly. It hurt every fibre of his being to be so weak, which only added to his determination that he would not be like this for long.

'That may well be,' Polly said, looking over her shoulder anxiously, 'but I can get us out of this "joint" faster.'

True to her word, she got them to the main entrance at breakneck speed.

An elderly gentleman saluted as he held open the main doors for them. Tommy returned the old man's address.

Once out in the fresh air, Polly carefully pushed the wheelchair down the ramp and onto the shale pathway.

'Made it!' she declared.

'Now, I can take it from here.' Tommy put his hands on the wheels and pushed down hard, but the gravel was damp. The wheelchair only moved a few inches forward.

'Let me,' Polly said. 'Just until we get around the corner.'

When they had made it a few hundred yards away from the main entrance, Polly stopped next to one of the wooden benches. It was dark, but they could just about see where they were.

Tommy looked up at the starry night and for a second was back on the lifeboat in the middle of the Atlantic. He wiped the thought from his mind.

'What a wreck.' He tried to make the words sound jovial, but he couldn't hide the sense of wretchedness he felt at his present situation. 'I thought I might be able to at least push myself in this damn thing.'

Polly caught his look of frustration in the light of the half-moon.

'Tommy, it's only Monday. On Saturday you could hardly sit up in bed, never mind get yourself into a wheelchair.'

'I know, but I had a great plan for this evening,' he said, causing Polly to chuckle.

'Do tell me,' she smiled. 'I'm intrigued.'

'Well, it's been three whole torturous days now since I have had you back in my life,' he said. 'And during that whole time, I've not once had you to myself.'

Polly chuckled again.

'I *know*. Every time I hold your hand, I can almost hear the matron tutting in her head. I'm sure she would ban *any* kind of physical contact if she could.'

'I think she missed her calling as a chaperone,' Tommy joked.

'Every time I've given you a kiss goodbye, I've felt her beady eye on us.'

'As well as just about every soldier on the ward,' Tommy added.

They were quiet for a moment as a young airman on crutches passed with his sweetheart.

'Which was why I wanted to be alone with you, just for a little while.' Tommy looked at Polly. He had dreamed of the day when he would take her in his arms and press her body against his own and kiss her.

'I so want to kiss you. Properly,' Tommy confessed. 'But I'm damned if the first time I do so is from the confines of a wheelchair.' His voice was deadly serious, causing Polly to laugh.

'So, does this mean I have to wait until you're well enough to do away with the chair before I get to kiss my future husband properly?' A smile played on her lips.

'I just ...' Tommy hesitated, finding it hard to talk so intimately. 'I just wanted to be able to at least *stand* and hold you in my arms.'

Polly was quiet. She understood. She could see how much it pained Tommy to be so incapacitated.

'Do you remember that time when we danced by the riverside? We'd both been working late, and we were saying we hadn't even been to a dance together or really on a proper date.'

Tommy nodded.

'And you told me that we were going to have a "Make Do and Mend" date.'

Tommy had thought of that night many times while he was away.

'And I asked you if you could hear an orchestra,' Polly said.

'Yes,' Tommy laughed. 'You said you thought it was playing the waltz, and I had no idea what a waltz sounded like, but I knew it was the kind of dance that was slow and I'd get to hold you.'

'And you said to me in the best King's English you could muster, "Would the lady care to dance?"'

For a moment they were both lost in the memory of what seemed like a totally different lifetime.

'Well,' Polly said. 'I think you should close your eyes and pretend you are there now.'

Tommy closed his eyes.

'And I want you to imagine that we're dancing by the river and you're holding me in your arms.'

Tommy could feel Polly's breath on his face. He could smell her freshly laundered clothes.

'And now that we're dancing ...' Polly leant towards Tommy, her thick brown hair falling forward and touching the side of his face, ' ... and you are holding me in your arms ...' she touched the side of Tommy's face ' ... you kiss me.' She whispered the words. Then kissed Tommy slowly.

Feeling the sensuousness of her lips on his own, Tommy responded, losing himself in her touch, her smell, her taste.

They were lips he could kiss for ever and a day.

Finally they were able to feel the love and passion they had for each other. A love that had not dwindled in the time they had been apart, but grown. Their fervour for each other even greater due to their doubts that this moment would ever come.

Dr Parker walked slowly along the windowless white corridors.

He'd walked up and down these corridors so many times he could do it blindfolded, if necessary.

A few minutes earlier Mrs Rosendale had come bursting into his office in such a flurry he'd imagined there must be an emergency on the ward. When she had breathlessly explained to him that Tommy had 'escaped' from the ward without permission in a wheelchair and with his fiancée, he had suppressed a chuckle. And another when she had related the misdemeanours of Percival, Shorty and Private Jones. All three of them had, rather cunningly, Dr Parker thought, orchestrated the breakout.

He had reassured Mrs Rosendale that he would recapture AWOL Watts and bring him back immediately.

Dr Parker idled as he headed towards the hospital's main entrance, wanting to give the two of them a little time together – but not so much that the cold autumnal air would be detrimental to the already precarious health of his patient. Tommy was still far from well and needed to be kept warm. With lots of rest and recuperation. Mrs Rosendale was already beside herself that Tommy was refusing any more medication. Dr Parker knew Tommy was still in considerable pain. He had been on morphine for quite some time. Ideally, he should gradually have been given lesser amounts so as to lessen the side effects of withdrawal. He had talked to Tommy about all of this, but he had been insistent. He wanted to get back to 'normal' as soon as possible.

As Dr Parker reached the main entrance, his thoughts, as they were wont to do, defaulted back to Helen. They'd spoken the morning after the air raid, when she had rung him at work.

As always with Helen, he could have chatted all day long. They'd had to break off their conversation when he'd heard his name called over the tannoy. She had asked about Tommy and he'd thought he'd caught a hint of embarrassment.

Realising just how much Helen still loved Tommy cut deep, as did the knowledge that his own love for Helen was doomed to be unrequited. They were friends. Good friends. God, he had been with her throughout her pregnancy and the trauma of her miscarriage. But they could never be anything more.

Helen created such a paradox of feelings within him. She was like an anaesthetic against the true awfulness of what his senses were assaulted with every day. She was his balm against the horrors of war's cast-offs.

She also, however, brought pain.

A terrible ache of longing that he was sure would never lift.

Walking out into the fresh but cold October night, it took Dr Parker a few moments to adjust to the darkness. Turning left, he walked for a hundred yards before he stopped on seeing the two young lovers. They were sharing the tenderest of kisses.

Dr Parker couldn't help but feel envious.

Why, oh why, did he have to fall so heavily in love with a woman whose heart belonged to another?

He started walking down the gravel pathway, coughing politely.

Chapter Thirteen

Four days later

Thursday 22 October

'Christmas? They're getting married at Christmas?' Dorothy's voice was verging on hysterical.

'On the actual *day*?' Polly asked, equally incredulous.

Rosie laughed and looked around the table at the women's shocked faces.

'Yes, on Christmas Day. The twenty-fifth of December.' Rosie took a sip of her tea. She was thankful the canteen was packed out and noisy so that no one could overhear their conversation. She still liked to keep all mention of Lily to a minimum.

'But I thought she was having it on the nineteenth?' Polly asked, blowing on a spoonful of stew to cool it down.

'Well, it's a rather long story, which I will try to keep short,' Rosie said.

'Yer make it as long as yer want, miss,' Angie said in all earnestness. 'We're all ears.'

Rosie looked at Polly, Bel, Dorothy, Angie, Martha and Hannah.

'Well,' she began, 'Maisie and Vivian were out with a couple of naval officers.' She looked at Bel. She hoped she'd made it sound like they'd been on legitimate dates as opposed to what Maisie liked to call 'escorting'.

'And it came out in conversation that the Grand had been told by the Ministry of War to expect a large influx of Admiralty and Royal Navy personnel in December.'

'Because the hotel is a "billet"? Is that right?' Hannah asked.

Rosie nodded.

'And when all of this was relayed to Lily ...' Rosie paused, thinking of the other evening when Maisie and Vivian had imparted the news to her. 'Well, let's just say the balloon went up.'

'Because?' Martha asked.

'*Because*,' Dorothy said, sighing dramatically, 'it meant there'd be no room for Lily's wedding reception.'

'Exactly,' Rosie said, topping up her tea from the pot in the middle of the table.

'So, what did Lily do?' Polly asked.

Rosie chuckled.

'She ordered George to get the car and they went straight to the Grand and demanded to see the manager.'

'And what did he say?' Bel asked. She had spent her wedding night at the Grand and had spotted the hotel's very pompous-looking manager.

'Apparently he was full of apologies. Said he had been going to contact them that very afternoon. To tell him of the unforeseen circumstances regarding their extra guests.'

Rosie smiled.

'Lily, of course, immediately realised she could use the situation to her advantage and continued to play holy war, demanding to know what he was intending to do about the matter.'

'What did he say?' Hannah asked.

'I think there were various options bandied about. Offers of compensation and the like. But when the manager told her that the hotel would be more or less back to normal by

Christmas, Lily, being Lily, decided it would be a great idea to tie the knot on Christmas Day!'

'That's like my aunty Gwen,' Angie chirped up. 'They got married on Christmas Day.'

'Why did they do that?' Dorothy asked.

'It was the only day of the year her 'n my uncle Bobby could get off.'

Everyone looked at Angie, curious to hear more.

'And,' she added, 'in those days the church always married people fer free on Christmas Day. Aunty Gwen always gans on about how she had a "penny wedding". Course that was years ago. They're both in their sixties now.'

Everyone was listening intently.

'Well, another interesting socio-economic fact from welder Angie Boulter.'

Angie frowned at Dorothy.

'English, Dor.'

'I think Dorothy just means how people's income affects what they do in life,' Hannah explained.

'Well, we'd better not tell Lily that, otherwise she'll be changing the date again,' Rosie said.

'So, I'm guessing the registry office will be open?' Polly asked.

'Yes, the manager, Mr Pollard, I believe he's called, rang the registrar there and then and got the date changed.' Rosie chuckled. 'According to George, he would have done handstands for Lily if she'd asked.'

Rosie didn't say anything to the women, but Lily had also negotiated a decent discount for the inconvenience and had accepted the offer of a goose and a large gammon joint for the wedding breakfast.

'So,' Dorothy looked at Polly, 'I don't suppose you and Tommy have settled on a date yet?' She widened her eyes and looked around at the women. 'Imagine – we might get two weddings in the space of two months.'

'Give them a chance,' Martha guffawed. 'Tommy's only just got back. He's not even out of hospital yet.'

Martha was glad she herself was out of hospital and back at work. Back with her friends. Back to normality – even if she *was* still feeling a little shell-shocked.

'Exactly!' Polly agreed rather too enthusiastically.

They all started getting ready to leave.

'Well, at least you've got the money set aside for when you *do* decide to get hitched, eh?' Rosie said.

Polly looked at her blankly.

'You know. Tommy's pay. What's it called again?'

'His gratuity pay,' Polly said.

'That's right. You told me that he'd been saving it for your wedding?'

All of a sudden, Polly looked around as if she'd lost something.

'Did you say Charlotte's working in the kitchen today?'

Her question had the desired effect. Everyone hurried over to the main counter, from where they could see into the back kitchen.

Charlotte was standing with her back to them in front of a large stainless-steel sink.

Angie put her thumb and forefinger in her mouth and let out an ear-splitting whistle.

It did the trick.

Charlotte spun round. Seeing the women, she lifted a handful of soapy suds and waved back.

'She's a good little worker that one.' Muriel came over to see the women. 'Doesn't stand around gassing. Just gets on with it.'

'Good to hear,' Rosie said. She'd warned Charlotte about Muriel's knack for squeezing information out of people and turning it into yard gossip.

'So, how's things going with Charlotte?' Hannah asked as they left the canteen. 'Is she going to stay or are you sending her back at the end of half-term?'

Rosie grimaced.

'I've told her that I understand that she's homesick and that she can come back during the holidays and at half-term, but she has to go back to school.'

'And did she agree?'

'Not exactly, but it's not up to her. She's going back whether she wants to or not. I'm hoping that after a week working here, she'll look more favourably on my suggestion and might even go willingly ...' Her voice trailed off as she looked around. 'Ah, Martha ... Helen's asked if you could pop and see her after lunch.'

Martha gave a puzzled look.

'Nothing to worry about. Think she just wants a quick chat. We'll be over on *Brutus* when you're done.'

Rosie watched Martha plod over to the admin building. It was strange seeing her in a turban. She'd been given strict instructions by the doctor at the hospital to keep her wound covered up during the day, especially when she was at work.

Dorothy and Angie looked at each other and then at Rosie and Polly.

'What?' Rosie asked.

'It's just strange – Helen. Us all being "friends" now.'

'I know,' Polly said. 'Do you think she's always been all right and we've all just demonised her? Or do you reckon she's changed?'

They were all quiet for a moment.

'Probably a bit of both,' Rosie said, just as the klaxon sounded out the start of the afternoon shift.

*

Helen was sitting at her desk, the receiver of the black Bakelite phone jammed into the crook of her neck as she topped up her tea.

'I know,' she agreed. 'And did you read *The Times* today? Did you read what Mr bloody Bevin said in the House of Commons?'

She listened for a moment.

'Well, let me tell you, I'm seething mad, as I'm sure every shipyard worker in Sunderland would be if they knew about it.'

Helen took hold of the receiver as she reached over her desk to get her Pall Malls.

'He made a big song and dance praising the shipyards on the Tyne and the Clyde.'

She paused for dramatic effect.

'But not a single mention about the yards on the Wear. Yards, I hasten to add, that have *not* been out on strike over some triviality.' Helen was building momentum. 'Yards which have been – *and still are* – making far more merchant ships than the Tyne.'

She quickly lit her cigarette.

'And is Mr bloody Bevin's memory as bad as his general knowledge? Forgetting that it was this very shipyard that designed the Liberty ship *and* showed the American yards how it's done!'

Helen cut short her rant, having just noticed that Martha was standing in the doorway of her office, looking like she was about to get six of the best.

When Mrs Crabtree's ginger tom trotted past her and into the office, Martha stared at the cat in open-mouthed disbelief.

'Sorry, John, I'm going to have to go. I've got Martha here ...'

Helen listened for a moment.

'Yes, yes, I'll tell her, although I'm sure she won't take a bit of notice.'

She was quiet again.

'Yes, of course, see you Saturday. Fingers crossed you don't get an emergency ... Great. See you then ... Bye.'

As soon as she'd hung up, Helen waved at Martha to enter.

'Come in, come in!'

Martha was still staring at the cat, which was now wrapping itself around Helen's legs.

'I know,' Helen said, scowling down and pushing it away with her leg. 'The damn thing's been stalking me ever since the air raid, so I brought it to the yard. Thought it might make a good rat-catcher, but it seems to prefer to be indoors ... Anyway, come in.'

Martha followed her orders.

'That was Dr Parker.'

Martha's face brightened up. She liked the doctor. He had a lovely way about him. Gloria had thought so too.

'He says you shouldn't really be back at work.'

Martha touched her headscarf. She'd be glad when she didn't have to wear it.

Helen looked at her and remembered the last time Martha had been in this office. It must have been about a year ago, she recalled guiltily, when she'd been trying, unsuccessfully, to split up Rosie's squad and force Martha to go and work with the riveters.

'How are you feeling, anyway? I did come to the hospital to visit but Gloria told me you'd just been discharged.'

'I'm fine, honestly,' Martha said, suddenly worried that Rosie might be sending her home.

'Well, just take it easy, won't you?' Helen said. 'And if you feel faint, head straight over to the first-aiders and they can get you across to the Royal in a jiffy.'

'I will. But I won't,' Martha said, before asking, 'Did you want me to help the riveters out?' She was perplexed as to why she was there.

'No, no.' Helen shook her head. 'Although any time you want to swap, you can do.' She laughed. Everyone knew Martha was a natural riveter, but she would never be parted from her women welders.

'I just wanted to say a proper thank you.' Helen looked at Martha. 'For saving my life. As well as Gloria's and Hope's.'

Martha nervously touched her turban again.

'If you hadn't have come into that building with me, Gloria and Hope would be dead. I couldn't have got them out of there on my own. And if you hadn't yanked me back when we were in Mrs Crabtree's lounge, I'd have been crushed under that beam. I certainly wouldn't be sat here now.'

'I wasn't trying to be brave,' Martha said. 'When I saw the beam going, I just grabbed you.'

'And in doing so,' Helen added, 'you cracked your head open because you were holding on to me and not breaking your own fall.'

'I probably would have bashed my head anyway. I can be really clumsy.' Martha smiled.

Helen looked at this giant of a woman sitting opposite her. She was such an anomaly. She'd never met anyone like her in her life.

'Well, I owe you my life. As do Gloria and Hope. A mere thank you hardly seems to do that justice.'

She stubbed out her cigarette.

'I want you to know,' Helen looked at Martha, deadly serious, 'that if there is anything – *anything* at all – I can do for you at any time, now or in the future, just ask me.'

Martha nodded.

'Will you promise me?' Helen said. 'If you ever find yourself in need of money, or you need help in any way, you must come to me.'

She paused.

'I want you to promise.'

'I promise,' Martha said, feeling a little overwhelmed by Helen's seriousness.

Helen got up, walked round her desk and took Martha's hand.

'You're a very courageous woman, you know?'

Martha blushed. Something she rarely did.

As Helen watched Martha leave the office and head back out to the yard, she felt the ginger tom brush against her legs.

'Come here, Winston.' She bent down, picked up the cat and gave it a stroke.

She stood there for a moment, petting the cat and thinking about the night she had heard her mother threatening to expose the women's secrets should Gloria and her father come clean about their love for each other. Helen had listened at the door and been taken aback.

Martha's secret, however, was by far the most shocking: she had been adopted as an infant after her mother was sentenced to death for the murder of at least five children – most of them her own. Crimes that had taken a while to come to light because she had slowly poisoned each of her victims, all the while making out that she was trying to nurse them back to health.

As Helen put a purring Winston back down and returned to her desk, she mused how such evil could have given birth to a brave and gentle soul like Martha.

It made her think of her own mother. It still shocked her that Miriam had intercepted Jack's letters to Helen, making her believe that he no longer cared. If she had known that her father hadn't forsaken her for his new family, she doubted very much she would have fallen so readily into Theo's arms and ended up in the hellish predicament in which she had found herself.

This past year her mother had revealed her true colours – and those colours were far from pretty. She mightn't be a murderer, but she was most certainly cold, calculating and cruel. A true narcissist.

Chapter Fourteen

Saturday 24 October

'Pleased to meet you,' George said as he shook Tommy's hand.

He had just arrived on the ward with Polly.

'You too, George. And thank yer for bringing Pol to see me. I hope you've not used up the rest of your petrol ration? I hear they've completely withdrawn fuel for private users.'

'They have indeed,' George said. 'But fortunately my little MG has been granted a special permit on condition she's available for "work deemed essential".'

George chuckled.

'And this is what I would deem "essential".'

Tommy smiled. He knew George had been the one to bring Polly to the hospital on the night of the air raid – and that he was a veteran of the First World War, although it was something he never talked about.

'Anyway, I won't keep you from your lovely lady here.' George winked at Polly.

Polly looked radiant. It didn't matter that she had visited Tommy every day for the past eight days; the thrill of seeing him had clearly not waned in the slightest.

'Now, am I right in thinking Arthur's accompanying me back into town?'

'He just went to use the facilities,' Tommy said, looking towards the entrance to the ward. 'Here he comes.'

They all looked as Arthur raised a hand and waved but stayed waiting by the matron's desk.

'Right, cheerio, then,' George said, turning to leave.

As he did so, he scanned the rest of the ward, taking in the dozen or so injured soldiers, most of whom looked as though they'd had surgery on at least one of their limbs.

Nothing changes, he thought bitterly.

As soon as George had left, Tommy took Polly in his arms and gave her a kiss.

His actions were accompanied by two loud wolf whistles from Percival and Shorty.

These, in turn, were met by a thunderous look from the matron, who was monitoring the ward like a headmistress on playground duty.

'Blimey, Pol,' Tommy said, looking down at the bag he'd only just noticed she had brought with her. 'No wonder you needed a lift here,' he ribbed. 'You're not thinking of moving in, are you? Not that I'd be complaining, especially as you'd have to bunk down with me.'

Polly batted his arm playfully. 'I think Mrs Rosendale might have something to say about that.'

She looked at him. He'd had to put his hand on the top of the bed to steady himself.

'Sit down,' she said, helping him to lower himself into the chair by the side. He was clearly still incredibly weak.

'I've brought you something,' Polly said. 'Something I did after I got that wretched letter from your commander.'

It still pained Polly to think back to that godforsaken day – and the four long months that had followed.

'Oh yes?' Tommy's face had gone serious.

Polly put her holdall onto the bed.

'Well, one evening, a week or so after I'd learnt you'd been declared missing, I was lying in bed, thinking about the day I'd just had.' She looked at Tommy and smiled. Sometimes she still had to pinch herself that he was back. That this was real.

'Arthur and I had been down to the docks and we'd been chatting about our favourite subject.' She laughed. 'You! And Arthur had been telling me about how your nana Flo could never keep you in because you always wanted to be outdoors. And I was thinking how I'd have normally enjoyed writing to you and ribbing you about causing your grandda and your nana no end of worries, when I suddenly thought to myself, so what if I can't *send* him any letters, there's nothing stopping me *writing* them.'

Polly looked at Tommy.

'So, I did. And I vowed that when you came back, I'd give you them and you'd know everything that happened while you were wherever it was you were.'

Tommy looked down as Polly pulled out a stack of letters from her bag.

'I reckon you must have written one a day?' He looked at the letters, which had been bound together by string and tied with a neat bow at the top.

'Thereabouts,' Polly said. She wondered if he'd notice that she'd stopped writing about six weeks ago, on the day his belongings had been sent back from Gibraltar.

'You never gave up hope, did you?' He didn't wait for an answer, instead pushing himself out of his chair and putting the batch of letters in his bedside cabinet.

Polly was relieved. She'd hate for him to know that she had, in fact, given up hope.

'Come on, time for our daily stroll.' He put his arm out and escorted his fiancée out of the ward.

'You must be very proud of that lad of yours,' George said as he steered the MG out of the hospital grounds, turning left onto Stockton Road. 'That's a bloody dangerous job he's been doing out there. Brave man. Very brave man.'

'Aye,' Arthur nodded.

They were quiet for a moment.

George drove slowly, enjoying the rarity of taking the 'old gal' out, and the fact that there was very little on the road.

'I just hope he's not got any madcap notion about going back out there,' Arthur added.

George looked at the old man and saw concern on his face.

'I presumed he'd been medically discharged,' George said.

Arthur sighed.

'I was asking him about it before you and Pol turned up and he said he'd asked them to hold off.'

George thought the old man might be worrying unnecessarily.

He doubted Tommy would ever be fit enough to go back to war.

'So, let me make sure I've got this right,' Tommy said, as he wrapped his arms around Polly and kissed her on the nose. They were outside, sitting on one of the benches dotted along the pathway that ran around the hospital grounds.

'George is engaged to Lily. And the two are old friends of Rosie's. And Bel's long-lost sister, Maisie, lodges with them in their house in Ashbrooke – along with Kate, Rosie's old school friend, and another woman called Vivian?'

'That's right,' Polly said, purposely not going into any more detail. There was so much Tommy didn't know. So many things these past two years that she hadn't been able to tell him in her letters. Rosie and the bordello being one of them.

'And thanks to the Admiralty, they're now getting married on Christmas Day?' Tommy continued.

'That's right,' Polly said again, this time following her words with a kiss.

After a few moments, Tommy touched Polly's face. He never tired of looking at her, being with her, talking with her – kissing her.

'So,' he said, 'isn't it time we decided on a date for our wedding?'

Polly didn't answer, instead closing her eyes and kissing him again.

Tommy kissed her back, then held her at arm's length and laughed.

'If I didn't know better, I'd say that you were avoiding the question, Mrs soon-to-be Watts.'

'I'm most certainly *not* avoiding your question,' Polly defended herself. 'I was thinking that perhaps we could get married in the New Year.' Her eyes lit up. 'Or better still, how about February the fourteenth – Valentine's Day?'

Tommy pulled her close.

'But I thought we agreed, when you woke me with a kiss ...' he kissed her neck '... that we'd waited long enough. That we'd get married *soon*.'

'January?' Polly suggested.

'*Soon*,' Tommy repeated.

Polly laughed loudly. Perhaps a little too loudly.

'Let's get you out of this place first, eh?' she said.

Hurrying into the canteen, Polly thought it seemed an age since she had been there last, when, in fact, it had only been a week.

The great constant time sometimes seemed terribly fickle.

'Dr Parker,' Polly called out, overjoyed at seeing the doctor sitting on his own enjoying a cup of tea and an iced bun.

During visiting times, if he wasn't in theatre, Dr Parker endeavoured to be in the cafeteria, available to the relatives of what he called his 'recruits'.

'Ah, Polly, come and sit down. How are you?'

'I'm good. More than good, thank you.'

Polly pulled up a seat.

'I just wanted a quick word about Tommy, if that's all right?'

'Of course, fire ahead!' Dr Parker looked at Polly. Seeing her for the first time without a dirty face and dressed in greasy overalls, he realised just how pretty she was.

'Can you tell me how Tommy's *really* doing? He's very good at making out he's absolutely hunky-dory, but you just need to look at him to see he's far from fit and healthy. There seems to be no doubt in his mind that he's going to completely recover. Back to how he was before he left. Do you think he's expecting too much?'

Polly paused.

'I'm asking, not because it matters to me, although it does.' She shook her head in frustration. 'I mean, I'll love him regardless, but I worry how he'll be in himself if he's not able to go back to work. It goes without saying he won't be going back to his unit in Gibraltar, but I know it would be the end of the world if he couldn't work again.'

Dr Parker took a moment to decide how best to answer the question. Polly wasn't just a pretty face; she was astute enough to realise that Tommy needed to recover enough to at least do some kind of work. If not, it would undoubtedly affect his mindset.

'That's a difficult question.'

He loosened his tie and took a deep breath.

'With Tommy there's a lot we don't know. The shock his body had. Underwater explosions have the potential to damage a person's internal organs. He's already had a ruptured spleen, but there may well be other issues that we don't know about. Add to the mix the fact that his body was given a secondary trauma when he nearly drowned in the Atlantic, and he spent a good part of his epic journey back here semi-conscious and fighting pneumonia.'

He thought for a moment.

'Only time will tell. It really is a case of a day at a time.'

Polly nodded, digesting what had been said.

'Thank you, Dr Parker. It's good that I know all this.'

'I have to say, though,' Dr Parker added, 'that Tommy is a very resilient man. He came off his pain medication earlier than I would have liked, and he's up and about, going for walks in the grounds when most men would still be bed-bound.'

'That's his stubborn streak,' Polly said. 'And his obsessive need to be outdoors.'

Dr Parker murmured his agreement. He'd seen both in Tommy this past week.

'He's on about setting a date for the wedding,' Polly added, a little shyly, 'but I wasn't sure how long it would be before Tommy was up to it?'

Dr Parker barked with laughter.

'I think Tommy would drag you down that aisle tomorrow if you'd let him!'

It wasn't quite the answer Polly had been expecting.

Seeing an elderly couple waiting a few yards away, Polly thanked Dr Parker once again and left.

Dr Parker stood up as Polly took her leave. It had been on the tip of his tongue to mention the night terrors that Tommy was having, but something stopped him.

They weren't uncommon in soldiers coming back from war.

Hopefully, they'd die down the more he adapted to being back home.

Chapter Fifteen

'Ah, good afternoon, Miss Crawford.'

Kate had seen Helen looking in the window, so when the bell above the door jangled, her nerves hadn't followed suit.

'How are you?'

'I'm very well, thank you.' Helen cast a glance back at the window display. 'Every time I come here, I keep meaning to ask you about that dress. It really is so gorgeous.'

'Ah,' Kate said, 'that was one of my first proper commissions. We decided on the pale pink because it was the bride's second marriage. She'd been widowed but was lucky enough to find love again.' Kate was always careful never to mention names when talking about other customers. She wanted to be known for her professionalism and discretion as much as for her skills as a seamstress.

'This is just a quick visit,' Helen said, putting a paper bag on Kate's workbench and pulling out the red dress she had been wearing the night of the air raid. 'I've had it dry-cleaned but there are still some marks on it, so I thought you could have it. What with all this make-do-and-mending going on.'

'Would you like me to make something out of it for you?' Kate asked.

'No, no, definitely not,' Helen said. As much as she was thankful that everyone had survived the Tatham Street bombing, she didn't want to be reminded of it.

'Thank you,' Kate said, putting it on a hanger and placing it on her rack of second-hand clothes. She knew why the dress was no longer wanted but would never say so. She also knew not to offer Helen any money for the dress. People of Helen's standing would take it as an insult. They would, however, expect priority service in return.

Kate looked at the dress.

'I have an idea what I might do with it.'

'That doesn't surprise me.' Helen smiled and turned to leave. 'I'll be in next week to chat to you about a rather special outfit I'd like made for about a week or so before Christmas.'

'For a party?' Kate asked.

'No, for a launch,' Helen said, feeling a swell of excitement that *Brutus* was well ahead of schedule. 'It's a particularly special launch, so I want something to reflect that.'

She thought for a moment.

'I want something stunning, but also professional. It has to say, *this is a woman who expects to be taken seriously.*'

Kate smiled as Helen opened the door.

She loved a woman who knew exactly what she wanted.

Kate was just having a closer look at the red dress when the bell above the door tinkled again.

This time she did jump.

On seeing who it was, though, she immediately relaxed.

'Charlie! How lovely to see you!' Kate hurried over and gave her a hug.

'I got finished early today,' Charlotte said. 'Rosie's doing a full shift, so I thought I'd come and see you, if that's all right? I won't stay long.'

'Of course it's all right. You're always welcome here, Charlie. You're part of the family.'

It gave Charlotte an immediate feeling of warmth to hear Kate's words. It was the second time she had been told this.

'I've just seen Miss Crawford leave here,' she said. 'She's my boss, you know? She's a right cow.'

Kate managed to keep a straight face. Rosie had told her of her plan.

'So, how's work gone this week?' she asked instead, walking to the back room.

'Loved it!' Charlotte said.

Again, Kate suppressed a smile. Rosie had clearly not succeeded.

'Tea?' Kate looked at Charlotte and saw she had been distracted by Lily's wedding dress, which was taking shape on a mannequin in the centre of the shop.

Charlotte nodded enthusiastically. 'Yes, please.'

'Do you like it?' Kate asked, standing at the entrance to the back room, watching Charlotte's reaction.

'It's amazing,' Charlotte said. 'It's like something you'd see on a film – or on stage.' She continued inspecting the flamboyant plush green velvet dress. 'What's the occasion?' she asked.

'A wedding,' Kate said.

'Really? It seems a little over the top for a wedding?'

'Not when it's for the bride,' Kate said.

'What? This is the actual *wedding* dress?' Charlotte asked. She looked at Kate, eyes agog.

'It certainly is,' Kate said, going into the snug to put the kettle on.

'How do you feel about going back to school on Monday?' she shouted through.

'I'm not going!' Charlotte's voice was resolute. 'Rosie can't make me.'

Kate didn't say anything. She thought that perhaps Rosie could – and would.

Charlotte was still inspecting the dress when the bell rang out for a third time and the front door was flung open with gusto.

'Oh, *mon Dieu!*'

Lily had stopped in her tracks on seeing a young girl who, from the description Kate had given her, she was sure was Rosie's sister.

'Est-ce Charlotte?'

Charlotte stared at the apparition standing in the open doorway and nodded. Never before had she seen such a woman. Titian hair piled high. A heaving cleavage on the verge of escape. A luxurious fur stole draped around her neck and shoulders. And a packet of Gauloises gripped in a manicured hand that was weighted down by the biggest diamond engagement ring Charlotte had ever seen.

'Mon cher enfant!' Lily gushed.

'Bonjour, madame,' Charlotte said, perplexed. *'Mais j'ai peur je ne vous connais pas.'* She explained that she was afraid she didn't know her.

'Ma chérie, je suis Lily!' And with that she took hold of Charlotte's shoulders and kissed her on both cheeks before enfolding her in her arms and giving her a big hug.

Charlotte was taken aback, as well as engulfed in the most gorgeous perfume.

'Ah, Lily,' she said.

Why had Rosie or Kate not mentioned what a colourful character Lily was?

Or that she was French?

'Je suis vraiment désolée, Rosie et Kate n'ont pas mentionné que vous êtes française.'

'Oh, I think I've died and gone to heaven,' Lily declared, her hand going dramatically to her heart, as though to check that this was not actually the case. '*Non, ma chère*, I'm English, although I did live in Paris for a while, before all this awfulness.

'So,' Lily looked over to Kate with a look of pure glee in her eyes, 'this is Charlotte!'

She looked back at Charlotte, scrutinising her from head to toe.

'Finally,' she breathed in dramatically, 'finally I get to meet you!'

Charlotte was now feeling a little overwhelmed and more than a little puzzled. She had only heard about Lily last week, when she had been here with Rosie and Kate after her first day at work.

'Come on through the back, Lily. I was just making a pot of tea,' Kate said. Her tone was not the most welcoming.

Lily flung off her fur stole and put it on Kate's workbench.

'Is it me or is it hot in here?' She fanned her face, which had suddenly flushed. 'I saw you admiring my wedding dress,' she said. 'Kate's doing a *formidable* job, *n'est-ce pas*?'

Charlotte nodded enthusiastically.

'*Allons-y. Allons-y!*' She ushered Charlotte into the back room. 'Let's have a nice cuppa and you can tell me all about yourself.'

'So,' Lily said, lighting up a cigarette and blowing smoke to the ceiling. 'Tell me about your week back in your home town. Have you enjoyed it?'

Charlotte nodded.

'It's been brilliant. I've been working at Thompson's, doing all types of different jobs. The yard manager's a bit of a slave-driver, but I've been in the kitchens the past few days and that's been a right laugh.' She hadn't, of course, told Rosie just how much fun she'd had with Muriel and the rest of the women who worked there.

'And I've also met some really nice people,' Charlotte added.

'Oh yes, and who would they be?' Lily asked. Rosie had been very tight-lipped about Charlotte after they'd had their 'words'.

'I've met all her squad. And they seem really nice. Especially Dorothy. And Hannah.' Charlotte was still a little scared of Angie, but would never admit it.

'Hannah's from Prague. She was working as a welder, but it was too much for her so Rosie got her a job in the drawing office. We had lunch together the other day, just the two of us, and we sat for a whole hour and talked about Cicero. He's Hannah's favourite philosopher.'

'Really?'

Lily, of course, had no idea who Cicero was, not that it mattered – what was clear was that Charlotte was obviously loving being back home.

'Oh, I forgot, I also went to Rosie's old flat and met Gloria and Hope. And I've been to Tatham Street and met everyone there.'

'Well then,' Lily said, looking across at Kate, 'as my humble abode is the only place you haven't been to, you'll have to come and have tea *chez moi* and meet my fiancé, George.'

'Oh, I'd love that,' Charlotte said. Her eyes were glued to Lily. She missed Kate giving Lily the daggers.

'So, tell me,' Lily tapped her cigarette in the ashtray, 'Rosie says you want to come back here to live?'

Charlotte nodded gravely. 'I *do*.'

'You're not worried about all the bombs being dropped on the town?'

Charlotte shook her head.

'So, the problem with coming back here to live full-time *is*?' Lily asked.

'Rosie is set against it.' Charlotte looked nervously at Kate, unsure how much she should say. She might be at loggerheads with her sister, but she'd never be disloyal to her.

'And why is that?' Lily probed.

'I think she wants me to stay at the school I'm at in Harrogate. It's very good, you see.'

'But you don't like being there?' Lily asked, stubbing out her cigarette.

'No, I hate it.' Charlotte couldn't stop herself.

'And have you told Rosie why you hate it so much?' Kate butted in.

Charlotte looked at Kate and then to Lily.

'Not really,' she said.

'Well, perhaps you should be totally honest with her,' Kate suggested, topping up their cups of tea. 'Rosie loves you to pieces. She'd want to know if something was troubling you.'

Charlotte blushed. She'd said too much already.

Lily looked at Kate and then at Charlotte.

'So, Charlotte,' she said, 'I'm guessing you don't fancy going to the Sunderland Church High School?'

Charlotte stared at Lily.

'I don't know of it,' she said, her senses on full alert.

A private school in Sunderland?

How come Rosie had never mentioned it to her?

'It's a very good school, by all accounts,' Lily said, ignoring the look of thunder coming from Kate. 'I believe they offer boarding, but most of the pupils appear to be day students.'

Charlotte felt like jumping up and down with excitement. She couldn't believe what she was hearing. 'Really?'

She looked at Kate, who had suddenly started to clear the table.

'Well,' Kate glared at Lily, who was looking all wide-eyed and innocent, 'we'd better get started on that wedding dress. Only another seven weeks to the big day.'

'Where's the school?' Charlotte asked.

'Mowbray Road. Right next to the art school,' Lily said.

'What? Just across the road from Christ Church?' Charlotte asked.

'That's it,' Lily said, doing her best to ignore the racket Kate was making clattering the cups and saucers about. 'I believe the church is affiliated with the school.'

Charlotte was just about to ask another question when Kate interrupted.

'Well, Charlie. It's been lovely seeing you. Have you got much planned for the rest of the afternoon?'

'I have now. Lots,' she said, getting up and putting on her mac.

After saying her thank-yous and goodbyes, Charlotte walked out of the boutique.

Her head was swirling with four words.

Sunderland Church High School.

Her prayers had been answered!

And just in the nick of time.

'Something smells nice.'

Rosie walked through the front door and was hit by the smell of steak and kidney pie. She took off her coat, hung it up in the hallway and dumped her haversack and gas mask by the door.

'I'm afraid I cheated and bought it from Jacky White's market,' Charlotte shouted from the kitchen.

Rosie poked her head into the lounge and saw that the fire had been neatly stacked and was ready to spark up.

The room looked immaculate. Carrying on down the hall-way and into the kitchen, she saw that Charlotte had set the table and put a little bunch of wild flowers in a milk jug in the middle – something their mother used to do.

'I have, however, made the gravy myself,' Charlotte added. 'And amazingly, it's pretty much lump-free.'

Rosie thought her sister looked strangely chirpy, especially as she was due to head back to Harrogate tomorrow. She would have liked to believe that now Charlotte had had her fun playing at having a job and meeting everyone her big sister knew, she was ready to get back to her studies and be with her own friends.

Rosie had to laugh at herself. *Who was she kidding?*

'Muriel taught me how to make proper gravy from scratch,' Charlotte said as she cut up the pie and put two large pieces on their plates.

'As long as she didn't manage to squeeze anything out of you that she could turn into a good bit of gossip,' Rosie said, watching Charlotte pour the smooth, dark gravy over their dinner.

'I'm not as daft as I look!' Charlotte put both their plates on the table and sat down.

'This is lovely, Charlie,' Rosie said, suddenly realising she was starving. It had been a long day. 'But,' she eyed her sister, 'much as it's appreciated, it won't make me change my mind about you going back to school.'

Charlotte looked as though she was going to say something but stopped herself.

'So,' Rosie asked, forking up a big piece of beef and pastry, 'what did you do this afternoon?'

'You first,' Charlotte said. 'Was it mad busy at the yard? Do you think *Brutus* is going to be ready for Christmas like Miss Crawford wants?'

Rosie felt uneasy. Charlotte was far too cheerful.

'Well, it was busy,' Rosie said. 'And it does look like *Brutus* is going to be ready earlier than expected, which is good news all round.'

She looked at Charlotte, who was making a great show of being very attentive and interested.

'But not just because Miss Crawford wants it to be ready,' she added. 'You understand why it's imperative to get as many ships built as quickly as possible, don't you?'

Charlotte swallowed her food and took a long drink of water.

'Of course I do, Rosie.' She put her glass down on the table. 'We need to get the ships built as fast as Jerry is sinking them, otherwise we're not going to win the war.' Charlotte quoted her sister verbatim.

'Just as I know,' she added, trying to impress, 'that we're the "Biggest Shipbuilding Town in the World", and at the moment we're launching, on average, a ship a week.'

'I'm impressed,' Rosie said.

It hadn't escaped her notice that Charlotte had said 'we're'.

Her unspoken message was clear.

I belong here.

After they'd eaten and washed and dried up, Rosie turned to Charlotte.

'Right, let's get us both a cup of tea and you can tell me whatever it is you want to tell me.'

Charlotte looked taken aback.

'How did you know I wanted to tell you something?'

'Charlie, I am your sister.'

When the tea had been made and they'd taken it into the living room, Rosie lit the fire before turning her focus to Charlotte.

'Right, go on then, fill me in.'

'Well …' Charlotte said, sitting up straight on the sofa. She couldn't hide her excitement. 'When I finished work this afternoon, I went to the Maison Nouvelle to see Kate.'

Rosie's feeling of unease from earlier on returned.

'That's nice,' she said. 'Was she all right?'

'Yes, yes, she was fine,' Charlotte said dismissively, before taking a big breath. 'But guess who came in while I was there?' she asked, her face animated.

Please, no! Rosie begged silently.

'I've no idea,' she said, trying to sound naturally curious.

Charlotte took another deep breath before declaring dramatically, '*Lily!*'

There was a pregnant pause.

'And?' Rosie asked, straight-faced.

'And!' Charlotte exclaimed breathlessly. 'You didn't say she's such a character! Why didn't you tell me about her before?'

Rosie didn't answer but cursed inwardly. She'd just about got Charlotte to the end of the week without her getting a sniff of her 'other life', then bingo! Up popped Lily.

'She can speak French!' Charlotte enthused. 'And that hair! And,' she added breathlessly, 'have you seen her wedding dress?'

Rosie just looked at Charlotte.

She had, of course, seen Lily's rather unconventional wedding dress, but that was the last thing she wanted to talk about.

'It's green!' Charlotte declared, her eyes wide. 'She's a right hoot, isn't she?' she gushed.

Rosie still seemed unwilling to enter into a discussion about Lily – or how wonderfully eccentric she was.

'It sounds like she's been wanting to meet me for ages,' Charlotte said, looking askance at Rosie.

Again, there was no response.

'Anyway,' Charlotte said, 'she's invited me round to hers for tea so I can meet her fiancé, George.'

The hackles on Rosie's back were now standing on end.

'Has she now?' she said through gritted teeth, before continuing as calmly as possible: 'Well, it's a shame you won't have time to visit her, seeing as you're travelling back tomorrow.'

There was another expectant pause.

Charlotte took a nervous sip of her tea.

'Well, Rosie, that's what I've got to talk to you about.'

'Mmm?' said Rosie.

'Well,' Charlotte went on, trying to be as composed and as convincing as possible, 'Lily was telling me about the Sunderland Church High School.'

Charlotte looked at her sister, trying to gauge her reaction, but Rosie's face was like a blank page.

'She says,' Charlotte continued, 'that it's got day students as well as boarders. She says it's a good school, by all accounts.'

'Does she now?' Rosie asked, raising her eyebrows. It was taking every bit of willpower to stop herself banging down her cup of tea, stomping the half-mile to West Lawn and wringing Lily's neck.

'Did you know about the school?' Charlotte asked, trying to keep her tone non-accusatory. On the way home she'd taken a detour to go and look at it. She'd vaguely recalled walking past it once, years ago, but had presumed it was part of the art school. Her sister, however, *must* have known about it – especially since moving to this part of town.

'I do know about the school, Charlie.' Rosie was having to think on her feet.

Bloody Lily, she'd murder her when she saw her.

'But it's no good for you,' she added nonchalantly.

Charlotte looked at her sister as though she had just chucked a pail of cold water over her.

'Why?' She could hear that annoying whine in her voice again but couldn't stop it, nor the tears of frustration that had started to sting her eyes.

Rosie took a drink of her tea, stalling for time.

'Charlie, like I said to you the day we went to Tatham Street, it's too dangerous here.'

Rosie paused.

'This is one of the most heavily bombed towns in the country.'

'I know, you've told me several times already,' Charlotte said, tears now pooling in her eyes. 'But if everyone thought like that – that it was too danger-ous to live here,' she argued, her voice growing steely, 'there'd be no one left. We'd all be hiding in the hills, like cowards. And there certainly wouldn't be any ships getting built. And if that was the case, it would just be a matter of time before I'd be learning German instead of French.'

Rosie looked at her sister. She often saw her mother in Charlotte, but there were other times, like now, when she saw herself.

Determined.

Stubborn.

'And besides,' Charlotte continued, 'the school's nowhere near the yards or the colliery. And here's pretty safe too.'

Rosie sighed inwardly. Peter had argued a similar case when convincing her to move there from her flat in town.

God, how she missed him. If only he were here now. She could do with the support.

'And Mrs Jenkins has a great Anderson shelter,' Char-lotte added, sensing victory. 'She caught me the other day and insisted on showing me. She said you were always working late whenever there'd been an air raid and hadn't used it.'

This was exactly why Rosie didn't want Charlotte here. It wouldn't be long before she was asking why she always had to work so late at Lily's.

'I just don't understand why I can't go to school here,' Charlotte continued to argue. 'I won't have to board. And I'll bet it's much cheaper than Runcorn.'

'But Runcorn is one of the best in the country. And is about the safest place for you to be at the moment.' Rosie knew her reasons sounded feeble.

Suddenly she had an idea. It was a delaying tactic, but at this stage of the game, she'd grab it with both hands.

'Look, Charlie.' Rosie tried to sound upbeat. 'You have to go back to Harrogate, at least until the end of term. Your fees are all paid up. There's no other option. Why don't we take stock of the situation when you come back for the Christmas break? It's only – what – another six weeks?'

'Seven,' Charlotte corrected.

'And then,' Rosie said, trying to push down another rush of anger towards Lily – *this was all her fault* – 'you can be my "plus one" to Lily's wedding. See her in her green dress. It's going to be quite a do at the Grand.'

Charlotte ignored the enticement. She'd be going to the wedding anyway.

'Can't you get a refund from the school?' Charlotte asked.

Rosie took in a deep, controlled breath.

'I doubt very much Mrs Willoughby-Smith will agree to pay back the fees just because you're feeling homesick and have decided you don't want to go there any more.'

'Well she should!' Charlotte exclaimed.

Rosie caught anger in Charlotte's voice.

Something wasn't right.

'Charlie, that's the way of the world. It you pay for a cake and eat half of it, you can't then return the other half and demand your money back.'

'That's not the same!' Charlotte snapped.

There it was again. The anger.

Hearing it brought to mind the fight Charlotte had been in. The one she'd said had nothing to do with her wanting to leave Runcorn.

'Charlie, my instinct tells me that there's something more to this than simply being homesick.'

Charlotte wished she hadn't got so irate and had started crying instead. It would have tallied more with being homesick. Also, it might have softened Rosie up. But she just couldn't help it. She *did* feel angry. And she couldn't hold it back.

'For heaven's sake,' Rosie cajoled, 'just tell me what's really going on.'

They were both quiet.

Charlotte thought of Kate's words from earlier on, telling her to be truthful with her sister. She knew deep down that Kate was right. Her sister did love and care for her. She was the only person in the whole world who did. If she couldn't be honest with her, who could she be truthful with?

Rosie saw her sister falter.

She moved and sat next to her on the sofa, putting her arms around her shoulders and squeezing her tight.

'I don't want you to give that school or Mrs Willoughby-Smith another penny,' Charlotte begged. 'They're horrible!'

Rosie was now really concerned.

'Why are they horrible?' she coaxed, trying her hardest to suppress her own anger. *Had they done something to Charlotte?*

'They're just horrible, horrible people and I don't want to see them ever again!'

Rosie could hear the beginnings of tears in her sister's voice.

'Charlie,' Rosie said gently, 'please tell me *why* they are horrible ... Nobody's done anything to you that they shouldn't have? Have they?'

Rosie felt queasy just saying the words. If anyone had interfered with Charlotte, she would never forgive herself.

'No, no,' Charlotte said. 'It's nothing like that.'

Rosie breathed a huge sigh of relief.

'It's a bit of a long story,' Charlotte said, looking up at Rosie.

'Well, I'll get us fresh cuppas and you can start at the beginning,' Rosie said.

Charlotte watched as her sister left to make the tea.

She knew that what she was going to tell her was going to hurt and humiliate her sister as much as it was going to make her angry.

Chapter Sixteen

At just after half-past ten, Dr Parker was saying a chaste goodbye to Helen at the bus stop after their evening at the King's Theatre on Crowtree Road. They had gone to see *49th Parallel*, starring Laurence Olivier – a film Helen had told him she had wanted to see for a while.

In the east end, Pearl was emptying the slops from the beer trays and chatting to Bill as well as to her neighbour, Ronald, who was trying to persuade her to go back to his for a nightcap.

In town, Dor, Angie and Marie-Anne were out celebrating Dorothy's twentieth birthday. They were presently being chatted up by three merchant-navy sailors in the Ritz.

Gloria was sitting with her leg up on a pouffe in her flat on the Borough Road, enjoying a cup of tea and writing a letter to Jack. She'd rung him from the hospital the day after the air raid and convinced him that she was fine and a visit was just too risky. If Miriam found out, the consequences would be far worse than a gash on her leg.

And at 34 Tatham Street, with Arthur and Agnes having just gone to bed, and Joe out with the Home Guard, Polly and Bel were enjoying a girly night in on their own.

Bel had commandeered Arthur's worn but comfy armchair, with Tramp and Pup nestled by her feet. Polly was sitting on one of the kitchen chairs, which she had positioned in front of the warm range. Both had hands wrapped around mugs of steaming Ovaltine.

'Come on, then,' Bel implored. 'I'm ready for the latest instalment. How was Tommy today?'

'He's doing really well,' Polly said. *'Really well.* He's on about setting a date for our wedding.'

Bel laughed. 'I bet you he is!'

She blew on her hot milk.

'So?'

'So what?' Polly asked.

'So, have you set a date?' Bel chuckled.

'No,' Polly said. 'I told him he needs to get out of hospital first.'

'Yes, but that doesn't stop you setting a date, does it?' Bel looked at Polly. 'I would have thought you'd have been dying to set a date. Come to think of it, I'm surprised you haven't already.'

Polly just smiled but didn't say anything. Instead she took a big slurp from her mug.

They were quiet for a moment.

'Tommy told me to say thank you to you and Maisie for asking George to give Arthur a lift home. All this toing and froing to the hospital on the buses is definitely taking its toll. Tommy's told him to have a rest tomorrow.'

Bel gave her best friend a puzzled look. *Was she trying to change the subject?*

She took a sip of her drink.

'Have you told Tommy about Lily's yet?'

Polly shook her head.

'Not yet. Not sure how to tell him, really. But we've got plenty of time. There's no rush.'

'It's a bit of an awkward one, isn't it,' Bel agreed. 'But he knows about their wedding? And that it's on Christmas Day?'

'Oh, yes,' Polly said, bending over to stroke Pup.

Bel looked at her.

133

'I would have thought Tommy would be wanting to beat them down the aisle,' she probed.

'Mmm.' Polly continued to pet the dog.

'What do you mean, *mmm*?' Bel asked, her suspicions growing by the second now.

Polly looked up. 'Yes, I think he probably would,' she agreed, sounding nonplussed.

'God, Pol!' Bel couldn't help but show her exasperation. 'I'd have thought you'd be a bit more excited. This is your *wedding* we're talking about!'

Bel saw the worried look on her sister-in-law's face and leant forward in her chair. 'What's wrong Pol?' she asked, putting her hand on her friend's knee and squeezing it.

Polly looked at her. She knew she was going to have to tell someone and Bel was the least likely to give her an ear-bashing.

She was also the only person she could really trust with keeping a secret.

Not that she'd be able to keep what she'd done a secret for much longer.

Chapter Seventeen

'You've got a right to look nervous, my dear.' George puffed on a cigar and eyed his future wife. Lily had just snapped at one of the girls and George had suggested they go for a cup of tea in the kitchen.

'I don't know what you mean, George. What do I have to be nervous about?' Lily walked over to the armoire and retrieved two glass tumblers.

'I thought we were having a cup of tea?' George said, easing himself down onto one of the wooden chairs with the aid of his walking stick.

Lily didn't answer, instead pouring out two cognacs.

George took his glass and gave Lily a look like the summons.

'The very fact you didn't tell me what you'd said when you were waxing lyrical about meeting Charlotte and how wonderful she was, and I only got to hear about it from a rather shocked Kate, says to me that you know what you did was wrong. Very wrong.'

George swilled the brandy around in his glass but didn't take a drink.

'I hate to say this, my dear, but you are now going to have to face the consequences.'

'And the consequences are?' Lily's face was blank. George knew whenever she was worried, her face lost all expression – it was her 'tell'.

'The wrath of Rosie for starters,' he said. 'To say she's going to be furious is an understatement. My guess is that

Charlotte would have checked out the school more or less straight after she left you and Kate at the Maison Nouvelle. I would say it will have taken her all of half an hour – tops – from Rosie walking through the front door after work for Charlotte to bring up the subject of the Church High School.'

George looked at his pocket watch.

'That's given her a good couple of hours to deal with the repercussions of what you've done and to concoct a suitably slow and painful death for you.'

George finally took a swig of his drink. He placed it carefully back down on the kitchen table and rotated it slowly.

'Honestly, George, you say I'm the drama queen!'

'Lily,' George said with a heavy sigh, 'what on earth possessed you to tell Charlotte about the school?'

Lily didn't answer. Instead she lit up another Gauloise.

The French grandfather clock out in the hallway chimed seven.

'Perhaps we should go out to dinner?' Lily suggested, nervously tapping her cigarette into the crystal ashtray.

'There's no running away from it, dear,' George said. 'It's time to face the music – or should I say, the firing squad?'

On hearing the front door slam shut, Lily jumped.

'Gawd! I'm getting as bad as Kate,' she mumbled under her breath, just as Rosie came marching into the kitchen.

Rosie stopped and glared at Lily.

She said nothing.

'Honestly, Rosie, if looks could kill.' Lily tried to sound jocular, but the tremble in her voice betrayed her nervousness.

'If only they could!' Rosie finally spoke.

136

'Shut the door, *ma chère*.' Lily waved a hand over at the door. She did not want anyone other than George to be privy to the inevitable dressing-down she was about to get.

Rosie turned to look at the door. Ignoring Lily's request, she went over to the armoire, got herself a glass and sloshed brandy into it. While she did so, Lily hurried over to the door and closed it.

'Well, let's make a toast.' Rosie raised her glass. 'To the victor!'

Lily looked at George, who appeared equally puzzled.

'You'll be pleased to hear, Lily, that you have won.' Rosie glared at her. 'You told her all about the damned school – knowing that doing so would give her the necessary ammunition to demand that she goes there and moves back here permanently.'

Rosie continued to fix Lily with a look of pure fury.

'Have you any idea what the backlash is for me? Did you once think about what I wanted?'

Neither woman spoke for a moment.

Lily broke the stand-off.

'You're right, *ma chère*,' she said, her voice eerily calm. 'I didn't think about what *you* really wanted, nor did I think about what *I* wanted, but I did think about what your little sister wanted, and what she obviously – *desperately* – wants is to be back here – *with you* – where she *belongs*.'

Rosie looked at Lily and then at George, who had been sitting quietly, sipping his drink and wisely keeping his mouth shut.

'That's not the point, Lily,' Rosie said, exasperated. 'I asked you – *trusted you* – not to say anything about the school and you flagrantly ignored my wishes.'

Lily felt herself flush. Feeling a little hot and light-headed, she sat down at the kitchen table.

Being trustworthy was one of the few virtues she claimed to possess. Rosie was right, she *had* betrayed a trust. It didn't matter how much she tried to convince herself, or anyone else, that she was justified in telling Charlotte about the Church High School, ultimately she had done wrong.

Lily looked at Rosie, who was still standing, giving her the death glare.

'I'm sorry, Rosie,' she said simply but sincerely.

She pulled out a chair and gestured for Rosie to sit down.

'You're right,' she said. 'I shouldn't have said anything. I broke a promise. And you know me, I pride myself on being a keeper of secrets. Someone you can trust. So, I apologise.'

Lily looked Rosie in the eye.

'I really don't know what came over me,' she said somewhat wearily. 'It was like the devil just crept into my head and opened my mouth. And the next thing I was blathering on about the school.'

She paused.

'I'm so sorry. I really am.'

Another pause.

'Do you think you'll be able to forgive me?'

Rosie looked at Lily and could see she meant what she said.

'Mmm,' she murmured. It was neither a yes nor a no, but it was good enough for Lily.

Rosie felt herself sag. Finally she acquiesced and sat down in the chair Lily had pulled out for her. Glancing at Lily and then at George, who had a look of relief on his face, she took a sip of her drink.

'You know what,' she said after a few moments' contemplation. 'I don't know who I'm angrier with.'

There was a pause.

'You, Lily – or that bloody school.'

'What, the Church High School?' Lily asked.

'No, the bloody Runcorn School for Girls,' Rosie said with venom.

Lily and George gave each other puzzled looks.

'Tell us more,' George said.

He'd always known there was more to all this.

And with that Rosie started to tell them what Charlotte had finally told her.

Chapter Eighteen

'Are you worried about the wedding night?' Bel asked, trying to be as tactful as possible.

'Well, yes,' Polly admitted. 'I mean, every bride's nervous about the actual wedding night, isn't she?'

Bel nodded. 'I was terrified before I married Teddy. I loved him so much, but it was still all rather foreboding.'

They were both quiet for a moment.

'Is that the reason you're putting off setting a date?' Bel asked tentatively.

Polly looked at Bel.

'No, if only that were the reason,' she said forlornly.

It was the first time Bel had seen Polly look down in the dumps since Tommy's return.

'You're starting to worry me now, Pol. Come on, just spit it out.'

Polly took a deep breath.

'Can you remember when I got notification that I was due Tommy's gratuity pay?'

Bel nodded. 'Yes. We were all surprised that they paid it out even though Tommy hadn't been officially declared dead.'

'Exactly,' Polly said.

Bel looked at her lifelong friend. It still hurt her to recall how devastated she had been that day and in the ensuing weeks.

'I tried to carry on as normal,' Polly said, her eyes tearing up. 'But inside I was in bits. I hate to admit it,' she looked at Bel, 'but the moment I got the letter ... At that very moment, all hope that Tommy was alive just left me.'

A tear ran down Polly's cheek. She brushed it away.

'I gave up hope. I gave up all hope I had of ever seeing Tommy alive.'

'I know,' Bel said.

They had all watched helplessly, wanting to make Polly feel better, but knowing there was absolutely nothing they could do.

'And what made it even worse,' Polly continued, 'was that Tommy had told me he was saving his pay for our wedding. So that we didn't have to scrimp and save. So we could get married when we wanted. *So that we didn't have to wait.*'

Bel looked at Polly.

'And then,' Polly continued, 'to make matters worse, the day I got the notification in the post, Rosie came into work and handed out the invites to Lily's and George's wedding.'

'Yes, I remember.' Bel thought she saw guilt in Polly's eyes.

'Can you remember me saying to Ma that I just wanted to give it all away?'

Bel nodded. 'I do.' Her eyes were fixed on Polly.

'And Ma said she'd have my guts for garters if I did any such thing and to stop talking like "an eejit".'

'Mmm,' Bel said. She had an awful feeling she knew what her sister-in-law was about to tell her.

Polly looked at Bel and grimaced.

'Well, I did,' she said.

'Did what?' Bel asked the question, hoping to hear a different answer to the one she was expecting.

'I gave it all away,' Polly confessed.

'You gave it all away?' Bel repeated.

Polly nodded.

'Oh, my God! I don't believe it.'

'I know,' Polly said, guiltily. 'I don't either.'

'Oh, my goodness. No wonder you don't want to set a date,' Bel gasped. 'Poor Tommy's been saving every penny for a top-notch wedding for the woman he loves – and you've gone and given it away!'

'Stop it, Bel,' Polly commanded. 'You're not helping.'

Bel looked at Polly's guilt-ridden face. All of a sudden, she just erupted into laughter.

Polly looked at Bel as though she had gone mad, but then Polly's face suddenly creased up and she too started to laugh.

Before long they were both crying with laughter, unable to stop themselves.

For the next few minutes neither woman could speak as they held their sides. Tears blurred their vision.

Finally, when they had both just about managed to control themselves, Bel asked Polly, 'So, pray tell,' she wiped underneath her eyes, 'who or what was the lucky recipient of poor Tommy's hard-earned money?'

'Don't, Bel, I feel bad enough as it is,' Polly said, sitting back on her chair and wiping her cheeks dry.

'No, seriously, though,' Bel said. 'Who did you give the money to?'

Polly took a drink from her Ovaltine, which was now lukewarm.

'Well,' she began, 'you'll be pleased to know I didn't just chuck it away. I did think about it.'

Bel couldn't help another burst of laughter.

'Ah well, that makes it all right then?'

She took a deep breath and forced herself to be serious again.

'Go on. What did you do?'

'Well, I donated some of it to the Red Cross. I'd been reading about all the good they've been doing and how many lives they've saved. As well as risking their own.'

'That's kind of you,' Bel said. 'And particularly poignant after what happened to Tommy.'

Polly nodded. The same thought had occurred to her more than once lately.

'Then I gave some to the King George's Fund for Sailors,' Polly said.

'Oh yes?' Bel asked, curious. She'd not heard of the charity before.

'Tommy told me about it. It was set up because there were so many maimed or lost at sea during the First War. It's to help the maritime community – those in need and their families.'

'Like those in the Royal Navy and the Merchant Navy?' Bel asked.

'Yes, and fishing fleets,' Polly added. 'I knew Tommy would like it if some money went to them.'

'Ah, that's nice,' Bel said. 'And what about the rest? There must have been a fair amount?'

'Well,' Polly said, 'I wanted someone from here to benefit from it.'

'What? From Sunderland?' Bel asked, intrigued.

'Yes,' Polly said. 'Tommy was always so proud of where he came from. It got me thinking about how it would be nice to help someone local.'

Bel listened.

'Do you remember that poor girl who lost both her hands when a German bomber crashed into her home just down the road in Suffolk Street?'

'Yes,' Bel said, sadly, 'the one who worked at the GPO as a telephonist. I think her mam was killed as well?'

'That's right. Well, I heard a while ago, from Muriel of all people – ' Polly rolled her eyes ' – that doctors were trying to get her fitted with some kind of artificial hands.'

Bel gave a look of amazement.

'I know. Incredible, isn't it?' Polly said. 'Anyway, there was a bit in the *Echo* about her, saying that they were trying to get her better and back to normal – well, as much as anyone can get back to normal after something like that happening.'

Bel nodded in agreement.

'So, I just put the money in an envelope,' Polly said, 'found out which hospital she was in, and asked the matron on her ward to give it to her.'

'You didn't tell her who it was from?' Bel asked.

Polly shook her head.

Bel stared. She shook her head slowly.

'Pol,' she said, 'you're a very special person, you know that?'

Tears welled up in Bel's eyes. She got up out of the arm-chair, went over to Polly, and wrapped her arms around her.

'The world,' she said, 'would be a lot better place if there were more people like you in it.'

She squeezed her sister-in-law tight.

Polly hugged her back.

'I hope Tommy thinks the same as you do, Bel.'

'Well, he'd be mad not to,' Bel said. 'He's lucky to have you. Very lucky.'

Chapter Nineteen

'Make sure she gets her bleedin' money back,' Lily whispered in George's ear as she hugged him goodbye.

George nodded, walked over to his MG and got into the driver's seat.

Lily tottered from the front gate to where the car was parked. She looked about her and was glad to see the street was empty. It had just gone eight o'clock and was only starting to get light. Most of the other residents on West Lawn were elderly and rarely left their homes, so she could risk leaving the house in her dressing gown with her hair still in rollers. Not that she would have been too concerned had any of her neighbours seen her. They all believed her to be French and as a result she was relieved of the burden of being either 'normal' or 'respectable'.

Bending down, she poked her head into the car. Charlotte was sitting scrunched up in the back seat. Rosie had made her wear her school uniform for the last time.

'Do as your sister says, you hear?' Lily commanded.

Charlotte nodded, her face a mix of excitement and apprehension.

Lily then turned her attention to Rosie, whose face was bare of make-up, save for a thin layer of foundation and a light brush of powder to cover her scars. She was a little taken aback to see that she was wearing her faded blue denim overalls, which were covered with a scattering of pinhole burns.

'See you when you get back,' Lily said simply, before stepping backwards. 'No need to tell you to drive carefully,' she said to George.

'No need at all, my dear,' he said, adjusting his rear-view mirror. He gave Lily a wink and a half-smile before pushing the gear stick into first and pulling away.

With both hands stuck in the pockets of her plaid night robe, Lily watched as the MG drove to the end of West Lawn.

Seeing Charlotte's smiley face looking out the back window and waving at her, Lily waved back.

She couldn't have wished for a better outcome had she actually planned it.

The journey to Harrogate passed quickly. The noise of the car engine made conversation practically impossible, which Rosie was glad of. She wanted to be totally focused on what she was about to do. Going up against someone as educated and as well-to-do as Mrs Willoughby-Smith was a little intimidating. She didn't want to stumble over her words or make a fool of herself, plus she wanted to take the deputy head down a peg or two. If she could also leave with a cheque for the fees she had paid for the rest of the term, then all the better. She was damned if she was going to beg for it, though.

As they made their way down the A1, Rosie looked at the passing landscape and the patchwork of fields – so lush and green, so unlike the grey metal and concrete terrain she was used to. She looked down at her overalls and recalled her first day at Thompson's. She'd been given a pair of men's overalls that were far too big for her, but she had not dared to ask if there was a smaller pair. She'd just been so thankful to be taken on. She hadn't realised at the time that it was thanks to Jack that she'd got the job. He had argued with management that they should give her a chance, despite her gender. He had tipped the scales in her favour by reminding them that they had recently taken on a girl of roughly Rosie's age in the admin department – his own daughter. In doing so he had also subtly reminded them that he was the son-in-law of one of the town's most influential and powerful businessmen, Mr Havelock. It was a card he rarely played and one he only allowed himself to use for the benefit of others.

Seeing the signs to Harrogate, Rosie felt a slight fluttering of nerves. She thought about yesterday evening when she had gone to see Gloria. She'd felt bad asking her to cover for her on her first day back at work, but she knew she wouldn't be able to concentrate on anything else until she'd done what she needed to do.

When she'd walked into Gloria's flat, she'd been surprised to see Helen sitting on the sofa with Hope on her lap. She knew, of course, that Helen had become close to Gloria and Hope. But still, it was strange to see them together in such a domestic scenario.

They had both been aghast when she'd told them what Charlotte had told her, although Helen hadn't seemed particularly shocked. Her words were, 'Welcome to my world.'

'One mile to go!' George shouted above the noise of the engine. Charlotte and Rosie sat up straight in their seats.

Five minutes later they had turned off the main carriageway and were driving slowly along winding country roads and it wasn't long before they were crunching down the gravel driveway of the Runcorn School for Girls.

As soon as George had reversed the car into the parking place allocated for visitors, he climbed out. Using his stick, he hurried round to the passenger side.

'Thank you, George,' Rosie said, stepping out of the car and looking around her. She saw the large clock on the front of the main school building. It was twenty-five-past ten. Her appointment was at half past. Their journey had been timed to perfection.

'Right, Charlie,' Rosie said as her sister clambered out of the back seat. 'Get your bag out of the boot and get your stuff.'

Charlotte nodded, went to the car boot and hauled out her empty suitcase.

'And remember what I said,' Rosie said sternly. 'I don't want even a cross word – regardless of what anyone might say to you.'

Charlotte nodded again and headed off in the direction of her dormitory at the back of the school.

'After you, my dear,' George said.

Rosie took a deep breath and the pair walked up to the main entrance and into the expansive foyer. The deputy headmistress's office was to the left and the school secretary's office was on the right.

'Oh, excuse me!'

Rosie saw the school secretary, whom she knew to be called Miss Howey, hurrying towards her. She had a cup of tea in her hand.

'Tradesmen's entrance. Around the back!' the secretary ordered, using her free hand to shoo Rosie back out the front door. She made no effort to hide her disdain.

Rosie forced a smile onto her face.

'Ah, good morning, Miss Howey,' she said. 'Lovely to see you again.'

She paused.

Seeing that the secretary still had no idea who she was, she informed her, 'It's Mrs Miller. Mrs Rosemary Miller. Charlotte Thornton's sister.' Rosie put her hand out to greet the secretary, whom she had met on her last visit.

Miss Howey looked at Rosie's outstretched hand but made no effort to shake it. Instead her eyes flickered to George, who was standing behind Rosie, his walking stick in one hand, his fedora in the other.

'Sorry, can I help you?' she asked, throwing an irritated look in Rosie's direction, but giving the smartly dressed gentleman a welcoming smile.

'I'm with Mrs Miller,' George said politely. Unlike Rosie, he did not offer his hand in greeting.

Rosie looked at George and then back to the school secretary.

She undid the top button of her overalls. Her temperature was rising.

'Miss Howey,' she said, 'I think you'll find I have an appointment with Mrs Willoughby-Smith at half-past ten.'

At that exact moment, the door to the deputy head's office opened.

'Mrs Miller—' Mrs Willoughby-Smith stopped in her tracks. The look on her face changed in a split second from pleasantly professional to one of undisguised horror.

She nervously scanned the immediate vicinity, terrified that others might have seen a labourer standing on the polished parquet flooring in an area only teachers and parents were allowed to tread. Even the pupils had to use a side entrance.

'Ah, Mrs Willoughby-Smith,' Rosie said, this time dispensing with the niceties of a handshake. Instead she stretched out her arm and signalled towards the deputy head's office door.

'Shall we? I believe it's almost half-past ten.' Rosie pulled up the sleeve of her overalls to look at her watch. The only belonging she had left of her mother's. 'Of course, I can sit and wait if you'd prefer.'

Rosie looked over Miss Howey's head as though she had just spotted someone she knew. She raised her hand in a wave.

'Oh, is that Charlotte's Latin teacher?'

She looked at Mrs Willoughby-Smith and then to Miss Howey.

'Gosh, I always forget her name.'

'Please come into my office!' The deputy head moved aside and pushed the door wide open.

'Are you all right to wait?' Rosie turned to look at George.

George nodded and sat down on a hard wooden chair in the foyer.

Having ushered Rosie into the confines of her office and quickly shut the door, Mrs Willoughby-Smith's demeanour changed.

'I have to say, Mrs Miller, that this is most improper of you.'

She pulled her chair closer to her desk and put her hands palms down on the embossed leather top.

'And I really must point out that if you come here again dressed like some lowly labourer fresh from the factory, we will not be able to allow you over the threshold. If any of my girls were to see you wearing such attire, what kind of example would that be setting?'

If there had been a shred of doubt in Rosie's mind that she was doing the right thing, Mrs Willoughby-Smith's last comment successfully obliterated it.

Rosie bit her tongue and pointed to the chair in front of the desk.

'May I?'

Before Mrs Willoughby-Smith had a chance to object, Rosie sat down, pulling up the trousers of her overalls as she did so and crossing her legs. She put her clasped hands on her lap.

'First of all, Mrs Willoughby-Smith, you need have no worries about me turning up here ever again, let alone dressed in what you refer to as "such attire".' Rosie smiled pleasantly.

Mrs Willoughby-Smith looked at Rosie and furrowed her brow.

'As of today,' Rosie explained, 'I am withdrawing Charlotte from this school.'

'I'm guessing,' Mrs Willoughby-Smith said, her eyes focused on Rosie's overalls, 'that the reason for you doing so is because you can no longer afford to dress yourself properly, never mind pay the fees to keep your sister here?'

Rosie glared at the deputy head.

'Far from it!' she retorted. 'In fact, Charlotte will be starting at another independent school – a school, I hasten to add, that runs its affairs with a far higher level of professionalism than Runcorn does.'

'Oh,' Mrs Willoughby-Smith said, sitting back in her chair. 'And which school might that be?'

Rosie looked at the deputy head.

'That's none of your business,' she said simply. 'What is your business, though,' she continued, 'and which I feel you have a right to know, is the reason why I have decided to remove my sister from the school.'

'Pray tell, Mrs Miller. I'm all ears.'

Rosie looked at the woman sitting in front of her and realised that nothing she said would make any difference, but she didn't care, she was going to say it anyway.

'When I was here last and we were discussing the possible reasons why Charlotte and the other girl in her year had ended up fighting, you knew all along what was really going on, didn't you?'

Mrs Willoughby-Smith didn't answer.

'You knew that Charlotte's classmates had found out that I was a shipyard welder and that she was being relentlessly bullied, didn't you?'

Again silence.

'You also knew that Charlotte had, in fact, endured a rather long and consistent campaign of bullying since first coming here due to the fact that she has neither a mother nor a father.'

Rosie paused.

'I only wish she had felt able to tell me about it at the time, but – and it hurts me to say this – in her words, she "just got used to it" and decided, for whatever reasons, not to tell me.'

Rosie looked at the deputy head's face, which was impassive.

'But then the bullying escalated,' Rosie said, trying her hardest to keep her anger at bay. 'The little gang of girls – who are, from what I can gather, known bullies – got their hands on a letter I sent Charlotte which made reference to my job and one of the ships I was working on. This had the effect of adding fuel to what had become, at that point, a dwindling fire.'

'Perhaps,' Mrs Willoughby-Smith interrupted, 'Charlotte should have been more careful with her personal possessions and not left them lying around for others to read.'

Rosie felt her face flush.

'The girls in question didn't find the letter by chance, or through any carelessness on Charlotte's part. They snatched it out of the hands of her best friend – a young girl called Marjorie – after Charlotte gave it to her to read.' Rosie took a deep breath. 'The bullies then proceeded to read it out to the whole dormitory whilst – again in Charlotte's words – "laughing like hyenas".'

Rosie glowered at the deputy head.

'The whole episode ended up in a fight, with Charlotte trying to reclaim her letter, and worse still, with Marjorie suffering an asthma attack. Thank goodness the poor girl's no longer a pupil here.'

'I'm afraid,' Mrs Willoughby-Smith said, a condescending smile stretched across her face, 'bullying is simply a part of life – be that at school or outside in the real world. The girls have to learn to deal with it. It's part of growing up. They just have to toughen up.'

Rosie couldn't believe what she was hearing. It took her a moment to unjumble the myriad of arguments fighting to break free to show just how wrong this was.

'Just because it's a part of life does not mean it's right, or that we should condone it by doing nothing!' Rosie couldn't stop the mix of anger and exasperation from breaking through.

'Mmm,' Mrs Willoughby-Smith mused. 'I suppose we are all entitled to our own opinions, but I have to say, Mrs Miller, that had you not lied about what you did for a living, in all likelihood none of this would ever have occurred. So, if the blame has to be placed on anyone's doorstep, I'm afraid it would be yours.'

Rosie looked at the deputy head sitting in her oak-carved chair, her hair swept back in a neat roll, make-up perfectly applied and a picture of the King on the wall behind her, and realised that she would never make this self-righteous woman see sense.

Rosie sighed.

'You're right, Mrs Willoughby-Smith, on one point, and that is I *should* have been honest from the start. I wish I had been. I really do. I should have been proud of my job and had the courage to stick my neck out and face the ridicule for doing a job those with closed minds think is for men alone. But I didn't, and my little sister has had to suffer the consequences of my lack of courage.'

Rosie took a breath. She could feel her heart pounding.

'However, what infuriated me perhaps even more than your inability to deal with the bullying and intimidation taking place,' she continued, 'was when Charlotte told me that she'd heard *you* laughing and snickering about the fact that I work as a welder in a shipyard.'

'Really?' Mrs Willoughby-Smith asked. The epitome of innocence.

'Yes, *really*,' Rosie said. 'You might recall asking to see Charlotte after my last visit, when I was summoned to come and talk about the problems you were having.'

'Yes, I spoke to both girls after our meeting that day,' Mrs Willoughby-Smith said. 'Gave them both a good dressing-down.'

Rosie straightened her back and leant forward in her seat.

'You'll recall, then, that you also had a meeting with the other girl's father. I believe his name is Mr Malcolm White-head?'

Mrs Willoughby-Smith started to move around uncomfortably in her chair.

'I did,' she said.

'And that you and Mr Whitehead had a good old chuckle over the fact that I am a shipyard welder and not a secretary, as I had purported to be. You were also keen that Mr Whitehead understand that he was to have no concerns about his daughter receiving any kind of disciplinary measures.'

Rosie breathed out.

'How do you think that made Charlotte feel?' she said. 'Sitting there, outside your office, hearing the person she was meant to respect and look up to bad-mouthing the

154

only living relative she has? Knowing that the bully was going to get off scot-free?'

The two women sat, both silent, staring at one another.

'So,' Rosie said, standing up, 'as Charlotte will not be spending another minute under this roof, I will expect to be refunded the fees I have already paid.'

Mrs Willoughby-Smith let out a bitter laugh.

'You have a good sense of humour, Mrs Miller, I will give you that.'

Mrs Willoughby-Smith stood up, moved around the desk and walked over to the door to open it.

Rosie knew this was one battle she would not win. If the school refused to give her back the fees, there was nothing she could do about it.

'And ...' Mrs Willoughby-Smith moved towards Rosie and spoke quietly ' ... I wouldn't be repeating anything we have discussed in this room to anyone. It wouldn't be wise. I'm sure you've heard about the laws regarding defamation? After all, who is going to believe a fourteen-year-old girl who's got a reputation for bare-knuckle fighting and has no parents to speak of, and her sister who works as a welder in a shipyard?'

The deputy head wisely took a step back and looked out into the hallway.

Seeing George push himself out of his chair with his walking stick, and her secretary's concerned expression, she forced a convincing smile across her face.

'So, good day, Mrs Miller,' she said, turning to Rosie, her voice saccharine sweet. 'I'm so glad we managed to sort everything out.'

And with that, Rosie found herself being ushered into the foyer, the office door closing firmly behind her.

Following the deputy head's lead, Miss Howey also got up and shut the heavy oak door to her office.

George looked at Rosie.

'Home?'

Rosie nodded, her face like thunder.

As they made it down the stone steps, George asked, 'How did it go?'

'Not quite how I had expected,' Rosie said.

'Did you say what you came here to say?' he asked as they reached the car. He looked about but could not see any sign of Charlotte.

'Yes.' Rosie paused. 'Yes, I guess I did.'

'Well,' George said, 'that's the main thing.'

He walked over to the passenger door and opened it wide.

'And did she agree to pay back the fees?' he asked as Rosie stood with her hand on the open door.

Rosie let out a bark of laughter.

'I think her words were "you have a good sense of humour, Mrs Miller".'

George looked at Rosie.

'Damn it!' he suddenly said, putting his hand to his head. 'I've left my hat in the lobby.'

He turned to head back to the school.

'I'll be back in a jiffy.'

Rosie was standing by the car, breathing in the fresh air, calming herself down and going over the exchange of words she'd just had with the deputy head. She hadn't really managed to take her down a peg, but did it really matter? She knew Peter would be proud of her and that provided her with some solace.

She also knew that Peter would be glad that Charlotte was coming to live at home. He'd always been a good listener while she'd regurgitated all the reasons Charlie couldn't possibly come back. His lack of words, though, had spoken volumes. She knew that he believed a family should be together. Regardless.

Seeing Charlotte appear from the side entrance of the main building carrying her suitcase, Rosie had to admit that, deep down, she too had always felt the same.

'You got everything?' Rosie asked.

'Yes,' Charlotte said, heaving the case.

'Here, let me give you a hand,' Rosie said.

'No, honestly, I can manage,' Charlotte insisted, shoving the case into the boot of the MG.

Charlotte was just getting into the back seat when she saw George making his way towards the car.

'Where's George been?' she asked Rosie.

'He forgot his hat.'

'Tally-ho!' George said as he reached the car, lifting his fedora in the air. 'Off we go! Home sweet home, and all that!'

He eased himself into the driver's seat and shut the door. Rosie followed suit.

'Everything all right?' Rosie asked, thinking George looked unusually chipper.

'Couldn't be better, my dear,' he said, allowing himself a little rev of the engine before they set off.

Chapter Twenty

Leaving Vivian and Maisie to deal with the last clients of the evening, Lily grabbed her packet of Gauloises and tumbler of cognac and padded up to what she liked to refer to as her 'boudoir' on the second floor.

'Thank goodness I've finally got you on my own,' she said, bustling into the room and seeing George getting changed. 'So, come on, I want every cough and spit. I've been busting to know all day.'

She plonked herself down on the stool in front of her vanity and lit up a cigarette.

'What did they say when they saw Rosie in her raggedy overalls?' She eyed George in the mirror as she blew out smoke. 'Gawd, I wish I'd been a fly on the wall.'

George laughed.

'So do I, my dear, so do I.'

He unwrapped a cigar and smelled it.

'Well, let's just say I think they would have happily thrown a blanket over Rosie and bundled her out of the building, away from prying eyes, if they'd had the opportunity.' He laughed, recalling the look on the secretary's face. 'I think the only reason they allowed her into the office was out of fear that someone would see her standing in the foyer.'

'So, what did you do when she went in there?' Lily started to remove her make-up with large dollops of white cream.

'Nothing. I just sat there on the "naughty chair" outside the secretary's office and waited,' George said, lighting up his cigar and puffing hard. 'I asked Rosie how it had gone when we walked back. She didn't seem exactly over the moon, but she said that she'd managed to say what she'd wanted to say.'

'Do you think Rosie got the better of her?' Lily asked.

'Mmm,' George pondered, putting his cigar on the side of the ashtray. He went over to Lily, unclasped her thick gold necklace and kissed her neck.

'I don't think you can really get the better of people like Mrs Willoughby-Smith. But I do think Rosie managed to at least get her point across, even if it was dismissed without a second thought.'

George proceeded to unzip the back of Lily's black dress.

'Well,' Lily said, standing and shaking herself out of her dress, 'it will have been good for Charlotte to see her sister do what she did. It took some nerve turning up there in her work overalls.'

Lily stepped out of her dress, now a mound on the floor.

'I'm guessing Mrs Deputy Head didn't give Rosie her refund?' she asked, putting on her dressing gown and taking a sip of cognac.

George shook his head as he had another puff on his cigar.

'So, you did as planned?' Lily asked. 'Went back for your fedora?'

'I did indeed, my dear.'

George puffed some more.

'I was, of course, very polite and very professional.'

'Of course,' Lily said, 'I wouldn't have expected anything less. So, what exactly did you say?'

'As discussed,' George said, 'I mentioned that I had been interested to hear from Mrs Miller that Mrs Willoughby-Smith, in her capacity as the deputy head of one of the country's top girls' schools, was on such friendly terms with the former prospective parliamentary candidate Mr Whitehead. And how I would guess that most of the parents with pupils at the school – and probably a good percentage of the staff – would be less than happy to hear that anyone from the school, never mind someone of Mrs Willoughby-Smith's standing, would be fraternising with a politician with such far-right leanings. Someone who had only just missed being interned along with Sir Oswald Mosley and the rest of his British Union of Fascist cronies.'

'Oh, George, you *are* good,' Lily said proudly. George had told her how the name had rung a bell when Rosie had mentioned it. When he'd repeated the name to the Brigadier, the old man had nearly choked on his brandy, gone bright red and relayed Mr Whitehead's entire tawdry history to them both. Lily had made a conscious decision to have more patience with the Brigadier in future, or at least to make sure the girls paid him plenty of attention.

'After which,' George said, 'I simply told her that it would be appreciated if she could write out a cheque for the money paid by Mrs Miller for the remainder of the term.'

'I'm guessing she did just that?' Lily said.

'She certainly did. Cool as a cucumber she was. Didn't say a word, simply opened her drawer, got the chequebook out and did what she should have done from the off.'

George bent down to pick up his discarded shirt.

'And,' he added, leaning on his walking stick as he stood up, 'I also told her that should Charlotte's new school need a recommendation regarding their new pupil, then they would receive such a reference and that it would be exemplary.'

'Good thinking,' Lily said. 'So, was that it? You just took the cheque and left?'

George took another puff of his cigar, blowing out a swirl of smoke.

'Mrs Willoughby-Smith might also have been given a short lecture on the importance of the shipbuilding industry and particularly how vital its role is at this tumultuous moment in time.' He paused. 'That is, *if* winning the war was what one wanted.

'And,' he added, 'how really she should be parading Mrs Miller around the school in her overalls and boots, praising her and other women like her for doing the invaluable jobs they are doing.'

Lily clapped her hands in glee.

'Well bleedin' done, George!'

Taking off her dressing gown, Lily climbed into bed.

She opened her arms.

'Now, stop puffing on that cigar and get yourself into bed. Your future wife wants to show you just how much she loves you.'

George laughed and stubbed out his cigar.

Chapter Twenty-One

Tuesday 27 October

'So, let's hear all about it,' Dorothy demanded as they settled down for their lunch in the canteen.

'Gloria here wouldn't tell us a thing, miss,' Angie groused.

Gloria looked at Rosie and rolled her eyes heavenwards.

'Just that you'd gone to Harrogate to see that Mrs Willoughby-what's-her-name,' Martha said.

'And that it was something to do with Charlotte being bullied,' Polly said, taking a bite of her sandwich.

Everyone looked at Rosie expectantly.

As Rosie began to relay the real reason for Charlotte's refusal to go back to Runcorn, their expressions changed to ones of outrage.

'Poor Charlotte,' Hannah said, her big brown eyes pooling with empathy. 'Why would anyone pick on another person because they'd suffered such a terrible tragedy – and at such a young age?'

'They should have been *nicer* to her because she didn't have a mam and dad, not *nastier*,' Olly said.

Hannah nodded vigorously.

'Perhaps in an ideal world,' Rosie said sadly.

'And Charlotte's friend with the asthma – what's her name again?' Polly asked.

'Marjorie.' Dorothy beat Rosie to it.

'Poor Marjorie,' Polly said. 'Thank goodness she's not there any more.'

'I know,' Rosie said. 'I think that was when Charlotte decided she'd had enough.'

'When she was totally on her own,' Martha surmised.

'Exactly,' Rosie said. 'It sounded like no one wanted to be friends with Charlotte after the fight for fear of being bullied themselves.'

'Honestly,' Polly said, 'makes me glad I went to Hudson Road School.'

'I just can't get the image of them all taunting Charlie and laughing at her.' Rosie dropped her voice on seeing Gloria nod her head at the counter, warning her that Muriel was about.

'And,' she added, 'I do feel a bit guilty for being so hard on her. Especially as the reason she didn't tell me was because she was worried about hurting *my* feelings.' She sighed. 'I should have realised that there was more to it than she was letting on.'

'Well, I don't think there's been any permanent damage done,' Gloria said, taking a sip of her tea. 'I think Charlotte's a chip off the old block. Like her sister – got broad shoulders.'

Everyone murmured their agreement. They were all glad Gloria was back in the fold. Their mother hen had returned to rule the roost.

When Rosie told them she had worn her overalls and boots, there were cries of disbelief, a huge guffaw from Martha, and an actual scream from Dorothy.

'Sorry.' Dorothy belatedly put her hand across her mouth and looked around her.

Dozens of nearby workers had swung round to see what the emergency was.

'Eee,' Polly said. 'I wish I'd seen you.'

'I wish I'd seen the looks on their faces,' Gloria said

Rosie thought for a moment and then laughed.

'In hindsight, it was a bit of a crazy thing to do.'

'I'd say! Wouldn't you, Ange?' Dorothy nudged her friend.

'Too bloomin' right,' Angie agreed. She hadn't thought it possible to idolise her boss any more than she did already.

'Oh, I forgot,' Rosie said, rummaging around in her bag. 'Charlie asked me to give you this, Hannah.'

'Oh,' Hannah said, taking the brown paper bag and looking inside. 'A book!'

She carefully took it out.

'Cicero,' she said, touching the hardbacked book as though it was newly discovered treasure.

'Who's he when he's at home?' Angie asked.

'He's Hannah's favourite philosopher,' Olly explained.

Hannah opened the book but hastily shut it again.

'I'll read it properly when I'm at home,' she declared. 'Please tell Charlotte "Thank you thank you thank you!"'

'But how was it that Charlotte ended up telling you the truth in the end?' Polly asked, puzzled.

Rosie groaned.

'A story for another time.'

Seeing Bel and Marie-Anne coming into the canteen, she waved to them.

'Hi, everyone,' Bel said as she and Marie-Anne reached their friends. They pulled up a couple of chairs and sat themselves at the top of the table.

'Just in time,' Rosie said, wanting a change of subject. Much as she liked Marie-Anne, she still didn't want her to know too much about her personal life. 'Dorothy was just on the verge of grilling Polly about her wedding.'

'How did you know?' Dorothy looked at Rosie in amazement.

'Just a guess,' she said, looking across at Polly, whose face had dropped at the mention of her nuptials.

They all caught Bel raising her eyebrows at her sister-in-law.

'Oh, that's a look if ever I saw one,' Marie-Anne said.

'Yes, it was!' rose Dorothy's voice.

Polly sighed and looked at Bel.

'Come on, Pol, you've got to tell them,' Bel said. 'It'll be good practice for when you confess all to Tommy.'

Now all the women were enrapt.

'Eee, yer not ganna call it off, are yer?' Angie said, aghast.

There was silence as they all awaited Polly's answer.

'Well,' she said. 'Not exactly.'

'What you mean, "not exactly"?' Martha asked, her face deathly serious.

Polly let out a nervous laugh.

'Oh, it's not bad news. I'm not calling the wedding *off*.' Polly paused. 'But there might be a bit of a delay.'

'A delay?' Gloria asked.

'Why?' Rosie asked.

Polly took a deep intake of breath.

'I still can't believe you did what you did,' Dorothy said to Polly as they all headed back to the dry basin. 'But I don't think you should put off the wedding just because you've *given away* all of Tommy's wages, don't you agree, Ange?'

'I agree,' Angie said automatically. She was still slightly dumbstruck that anyone could give that amount of money to charity. And Polly of all people. She was meant to be the sensible one.

'What about you, Martha?' Dorothy asked.

Martha nodded her head in silent agreement. She, too, had been gobsmacked by Polly's revelation, but more so about the poor girl who had lost her hands. She kept looking down at her own hands, imagining what it would be like to have false ones.

'I suppose you could do what Rosie did,' Gloria suggested.

'What? Run away and get married in a registry office?' Angie asked.

'It wouldn't cost much,' Martha said.

'I'd be up for that,' Polly said. 'More than up for it, but I think my ma would have me hung, drawn and quartered for even thinking about it. Mind you, she's probably going to do that anyway when I tell her about the money.'

'Oh. My. God.' Dorothy said. 'You've not told Agnes?'

Polly turned pale.

'No, and I'm not telling her until I've told Tommy.'

'When yer gonna tell Tommy?' Angie asked. 'He's gonna go bonkers, isn't he?'

'Ange,' Dorothy reprimanded. 'That's not really what Pol wants to hear.'

'I'm sure Tommy won't go "bonkers",' Gloria said.

'I hope not,' Polly said. 'Although I bet you he'd be up for doing a Rosie and Peter.'

'It did sound very romantic, didn't it?' Dorothy mused, a dreamy look on her face.

'Yes, I thought so,' Polly said. 'Just the two of them. In a whirlwind romance, like they were eloping. Although,' she added thoughtfully, 'I wouldn't have liked the end bit – my new husband going off to war. Imagine getting married, then two days later kissing him goodbye, not knowing if you're ever going to see each other again.'

'It's not unheard of these days, though, is it?' Gloria said.

'It must be awful,' Marie-Anne said.

Polly gave an involuntary shiver, thinking of her own heartache when she'd waved Tommy off to war after just getting engaged.

'I know,' she said. 'I keep telling myself how lucky I am. At least I've got Tommy back for good.'

166

Chapter Twenty-Two

As Rosie made her way over to see Helen in the admin building, she looked up at the squawking seagulls settling on top of one of the cranes that wasn't in use.

So that was why Polly had been so evasive the other day. She must have been out of her mind with grief to have done something so insane. Rosie wished she'd known; she might have been able to talk her out of it.

Rosie had known Tommy for years during his time working for the Wear Commission and she knew he'd not make a song and dance about it all, but she'd wager he'd secretly be gutted. There was no way he'd be able to afford a ring, never mind pay for an actual wedding. And it wasn't as if Agnes had any money.

'All right, Jimmy!' Rosie waved over to the head riveter. He opened his mouth to speak but before he could say anything, she beat him to it.

'No! You can't have her!'

It was their regular banter concerning their long-standing tug-of-war over Martha.

Opening the door to the main entrance to the admin department, Rosie was hit by a blast of warm air. Taking the stairs two at a time, she felt lighter for having told the women about her meeting with the deputy head. They'd made her see the funny side of it all.

Rosie spotted Helen in her office as she opened the inner door. She was on the phone and her face looked serious.

She hung up and gestured at Rosie to come in.

'There's been another accident at Doxford's,' she said, lighting up a Pall Mall and waving at Rosie to sit down. 'A rope from a ship being launched wrapped around a ship in the next berth and dislodged a ladder, which landed on top of some poor bloke. Fractured his skull ... He was only forty-five.'

'Dead?' Rosie asked, aghast.

Helen nodded solemnly.

'Leaves a wife and nine children.'

'Oh God, that's awful.'

'I know,' Helen said. 'They'll end up ruling accidental death, but in my opinion that was negligence.'

Just then, Rosie felt something brush against her leg. She jumped and looked down to see Mrs Crabtree's ginger cat. She gave it a stroke before it sauntered over to a saucer of water in the corner of the room.

'Does Gloria know?' Rosie said, nodding at the cat.

'Yes ...' Helen blew smoke up to the ceiling ' ... she does. They were reacquainted yesterday.'

'And?' Rosie asked.

'And she was not at all amused. I think her words were something along the lines of, "It's your choice if you want that flea-bitten moggy getting under your feet and tripping you up, as long as you don't go chasing after it if there's a bloomin' air raid." I did, of course, try and argue the case that I'd really done her a favour since the cat had taken up permanent residence on her doorstep and would not leave. There was also a practical reason for bringing the cat to work.'

'As the resident rat-catcher?' Rosie asked.

'That's right,' Helen said.

'And has it many scalps to its name as yet?' Rosie looked at the marmalade-coloured cat now making itself comfy right next to the heater.

'Not that I'm aware of,' Helen said, getting up to pour a cup of tea from the tray on the side. She pointed to the pot, but Rosie shook her head. 'Anyway,' she said, 'how did it go yesterday?'

Rosie let out a slightly bitter laugh. 'As well as to be expected, all things considered.' She thought of the cheque that George had given her when he'd dropped her and Charlotte off. It had made her feel a lot better about the outcome.

'Which is why I'm here,' Rosie said. 'First of all, thank you for having Charlotte work at the yard last week *and* paying her—'

'But,' Helen interrupted, 'you're going to tell me she won't be coming back as she'll be starting at the Church High School.'

'That's about the sum of it,' Rosie said. She had mentioned the school when she'd popped in to see Gloria on Sunday. 'If I can get her in there. I don't know if they've got any places, or if they'll have her,' she added.

'Oh, they'll have her,' Helen said, taking a sip of her tea. 'They'll be jumping at the chance to have someone like Charlotte – with brains, and I'll bet you she's good at sports as well.'

Rosie had to think. She wasn't sure about her sister's sporting prowess.

'Plus, they'll need all the pupils they can get at the moment,' Helen added. 'I'll bet quite a few of the parents have packed their little Jezebels off to stay with relatives in the country for the duration.'

'To be honest, that would have been my preference. But as Charlotte has no relatives, never mind any in the country, I'm going to have to risk her staying here.'

Helen wondered again how on earth Rosie was able to afford paying for her sister's private education.

'I went there, to the Church High School, you know?' Helen said.

'Did you?' Rosie did, in fact, know Helen had attended the school. 'Would you recommend it?' she asked, suddenly realising that the two of them – formerly silent foes at the yard – were now chatting like good friends.

'I'm sure Charlotte will love it there,' Helen said. 'And it does have a good reputation. If your sister wants to go on to university, they'll get her in.' She knew Charlotte would get the grades she needed. She'd seen how quickly she'd picked up anything she was asked to do at the yard. The girl was as bright as a button.

Rosie pushed herself out of her chair.

'I better get back. Poor Gloria's meant to be on light duties. I've leant on her heavily these past two days.'

'Oh, Gloria's as tough as old boots,' Helen laughed. 'But if you're worried about her for any reason, come and see me. Just put her wherever they need a spot-welder and make sure whichever squad she's with knows that she has to rest her leg as much as possible. And if you get any gyp from anyone, just send them my way.'

'I will.'

Rosie made to leave, then stopped, thumping her head with the base of her palm.

'I forgot. The main reason for coming here. I need to take a few hours off later on in the week to go and see the head at the Church High School. I'll work overtime on Sunday and make it up then, though.'

'Yes, of course, that's fine. And put the word out that from now on in, there'll be all the overtime anyone wants.'

'You on target for *Brutus*?' Rosie asked.

'Yes.' Helen's face lit up. 'Fingers crossed she'll be going down the ways a week before Christmas.' Her joy, though, was immediately dampened when she thought about her father. If only he could be there to see what she had achieved. He'd be so proud of her. God, she missed him.

Rosie made to leave for the second time.

'Actually,' Helen said, 'when you go up to the school, send the head my regards, will you?'

Rosie looked at Helen.

'Are you sure? I'm going to be honest about what I do for a living. I don't intend to make the same mistake twice. They'll know I'm a welder here.'

'Oh, I'm *very* sure,' Helen said, a slightly mischievous look on her face. 'In fact, send her my "warm regards", and tell her that I might be popping in for a visit sometime soon.'

Rosie smiled her thanks. She had no idea that on hearing Helen would be 'popping in', the headmistress would be rubbing her hands with glee. Any visit by a member of the Havelock family meant a sizeable donation to the school.

What Rosie did know, however, was that if the head-mistress was harbouring any doubts about taking Char-lotte on, the mere mention that Rosie knew Mr Havelock's granddaughter would have the head pushing Charlotte through the school gates faster than a ship careering down the slipway on launch day.

Chapter Twenty-Three

Over the next two weeks, like all the workers at the North Sands yard, the women welders notched up as much overtime as they could in the push to get *Brutus* ready before Christmas.

As soon as Dorothy and Angie got back to their flat in Foyle Street it was a case of bathe, eat and bed. Angie liked to joke that she could hear Dorothy snoring in the next room, but in reality she had no idea what kinds of sounds her best mate made in her sleep. As soon as her own head hit the pillow, she was out like a light.

Once a week they'd meet up with Marie-Anne and go dancing at the Ritz. But that was it. There was neither the time nor the energy for anything else. They only got to know that their 'neighbour with the posh name', Quentin, whom they'd yet to meet, had been home for a few days after being informed of it by their other neighbour – a kindly old woman they'd nicknamed Mrs Lavender as her real name was too difficult to pronounce.

Martha's daily routine paralleled Dorothy's and Angie's, minus the weekly knees-up at the Ritz. When she wasn't doing overtime, she was carrying out her ARP duties.

The worries her mam and dad had about their only child working at Thompson's were only marginally less than their anxieties about her pulling people out of collapsing buildings. Anxieties that had been exacerbated since the Luftwaffe had bombed Canterbury. It had been one of the heaviest raids on Britain since the Blitz.

Gloria, in the meantime, had taken herself off light duties despite objections from Rosie and Helen, reassuring them that her leg was well and truly on the mend. She wanted to get back to normal, immerse herself in work – and be with her own squad. She needed more challenging work, and the company of her friends. Since the air raid she seemed to be missing Jack more than normal.

The women had subtly tried to find out more about her friendship with Helen and how they had become so close, but Gloria was keeping tight-lipped. There was no way she could tell them that their friendship had been forged when Helen turned up on her doorstep the day she'd found out she was pregnant.

At least, Gloria consoled herself, her workmates had stopped asking when Jack was coming back. They'd either got tired of asking or had believed her when she'd claimed his presence on the Clyde was needed for the foreseeable.

Following her meeting with the headmistress of the Sunderland Church High School, and after Charlotte had passed the required test, Rosie was informed that the school would be willing to accept her sister as a day pupil. The headmistress, a Mrs Longbottom, an odd woman with an even odder name, had tried to hide her surprise when Rosie had informed her that she was a welder. Rosie thought this might well have been because she had mentioned her friendship with Mr Havelock's granddaughter *before* disclosing what she did for a living.

When she'd waved Charlotte off on her first day at her new school, she had felt more like a mother than a sister as she'd tried not to fuss too much. Charlotte had agreed Rosie could walk her as far as Christ Church, but had insisted on saying her goodbyes before she crossed the Ryhope Road. It was only then that Rosie had realised she was, in fact, more nervous than Charlotte.

Rosie now just needed to work out how she could keep hidden the truth about her 'other life' at Lily's – past and present – from Charlotte. It was not going to be easy, but Rosie had convinced herself that it was not impossible.

Polly, meanwhile, had cut down her visits to Tommy to every other day. Tommy had been adamant, reassuring her that it wouldn't be long before he was discharged. He had taken to walking around the entire grounds of the hospital three times a day in his determination to get his fitness back, and was eating whatever was put in front of him in order to put on weight.

Dr Parker had been a little concerned that he was pushing his body too hard too quickly, but he had learnt that Tommy wasn't one to take orders. It made him wonder how he had got on in the navy, but the more Tommy told him about his unit in Gibraltar, the more he understood why it had been a perfect fit for his patient. Tommy's specialised diving unit sounded as though it was made up of a mishmash of wayward characters, led by a commander who sounded unconventional and had little regard for those higher up the chain of command.

As Arthur visited his grandson on the evenings that Polly was doing overtime, it meant she was still able to regale her friends with daily updates on her fiancé's progress.

The women never tired of listening to their workmate chatter on about the man she loved, but neither did they tire of admonishing her for not plucking up the courage to tell Tommy about the non-existent gratuity pay.

Polly insisted it was hard finding the 'right moment'.

She knew that she was on borrowed time, though.

She had to confess and she had to do it soon.

It was the only blot on her otherwise perfect landscape.

Chapter Twenty-Four

Wednesday 11 November

'Bloody hell,' Percival shouted across the ward. 'Listen to this.' He shook open the newspaper he was reading.

'"All traffic into and out of the world's busiest port has been brought to a complete standstill after it was discovered that the Germans have mined waters off New York Harbor."'

Tommy was sitting up in his bed, listening intently. He knew there were hundreds of ships anchored there waiting assignments. The harbour was massive. There were thirty-nine shipyards and hundreds of piers and docks. This was not good news.

'What's it say in there about North Africa?' Shorty asked. He, like most of the men on the ward, had served with the Durham Light Infantry and had fought in the so-called 'Desert War'.

Percival turned to the next page.

'Here we are,' he said. He read for a moment, his face dropped with disappointment. 'Looks like Jerry and the Eyeties have occupied Tunisia ...' He paused. '"Without opposition from the French colonialists",' he quoted.

'And Jerry has also occupied Vichy France.' He read for a moment. 'Apparently they're in violation of the 1940 armistice, but they've done it,' he read on, 'because the French admiral François Darlan has made a deal with our lot in North Africa.'

'Come on, Percy,' Smithy shouted from the other side of the ward. 'There must be some good news?'

Tommy swung his legs out of the bed and put on a thick woollen dressing gown that had once belonged to Arthur.

He walked over to the swing doors of the ward.

'Just need a breath of fresh air, Matron.' Tommy smiled at Mrs Rosendale.

'Don't be long,' she said sternly, pretending she had some authority over Tommy's comings and goings. It was all show, though. She'd given up trying to keep the lad within the confines of the hospital, never mind the ward.

As was usual these days, when Dr Parker was doing his morning rounds he found Tommy's bed empty. He didn't need to ask where he was.

'So, yer ready to discharge me?' Tommy shouted out to Dr Parker when he saw him walking towards him along the shale pathway.

Dr Parker sighed as he reached Tommy and sat down next to him on the bench. Every day Tommy would ask the same question and every day he would give the same answer.

'I don't want to sound like a broken record, but let's just see how you get on this week. But when you *do* get out,' Dr Parker said, thinking it sounded like they were discussing a breakout from prison, 'will you be staying at Polly's?'

He asked not through politeness, but because it would help him decide if he could discharge Tommy a little earlier than normal.

Tommy shook his head. 'No, I don't think it's proper. Not until we're married.' He wondered if Dr Parker would hear the lie in his voice.

Dr Parker didn't, but he did think Tommy was a strange chap. He couldn't quite work him out. Most blokes would have jumped at the chance of moving in with their fiancée and future in-laws.

'Any idea where you might end up?' Dr Parker asked.

'Aye, it's all arranged,' Tommy said. 'Major Black's going to put me up for a while. He's got a spare room in his flat in town.'

'Major Black?'

'Joe's superior. Zone commander in the Home Guard. Sorry, I thought Joe'd told yer about him when yer met him the other day.'

Joe had caused a stir when he'd visited Tommy, joking with the other lads and saying it was about time he checked out his future brother-in-law.

'Major Black's the war vet who lost his legs at the Battle of the Menin Road Ridge.'

'That's right ... Belgium ... 1917,' Dr Parker recalled. 'Got me talking about the latest in prosthetics, I remember.'

'So, yer see, Doc,' Tommy said with a wide smile, 'I've got my digs all sorted. I'm all ready to go.'

Dr Parker looked at Tommy.

'All right,' he relented.

'Brilliant, I'll tell the Major,' Tommy said with a cheeky smile.

'I didn't mean that it's a done deal,' Dr Parker retorted, standing up.

'Actually,' Tommy said, his face serious now, 'I wanted to ask yer something about this spleen malarkey.'

'Oh, yes?' Dr Parker said, curious. Tommy rarely asked questions about his health, making out that he was perfectly fit and healthy.

'I know you've already told me,' Tommy said, 'but what exactly does the spleen do?'

'Well, put simply,' Dr Parker said, 'it's part of the body's immune system.'

'So, what effect will it have, me not having one?' Tommy said.

'It means you're going to have to really look after yourself. The absence of a spleen makes the body more prone to infections and illnesses like pneumonia, which you have already experienced first-hand, and which you're still recovering from.'

'But other than that, it's fine,' Tommy said.

'Mmm.' Dr Parker was loath to sanction Tommy's somewhat dismissive attitude. 'Is there a reason you want to know?' he asked.

'Aye, there is actually, Doc.'

Tommy stood up.

'Come on, I'll walk back with yer 'n tell yer.'

At seven o'clock on the dot, Tommy was standing at the top of the hospital steps, waiting for Polly. He'd been given a pair of khaki trousers that were no longer needed by their original owner, as well as a thick polo-neck jumper. Both were a little on the baggy side. One of the lads had lent him an army jacket and Mrs Rosendale had given Tommy a purple woollen scarf, muttering that if he insisted on going outside all the time, the least he could do was make sure he was well wrapped up.

When Polly appeared through the darkness, hurrying down the last stretch of gravel pathway, a wide smile spread across her face. This was the first time she'd seen Tommy fully clothed.

'Oh, are we off on a date?' she joked.

'It won't be long before we are,' Tommy said, walking down the stone steps to greet her. He pulled her towards him, and they kissed each other as though it was the first time in weeks.

'Guess what?' Tommy said when they finally parted. He took Polly's hand and guided her away from the entrance.

'What?' Polly said as they walked to their favourite spot at the side of the hospital. She leant into him and kissed him on the cheek.

Tommy stopped and looked down at Polly, who was just a few inches shorter than he was.

'I'm being discharged on the weekend,' he said, his eyes dancing. He'd managed to twist Dr Parker's arm.

Polly flung her arms around his neck and kissed him full on the lips.

'That's fantastic news,' she said, kissing him again. 'I can't believe it!' She stared at Tommy's face, which was still a little gaunt but had lost that awful skeletal look. 'I didn't think Dr Parker was keen on letting you out of here for a while?'

Tommy gently tugged her across to one of the huge sycamore trees dotted around the hospital grounds.

'It's all been agreed,' Tommy said. 'I leave on Saturday. I just need yer to tell Joe 'n make sure it's still all right to go stay with the Major.'

Polly looked at Tommy, a puzzled expression on her face.

'I still can't understand why you won't live with us in Tatham Street. You'd have your own room. Me and Arthur'll be there. And there's the added bonus of Ma's cooking.'

Tommy put his hands on Polly's narrow waist and pulled her towards him, kissing her into silence. As he pressed her body against his own, they abandoned their words to kisses and caresses.

When they felt the first splodges of rain land on their faces, they finally pulled themselves apart.

'Come on,' Tommy said. 'Let's get a cup of tea in the canteen.'

As they hurried back to the hospital and out of the rain, Polly thought Tommy looked shattered. Reaching the canteen, she saw the relief on his face when they found a seat and he was able to sit down and rest.

'Stay there while I get the tea,' Polly commanded. She was gone before he had time to object.

A few minutes later, having returned with tea for two and a couple of scones, Polly sat down and looked at Tommy.

'Are you absolutely sure about staying with the Major? I mean, you don't know him. You've never even met him,' Polly said, transferring the cups and saucers onto the table. 'And I have to tell you, I think Ma's a little put out that you're not coming to us,' she added, putting the empty tray to one side.

'Trust me,' Tommy said, taking a sip of his tea. 'It'll be better all round if I'm with the Major.' He looked at Polly. 'And from what yer Joe says, he's a great bloke.'

'I know Joe thinks the world of him,' Polly said.

'And,' Tommy said, picking up his scone, 'I've told Joe to tell him that I'll give him money for food 'n lodging. I've told him I've got my gratuity pay, which I know has been put aside fer our wedding, but I'm sure there'll be a little left over.'

Polly blanched.

She hoped Tommy hadn't noticed.

Tommy took a bite of his scone and washed it down with a big glug of tea.

'Not that it sounds like the Major will take a penny. Says it's the least he can do for anyone who's risked life 'n limb for King 'n country.'

'The army is his life, that's for sure,' Polly said distractedly.

'He sounds like quite a character,' Tommy said. 'Joe said it was the Major who got him involved with the Home Guard after he got back from the war.'

'Joe wasn't in the best state when he came back,' Polly said. 'Not surprising really. After everything he'd been through in North Africa. And losing our Teddy.'

Polly thought for a moment.

'And he was having these terrible nightmares. It was awful. I think the whole street could hear him screaming out in his sleep in the middle of the night.'

Tommy tensed.

'I remember yer telling me in one of your letters,' he said, taking another mouthful of tea.

'It was only when the Major signed him up with the Home Guard,' Polly continued, 'that the nightmares eased off and then stopped completely.'

'Really?' Tommy said. 'That's interesting. I wonder why.'

'Arthur reckons it was because he was able to talk to the Major about what he'd seen out in the desert. Them both having served on the front line.'

Tommy nodded.

'Makes sense.'

He thought for a moment.

'Talking about his demons rather than keeping them trapped inside.'

Polly nodded sadly.

'Bel said that Joe has accepted that he might always be haunted by the awful things he's seen, that the images – the memories – might well be with him his whole life. But at least his nightmares have stopped.'

'With acceptance comes freedom,' Tommy said quietly.

Polly looked at Tommy and thought he seemed a million miles away.

'Are you all right?' she asked.

Tommy rubbed his hands over his face.

'Aye, course, I'm fine,' Tommy smiled. 'Absolutely fine.'

He looked around the canteen and then leant forward across the table.

'Enough morbid talk,' he said.

Polly saw a twinkle had come into his eyes.

'Let's speak about me 'n you,' he said, taking hold of her hand. 'Yer know what me getting out of here also means?'

Polly felt her heart hammering.

She knew what Tommy was going to say next.

'Mmm,' she stalled, something she had been doing a lot of lately. Particularly these past two weeks, since the subject seemed to be cropping up with increasing regularity.

'It means,' Tommy said, 'that as I'm no longer confined to the perimeter of this hospital, I'm now free to walk yer down the aisle.'

Polly knew her face should be lighting up with joy and happiness.

But it wasn't.

Worse still, she felt her forced smile probably looked more like a grimace.

Judging by Tommy's reaction, her supposition was right.

'God, Pol!' Tommy couldn't hide his disappointment. 'If I didn't know yer better, I'd think that yer didn't *want* me to walk you down the aisle.'

'No, Tommy!' Polly said. 'That's not true. That's about the furthest from the truth you can get.'

Tommy looked sceptical

'So why do you keep avoiding talking about us getting married?'

He looked Polly in the eyes.

'And why is it yer look so guilty?'

He sat back in his chair. He'd tried to ignore Polly's reticence in talking about getting married. His gut instinct had told him to hold off, that there was an explanation. He'd thought that perhaps Polly just needed to see him get better and out of hospital before they arranged the wedding, but clearly that wasn't the case.

'You've not met anyone else, have yer?' He scrutinised her face. The sane part of him said that this was nonsense, but the other, less stable part of his brain was pushing the case for possible infidelity.

Polly sat bolt upright.

'Of course I haven't!' she said indignantly. 'Do you think I'd be able to be with you the way I am if I had some other bloke?' Now anger was impinging on her guilt. 'I thought you knew me, Tommy? I thought we knew *each other*?'

'So did I,' Tommy said. His voice had hardened. 'But I saw something in yer just now that I couldn't read.' His mind was now racing. 'Every time I've mentioned the wedding you've either been a bit off, or you've changed the subject.'

It had come to the crunch.

Whatever it was needed airing.

'I thought yer wanted to get married as soon as we could? We both said – agreed – that we'd waited long enough. Remember?'

'Of course I remember,' Polly said, her anger dying down, remembering the joy and love she'd felt on seeing Tommy in his hospital bed. Alive.

Seeing his hurt and confusion, she knew she couldn't put it off any longer.

'So, tell me,' Tommy said. 'What is it? I know yer well enough now to know that something's wrong, but I'm not a mind-reader.'

Polly looked at her watch.

'Visiting time's nearly over,' she said.

'I don't give a damn,' Tommy said, his eyes searching the face of the woman he loved. 'You're going to stay here until I know exactly what's the matter,' he said.

'Let me get another tea then,' Polly said resignedly. 'And I'll explain.'

'You know the letters I wrote to you after I learnt that you were missing?' Polly asked.

Tommy nodded. He had asked Polly if he could keep them. Had read them all twice over.

'Did you look at the dates?' Polly asked.

Tommy nodded.

They were both quiet for a moment.

'Yer stopped writing at the end of August,' Tommy stated. 'I did wonder why yer had stopped then. It wasn't as though there were bigger 'n bigger gaps between the letters 'n then they just dwindled off.'

Polly put both hands around her teacup and took a deep breath.

'When I heard you were missing, I was devastated. I remember the postwoman giving me the letter and after that it was all a bit of a blur. I vaguely remember going to work and seeing everyone, them all saying I shouldn't give up hope – that there was still a chance you were alive.'

Polly looked at Tommy, her eyes filling with tears as she remembered that awful day.

'And I did. I kept on hoping and praying. I think my writing you letters that I couldn't send was my way of rebelling. My way of railing against everything.'

Tommy moved his chair around the table so he was adjacent to Polly.

He touched her hand, but she kept them both firmly clasped around her teacup.

'I couldn't give up on you. It was as though if I did, it would be a betrayal. As if by giving up on hope, I was giving up on you. It sounds stupid, but I felt as though my hope might keep you alive – or perhaps it was really the other way around. Believing that you were alive was keeping *me* alive.' Polly's voice started to crack with emotion. 'Because I felt like I would die inside if you weren't to come back.'

For the first time Tommy saw the reality of what life had been like for Polly, how heartbroken and worried she had been. He had been so wrapped up in his own recovery, in getting himself back to normal, that he had not really thought about the hell Polly had been through.

'Even though I didn't hear anything, I still kept writing. It was like I was saying, "I am *not* going to be beaten."' Polly laughed sadly. A tear crept down her cheek and Tommy stopped it with his thumb. It hurt and angered him to see just a glimpse of the heartache he had caused.

'But then,' Polly looked at Tommy straight in the eye, 'they sent your belongings back, and then a while later, the notification of your gratuity pay arrived. The money you had told me you were saving for our wedding. And it was ... well, it was like the straw that broke the camel's back.'

More tears began to fall down Polly's pale face.

'I'm so sorry, Tommy.'

Tommy saw the guilt, but still had no idea of the reason for it.

'I feel ashamed to admit it,' she said, relinquishing her teacup and using the sleeve of her cardigan to wipe under her eyes, 'but I gave up hope ... I gave up on you being alive.'

Polly started to cry properly.

Tommy went to put his arms around her.

'Don't,' she said, moving away. 'Don't. Please don't.'

Tommy sat back, hurt at the perceived rejection.

'I don't think you'll feel like hugging me when I tell you what I've got to tell you.'

Tommy felt his heart beating faster and the paranoia started to creep back.

Had Polly been with another man? Had her grief – her lack of hope – driven her to seek solace with someone else?

'Just tell me, Pol. What is it? What have yer done?'

Polly took a juddering breath.

'I'm so, *so* sorry, Tommy.'

She sat up straight and looked at him, needing to see his reaction.

There was a moment's silence before Polly finally spat it out.

'I gave it all away,' she said simply.

Tommy looked at her in confusion.

'I don't understand. *What* did yer give away?'

'Your *money*,' Polly said. 'Your gratuity pay. Every single penny of it.'

Tommy looked at Polly as his brain registered what she was saying.

Then he let out a loud guffaw.

'*That's* what you've been so worried about telling me?' he asked, cupping her tear-stained face in his hands.

Polly nodded.

'Honestly,' he said, letting out a huge sigh of relief, 'I thought yer were gonna tell me you'd been off with someone else.' He kissed her on the lips. He kissed her again and she kissed him back.

'No. Never! I've never even looked at another man, never mind *been off* with one!'

'Or you'd got cold feet. Changed yer mind about getting married.'

Polly laughed through the tears.

'Oh, Tommy, if only you knew. The hours I spent wishing we'd got married before you left. I meant every word I said that day about getting married as soon as possible. I just felt so awful about giving away your pay. I didn't know how to tell you.'

Tommy moved his chair so that it was next to Polly's and put his arms around her.

'First 'n foremost, yer must not feel guilty about giving away my pay. I don't give two hoots about money. Never have done 'n never will.

'On top of which it's never sat easily with me earning money from being at war. Probably why I didn't want to spend any of it.'

Tommy smiled.

'Actually, I'm *glad* you've given it away.'

Polly batted away his words. He was just trying to make her feel better.

'Yer know, Pol,' Tommy said. 'Yer must never feel guilty about having given up hope that I was still alive.'

He had seen the pain and guilt etched onto Polly's face when she had told him.

He kissed the top of her head and squeezed her.

'Yer had every right to give up hope. There was nothing wrong with that. I don't know why yer felt so bad about it.'

He leant back a little so that he could look at Polly.

'Sometimes, yer know, you have to give up hope. It's not being defeatist. I know this might sound odd, but sometimes yer have to give up hope to keep going, to move on and carry on living.'

His face became serious.

'And yer know, if anything were to happen to me at any time in the future, yer must carry on. Yer must live yer life.'

Polly pulled away and looked at him.

'Well, I won't have to, will I?' she said. 'Nothing's going to happen to you. You're here now and we're going to be together for the rest of our lives.'

Tommy gave Polly a look she couldn't quite fathom, before his face broke into a smile and the twinkle returned to his eyes.

'So,' he said. 'Come on, tell me who yer gave the money to?'

The canteen had closed for the evening, but the staff had spotted Polly and Tommy while they were clearing up and had seen that whatever they were talking about was serious. They'd left the lights on and asked Polly and Tommy to flick them off and close the door on their way out.

Feeling more relaxed now her secret was out, it was easier to tell him exactly what she had done with his pay.

Tommy wasn't one for tears, but Polly could have sworn he was holding back when she explained that a portion of the money had gone to the Red Cross. He stopped her talking and kissed her with such tenderness that it took her aback.

When she told him about the King George's Fund for Sailors, a big smile replaced the sadness.

'That's exactly who I would have given it to,' he declared. 'I'm so glad you thought to give them a share.'

When Polly told him that the rest of the money had gone to the local girl who was going to be fitted with artificial hands, his eyes once again teared up and he took her in his arms and kissed her.

'Pollyanna Henrietta Elliot,' he said, looking at her proudly. 'I didn't think it was possible to love yer any more than I have done these past two years, but I do. I am so proud of yer. So proud.'

Polly forced back the tears. The love she felt for this man was overwhelming.

In the quietness of the canteen they kissed and then kissed some more, before Tommy pulled away and looked at Polly.

'So, when we gonna get married?'

'Yer working late, pet?' Mrs Killochan the cleaner stuck her head round the door to Dr Parker's office.

Dr Parker smiled. Mrs Killochan called everyone 'pet' regardless of where they were in the hospital hierarchy.

'I *am*, Mrs Killochan,' Dr Parker said, keeping his hand on the page he was reading. 'Don't worry about the office. I'm sure no harm will come from leaving it another day.'

The cleaner eyed the desk covered in stacks of books and files, and then at the floor, which was catering for the over-spill.

'Not that I can ever get at anything to clean anyways,' Mrs Killochan huffed good-naturedly.

'I'll try and have a tidy-up tomorrow,' Dr Parker promised.

The old woman laughed.

'Aye, you do that,' she said. 'I'll believe it when I see it.' She chuckled.

'I'll leave yer to it, pet,' she said, shutting the door.

Dr Parker looked back at the page he'd been reading. It had taken him ages to find what he had been looking for. He'd asked his colleagues, but they'd all shaken their heads and admitted their extensive knowledge of human biology did not extend to this particular area. He had even rung a specialist in London, who had offered his opinion. But it was just that – an opinion. There had been no documented cases on the effects of deep-sea diving following a splenectomy.

Reading the few paragraphs he had found just before Mrs Killochan's interruption, it would seem it would have to be a case of giving it a go and hoping for the best.

God, the man was annoying!

It was now a little over a month since Tommy had been operated on. Why couldn't he just sit back and let his body recover in due course?

From the moment he'd opened his eyes, he'd been in a rush. A rush to get off his pain meds. A rush to get out of bed. A rush to get back on his feet.

And now a rush to get back in the bloody water.

Chapter Twenty-Five

'Are you two staying up for a while longer?' Vivian stuck her head round the door to the back parlour. She had just seen off the last client and was doing her usual end-of-evening check and lock-up.

'Yes, *ma chère*, we're going to have a little nightcap before heading up. You get yourself off. And Vivian ...' Lily called her back. 'I just want to say you're doing a great job as head girl.'

Vivian's face lit up.

'Well, I aim to please,' she said in her best Mae West drawl.

Lily looked at her longest-serving girl, with her platinum hair and voluptuous figure. She had changed a lot from the skinny, mousy runaway who had come knocking on her door late one night five years ago.

'You have great professionalism. You keep the rest of the girls in line –' Lily poured out two cognacs ' – as well as the clients.' She handed one of the drinks to George, who was sitting in the armchair next to the open fire. 'And you've been great with the Brigadier of late, who I know can be a terrible bore and rather a challenge to talk to.' The old man had a habit of spitting when he talked.

Vivian smiled a little self-consciously. She didn't take compliments well.

'And,' Lily added, 'now that the Gentlemen's Club is really starting to get going, I think we'll sit down and have a longer chat about your and Maisie's idea to develop this "escorting" side of the business. I've been mulling it over. If it's done properly, it could work well all round.'

Vivian nodded, smiled and said her goodnights.

She couldn't wait to tell Maisie what Lily had just said.

'So, George.' Lily turned and sat down in the armchair next to her future husband. 'Tell me how it went at Blacketts today with your fitting?'

'All good, all good,' George said.

Lily looked at him and then at the nest of tables next to his chair on which lay a hardback copy of a book emblazoned with the title *Men at War*.

'Mmm,' she said, eyeing the book. 'Let me guess, you spent all of about fifteen minutes at the fitters and at least fifty in the bookshop? Hence the new read.'

Lily picked up the thick volume of short stories edited by Ernest Hemingway.

'A strange choice for someone who purports to hate anything and everything to do with war.' Lily looked at her fiancé.

'You are right, my dear, in that I do indeed hate all things to do with war, but that's not to say the very nature of war and the psychology of human violence do not interest me.'

Lily wasn't sure whether this was quite the right start to the conversation she had planned to have with her fiancé that evening.

'So, tell me my love,' George said, looking at Lily and taking a sip of his cognac, 'what's on your mind? I know something is going around that very lovely but very complex and, dare I say it, calculating head of yours?'

'George, *mon cher*, you know me *too* well.' Lily stood and picked up her packet of Gauloises from the mantelpiece.

'Well,' she said, taking out a cigarette. 'As you are more than well aware, I've been organising our wedding.' She stopped and lit her cigarette. 'Which, I hasten to add, is going to be rather spectacular. And I have to admit, despite my initial ranting and raving about us having to move the wedding to Christmas Day, I now wouldn't want it on any other day. It's somehow made the whole event doubly exciting. And doubly extravagant.'

George took a slightly nervous sip of his brandy. He wanted Lily to be his wife more than anything, but he would happily forgo the actual wedding itself. He envied Peter and Rosie their simple, and very private nuptials in Guildford.

He looked at Lily, who was now sitting back down in her armchair. 'Spit it out, my dear. You make me nervous when you start beating about the bush. It says to me that you're about to ask me something – or tell me something – that I'm not going to view favourably.'

Lily took a long drag on her cigarette.

'Gawd, George, I wish you weren't so perceptive,' she said. Cockney was trumping *français*, as was the norm whenever Lily became angry or exasperated.

'So, come on.' George smiled.

'Well, much as I adore the suit that we've chosen for you to get married in, and which will still come in handy as you were in desperate need of a new one anyway ...' Lily crossed her legs and leant forward so that she could touch George's hand. ' ... what would make my day even more special than it's already going to be ...'

Lily paused.

'Yes?' George asked, scrutinising Lily suspiciously. He had a horrid feeling he knew what was coming next.

'Would be ... if ... on our wedding day, you would wear your uniform.'

The room was quiet for a long moment.

'Lily, my dear.' George turned to his fiancée with sad eyes. 'I love you dearly, more than anything or anyone in

193

this world. And you know I'd do anything for you. But this, I'm afraid, is something I can't do. I don't even know where my uniform is – or if it's still in one piece – but even if I did, I wouldn't.'

Lily smoked for a moment silently, undeterred. She knew exactly where his uniform was and precisely what state it had been in.

'What I don't understand about you, George ...' Lily blew out smoke as she talked ' ... is why you seem to believe that what you did in the last war was something to be ashamed of.'

'I don't feel shame, my dear,' George said. 'I just don't see that there was anything to be proud of either. And when one wears a uniform it should be with a sense of pride.'

'But *I'm* proud of you, George,' Lily said with a rare show of sincerity. 'I – and many others – think what you did was incredibly brave.'

She looked at George, who was staring into the fire, lost in another world.

'For heaven's sake, George, they don't just hand out Distinguished Service Order medals willy-nilly. You're a *war hero*.'

Lily walked over to George, took hold of his hands and squeezed them.

'Please, just for one day don't hide your light under a bushel. Let me show people what a great man I am marrying.'

George got up and kissed Lily tenderly on the lips.

'Come on, my dear. Let's go to bed.'

Lily stubbed out her cigarette and took her future husband's hand.

She knew by his silence that the answer was no, but that didn't mean she was going to give up.

Chapter Twenty-Six

The following day

Thursday 12 November

The wind was whipping up, snaking its way around the crammed ravine of the Wear and bringing a cold blast from across the North Sea. It was a taste of the winter now lurking around the corner, eager to descend on the town and torment those who worked under the canopy of an unforgiving sky.

'Platers' shed,' Rosie said, pointing over to the huge metal warehouse where the metal scales of the ships-to-be were stored.

Polly, Gloria, Martha, Dorothy and Angie nodded and leant forward as they hit a wind tunnel that stretched the hundred yards to the entrance of their lunchtime sanctuary.

'Bloomin' weather!' Dorothy complained as they almost fell over the threshold.

'I *do* hate the wind,' Gloria said.

'Yeah, cold over wind any day,' Martha added, rubbing her eyes, which had just got some dirt in them.

Spotting a five-gallon barrel fire, Rosie led the way, dumping her haversack on the ground and waving across to a group of caulkers who had also decided to swap the canteen for the airier domain of the platers' shed.

The women got to work, pulling up wooden boxes and pallets as makeshift seats, and getting out their packed lunches.

'So ...' Dorothy looked across at Polly. 'Do I even need to ask?'

Polly had her sandwich in both hands. She looked round her circle of friends, all staring at her expectantly.

'Yes!' she declared. A big smile on her face. 'You'll be pleased to know I finally did it! I finally told Tommy!'

'Hurrah!' Dorothy exclaimed.

'About bloody time,' Gloria said, delving into her haversack to get her sandwiches.

'Oh my God, Pol.' Angie's expression was grave. She still couldn't believe what Polly had done. 'What did he say?'

'He was fine about it ... Thank goodness,' Polly said, taking a bite of her sandwich.

'*Fine*?' Rosie said curiously, unscrewing the top of her tea caddy.

'Actually ...' Polly said through a mouthful of bread and spam.

The women all looked at her in great expectation.

Polly swallowed.

' ... he burst out laughing!'

'He laughed?' Angie couldn't believe her ears.

'Not laughed in a way that he thought it was funny,' Polly explained, wiping her mouth of crumbs. 'It was more like he was relieved.'

'Relieved?' Martha asked, puzzled.

'Yeah, what do you mean "relieved"?' Angie said, now totally confused. 'Why would anyone in their right mind be "relieved" 'cos you'd just chucked away a load of their hard-earned dosh?'

'I think he thought there was a chance I might have gone off with someone else ... you know ... when he was declared missing,' Polly explained.

'As if!' Gloria said, blowing on her tin cup of steaming hot tea.

'I don't understand.' Martha looked baffled. 'What's giving his money away got to do with you having another bloke?'

'Because,' Dorothy butted in, 'Polly's reticence about setting a date for the wedding must have made Tommy wonder if she'd gone off with someone else. You know? While the cat's away, the mice will play?' She looked at Polly. 'Am I right?'

'That's about the nub of it,' Polly said.

'So, what are you going to do?' Rosie asked, unsurprised by Tommy's reaction.

'About?' Polly asked, taking care not to spill her tea as she poured it into her cup.

'About *getting married*,' Gloria said. She had told Jack about Polly's charitable donations when they'd spoken last night. At the end of the call he had suddenly blurted out that he longed for the day when he could free himself from Miriam, marry Gloria and be a proper father to Hope. It had made her feel so happy – and also so sad.

'Well,' Polly said, taking a slurp of tea, 'we decided we were no worse and no better off than most couples who want to get married these days, and that we'd just have to do it on the cheap. I mean, you don't have to have a load of money to have a great wedding, do you?'

The women murmured their agreement, but it lacked conviction.

'I suppose you could wait a while till you're able to save up a bit of money,' Gloria proposed.

'Mmm, I did suggest that,' Polly said, 'but Tommy said he didn't want to wait. And if I'm honest, I don't really want to wait either, especially as it'd take us ages to save up. Even if Tommy's well enough to work again and we've two wages coming in, it'll still take us ages to make up what I gave away.'

'Cheap 'n cheerful. And better sooner than later, eh?' Gloria said, sensing the woman's slightly deflated mood. Polly had been everyone's happy-ever-after. They'd all agreed that their workmate would make a beautiful bride and look amazing in white, floating down the aisle towards the man she was batty about.

'You know that Kate will make you a wedding dress, don't you?' Rosie said. 'And she won't expect paying.'

'I know she would,' Polly said. She had dreamed of the kind of beautiful wedding dress she knew Kate could create for her, but she would never admit it. 'But that's not fair on Kate. Especially as she's got her hands full with Lily's wedding dress and all her seamstress work. No, I'm going to ask around. See if perhaps I can borrow one. Or get a second-hand one cheap.'

'So, have you both thought of a date?' Martha asked.

'Well,' Polly said with a big smile, 'Tommy's getting out of hospital this weekend ...'

'That's great news!' Gloria said, surprised.

'That's soon,' Rosie said. 'I thought they were going to keep him for a while longer?'

'I know, so did I,' Polly said. 'But he said Dr Parker's discharging him this weekend.'

'That doesn't mean you're getting married this weekend, does it?' Martha asked.

Dorothy and Angie hooted with laughter.

'Course she's not, yer dafty!' Angie said, nudging Martha, who didn't budge an inch. 'Even if they've got no money, they've still got lots to plan. And yer gorra get booked in – even if it's at the registry office. Isn't that right, miss?' Angie looked at Rosie.

'That's right, Angie.' Rosie tried to keep a straight face. 'And the only reason I got married so quickly was because Peter got us a special licence, but even that took some organising. And you have to give a reason for wanting to get married so quickly.'

'Anyway, you're still going to get married in a church, *aren't you?*' Dorothy's question was more a plea.

'Oh, yes,' Polly said. 'Definitely. We're going to go and see the vicar at St Ignatius and ask when he can fit us in.'

At the mention of St Ignatius, Gloria had a flash of Hope's christening and the drama of Jack turning up in the middle of the ceremony. That day had been the start of Jack getting his memory back. They had been reunited. It was the first time he'd held Hope. She knew she had a lot to be thankful for, but still, the longer they were parted, the more she yearned for him. They might speak on the phone and write to each other, but they still hadn't actually seen each other, held each other, since the start of the year.

'So, when do you think you'll be getting married?' Martha asked, having listened intently to what everyone was saying. She'd never realised it was all so complicated.

'We reckon by the time it takes him to read the banns out—'

'Which the vicar has to do three Sundays before the actual ceremony,' Dorothy informed Martha.

'And with the time it'll take us to organise everything,' Polly continued, 'hopefully we'll be able to set a date in the first two weeks of December. At the very latest a week before Christmas.'

Dorothy clapped her hands in glee.

'Two Christmas weddings!'

As they all started to tuck into their lunches and discuss other ways Polly could still have a fabulous wedding on a shoestring, Gloria suddenly looked at Polly.

'Have you told Agnes?' she asked.

'About the money?' Polly said.

Gloria nodded.

Everyone stared at Polly and she shook her head.

'Oh dear,' Martha said.

'Oh dear, indeed,' said Dorothy.

Chapter Twenty-Seven

'Yer what?'

Agnes and Pearl spoke at the same time, Agnes's Irish brogue slightly louder than Pearl's broad north-east accent. The looks of disbelief they both had plastered on their faces, though, were equal.

Agnes banged the pot of tea down on the kitchen table.

'Please tell me that I didn't hear right?' Agnes demanded, glowering at her daughter.

Polly didn't say anything.

Pearl looked at Bel, who was by the sink in the scullery. She jerked her head towards the back door and for once Pearl did as she was told. Grabbing her fags off the sideboard, she hurried out. They all knew to keep out of Agnes's way when she was ready to pop. She could quiz Bel later.

Agnes turned to look at Arthur, who had just got settled in his armchair, then at Bel, now busy stacking up the plates, and finally at Joe, who was playing snap with Lucille.

'As none of you have uttered a word, I'm guessing I *did*, in fact, hear right?'

Agnes scowled at Polly, still in her overalls, standing by the kitchen doorway and looking ready to make a run for it if necessary.

'Yes, Ma, you heard right,' Polly said finally, keeping her voice level. 'I gave the money away, like I said, to charity. The Red Cross, the King George's Fund for Sailors and that poor girl from down the road.'

Agnes shook her head slowly to show her utter disbelief.

'I suppose if it went to charity that makes it all fine and dandy!' Her voice rose dramatically.

She looked at Polly and then to Arthur.

'Does Tommy know?'

They nodded in unison.

'And he still wants to get married?' Agnes's eyes were wide with disbelief.

'Yes, Ma, he still wants to marry me,' Polly said, keeping her words to a minimum so as not to further fan the flames of her mother's growing fury.

Agnes looked at Arthur for a second opinion.

'He does, Agnes,' the old man confirmed.

'Well, then,' she said, her attention still on Arthur, 'they're both as daft as each other!'

She looked back at Polly.

'So, you gonna walk down the aisle in your overalls? 'Cos that's all you'll be able to afford.' She paused for a moment. 'I suppose we could bleach them white.'

There was a clatter from the kitchen. Bel cursed under her breath as a plate slipped from her hand into the porcelain sink.

Agnes turned to glare at Bel.

'And I'm guessing you knew all about this as well?'

Bel nodded.

Agnes's focus turned to Joe, who was pushing himself out of his chair with the aid of his stick and putting his hand out to Lucille.

'You too?' she asked.

Joe ignored his mother's question. 'I'm just gonna get the bairn ready fer bed.' He made his way out of the kitchen with Lucille.

'There are worse things, Ma,' he said.

Polly threw her brother a look of thanks.

'Unbelievable.' Agnes spat the word out. 'Call me selfish, but that was the one bright spot on the horizon. Amongst all this doom and gloom and warmongering. Seeing my daughter getting married 'n having a lovely wedding.' She blew out air. 'Being thankful my only daughter had got herself a good man who'd had the sense to save what little money he had for a half-decent wedding.'

Agnes shook her head and took off her pinny. She gave Polly a dark look.

'I'm sorry to have to say this, Pol.'

Another exhalation of air.

'But I'm disappointed in yer. I thought I'd brought yer up with more sense.'

Agnes hung her apron on the hook by the side of the range.

'I'm going to see Beryl,' she said, stomping out of the kitchen.

Her angry footsteps could be heard clomping down the tiled hallway.

A few seconds later the whole house shuddered as she slammed the front door.

When Joe came back downstairs in his Home Guard uniform, ready for his night shift, he looked through the kitchen door to see Polly nursing a cup of tea. She looked crestfallen.

'Give Mam an hour,' he said, sitting at the bottom of the stairs to tie his bootlaces. 'She'll have come down off the ceiling by then.'

He pushed himself back up and looked at his little sister.

'For what it's worth, I think what yer did was incredibly kind.' He paused. 'I know what our Teddy would have said, mind yer.' He chuckled, more to himself. '"Mad as a March hare."'

Polly felt herself well up at the mention of her brother.

'But that's why we both love you so much.'

Polly had to choke back the tears as she got up, walked over to her brother and hugged him.

Joe often talked about his twin in the present tense, as if he were still there with them all.

Perhaps he was.

When Polly came back from seeing Tommy shortly after ten, she found Agnes on her own, sitting in Arthur's armchair. Tramp and Pup were lying outstretched in front of the range. They barely moved, only raising tired eyes to see who had come into the kitchen and brought a draught of cold air with them.

'Shut the door,' Agnes said, seeing Polly hesitate. Normally at this time it would just be Bel up. Joe was out late most evenings with the Home Guard, Pearl was at the Tatham, and Agnes tended to go to bed shortly after Arthur, at around half nine. Tonight, though, after returning from Beryl's, Agnes had asked Bel if she wouldn't mind giving her some time alone with her daughter.

'There's a spare cuppa going.' Agnes cast her eyes over to the kitchen table, which had been cleared save for a pot of tea, a small jug of milk, a bowl of sugar and a cup and saucer.

Polly looked and breathed a sigh of relief.

This was her ma's peace offering.

'I'm sorry, Ma,' Polly said, pouring her tea and pulling a chair out from under the table and positioning it in front of the range so that the dogs were by her feet. 'I know we're not exactly flush.' She looked at Agnes, who was wearing the same clothes she saw her in every day.

'I know I should have given you the money for housekeeping,' Polly said, guilt creeping into her voice. 'You're right, I should have had more sense … I'm sorry you think I'm a disappointment.'

Agnes leant forward and took hold of Polly's free hand.

'Oh, Pol, yer not a disappointment.' She sighed and looked into her daughter's pretty blue-green eyes, which never failed to remind her of Harry. She still missed him, even now, after all these years.

'I'm sorry for saying that. I didn't mean it. Yer the best daughter any mother could ask for.' She looked at Polly and could feel tears beginning to pool. 'I mean that, I really do. I think what yer did was the kindest thing I've ever heard of anyone ever doing. If not the craziest.' Agnes squeezed her daughter's hand and gave her a sad smile.

Polly felt her body sag with relief. She hated falling out with her mother, and more than anything she hated feeling that she had let her down.

'It's just,' Agnes continued, 'I kept thinking of when yer father 'n I got married.'

Polly looked at her mother in surprise. She rarely talked about her father.

'We were so poor,' Agnes said. 'I wore my mother's old wedding dress 'n yer dad borrowed a mate's suit that was too small for him.' Agnes let out a soft chuckle. 'He kept pulling the sleeves down as if that'd somehow stretch it 'n make it fit.

'When you came along after the twins – *a girl* – I was so chuffed, I remember thinking to myself, this little mite's gonna have a proper wedding. With a proper dress, and a proper wedding breakfast, even a little party afterwards.'

Agnes let go of Polly's hand, got up, topped up her tea and sat back down.

'I didn't say anything, but when Tommy came back, I kept thinking of the gratuity money you'd got.' She thought for a moment. 'I should have known something was up because yer never mentioned it.'

Polly didn't say anything. It was rare her mother opened up about her own feelings.

'I felt so happy that Tommy was alive and that you were going to get married – and that you'd have the kind of wedding day I'd always wished for yer ... Perhaps even have enough left to get yourselves a little flat somewhere nearby.'

Agnes looked down at the dogs, now gently snoring.

'I was so angry that was never going to happen, I let my tongue run away with itself.'

Agnes took in a deep breath.

'But when I went round to Beryl's 'n I heard myself rant on, I saw the look on her face and realised I was being self-ish. And not only selfish – what I said to you was unkind. But most of all, it was untrue.'

Polly put down her tea, got up and put her arms around her mother. She looked tired.

'And the funny thing is,' Agnes hugged her daughter back, 'I know if Harry was alive now, he'd be as proud as punch of yer, he would.'

Agnes allowed a tear to escape unchecked.

'And I hate to admit this, but yer da would be just as proud of yer for doing what you're doing – trooping to that yard day in day out, all kinds of weather, building them ships. Doing your bit to win this war.'

Polly felt her chest swell.

Those words meant the world to her.

More than her ma would ever know.

Chapter Twenty-Eight

Four days later

Sunday 15 November

'Don't forget,' Charlotte told Marjorie as they got ready to leave the house, 'use the toilet before we go. And squeeze out every last drop, because believe you me, you do *not* want to be using the lavvy at the yard.'

Marjorie giggled at her friend's use of the word 'lavvy'. Charlotte had always had a slight accent – another reason she'd been picked on at Runcorn – but now she was back home, it was stronger.

'Gosh, yes, I nearly forgot!' Marjorie dumped her handbag and gas mask, and headed off to the toilet next to the back door.

'And remember, nil by mouth,' Charlotte shouted after her friend. She reckoned they'd probably already drunk too much tea this morning.

When Marjorie returned, Charlotte noticed her wiping her mouth.

'You've had some water!'

'Oh golly, I forgot,' Marjorie said, putting her hand on her mouth. 'Force of habit.'

'Don't worry. If you think you might need the loo again, we can pop into the public ones by the park.'

Marjorie pulled a face.

Charlotte laughed.

'God, Marge, if you think that one's bad, you *really* need to see the one at the yard!'

Charlotte put her hand on the front-door Chubb and turned back to face her friend.

'Now remember, full sprint from the moment we get out the door. Mrs Jenkins can sense you're going to leave the house before you know you're going out yourself.'

'Righty-ho,' Marjorie said, checking her pocket for her inhaler.

A few minutes later they'd made it out the gate at the bottom of the private road and had stopped to cross Tunstall Road.

'You all right?' Charlotte looked at her friend, who was out of breath but not struggling.

'Yes, yes, all good,' Marjorie said. 'Oh, I do miss you, Charlie,' she went on as they hurried across the road and made their way up Tunstall Vale.

'I miss you too, Marge,' Charlotte said. 'But I actually think it's going to be so much better now we're *both* back home. We can see each other lots.'

Marjorie had jumped for joy when she'd got Charlotte's letter telling her she had succeeded in escaping 'the castle' and was now a new girl at the Sunderland Church High School – the sister school to the one Marjorie was now attending in Newcastle.

'And,' Marjorie said, pulling her hat further down past her ears, 'our schools will be in tournaments against each other.'

'Yeah,' Charlotte said. 'Miss Launder, our PE teacher, says she wants me to play centre forward.'

'And I'll ask my PE teacher if I can come and support our team.'

Both girls knew there was no way Marjorie would ever be chosen to play hockey for the school, or any kind of sports for that matter, but she would be able to wangle herself a seat on the school bus as their mascot.

As they reached the corner of West Lawn, Charlotte stopped.

'Follow me.' She turned right and Marjorie followed suit.

'Where are we going?' Marjorie asked.

'Look,' Charlotte said. 'See that house there?' She pointed to the second house in.

'Yes, I see it,' Marjorie said, staring at the grand, three-storey, turn-of-the-century terraced house.

'Well, that's where Lily and George live.'

'Oh, it looks nice,' Marjorie said. 'A bit like my house in Jesmond.'

Charlotte had never been to her friend's house in Newcastle, but she was going to find out soon. Marjorie's parents had invited her to stay overnight during the holidays.

'Why don't we pop in and see them both? Introduce you quickly,' Charlotte said.

Marjorie thought for a moment. She was intrigued but also a little nervous. George sounded nice – just like her great-uncle Bertie – but from what Charlotte had told her, Lily was very eccentric.

'Come on,' Charlotte said, dragging her friend towards the house.

They were just a few yards away when they stopped in their tracks as the door opened and a man who wasn't George stepped out. The large black front door closed behind him and he stood and lit a cigarette.

'I think we should leave it,' Marjorie said. 'It's not polite to turn up unannounced.'

Charlotte stared at the man. He looked a little dishevelled.

'Maybe you're right,' she conceded. 'Guess I'm just curious to see inside. Especially as Rosie works there.'

'Doing the books?' Marjorie said.

Charlotte nodded.

'What business does Lily have?' Marjorie asked.

'I'm not sure,' Charlotte said, suddenly realising that no one had really explained. 'I've only been here the once. And then I didn't even make it past the gate.'

Charlotte watched as the man hurried down the stone steps and down the long pathway.

'When was that?' Marjorie asked.

'The morning George took us to Harrogate.'

Marjorie was still overawed by what Rosie had done that day. *Going to the school in her overalls!* She couldn't believe it when Charlotte had told her. She kept asking her to go over and over each part of the day in the minutest of details so that she could imagine that she too had been there.

'Anyway,' Marjorie said, looking at her watch, 'we've not got time. Rosie's expecting us at noon, so we're best not to be late – and you said you were going to show me the school en route.'

Charlotte agreed and after a brisk walk back onto Tunstall Vale, across the Ryhope Road and down Mowbray Road they were standing facing Sunderland Church High School.

'That's my form room there.' Charlotte pointed to the left of the red-brick building, which looked more like a huge detached house than a school. 'The headmistress's room is there on the left, just as you walk through the main entrance, and the deputy head's is on the right.'

'It looks like my school, only smaller,' Marjorie said. 'Rosie must have to work all hours to send you here,' she said. She'd heard her own parents discussing her school fees the other day and how it was probably for the best that they'd only had the one child.

'Yes,' Charlotte said thoughtfully. 'Now you mention it, I suppose she does.'

They were quiet for a moment.

'Come on, then!' Charlotte said, hooking her arm through her friend's. 'To Thompson's!'

'Yeah! To Thompson's!' Marjorie repeated.

The two girls looked at each other, and putting one foot forward and taking a deep breath, they began singing and marching in step:

Follow the yellow brick road,
Follow the yellow brick road,
Follow, follow, follow, follow,
Follow the yellow brick road.

It was, of course, their favourite film.

Chapter Twenty-Nine

Twenty minutes later, after following the cobbles rather than a yellow brick road, and revelling in a trip across the Wear on the ferry, Charlotte and Marjorie, like Dorothy and her three companions on their arrival at the Emerald City, found themselves looking up at a huge pair of metal gates.

They had timed it to perfection – it had just gone midday and the deafening clanging and clanking noise of the shipyard, as well as of all the other yards along the river, had just stopped.

'Golly me!' Marjorie said, her hand fidgeting with the inhaler in her coat pocket. 'This place is incredible.'

They both looked into the expanse of the yard to see groups of men and the occasional woman sitting down on makeshift seats, chatting to their fellow workers as they got out their lunch boxes and started tucking into their sandwiches.

'Aren't they freezing?' Marjorie asked, pulling her coat up to her chin. The temperature had dropped today and there was a distinct feel of frost in the air.

'See those half-barrels everyone's standing around?' Charlotte pointed over to a group of caulkers smoking. The occasional lick of fire could be seen escaping from the top of what looked like an oversized metal can.

She nodded.

'They're like mini furnaces,' Charlotte said.

'Look, there's Rosie!' Marjorie said, as she spotted her friend's older sister striding across the yard in dirty overalls and big leather boots. She was struck yet again by the image of Rosie sitting in Mrs Willoughby-Smith's office in all her work gear.

'Hi, you two,' Rosie said, before looking up to Alfie, who smiled and gave her the nod.

Rosie looked at Charlotte and her best friend. She didn't think it possible to get two more different girls. Chalk and cheese, but they got on like a house on fire. They'd kept her awake half the night with their chatter and giggles; she'd not had the heart to tell them to be quiet.

'Now, Marjorie, are you sure your parents are all right about you visiting the yard?' Rosie had never met Marjorie's parents, but she had the impression that they were a little overprotective of their only daughter.

'Oh, yes, Rosie,' Marjorie said, her face the picture of innocence. 'Mummy and Daddy think it's a great idea.' Marjorie wasn't one for lying, but nothing was going to stop her coming there today and seeing everything that Charlotte had told her about.

'Come on then,' Rosie said. 'Let's go straight to the canteen. We'll have a quick bite to eat, and afterwards I'll show you around.'

Both girls almost skipped behind Rosie as she led the way.

As they reached the main doors, Rosie turned to her two charges.

'If you need the loo, Marjorie, just ask Charlie, she knows where they are.'

'Oh, there won't be any need,' Marjorie said, quick as a flash. 'We made sure we went before we left.'

'Well, you never know,' Rosie said as she opened the door and walked into the cafeteria. 'You might do after a nice big pot of tea. I know how much you two love your fresh brew, and I must say, you get a good cuppa here.'

Rosie looked around the canteen at the workers, most of them with a cup in one hand and a fag in the other.

Marjorie gave Charlotte a panicked look.

'We might just stick with water,' Charlotte said as casually as she could. 'We must have drunk nearly a pot each before we came out.'

Rosie couldn't help smiling as she turned and led the way to where she knew her squad were sitting.

When she reached their table, though, her smile dropped. The women all looked unusually serious.

Something was wrong.

'Hannah?' She walked round and sat on the empty chair next to her. She looked at Olly, who was sitting next to Hannah, holding her hand. He too looked incredibly sad.

'What's wrong?' she asked.

The pale face of their 'little bird' was streaked with tears.

'Hannah's just got some bad news,' Olly said.

Rosie looked at Olly and then at the faces of the women.

'Her mam and dad?' she asked quietly.

'They're not dead,' Hannah blurted out. 'Well, we don't think so.'

Rosie breathed a sigh of relief. They all knew the situation with the Jews was becoming dire, not so much through the newspapers or wireless, but from Hannah's aunty Rina who was privy to a lot of information that was not yet public. She'd recently travelled down to London with the rabbi to a big protest meeting at the Royal Albert Hall. Hannah had relayed to them what her aunty had told her, and she'd shown them a copy of the *News Chronicle*, a Jewish newspaper she'd brought back with her. They had all sat and listened as she read them an article about this new atrocity being referred to as a 'holocaust'. No one had said anything for fear of showing their own anger and upset, but they'd all quietly agreed to keep an eye on Hannah. Olly had also been instructed to tell them straight away if he thought there was anything wrong.

He had clearly done as they'd asked.

'You know I told you my parents were in the Theresienstadt ghetto?' Hannah said, forcing herself to keep her emotions at bay.

The women all nodded, their faces sombre.

'And that although it was awful, their chances were better if they remained there?' Hannah pulled a hanky from her sleeve and put it to her eyes. She started to cry silently.

'Hannah's just heard they've been moved,' Olly said. 'To a place called Auschwitz.'

The women didn't know where the place called Auschwitz was, but guessed by Hannah's distress and the desolate look on Olly's face that this was one of the so-called 'death camps' she'd told them about.

'I will be fine,' Hannah said, wiping her eyes. 'I must be strong. And brave. *Můj mami a táta* would want that.'

It was the first time they had all heard Hannah refer to her mother and father in her native tongue.

All of a sudden, Hannah looked up and saw Charlotte and Marjorie standing quietly behind Rosie.

'*Ach, můj Bože,*' she said. 'Charlie, come here.' She put out her two skinny arms to give Charlotte a hug. 'Here you are with your friend and I'm being all morbid ... I'm guessing that this is Marjorie.'

Hannah put her arms out once again.

Marjorie stepped forwards and the two embraced. It did not escape anyone's notice that the two were as skinny as each other and not dissimilar in looks, only one had short blonde hair and the other thick, dark hair.

'Come sit down!' Hannah commanded.

Charlotte and Marjorie sat in the two remaining seats between Rosie and Angie. Charlotte grabbed the one nearest her sister, forcing Marjorie to sit next to Angie.

'So, Marjorie,' Hannah said. 'Charlie here has told me all about how you were first to escape "the castle", paving the way for her return to her home town.'

Marjorie blushed.

'Oh, I'm not so sure about that. I think Charlie rather made good her own escape.'

'So, let me introduce you, Marjorie,' Hannah said. 'This is Polly, Martha, Dorothy and Angie. And Olly.'

The women all smiled, even though their minds were still in a place called Auschwitz.

'So, what yer both been up to this morning?' Angie looked at Charlotte and Marjorie.

'Oh ... Umm ...' Marjorie hesitated. They'd spent most of the morning chatting, drinking tea and eating toast, and running around the house. 'We went for a walk.'

'Where did you go?' Polly asked, genuinely interested.

'Mmm ...' Marjorie hesitated again. They hadn't exactly been on a proper walk as such. 'Well, we walked to Lily's.'

The women's faces flashed concern and they automatically looked at Rosie.

'Did you?' Rosie tried to keep her voice casual, but her words were clipped.

'Yes, but we didn't *go* to Lily's,' Charlotte said, suddenly panicking. Her sister had more or less forbidden her to go there without her say-so.

'What do you mean? Did you go or didn't you?' Rosie snapped. *God, why was Lily and her bloody abode like a magnet to her little sister?*

'Well, we didn't pay a visit to Lily's,' Marjorie said, sensing that they had done something wrong, although unsure

216

what exactly. 'It was more a case of us passing since we decided it was rude to call unannounced.'

'I should think so too!' Angie said, causing Charlotte and Marjorie to jump. 'Yer dinnit just go 'n knock on someone's door without being invited!'

Dorothy looked at her friend, who had no qualms about knocking on anyone's door uninvited.

'Oh, I almost forgot,' Hannah said, turning to Charlotte. 'Thank you so much for my book!' She bent down and scrabbled around in her bag. 'See, I take it everywhere with me!'

Marjorie's face lit up as she took the proffered book.

'Oh, I adore Cicero. "Philosophy is the mother of all arts. The true medicine of the mind",' she quoted.

'It is indeed,' Hannah sighed. She looked up at the women sitting around the table. Tears had once again started to blur her vision.

'A true medicine of the mind, just like my friends here – a medicine I could not survive without.'

As Hannah spoke, Marjorie opened the book and was hit by what she saw on the first page. It was a library card on which had been stamped: *Property of the Runcorn School for Girls*. Across it was scrawled, *Enjoy! Love Charlie x*.

She immediately shut the book and handed it back to Hannah.

'Why don't you two go and get yourselves something to eat?' Rosie said to Charlotte and a flushed-looking Marjorie. 'Before there's nothing left. Muriel tends to shut up early on a Sunday. Then I can give you a quick tour of the yard before the start of the afternoon shift.'

Charlotte and Marjorie hurried off just as Helen walked into the canteen.

'Helen!' Rosie waved at her, more to show she was welcome than their whereabouts.

'Hi, everyone,' Helen said, immediately seeing Hannah's wan, tear-stained face.

'Have a seat,' Rosie said, pulling out the chair that Charlotte had just vacated.

'Cuppa?' asked Martha, taking hold of the teapot dominating the middle of the table.

'No, thank you, Martha. I think I've already drunk enough to sink a ship.' Helen smiled. 'I just wanted to come and say a quick thank you to you all.' She looked at the women. Out of the corner of her eye she caught Dorothy giving Angie a nudge. 'To thank you for all the overtime you're doing. I know you're all working your socks off, and let's face it, they're not exactly ideal conditions.'

Everyone glanced out the canteen window. The sky was dark and the windowpanes were starting to rattle as the wind got up.

'Providing there are no hiccups, it's looking more and more likely that we're going to hit a new production record, which is just brilliant.'

There was a murmur of agreement.

'Are we still on schedule to launch *Brutus* before Christmas?' Rosie asked.

'Most definitely,' Helen said, relaxing. She felt much more at ease with Rosie. Had even started to feel that there were the beginnings of a real friendship. 'That's the other reason I wanted to see you all.'

Again, Helen looked at the women's expectant faces.

'To tell you that I've set a launch date. Friday the eighteenth of December. Exactly a week before Christmas.'

'Oh,' Polly exclaimed. 'That's so exciting!'

Everyone's focus diverted to Polly.

'Tommy and I'll be getting married the next day. On Saturday the nineteenth.'

Polly had wanted to tell them her news during the lunch break, but had held back after hearing the terrible news about Hannah's parents.

'Hurrah!' Dorothy couldn't contain herself.

'Eee, that's brilliant, Pol!' Angie said. 'That's two weddings in one week!'

Helen looked at her former love rival and gave what appeared to be a genuine smile. 'Congratulations, Polly!'

Everyone looked at their workmate and then at their boss. It was still strange to see Polly and Helen within arm's length of each other, never mind celebrating the fact that Polly was going to marry the man Helen had desperately wanted for herself.

'Thanks, Helen,' Polly said, feeling a little awkward. *Did Helen still harbour feelings for Tommy?* She was unsure.

'You've not left yourself much time, have you?' Helen paused while she did a quick calculation. 'Four weeks and four days exactly.'

'Well, there's not that much to organise really,' Polly laughed. 'It's going to be quite a simple, low-key affair.'

'But you're still getting married in church?' Helen asked.

'Of course!' Angie said, as if to suggest otherwise was an insult.

'The vicar has to read out the banns for three weeks,' Martha informed Helen. 'To give people a chance to object if they want to.'

There was an awkward moment.

'Not that anyone will be objecting,' Hannah chipped in.

'Of course not,' Helen said.

There was another slightly strained silence.

'And Tommy's been discharged?' Helen asked, wanting to fill the gap in the conversation.

'Yes,' Polly said. 'He came out yesterday. I think he was going stir-crazy in there.'

'Am I right in saying he's not staying with you in Tatham Street?' Helen asked.

'No, he said he didn't feel it was right to be under the same roof as me until after we were married.'

'Oh.' Helen couldn't keep the surprise out of her voice. She glanced at Rosie, who returned her look of astonishment.

'I know,' Polly said, catching the look. 'Everyone keeps saying the same thing. He must be mad, especially as he'd be fussed over no end by my ma – and fed stew and dumplings till it's coming out of his ears.'

Helen and Polly both chuckled, knowing this had always been Tommy's favourite meal since he was a child.

As the women started to quiz Polly about every detail of her wedding, Helen made her excuses and headed back to her office.

As she hurried across the yard to the main admin block, she felt a huge sense of relief. She had been terribly nervous about going across and seeing the women, Polly in particular. She had no idea if Tommy had remembered her ridiculous declaration of love on the night of the air raid, and if so, whether or not he'd told Polly. Judging by how friendly Polly had just been, Helen thought she was right to believe that Tommy hadn't said a thing, even if he *had* remembered.

As Helen forced the main door to the admin building closed against the growing winds, the image of Hannah's pale, tear-stained face came to the fore. She would have liked to have asked her what was wrong, but hadn't felt at ease doing so in front of an audience.

The sadness that she had seen etched onto Hannah's pretty face, though, had exacerbated her own guilt at the way she had treated the squad's 'little bird' when she had first started at the yard. Making her do the hardest, most labour-intensive welding jobs in an effort to get shot of her – her ultimate aim being to break up Rosie's squad as a convoluted way of getting back at Polly for stealing the man she had set her heart on.

She felt embarrassed just thinking about her past behaviour.

Had she really been that person? So selfish? So shallow? So heartless?

She felt like a different person now.

She *was* a different person now.

Everything she had been through this past year had changed her: finding out she had a baby sister; her father's banishment to the Clyde; realising her mother's love was, and always had been, purely conditional; being conned and abandoned by Theo – a married man with two children, and his wife expecting a third.

But she knew that what had really changed her, more than anything else, was losing her baby.

At the end of the shift, Rosie caught up with Dor and Angie.

'You two off home?'

'I'm just gannin to see my mam 'n dad 'n the little 'uns,' Angie said.

'And I'm going to see my mum and the four terrors,' Dorothy said.

'Duty calls, eh?' Rosie smiled. Both women had less than perfect families, although for very different reasons.

'Once a week is once too much,' Dorothy huffed.

'At least with all this overtime we've got a good excuse not to gan round more often,' Angie said.

Rosie knew that Dorothy's family would probably not be too fussed if she only showed her face once in a blue moon, but Angie's would be less than happy. Angie's mam and dad relied on their daughter's weekly visit to look after the children for a few hours, cook the Sunday dinner and give the house a quick going-over, as well as on the money she gave them.

'Did Marjorie and Charlie enjoy their tour of the yard?' Dorothy asked.

'Yes, it was just a quick one, though,' Rosie said. 'I got Hannah and Olly to show them around the drawing room and up in the mould loft.'

'Good thinking, miss. That Marjorie looked like she might be blown out to sea. There's nothing to her.'

Rosie laughed. That had been part of the reason she had kept them indoors as much as possible. The other being that she had her doubts whether Marjorie's parents really had agreed to her being there.

'You going to meet up with them now?' Dorothy asked.

'I said I'd treat them to some tea at Vera's before Marjorie got the train back to Newcastle.'

'She dinnit sound like she's a Geordie, miss,' Angie said.

'I think she's been away from home most of her life. At boarding school.' Rosie smiled; there was no mistaking where Angie had been born and brought up.

'Yer ganna introduce her to Vera, miss?' Angie sounded concerned. Vera was known for being rather brusque and somewhat prickly, especially with those she didn't know.

'Rina's working today,' Rosie said. 'And Hannah and Olly are meeting us there as well.'

'Ah, they'll be all reet then, miss,' Angie said.

'It'll be good for Hannah too. Might take her mind off things for a little while,' Dorothy said.

'Exactly,' Rosie agreed.

They walked down to the ferry.

'You've still got George's uniform safe and sound in the flat, haven't you?' Rosie asked.

'Of course, miss,' Angie said.

'Still in its dry-cleaner's bag, miss,' Dorothy said. 'Any particular reason you're asking?'

Rosie sighed wearily.

'Oh, Lily reckons she's going to persuade George to wear his uniform for their wedding. I personally think this is one argument she's not going to win.'

'Ahh,' Dorothy and Angie said in unison.

They didn't say so, but they didn't rate Lily's chances of success very high either.

They'd seen the state of George's uniform when they'd found it on the day they'd moved into his flat. It had been stuffed up in the attic. Out of sight and out of mind. It certainly didn't look like it was something their landlord ever wanted to *see* again – never mind get married in.

Chapter Thirty

Dr Parker gently rapped on the open door to Helen's office. As he did so, he saw a ginger blur shoot past him and out into the main office.

'All work and no play ...' He let his voice trail off as he watched Helen look up from a pile of order forms on her desk. The rush of adrenaline that hit him was no surprise. He'd accepted that was how it was whenever he saw Helen. Just like he had accepted that the feelings he had for this woman would never be reciprocated.

Not as long as her love for Tommy dominated her heart.

'Oh, is it that time already?' Helen looked at her watch before raising her sparkling emerald eyes to the man who had become her closest friend.

'It is indeed,' Dr Parker said, getting Helen's coat from the back of the door and holding it out for her. 'And there's no time to be wasted if we're to make it to our favourite eatery before it shuts.'

Helen placed a Hartleys glass paperweight on top of the documents she had been checking. 'Well then, I guess these can wait until tomorrow.' She manoeuvred herself around the desk. Putting her arms through the sleeves of her coat, she sensed John's presence close behind her. For the briefest of moments, she felt like taking a tiny step backwards and relaxing her body into his outstretched arms.

As soon as the thought entered her mind, though, she gently pushed it away. She had got used to these imaginings. They were not uncommon. She had learnt to accept them for what they were. Flights of fantasy. She knew John could never be anything more than a friend. How could he, after what he knew about her? As her mother liked to tell her whenever she got the chance, she was 'soiled goods'.

Strangely enough, Helen thought as they made their way out of the main building, it didn't bother her. She would trade the feel of John's arms around her, even the touch of his lips on hers, for the ease of their companionship.

Besides, romantic love had hardly brought her happiness.

'So, tell me about your day,' Dr Parker said.

'Well,' Helen said, after a deep intake of breath, 'you'll be pleased to know I was very brave and went to see everyone in the canteen.'

Dr Parker turned to look at her. She had tied a scarf around her head in an effort to save her perfect victory rolls from being sabotaged by the winds. She looked, as always, incredibly glamorous.

'*Very* brave,' he said with a smile. For someone so outwardly confident, it always amazed him that inwardly Helen was so insecure.

'And did it all go well?'

'Yes,' Helen nodded, linking his arm and holding the ends of her scarf to ensure it did not blow away as they walked up the embankment to Dame Dorothy Street. 'I wasn't exactly sitting around having a good gossip with them all, but I did thank them for working so hard.'

'And were they all nice to you?' Dr Parker couldn't help feeling protective of Helen. He knew the women had been overwhelmed with emotion the night of the air raid, and that their declaration of a steadfast and long-lasting friendship might easily become a distant memory as life resumed some semblance of normality.

'Yes, they were.' Helen was quiet for a moment as they reached the top of the road and turned right. 'I know they'll always be *nice* to me because of what I did,' she mused.

'What you "did" – meaning risking your life for Gloria and Hope?' Dr Parker's question was rhetorical. Helen always seemed to trivialise her actions on that fateful night.

'Mmm,' Helen said. 'But one day I hope they'll be nice to me because they *like* me – not because they feel like they *owe* me, if that makes sense.'

Dr Parker nodded.

'Yes, it does, perfect sense. And I'm sure that day will come when they realise that you are a lovely person, as well as a brave one.'

Helen turned her head to the right and looked across the river.

'Oh, John, I think you're a little biased,' she said sadly, thinking of Hannah. 'I think we both know that I haven't exactly been a "lovely person" to date.'

Dr Parker knew by Helen's tone that there was something bothering her.

'What's wrong?' he asked.

Helen looked at him and thought how wonderful it must be to have a clear conscience. To be a genuinely good person.

'I still feel so guilty about Hannah,' she said as they walked along Harbour View.

'Why is your guilt stronger today?' he asked. 'Has something happened?'

Helen was quiet for a moment as she looked down into the darkness of the north dock.

'I think something might have happened – judging by the terribly woeful look on Hannah's face this afternoon. She'd obviously been crying. I would have liked to ask her what was wrong, but I don't feel like I know her well enough to start prying into her personal life.'

'The poor girl's probably worried sick about her mother and father,' Dr Parker said. 'There's more and more coming out about what's really happening over there.'

'What have you heard?' Helen asked. She knew John spent his spare time reading just about any and every newspaper he could get his hands on.

'There was an article in the *Guardian* recently,' he said, his face becoming serious. 'It was a report on a meeting that happened at the Royal Albert Hall. Well, it was more a protest than a meeting as such – about the Nazi persecution of the Jews.'

'Oh yes?' Helen said. 'What did it say?'

'It would seem that the Archbishop of Canterbury didn't beat about the bush. Said we are seeing – what were the words he used? That's it, an "eruption of evil". That there's been nothing like it for centuries, and that what's happening in Europe is so horrible we are refusing to accept it.' He huffed. 'That's if we're even aware of what's going on.'

Helen guided John over to the railings.

'And did he say what *is* happening over there?' Helen asked. 'It all seems very vague.'

'Well, Hitler initially claimed to be deporting Jewish refugees for labour, and that only men of working age were needed, then it was women – and now *children* are being deported. From two years old up.'

Helen felt a shiver go down her back as she thought of Hope.

'The fear,' Dr Parker said, 'is that a large proportion of those deported are destined for camps where thousands of Jews have already perished. The Archbishop didn't beat about the bush and said it's clear Hitler is hell-bent on "exterminating the Jewish people".'

'God!' Helen felt her anger shoot to the surface. '*Exterminating*. How can you want to *exterminate* people just because of their religion? Their culture?'

Dr Parker looked down at Helen's outraged face, which mirrored his own feelings.

'So, the chances are,' Helen said, 'Hannah's parents might well have been sent to one of these camps?' Her guilt came to the fore again, followed by a need to make amends one day.

If not for Hannah's sake, then for her own.

'So, what's it like, living with the Major?' Polly asked as she leant across their table and gave Tommy a kiss.

'Better than sharing a ward with half a dozen blokes – and soldiers at that!' Tommy laughed. 'Actually, the Major has said he would love to see his flat graced by the presence of a woman – whether he is there or not.' Tommy gave Polly a mischievous smile.

'In other words,' Polly said, 'he's happy for me to be there unchaperoned?'

Tommy nodded enthusiastically.

'Exactly.'

He took a sip of his tea.

'And I do believe he's going out tonight with Joe 'n the rest of his Home Guard squad. So, would the future Mrs Watts like to come back 'n drink yet more tea at my new digs?'

Polly made a face, as though deciding whether this was something she would like to do or not, before breaking into a wide smile.

'I think the "future Mrs Watts" would love to see your new digs and drink yet more tea.'

This time it was Tommy who leant across to give Polly a kiss.

'Yer know how much I love yer, don't you?' he said.

Polly nodded and kissed him back.

They parted just as the door of the café opened and a gust of cold air caused the half-dozen or so customers, including Tommy and Polly, to look at the culprits.

'Oh!' Polly couldn't help herself exclaim in surprise. 'Helen!'

'Polly!' Helen was also taken aback to see Polly and Tommy sitting at what was her and Dr Parker's favourite table.

The two women looked at each other.

'Honestly,' Helen said. 'As if you don't see enough of me at work.'

'And,' Tommy chuckled, 'as if I've not seen enough of this man over the past four weeks!'

Dr Parker walked over to where Polly and Tommy were sitting by the window, which would have given views out to the North Sea had the blackout blinds not been pulled down. He stretched out his hand and shook Tommy's by way of a greeting and tipped an imaginary hat to Polly.

'Have a seat!' Tommy said, pulling out the empty seat next to his. Polly smiled at Helen and did the same with the seat next to her. As Helen took off her scarf and coat before sitting down, Polly became conscious of her dirty overalls and that her hair was in need of a good brush. *Why did she always feel inferior around Helen?*

'So . . .' Dr Parker said, trying to keep his face from showing his disappointment that the few spare hours he had managed to get off, and which he had hoped to have spent solely with Helen, now looked as though they would be sacrificed to being sociable. 'I see my instructions to rest and recuperate have gone by the wayside?'

Dr Parker looked at Tommy and thought he still looked too pale and undernourished. He should never have agreed to discharge him. Although, who was he kidding? Tommy would have left the Ryhope with or without his permission.

'Tommy, it's lovely to see you,' Helen said. She had been dreading this moment. *Had he remembered?* She felt herself flush with a mix of humiliation and embarrassment as she recalled those few moments of insanity when she had believed Tommy had wanted her, and when she had thought she wanted him.

The irony, she realised, was that neither was true.

Looking at Tommy now, her heart went out to him, not with love, but sympathy. He looked terrible. She knew why John hadn't wanted to discharge him. Instinctively she went to squeeze his hand resting on the tabletop, but quickly retracted it.

It did not go unnoticed by either Dr Parker or Polly.

'I'm so sorry I've not been in to visit you while you've been in hospital,' Helen said guiltily, trying her hardest to think of an excuse.

'Dinnit be daft,' Tommy said. 'You've got better things to be doing with yer time. Not that you've got much time for yerself, by the sounds of it. Pol tells me you're going full steam ahead to get *Brutus* down the ways?'

Helen nodded. She was glad the ice had been broken and that they were on familiar territory.

'Another fresh pot, please,' she said, seeing the waitress coming over to them. As she turned back to the table, her face suddenly lit up.

'Oh John, I forgot to tell you the good news.'

She looked at Polly and then at Tommy – then back at Dr Parker.

'They've set a date.'

Helen laughed on seeing the puzzled look on John's face.

'For their wedding. Scatterbrain!'

'Really? When?' Dr Parker asked. His mind felt all over the place. Skirting between concerns about Tommy's health and his early discharge, and the fact that this was the first time he had seen Helen with Tommy since the day at the hospital when he'd realised she was still very much in love with a man she couldn't have.

'Saturday the nineteenth,' Polly said, taking hold of Tommy's hand across the table.

'Of December?' Dr Parker asked.

'A day after we launch *Brutus*,' Helen said. 'How's that for timing?'

Dr Parker looked at Helen. There was no resentment in her voice whatsoever. Helen was not only beautiful, but also a very good actress.

'So, obviously you're both invited,' Polly said, looking at Tommy for confirmation and then back at Helen and John.

'Aye, that goes without saying,' Tommy nodded.

'Oh, thank you, Polly,' Helen said, glancing at John. 'We'd love to come, wouldn't we?'

'Of course, wouldn't miss it for the world!' Dr Parker said, smiling at the happy couple and at Helen. Again, she'd done a grand job of sounding totally sincere.

'Well, we better get ourselves off now,' Polly said, and Tommy immediately got up and grabbed his leather motorcycle jacket off the back of the chair.

'Aye, doctor's orders,' he chuckled. 'Lots of rest and early nights.'

'Tommy, the day you follow an order, I'll eat my hat.'

The two men shook hands.

'And Polly, please just say if I can do anything to help with the wedding,' Helen said. 'Or if you need time off? It's not every day you get married.'

Helen knew about Polly spending Tommy's gratuity pay. Gloria had told her. She would have loved to give them some money for the wedding, but knew they'd be affronted by the very suggestion.

'And send my regards to yer dad, Helen. Tell him the Scots have had their pound of flesh. We need him back here now.'

Helen laughed.

God, if only he knew. Her father would not be coming back to the north-east any time soon. Not as long as her mother was living and breathing.

'I will,' Helen said as she and Dr Parker said their good-byes and watched Polly and Tommy leave the café.

'Well, that's the last place I'd have expected to see Helen,' Tommy chuckled as he pulled on his jacket.

'Me too,' Polly said.

'Looks like the Bungalow Café's not just our favourite place for a date.' Tommy smiled as he put his arm around Polly and pulled her close.

'Oh, I don't think they're courting,' Polly said. 'I think they're just friends. Even Gloria says so, and she should know.'

Tommy laughed. 'Just friends, eh?'

'You don't think so?' Polly asked, curious.

'Well, put it this way,' Tommy said, 'I don't know any red-blooded man who would troop all the way over from Ryhope during his few precious hours off to take a mere friend fer a cup of tea in a little café on the other side of the water. Helen might well see the good doctor as just a friend, but I'd bet Dr Parker's intentions are anything but chaste.'

Polly looked at Tommy, shocked.

'Thomas Watts,' she said, 'these days a man and a woman can be just friends, you know. I believe the word is "platonic".'

232

Tommy chuckled.

'Not when the woman looks like Helen.'

Polly felt a wounding stab of pure, unadulterated jealousy. 'I suppose she must be rather irresistible to all men.' She looked at Tommy for his reaction.

A wide smile immediately spread across Tommy's face.

'Not "all",' he said. 'This man's only got eyes for one woman and she's right here next to him.'

Polly pushed the green-eyed monster away.

'Remember our first date?' Tommy said as they reached the bus stop. He pulled Polly close and kissed her.

'How can I forget?' Polly smiled at the memory. 'You came up to me after work and asked if you could give me a ride home. I was so nervous because I'd never been on the back of a motorbike before.'

Tommy laughed.

'Not that it showed. You climbed on as though you'd done it a thousand times.'

He bent his head and kissed her.

'We rode all the way to Whitburn and back and all I could think of was the feel of your arms around my waist,' Tommy said, his mind drifting back in time.

'Then we stopped at the Bungalow Café and shared a big piece of cake. I was so nervous I could hardly eat,' Polly recalled.

'And all I could think of was kissing you.'

Tommy stopped walking and pulled Polly close.

'It was a little while before I got my wish,' he said, bending his head and kissing Polly gently on the lips.

He pulled away and looked at her.

'Which is why I believe we've got so much catching up to do.'

Polly laughed.

'Come on then,' she said, seeing the bus with its dimmed headlights approaching. 'Let's get back home and start catching up.'

When they walked through the door to Major Black's flat, Polly could see that Tommy was shattered.

'I'm making the tea,' she said. 'And you're going to do as you're told for once and sit in that nice armchair.'

Tommy opened his mouth to argue but Polly had already left the room.

When she came back five minutes later with the tea tray, Tommy was fast asleep.

She put the tray on the sideboard and took a throw that had been flung over the back of the sofa. She carefully put the blanket over him and kissed him ever so softly on the lips.

'Don't you worry, Thomas Watts, we've got all the time in the world to catch up.'

Chapter Thirty-One

John Street, Sunderland

One week later

Sunday 22 November

'So, they're that bad, are they?' Arthur said.

Major Black nodded.

'They are. That bad. I suppose they don't call them night terrors for nothing.'

The two men were in the front room of the Major's ground-floor flat on John Street.

Arthur was sitting in the armchair next to the large sash window overlooking the pretty cobbled street. The Major had wheeled himself over to the sideboard where he kept his decanter of whisky.

Splashing two good measures of single malt into heavy glass tumblers, the Major balanced one in his lap, held the other in his left hand, and used his right hand to push his wheelchair towards Arthur.

The old man stayed seated, knowing the Major would be offended if he got up.

He took the proffered glass.

'To our brave boys,' the Major toasted, his Scottish accent strong and proud.

'Aye, our brave lads,' Arthur said solemnly.

They were both quiet for a moment.

'The matron on Tom's ward told me,' Arthur said, looking out of the taped-up window. 'Took me aside one day. Said she thought I ought to know. That she didn't feel it was *appropriate* to mention them to Polly. Dripping sweat, she said. Every night. Without fail. She ended up leaving a spare towel on the chair by the side of his bed so he could wipe himself down. Said he spent half the night flinging his arms out, grabbing at imaginary objects.' Arthur took a sip of whisky. 'He says he doesn't want Polly hearing him in the middle of the night "wailing and howling like some dog that needs putting down". Says she's been through enough.'

'The thing is,' the Major said, 'he's not going to be able to keep it from her when they get married.'

'Aye, I know. The lad's worried sick he's going to scare the living daylights out of her on their wedding night.' Arthur took another sip of his whisky. 'I've told him he needs to be honest with Polly. Tell her the truth. That it's nowt to be ashamed of.'

'It's understandable, though, isn't it? The laddie's young. He's got his pride. He doesn't want to tarnish what they've got with the horrors of war,' the Major said, grimacing as the whisky burned. 'God, it makes me so angry.' The Major shuffled uncomfortably in his wheelchair. 'As if it's not enough that war takes live and limbs – but a man's peace of mind as well.'

Arthur nodded.

The Major's body suddenly sagged.

'Has he told you what terrors are tormenting him?' he asked.

Arthur took another sip of Scotch.

'Aye, he has.' His face was sombre. 'When Tommy was on the hospital ship, he was looked after by a Red Cross nurse. He told me his memory is vague as he was in and out of consciousness, but he could remember her face. The ship got hit. They were able to get into lifeboats, but a lone bomber emptied its load and they all went in. Tommy said it was chaos. One minute they were about to be rescued, the next they'd been chucked into the Atlantic. He saw the nurse struggling to keep herself from going under. Swam to her, but she was dragged under.'

'Her clothes,' the Major muttered, knowing it was often the heavy weight of sodden clothes that beat even the strongest of swimmers.

'Exactly,' Arthur said. 'Tommy said he dived. Found her and tried to get to her but she gulped in water and that was it. It was too late. Drowned. Dead by the time he reached her.'

The Major's face was flushed. His free hand was gripping the arm of his wheelchair.

'Tommy said it's her face he sees in his sleep – at the very moment that life leaves her. He says he spends his night swimming. Desperately trying to reach her, but failing. He can't forget her face. One of the things that gets him the most is that he never got to thank her for helping him.'

'And he can't remember anything more about her?'

'No, just that she was young.' Arthur paused. 'He remembered her voice. Sounds like she was from the Dales.'

'A Yorkshire lass?'

'Aye.'

The two men drank in silence, deep in thought.

After a little while, the Major drained his glass.

'I've got an idea,' he said as he wheeled himself towards the nest of tables by the side of the sofa.

Picking up the black Bakelite telephone from the polished wooden top, he put it on his lap. He lifted the receiver and dialled the operator.

Armed with just the name of the Red Cross ship that had been hit, the Major made a few calls to those in the know, as well to those who owed him a favour.

Half an hour later he had acquired the information he needed.

Handing Arthur a piece of paper on which he had scrawled a name and address, he leant back in his wheelchair.

'It's worth a try,' he said. 'And if it doesn't stop Tommy's night terrors, it might well help that lassie's poor parents. Give them some kind of solace that their brave and selfless daughter was saving lives to the bitter end.'

Chapter Thirty-Two

The Maison Nouvelle, Holmeside, Sunderland

'Arms up as though you are a bird in flight,' Kate told Charlotte.

The pair were standing in front of the workbench in the middle of the Maison Nouvelle.

'This just needs taking in here ... and here.' Kate spoke more to herself than to Charlotte as she carefully pinned in both sides of the dress.

'So, people just give you clothes they don't want?' Charlotte asked, amazed that someone could have voluntarily relinquished the lovely red dress she was now wearing.

'They do,' Kate said. 'Arms down.'

'But why didn't the person want this dress any more?' Charlotte asked.

'It's not my place to ask why,' Kate said. 'Turn around.'

Charlotte did as she was told and Kate put more pins into the back of the dress where she was going to make a pleat.

'Do you ever go back to Whitburn?' Charlotte asked.

Kate stood up straight, took a step back and inspected her handiwork.

'No,' she said.

Charlotte sensed this was a topic that was not up for discussion.

'I think this dress was destined to be yours,' Kate said. 'You're going to be the belle of the ball – or I should say, the weddings.'

Kate bent down to check the hem, which she had pinned earlier.

Charlotte looked around the shop at the rolls of fabric stacked up against the walls, and then back at Lily's green velvet dress, which was now hanging up on a hook.

'So, it's all right to wear red to a wedding?' Charlotte asked, looking down and thinking that she didn't care. She loved this dress and was going to wear it regardless.

'Of course,' Kate said, standing up straight again, her eyes still fixed on the hem. 'White is the big no-no, as only the bride should wear white – or green, in Lily's case.'

Charlotte watched as Kate walked over to the worktop and picked up her measuring tape. Just then the bell tinkled and the front door opened.

Kate spun round to see who it was.

They both stared as Alfie's head appeared around the door.

It took Charlotte a moment to recognise the face, having only ever seen it looming down at her from the timekeeper's cabin.

'Oh, Alfie.' Kate's voice sounded out her obvious relief. 'Come in, come in!' She turned back to Charlotte. 'Are you all right just staying like that for a few minutes, Charlie? This won't take long.'

Charlotte nodded, intrigued as to why Alfie was here – in a boutique of all places – and looking like he was just off to church.

'Here you are,' Kate said, bustling over to the rail of clothes and pulling out a pair of trousers.

'Ah, that's grand, thanks, Kate.' Alfie pulled out his wallet and took out a five-bob note.

'If you're not happy with them, just bring them back.'

'No, no, they'll be perfect.'

'Your nana keeping all right?'

'Yes, she's well. She sends her regards. And her thanks for "doing my job for me".'

'Tell your nana it keeps me in work, so it's me that should be thanking her,' Kate smiled, taking the money and giving Alfie his change.

'She was telling me there's a new movie in town called *Holiday Inn*.' Alfie started to shuffle about nervously on the spot. 'It's got Bing Crosby and Fred Astaire in it.'

'Oh, that's nice,' Kate said. 'Well, I hope she enjoys it. You can tell me if it's any good next time you're in.' She looked at Alfie, who didn't seem to be making a move. 'Well, you have a good evening.'

'Yes, you too.' Alfie reluctantly made his way to leave.

When he opened the door he turned and looked as though he was about to say something, but didn't.

'Bye, then,' he said, shutting the door carefully behind him.

Charlotte was still standing mannequin-like in the middle of the shop.

'I don't think it was his nana that wanted to see the film.'

'Really?' Kate said, distractedly. She was inspecting the scoop neckline on the dress. 'I hope Rosie doesn't think this is too low.'

'No, it's fine! Perfect the way it is,' Charlotte panicked. 'So,' she said, quickly changing the subject, 'Lily's dress is finished, is it?'

They both looked up at the stunning, emerald-green fishtail dress whose neckline was most definitely too low.

'Just about,' Kate said. 'Just a few little bits and bobs to add.'

'And,' Charlotte said, trying to sound as casual as possible, 'what is it exactly that Lily does again?'

For the first time Kate looked at Charlotte rather than the dress she was altering.

'What does Lily do?' Kate repeated.

Charlotte nodded.

'For a living?'

Charlotte nodded again.

'Mmm ...' Kate hesitated. 'Well ...'

'Only me!' Rosie's voice trilled out at the same time as the doorbell jangled and the shop door swung open. After Sister Bernadette's impromptu visit, Rosie always made a point of announcing her arrival.

'Ah, *Rosie*, perfect timing!' Kate said. 'You can see Charlie in her new dress before she takes it off.'

Rosie looked at her little sister, who, she realised, not for the first time, was not so little any more.

'Very grown-up,' she said. '*Too* grown-up for my liking ... And that neckline's a little low.' Rosie paused. Seeing the instant look of fear on Charlotte's face, she allowed herself a half-smile. 'But despite that, it does look rather lovely. And suits you to a T.'

Charlotte breathed a sigh of relief.

'Charlie was just asking what Lily does for a living.' Kate tried to sound nonchalant as she carefully unzipped the back of the dress.

'Oh, was she now?' Rosie gave Charlotte a puzzled look. 'Lily's doing the same thing as the last time you asked.' Rosie looked at her sister, a slight frown on her face. 'She has interests in a variety of businesses.'

'I was just wondering what *kinds* of businesses?' Charlotte said.

Rosie hesitated for a moment, not liking where the conversation was headed, but also not wanting to sound evasive.

'Lily's got a finger in a few pies,' Rosie said. 'This place being one of them.' She looked around the shop. 'And she owns a few properties, and a few stocks and shares here and there which she likes to play with.'

She looked at Charlotte.

'Why the sudden interest?'

'Just curious, that's all.'

'Well, curiosity killed the cat,' Rosie said. 'So why don't you just concentrate on your own *business* rather than everyone else's?'

'Go and get changed,' Kate said, walking over to the back room that also doubled as a changing room. 'But be really careful with the pins. I'll wait here and you can just pass it out to me.'

As soon as Charlotte was behind the curtain, Rosie and Kate exchanged looks.

'So,' Rosie said, delving into the pocket of her overalls, 'I've got everyone's clothing coupons.'

Kate's face lit up.

'That's fantastic!'

'What's fantastic?' Charlotte's voice sounded from behind the curtain at the same time as her bare arm appeared holding out the red dress. Kate took it.

'What did I just say about curiosity killing the cat?'

'What's *fantastic*,' Kate spoke through the curtain, 'is that Rosie and her squad – and just about everyone else Polly knows – have all donated their clothes rations so that I can make a decent wedding dress for Polly. Even Helen's put hers in.'

'Wow!' Charlotte drew the room divider back dramatically. 'That *is* fantastic. You can have mine as well.'

'Don't worry, yours have already been donated,' Rosie said.

Kate and Rosie both looked at Charlotte.

'A trip to the hairdressers might be a good idea sometime soon,' Rosie mused.

'No, it's fine the way it is.' Charlotte couldn't get her words out quickly enough.

'I think Charlie wants to grow her hair long.' Kate looked at Rosie, widening her eyes. 'Like Polly's.'

'Really?' Rosie teased. 'Rather than have a nice, practical bowl cut like Martha's?'

Charlotte scowled by way of response.

'I can tidy it up for her,' Kate said. 'I have some proper hairdressing scissors.'

'I think you've got enough on your plate,' Rosie said, glancing up at Lily's green dress. 'Two weddings to deal with, as well as your normal work.'

'Oh, don't worry about me,' Kate said. 'The busier the better. Anyway, I've more or less finished Lily's dress and to be honest, I thought Polly might have some bridesmaids that would need dressing – but it would seem not. Lucille's going to be the only bridesmaid, and she doesn't need a dress. Bel says she's obsessed with this one particular yellow dress she's had since she was two. Apparently, every time she grows out of it, Bel just gets her another one in the next size up.'

Rosie chuckled. She and the rest of her squad had all heard about Lucille and her yellow dress.

'Bel's going to be the matron of honour, but I don't even have to make her a new dress. She's going to wear her wedding dress.'

They all automatically looked towards the window where the dress was displayed.

'Actually,' Rosie said, 'I think everyone's a little disappointed that it's going to be a rather quiet, down-at-heel affair – everyone, that is, apart from the bride herself, who says she'd be just as happy walking down the aisle in her overalls as long as Tommy was waiting for her at the altar, although I have a sneaking suspicion that she'd secretly love to have a new wedding dress. Not that she'd ever admit it.'

'Am I right in saying they're not even going to have a proper reception?' Kate asked.

'Sandwiches and tea at Tatham Street. But I think everyone'll end up in the pub afterwards. Bill said he'd shut off half the bar and the snug.'

'Are they having a honeymoon?' Kate asked.

Rosie shook her head.

'Well,' Kate said, trying to sound positive, 'at least they have each other, eh? And Tommy's alive and back for good.'

'Exactly,' Rosie agreed. 'Polly says he's coming on in leaps and bounds. Putting on a bit of weight thanks to Agnes's cooking.'

Charlotte was standing quietly, taking in every word. She had been captivated by Polly and Tommy's love affair since first hearing about it.

'Come on, then,' Rosie said, turning to Charlotte. 'We've taken up enough of Kate's time. She's got another wedding dress to design.'

Kate gave Charlotte a hug.

'Drop by at the weekend. I should have your dress ready by then.'

Charlotte stood and stared through the brown anti-blast tape at Bel's dress while Rosie scrabbled about in her bag for her little electric torch. She'd just found it when they heard the sound of two pairs of high heels click-clacking on the pavement.

'*Rosie – is that you?*'

Charlotte and Rosie looked up to see Vivian and Maisie emerging through the darkness of the blackout. They were both done up to the nines. Rosie cursed inwardly.

'It *is*!' Vivian said in her usual Mae West drawl. 'And would I be wrong in guessing that this is the little runaway, Charlotte?'

Maisie flashed a weak beam of light from her own pocket torch, making Charlotte squint.

'Yes, it is,' Rosie said, turning to her sister.

'Charlotte, this is Vivian and Maisie, who lodge with Lily and George.'

Charlotte's mouth dropped open and her eyes widened as she stared at the two starlets who looked like they had just stepped off a Hollywood film set.

'Pleased to meet you, Charlotte.' Maisie stretched out a gloved hand.

'And you, too,' Charlotte said, shaking it.

'You working tonight?' Vivian asked Rosie.

'I'll probably do a few hours.'

'Oh, she's a cherub, isn't she? And what lovely hair.' She curled a loose strand of Charlotte's wayward brown hair around a long, glossy-red fingernail. 'Could do with a bit of a tidy up, though.'

She looked at Charlotte.

'I'm known for my skills with the scissors, amongst other things!' She let out a deep, throaty laugh.

Charlotte finally found her voice. 'I'm growing it long.'

'Of course, honeybun, but ya still need to keep it trim.'

'So,' Rosie interrupted, 'you two got dates tonight?'

'Yes,' Maisie said, gently taking Vivian's arm. 'We're just checking in on our Kate, and then we're off to the Grand.'

'Well,' Rosie said, turning on her torch, 'have a good night.'

'Rosie?'

'Yes?'

They were walking up Holmeside. Away from the boutique, heading for home.

'Doesn't Bel have a sister called Maisie?'

'Yes.'

'But that's obviously not her, is it?'

'What do you mean that it's *obviously* not her?'

'Well, obviously, because Bel is white, and Maisie is coloured.'

'Not if Bel and Maisie had different fathers.'

'Really?' Charlotte was intrigued. 'So Pearl was married to a black man?'

'I don't know about *married*, but from what I gather, she was in a relationship with a stoker from the West Indies.'

'Really?' The intrigue in Charlotte's voice was clear. 'But Maisie doesn't sound as though she's from here? She speaks like a southerner.'

'That's because she is.' Rosie checked the road and grabbed Charlotte's arm as they crossed over and began walking up Vine Place. 'Pearl had Maisie adopted. Down south.'

'Really?'

They walked on for a few moments.

Rosie could almost hear her sister's brain whirring at full speed.

'So, how come she's up here now?'

Rosie stepped up her pace.

'From what I gathered,' she said, 'Maisie wanted to find her birth mother, which obviously she did.'

Rosie deliberately left out the drama of Maisie turning up at Bel and Joe's wedding reception and declaring her parentage to all and sundry. A declaration that had sent Pearl off on a bender, culminating in her trying to end it all by taking a swim in the middle of the night down Hendon beach.

'What? And she decided to *stay* up here?'

'That's right.'

'So she got lodgings at Lily's? With Kate and the American woman, Vivian?'

'That's right.' Rosie decided not to enlighten Charlotte about Vivian's Liverpudlian roots.

'And what does Maisie do? For a living?' Charlotte asked.

God, why did Charlotte have to be so damned inquisitive?

'Honestly, Charlie. Why are you so obsessed with what people do for a living?'

Charlotte thought about it for a moment.

'I suppose I'm just curious.' As soon as the words were out of her mouth, she laughed. 'I know, I know. Curiosity … cats …'

They walked on. Charlotte hurrying to keep up the pace.

'I think,' Charlotte said, a little breathlessly, 'I'm just wondering about what I might want to do. You know, when I get older.'

'I think you've got plenty of time for that,' Rosie said. 'Anyway, I thought you wanted to go to university? Put that intelligent and overactive brain of yours to use?'

Charlotte smiled. She loved it when her sister gave her a compliment. Even if it was a backhanded one. And even if it was because Rosie was avoiding her question.

Why, though, did her sister seem so reticent to talk about Lily and anyone associated with her?

Chapter Thirty-Three

The following day

Monday 23 November

'Pol, I need to talk to you about something.'

Tommy saw the instant look of worry.

'It's nothing bad.' He paused. 'Well, it is, and it isn't.'

The look of worry on Polly's face deepened.

'Bloody hell, I'm not saying this right!'

Tommy sat up straight on the sofa and pushed his hand through his hair in frustration. They'd been out for a walk along the river and had just returned to the Major's flat.

'What I mean is that it's nothing *really* bad.' He paused again. 'Just might not be very pleasant. For you anyway.'

'What is it, Tommy?' Polly took hold of her fiancé's hand, forcing him to sit back. She let out a nervous laugh. 'Explain. You're talking in riddles.'

'It's something Arthur thinks I should tell you. Says it's not good to keep things from each other. "Be honest 'n open from the start," he keeps saying. "Begin as you mean to go on."'

'Yes ... And?' Polly was searching Tommy's face, trying to read him.

Tommy took a deep breath. He opened his mouth to speak but nothing came out.

'Why don't you start at the beginning?' Polly tried to help.

Tommy looked at her and nodded.

'Yes. The beginning.'

And so Polly listened as Tommy relayed everything that had happened that awful day on the Atlantic.

When he finished, he looked at Polly.

He took a deep, shuddering breath.

'Ever since, I've had these terrible nightmares. I see her die every night in my sleep. Every night I try and save her. Every night I fail.

'Arthur knows about them. Matron told him. He asked me about them. The Major knows ... Obviously ... I'm probably keeping the poor bloke awake at night.'

He looked at Polly.

'He claims he doesn't sleep anyway. Says that night terrors are normal – a "by-product" of war. Or so he says ...' His voice trailed off.

'I'm guessing that's why you didn't want to move into Tatham Street?'

Tommy nodded.

Polly looked at the man she loved, at the dark circles under his eyes, and now knew their cause.

'Nothing can change the way I feel about you, Tommy. You must know that?'

'Nothing?'

'Nothing.'

They held each other.

After a little while, Tommy put his hand in his trouser pocket and pulled out a scrap of paper on which was scrawled a name and address. He gave it to Polly.

'Her parents?'

Tommy nodded.

'You want to go and see them?'

'I do.'

Chapter Thirty-Four

Four days later

Thursday 26 November

Tommy felt a slight shiver of nerves. He had no idea whether his visit to this little two-up two-down terraced house in the village of Ruswarp, just a mile outside of Whitby in North Yorkshire, would be received well. He also didn't know whether the two-and-a-half-hour journey there would end with the slamming of a door in his face. Grief affected people in different ways. He knew that from his own personal experience. Losing his mother so suddenly and so unexpectedly when he was a boy had brought him anger rather than sadness. But that had been a different situation.

Tommy adjusted his uniform. He straightened the lapels and brushed the stiff shoulders with the palm of his hand. Not that it needed it. He looked impeccable. His Royal Navy petty officer's jacket and trousers had been cleaned and pressed by Agnes. She had taken great pride in doing so. Had told him what he was doing was both brave and admirable, but not to worry if he was not welcomed with open arms. Agnes had taken hold of his hands and held them in a firm grip. She had said that she was proud of her future son-in-law. Just as Arthur and Polly and all those he knew were proud of him.

Tommy had been taken aback by Agnes's words and for the first time since he was small, he'd felt what it must be like to have a mother.

Tommy raised his hand and knocked on the door, which looked as though it had recently been painted black.

He thought of Polly, whom he had left sightseeing in the seaside resort of Whitby. She had understood his wanting her company, as well as his need to see Catherine's parents on his own.

Taking a deep breath, Tommy could feel the pull of his starched navy-blue uniform against his chest. He had put on weight these past few weeks. His appetite had come back tenfold since leaving hospital. Thanks to Agnes's cooking, his growing hunger had been more than satiated. A part of him felt guilty for feeling so well.

'Good afternoon,' said the diminutive woman who answered the door. She was dressed from head to toe in black.

Tommy immediately took off his cap and pressed it against his chest.

'Good afternoon. Am I speaking with Mrs Reid?'

'Yes, you are, young man.' The woman's voice sounded familiar. It took Tommy a second to realise why. Like mother like daughter.

'My name is Tommy Watts. Petty Officer Tommy Watts. I wondered if Mr Reid was also at home?'

The woman's dark brown hair was scraped away from her face into a bun. Her face was pale and there were the beginnings of wrinkles around her eyes. She had the same kind, dark brown eyes that visited him every night.

'Yes, he's out back. In the garden tending vegetables.' Her Yorkshire accent was distinct. Her voice soft, almost gentle.

'Do you think it would be possible to speak with yer both?'

Mrs Reid's eyes dropped to look at Tommy's uniform and back up to his face. A face that looked nervous and sad.

'Is it about Catherine?' she asked. Tommy nodded. She opened the door and Tommy stepped over the threshold.

'Please, go 'n sit in the front reception room.'

She shut the front door and showed Tommy into the lounge.

'I'll go get Mr Reid.'

Tommy stood in the middle of the living room and looked out of the front window. It had not been covered in anti-blast tape. He heard the back door open, then close and then the sound of splashing water. His eyes strayed to the mantelpiece and he caught his breath. He knew that face so well. Had lived with it for the past five months. The night-time visitations made it feel much longer.

'Aye, she were a bonny lass.'

Tommy turned to see Mr Reid enter the room. The mud patches on the knees of his trousers showed he had come straight in from the garden. His clean, outstretched hand showed it had been him at the sink.

'Would you like a cup o' tea, lad?' Mr Reid asked. His handshake was firm. 'The wife says you've come from the north-east? She's good with placing dialects. You must have had a long journey. A few hours at least.'

'Thank you,' Tommy said. 'But I don't want to put either of yer to any bother.'

'Milk 'n sugar?'

Tommy nodded.

Mr Reid walked out to the hallway.

'Milk 'n sugar for the lad, pet.'

'Sit down,' Mr Reid said. 'I need to rest my legs even if you don't.'

Mr Reid asked Tommy where in the north-east he hailed from, and on hearing he was from Sunderland, County

Durham, the conversation naturally led to chat about the collieries and the shipyards and Tommy told him that he had been employed as a dock diver by the Wear Commission before he'd signed up.

Mrs Reid came into the room with two china teacups, handed them to her husband and their visitor and returned with her own.

Tommy took a sup of the strong Yorkshire brew before putting his cup and saucer down on the coffee table.

'I'm sorry to intrude,' Tommy said. 'On yer life, and also on yer grief.'

Mr Reid took his wife's hand and held it tight.

'And if at any point yer want me to stop talking, just say, and I will.'

They both nodded.

'I wanted to come here today to tell yer about yer daughter, Catherine.' As he started to speak Tommy suddenly felt overcome by emotion. He had to blink back the tears. *Be strong! This is their pain. Not yours.*

'Catherine looked after me when I was on the hospital ship. I was very ill 'n she nursed me. Looked after me. She was kind 'n gentle.'

Tommy paused.

Swallowed hard.

'I was in 'n out of consciousness, but it was her face that I saw, her voice that I heard telling me that I was going to be all right. That I was safe. That I was now in good hands … And I was.'

Tommy looked at the couple opposite him. Their eyes had filled with tears. Their attention was unfaltering. They continued holding hands.

'When the ship took a hit, it was Catherine who made sure I got on a lifeboat. It was yer daughter who put other lives before her own. She never once showed fear. She was calm, always speaking to me, telling me that help was coming. She must have been fearful, but not once did it show.'

Tommy noticed Mr Reid glance at the photo on the mantelpiece.

'She was truly courageous in every sense of the word,' Tommy said simply. 'When the lifeboat capsized, we all went into the water.' Tommy paused, looking at the couple. Tears were now streaming down both their faces.

'Carry on, lad.' The strength in Mr Reid's voice belied the devastation showing on his weather-beaten face.

'I'm a diver, as you know, Mr Reid.' Tommy looked at them both, watching for any signs that they wanted him to stop telling them how their child had died.

Surely there could be no greater torment.

'I tried to save her,' Tommy continued. He took a deep breath, desperately trying to keep the pressing sorrow that threatened to engulf him at bay. 'I would have given my life for hers if I could.'

He stopped.

'I'm so sorry, Mr and Mrs Reid. So sorry that I couldn't. That I wasn't able to save her. I am so sorry that it is me 'n not Catherine who is sat here now.'

Tommy's vision was now blurred. He blinked hard.

'I just wanted – needed – to tell yer how heroic yer daughter was. How caring 'n kind 'n loving she was to someone she didn't even know ... And I am certain I won't have been the only one she saved.'

Another pause.

'But I might be the only one who is able to come here 'n tell yer about yer daughter.'

Mrs Reid finally gave in to her grief. Her cries were muffled by her husband's chest as he held her tightly. His own tears continued to fall silently.

'Thank you,' Mr Reid said simply. 'Thank you for coming here and telling us.'

Mrs Reid sat up and pulled a hanky from her sleeve and dried her eyes.

She stood up and walked over to Tommy and took his hand.

'Catherine will be so glad you took the time to come here and visit us,' she said, a smile spreading across her face, now wet with tears as she spoke the name of her daughter.

'All she ever wanted was to be a nurse. Even when she was a little girl, she'd patch up her dollies. When she got older, she'd practise on me and her father.'

Mrs Reid straightened her back and looked at the sepia studio portrait of her only child.

'We've never had a body to bury,' she said. 'But I feel you've brought her back to us.'

She nodded. Gave Tommy a sad smile and left the room.

Mr Reid got up and walked over to the sideboard. He poured out two good measures of whisky and handed one to Tommy.

He sat back down and raised his glass.

'To my dear girl, Catherine.'

'To Catherine,' Tommy said.

For the next hour the two men chatted. Mr Reid had also been in the Royal Navy and had served in the First War. He told Tommy a little about his time on HMS *Neptune*, which Tommy knew had been the flagship of the Home Fleet.

As Mr Reid talked, his voice became addled with regret. He poured them both another Scotch and said that he believed it had been his daughter's love of hearing about his life at sea that had propelled her to volunteer to work for the Red Cross, and in particular to become a nurse on a hospital ship.

They sat quietly for a little while.

Tommy knew to respect the silence.

There was nothing he could say that would offer any kind of comfort that might ease the suffering of a parent who had lost their child.

Their only child.

Mr Reid exhaled a long breath before pulling out a packet of Player's from his shirt pocket. Offering one to Tommy, who declined with a shake of his head, he pulled the ashtray on the coffee table close, lit up his cigarette and asked Tommy about his work as a mine-clearance diver.

Through billows of smoke he listened as Tommy told him about the Italian frogmen, their limpet mines, and about naval life out in Gibraltar.

When Tommy got up to leave, Mr Reid shook his hand.

'You take care, lad.'

Tommy nodded.

He walked out into the hallway to see Mrs Reid appearing from the kitchen with a parcel tied with string.

'Sandwiches. For the journey,' she said.

'Thank you, Mrs Reid. That's very kind of yer. Thank you.'

Tommy knew why Catherine had become the person she was.

'Do you have a sweetheart?' Mrs Reid asked.

'Aye, a fiancée. We're getting married in a few weeks.' Tommy always felt his heart lift whenever he thought of Polly.

'Well, you make sure you both bring life into this world,' Mrs Reid said. Her words took Tommy aback. They were unexpected.

'You're a good man,' she continued. 'And I'm sure your fiancée is a good woman. If anything were to happen to you, she'll need a part of you to keep her going. To give her the will to live and remind her of the man she loved.'

Tommy nodded again. Knowing that the couple now standing saying their goodbyes would have given anything to have a grandchild to remind them of their daughter.

This couple, Tommy knew, would be in mourning for the rest of their lives.

He walked down the short pathway, turning back to give a brief salute.

As he walked away from the house, thoughts that had been creeping into his head of late were now starting to gain momentum.

Chapter Thirty-Five

The bus journey from Ruswarp to Whitby took a quarter of an hour.

Looking out the window, Tommy could see the trees had now been stripped of their leaves. Autumn was morphing into winter, making Tommy aware of time.

And how quickly it went.

It took Tommy another ten minutes to walk to their pre-arranged meeting place – a little cafeteria down from the ruins of the famous Whitby Abbey.

Spotting Polly sitting by the window of the café, he waved and increased his pace.

Polly, too, had seen her fiancé from afar, looking so dashing in his smart naval uniform. She returned his wave just as the waitress appeared at the table with a pot of tea for two.

This morning, when he had come to collect her from Tatham Street, it had been the first time she had seen him in full regalia. He had taken her breath away. Made her heart hammer more than it normally did whenever she saw him. But it had also given her a feeling of unease, although she was unsure why.

Heads turned as Tommy's entrance was heralded by a particularly loud brass bell above the glass-fronted door. He was oblivious to the stir he caused, his eyes fixed solely on Polly. Taking off his peaked cap, he manoeuvred his way around a handful of tables.

Reaching her, he bent down and kissed her full on the lips.

'Perfect timing,' he said, looking at the tea tray. 'How did you know I was due?'

Polly laughed as he pulled out a chair and sat down.

'It must be the Irish in me. I have the gift of foresight,' she joked in a convincing Gaelic accent. 'Or just an educated guess.'

Tommy put the greaseproof-paper parcel on the table.

'Sandwiches. From Mrs Reid. I thought we could have them on the train back.'

'Good idea.' Polly looked at Tommy, thankful that those in the café had finished ogling her fiancé and were carrying on with their own conversations. 'Hopefully it won't be so packed on the way back.'

She put a warm hand on top of his.

'So, how did it go?'

Tommy thought for a moment.

'It went well. Or rather, as well as could be expected.' He paused. 'I think they were glad I visited.'

Polly poured their tea, and asked more questions about Mr and Mrs Reid. Tommy told of their kind welcome, of their sadness, and also their stoicism on hearing of their daughter's last moments. Polly listened and forced back her own tears. Inwardly she railed against the injustices of this war that was killing so many innocents, bringing such unbearable grief to those who didn't deserve it. Again, she felt blessed that she had been spared. That the man she loved had lived and had come back to her.

As Tommy talked, he became aware of a strange feeling of release. Watching Polly refill their china cups, he felt as though the tight bond tying him to the woman whose name he now knew had loosened. He had finally been cast adrift.

Like Mrs Reid had said, Catherine was now with those she should be with.

Not wanting to leave the cosiness of the café and each other's company, they ordered another pot of tea and two scones, and Polly told Tommy about the hours she had spent without him in the little seaside town.

She had looked at the statue of Captain Cook, who had learnt his trade here working on the colliers, shipping coal from the port. She had walked through the famous whalebone arch that commemorated the town's whaling industry and strolled around the harbour. Last of all she had walked up the one hundred and ninety-nine steps and visited St Mary's Church, where she had said a prayer of thanks for the return of the man she loved.

When they left the café, it was dark. It took them a quarter of an hour to stroll back across the bridge, along New Quay Road, before arriving at the train station.

'No more trains this evening, I'm afraid,' the stationmaster announced on seeing them. The weariness with which he spoke suggested he had had to repeat the news several times already.

'What's the problem?' Tommy asked.

'Summat at Middlesbrough depot. Not sure what. Possible air raid. Or could just be technical.' He huffed. 'Course I'm always last t'know. Am only stationmaster, after all.'

'Buses?' Polly asked.

'Last bus left an hour ago. No more now till mornin'.' And with that the old man ambled over to the main entrance and closed the gates, having seen more travellers heading up the street.

'Well, that's a turn-up for the books,' Tommy said, looking at Polly.

'I think we're well and truly stranded,' she replied, looking around and trying to find a solution to their transport problem.

Tommy pulled her close.

'Well, you know what they say?'

Polly shook her head, enjoying the closeness of their bodies.

'Every cloud has a silver lining.'

'And our silver lining is?'

'We make our trip into a proper break. Get ourselves a bed and breakfast?'

Polly looked up at Tommy and laughed.

'I don't think we have much of a choice.'

Twenty minutes later they knocked on the door of a B & B on West Cliff that looked out over the North Sea. They had pooled the money they had on them. It was enough for a room, but not for two separate ones.

After they had explained that their train had been cancelled, the owner, an old woman with no teeth and wearing the traditional black dress and shawl of a widow, agreed they could share a room, but not before she had inspected Tommy's uniform from top to bottom, enquired about his rank and then scrutinised Polly's diamond and ruby engagement ring.

'Are you all right about all of this?' Tommy asked Polly when they went to freshen up. Their room on the first floor was spotlessly clean.

'Of course,' Polly said, trying to hide her nerves.

'What happens if I start screaming and shouting like a banshee in my sleep?' Tommy asked.

'Well then, I'll just wake you up,' Polly said matter-of-factly.

'All right. But I apologise in advance,' he said, although he doubted very much he would be able to sleep. Not only for fear of scaring Polly, but because he had dreamed of the day when he would share a bed with her for such a long time that sleep would seem a sacrilege.

'Well,' Tommy said, looking at the sandwiches he had put on top of the drawers. 'Thanks to Mrs Reid we aren't going to starve. And I reckon we have enough change for half a pint of beer and a gin and tonic.' He emptied his pockets of coins.

'Perfect,' Polly said, hoping the money they had left might stretch to an extra shot of gin. This was, after all, to be their first night together.

It didn't take them long to find a small tavern by the riverside where they were able to get a table in the corner and enjoy their shared sandwiches and drinks.

They both admitted they weren't terribly hungry and agreed that it felt rather lovely knowing they had the whole night together, not having to part at the end when all they wanted to do was be in each other's arms.

Tonight, they would be.

As stipulated by the old woman, they were back by ten o'clock.

When they entered their room, they saw she had left out an old nightdress for Polly and a pair of what might well have been her husband's pyjamas for Tommy.

'Now, I'm more than happy to sleep on the floor, if you'd feel more comfortable?' Tommy eyed Polly, keeping his fingers firmly crossed she would reject the suggestion.

'It's probably no harder than my bunk in Gibraltar,' he added.

'Well, thank goodness you won't ever have to sleep there again.'

Tommy looked as though he was about to say something, but didn't.

'So, no, I most certainly do *not* want you sleeping on the floor,' Polly said.

After they'd changed and climbed into bed, Tommy wrapped his arms around Polly and pulled her close.

'I think I've died 'n gone to heaven.' He looked at Polly and kissed her on the lips. 'I think I'll stay like this all night, just looking at you.'

Polly smiled, relaxing into the warmth of his body. 'Just think, we'll soon be able to be together like this every night for ever and ever.'

Tommy kissed Polly. He wanted to talk to her. Share what he was thinking and feeling. He knew that it was important that he was honest with her. Arthur's advice was right – be open and honest from the start. But this evening had been so perfect, so lovely, he couldn't – wouldn't – do or say anything to jeopardise it.

He kissed Polly again and she responded. They kissed and caressed, showing the love they felt for one another.

'I love you, Tommy. And I want to be with you in all ways.' Polly's voice was breathy with desire. 'But I want to wait until we're married.' She looked at Tommy and saw the fire of passion in his eyes. 'We've waited this long. Just another few weeks and then we can make love every night forever more if we wish.'

Tommy kissed Polly again, forcing himself to hold back his ardour.

'I understand,' he said, squeezing her gently.

What he would have given to simply click his fingers and for those weeks to have passed. For their wedding to have been celebrated and for this to be the night of their honeymoon.

He held her in his arms, fighting sleep, but failing.

After a while he heard Polly's breathing change and knew she too was losing the battle to make the night longer.

Chapter Thirty-Six

The following day

Friday 27 November

Polly rested her head on Tommy's shoulder as they sat squashed together on the train back to Sunderland. The old woman had given them a hearty breakfast of toast and kippers before seeing them off with a toothless smile, telling them to come back and stay when they were married. Polly had told her that they would. Tommy had shaken her hand and given her a kiss on the cheek, causing the old woman to blush.

It might just have been tiredness making her perception a little off-kilter, or the fact that her emotions were riding high, but Polly felt there had been a change in Tommy. A good change. But a change all the same. He seemed more at peace with himself after his visit to Mr and Mrs Reid. And last night, as they had both drifted in and out of sleep, there had been no thrashing around or crying out with nightmares.

The squeal of the steam engine as it pulled into Seaham station caused them both to sit up.

'You all right?' Tommy asked quietly.

Polly nodded.

'More than all right.'

'You?'

'Looking forward to making you my wife.'

Polly kissed him on the cheek and whispered, 'Me too.'

*

When they reached the front door of 34 Tatham Street, Tommy cupped Polly's face in his hands and kissed her gently.

'I'll come around for yer this evening. After you've got back from work,' he said.

'Will you rest today?' Polly had seen how tired he got after walking just short distances. She knew that behind the show of bravado, there was still a man who was far from back to his normal self.

'Don't you be worrying about me. Just take care in that yard. I don't want anything to scupper our wedding plans.'

Polly gently took the lapels of his jacket in her hands and pulled him towards her.

'Don't worry. There'll be no scuppering.' She kissed him.

The front door swung open just as Tommy started to kiss Polly back.

'Thank goodness yer both back!' Agnes looked at them. 'Go 'n get yerself a cuppa,' she told Polly.

'See you later.' Polly gave Tommy a quick kiss and disappeared indoors.

Agnes eyed her future son-in-law.

'Joe went to the station last night. Found out yer train had been cancelled.' She put her hands on her hips. 'I'm presuming yer both managed to find beds for the night. I stress the word *beds*. As in *more than one*.'

Tommy had to force back a smile. He loved Agnes to pieces. She was the archetypal lioness, forever protective of her cubs.

'We did,' Tommy said. His voice was deadly serious. 'You can rest assured. You have no worries there.'

Agnes continued to scrutinise him.

'Mmm,' she said. 'It's a good job the wedding's only a few weeks away.'

'Twenty-two days and counting,' Tommy said with a twinkle in his eye as he turned to go.

'Well, you just keep counting, young man,' Agnes shouted after him.

Polly stood in the hallway, listening to the interaction between her ma and fiancé before turning and going into the kitchen.

'Ah, yer back.' Arthur eased himself out of his chair, but gave up and sat back down. Polly leant over and gave him a big hug. He seemed so much older and more fragile of late.

Agnes bustled back into the kitchen. She gave her daughter a look like the summons and carried on into the scullery.

'How did it go with Mr and Mrs Reid?' Arthur asked.

'Well, they sounded like a lovely couple.' Polly bent down to stroke Tramp. 'I think it was a good thing to do. Tommy seemed a lot more at ease after he'd seen them.'

Arthur looked at Polly. He dropped his voice.

'No nightmares?'

Polly shook her head, looking back nervously to make sure her ma wasn't earwigging. Agnes was peeling potatoes rather zealously.

'No,' she said quietly.

'Good,' he said, putting his hand out to stroke Pup, who had bounded back into the room with Agnes and was now demanding attention from the old man.

'We have the Major to thank for that,' he said, ruffling the dog's head. 'And the love of a good woman.' He thought it might well have been Polly's presence next to his grandson last night that had buffeted away the terrors, as much as his chat with the nurse's mother and father.

'It's good that yer went with him,' Arthur added. 'Now we just need to make yer the second Mrs Watts.'

Polly looked down at the engagement ring that Arthur had bought Flo when they were just seventeen years old. She knew theirs had been a true love. A strong love.

'Actually, I've got something to ask you, Arthur?' Polly looked at the old man.

'Oh aye, and what might that be?'

'Would you give me away?'

Arthur's pale blue eyes lit up.

'I'd be honoured to, pet ... Honoured, I would.' This time he forced himself out of his chair and took hold of Polly's hands.

'You've made an old man very happy. Very happy indeed.'

Agnes continued to peel her potatoes in the scullery.

She couldn't think of anyone better to take the place of her Harry.

Chapter Thirty-Seven

Kate was looking out the front window of the Maison Nouvelle.

She could have gone and stood outside to wait for Alfie, but it was too cold and windy. She didn't know which she hated more. Both brought back awful memories that she would never get rid of, no matter how hard she worked. No matter how much she filled her mind with fabrics, fashion and haute couture. They would always be there. Lurking in the background.

Just as long as they stayed in the background.

Kate's ability to keep them buried – or at least partially so – had been so much harder since Sister Bernadette's impromptu visit back in January. The nun's hate-filled words had been vile, but it had been her presence that had instilled the terrible fear in her. Simply by walking into the boutique, Sister Bernadette had dragged the horrors of Kate's past into her present. A past she thought she had escaped.

Seeing Alfie cross the main road, straightening his hair with both hands, Kate took a deep breath. She had to do this. She had to be brave. She couldn't live her life in a bubble – bobbing between the safety of the boutique and the bordello. It was like Lily kept telling her – she was young, she had to spread her wings. Or at the very least be able to make the journey from the centre of town to Thompson's.

Kate opened the door just as Alfie reached the shop. He was wearing his Sunday best. He had been wearing it under his overalls all morning at work as there wasn't time to go home and get changed before going to fetch Kate.

'I'm all ready,' she said, forcing a smile she didn't feel.

She turned and locked the front door to the boutique.

'Right, let's do this,' she said.

Alfie offered her his arm.

She looked at it, hesitating, before slipping a gloved hand through its crook.

As Polly hurried to work, she felt light. Almost weightless and so extraordinarily happy. So totally in love. It didn't matter that the cold was biting and that the day was grey.

When she reached Thompson's she was surprised to see an old man in the timekeeper's office.

'One one one,' Polly shouted out. 'Is Alfie all right?' she asked, taking her time card.

'Aye, pet, he's on some sort of an errand. I'm just covering for the lad.'

Polly smiled and hurried across the yard. It was a quarter of an hour before the start of the afternoon shift.

The clamour of the canteen hit her as soon as she stepped through the door. She hurried over to where she knew the women would be.

'Polly!' Dorothy jumped up out of her chair with such excitement it clattered backwards.

'She's back!' Angie declared.

'Eee, we didn't know if you'd be in,' Martha said.

'Bel told us you'd got stranded in Whitby,' Gloria said.

'Yeah, right. Stranded my foot!' Dorothy said, righting her chair and sitting back down.

'As if we believe that,' Angie chipped in.

'Not everyone's like you two,' Gloria batted back.

Polly laughed at the women's banter. She sat down and poured herself a cuppa from the pot in the middle of the table.

'We really *did* get stranded there,' Polly said. 'The last train got cancelled.'

'Well, we'll believe you—' Dorothy said.

'—thousands wouldn't!' Angie chimed in.

'Did you have a nice time?' Rosie asked.

'Yes, we did,' Polly said, unable to stop herself blushing.

'Eee, Pol, yer've gone all red.' Angie nudged Dorothy.

'Well, that's great to hear,' Rosie said. 'Now, I hope you don't mind us interfering in your wedding plans, but—'

'But if you do, it's tough, because we've interfered!' Dorothy couldn't stop herself.

Polly looked at the women, confusion on her face.

'You know how you said about getting a second-hand wedding dress?' Rosie asked.

'Or borrowing one,' Angie said.

'Yes,' Polly said, forcing herself to sound enthusiastic. 'I was going to have a look this weekend. Beryl was also going to get her dress down from the attic and I was going to see if it would be any good.'

'So we heard,' said Rosie. There had been a near riot when Bel had told them of Polly's plan. Much as they all liked Beryl, none of them held out much hope that her dress would be anywhere near decent, even in the unlikely event that it fitted.

'Well, we all decided – and by *we* I mean this motley crew.' She looked around at her squad. 'And, of course, Hannah. And Charlie.' Rosie rolled her eyes at the mention of her sister. 'And Bel and Marie-Anne. And Helen too. We all decided that we'd pool our resources and give you a joint wedding present. And that our wedding present to you would be—'

'—your wedding dress!' Dorothy and Angie almost shouted in unison.

Polly's face lit up.

'Really?'

'We've all pooled our clothing coupons,' Rosie continued, 'and handed them over to Kate so that she can make
you a dress. *Maison Nouvelle* style.'

Polly's eyes were growing wider by the second.

'But as time is of the essence, Kate needs to get started as
soon as possible,' Gloria explained.

'So,' Martha chipped in. 'You're going to get measured
up today.'

'Today?' Polly asked, trying to take in what she was
being told.

'Kate's coming here,' Rosie said. 'She should be arriving
any minute.'

'Oh, my goodness!' Polly said, shocked. 'I can't believe
it. Kate's going to make my dress? And you're all paying
for it?'

They all nodded.

Tears welled in Polly's eyes.

'Are you sure? I mean, you all need your coupons for
yourselves?' She looked at Dorothy and Angie. She knew
this was a massive sacrifice for them in particular. They
were forever complaining about not having anything to
wear.

'The hours we're working at the moment,' Angie said,
deadpan, 'we've no need fer them. All we ever wear these
days is our overalls. And we dinnit need coupons fer
them.'

'Agreed,' Dorothy said. 'Besides, we couldn't bear for
you to walk down the aisle in something wretched and
second-hand. Or worse still, *Beryl's* wedding dress. We're
really doing this for ourselves, aren't we?'

The women all nodded.

'And Kate's got the time?' Polly said. 'I thought she was
working flat out on Lily's dress?'

'It's just about done,' Rosie said. 'And you know Kate, she's not happy unless she's got a needle in her hand and a new design in her head.'

'So, you see,' Gloria chuckled, 'this is not really about you, but about everyone else.'

'My own wedding dress,' Polly said, starry-eyed.

Rosie smiled. She'd been right.

'I don't know what to say!' Polly looked round the table.

'Don't say anything,' Rosie said. 'Just get yourself up to Helen's office.' She looked at the wall clock. 'You've got half an hour to get measured up and have a chat about what you'd like.'

'Oh, gosh, I have no idea what I'd like,' Polly panicked.

'Even better,' Rosie said. 'That means Kate will have free rein to do exactly what she thinks.'

A big smile appeared on Polly's face.

'It's going to be amazing, isn't it?'

Rosie chuckled. 'I think that goes without saying. Now go, and we'll see you over in the dry basin when you're done.'

Kate knew that this was Polly's surprise. Her wedding present. She had been over the moon when Rosie had explained to her what all her squad had agreed on. She wasn't sure it was entirely necessary for her to go over and do the measuring up at the yard, rather than have Polly come to the shop, but she hadn't argued the case. She had already turned down a few jobs with wealthy clients who had wanted her to come to their houses. She knew that if she wanted to extend her business and grow her clientele, she had to be prepared to venture to other parts of the town than Holmeside and Ashbrooke.

'There's Thompson's,' Alfie pointed out as they stood at the front of the ferry. There was pride in his voice. 'And next to it is Crown's.'

Kate felt as though she was travelling to the other side of the world, not just to the other side of the river.

It had been nearly thirteen years since she had been to the north side of town.

'Nearly there,' Alfie said. 'See that ship in the dry dock?'

Kate nodded. She now felt frozen to the spot. She had one hand on the railing; the other was holding her black velvet cloche hat, which offered only a modicum of protection from the harsh weather.

'That's SS *Brutus*. She's to be launched in a few weeks.'

Kate nodded again and tried to smile. She knew it was the cargo vessel Rosie and her squad were working on. And she knew about the launch through Helen, whose dress was just about ready. It was a design she was particularly proud of. A perfect meshing of professionalism and femininity.

'She's exactly four hundred and twenty-three feet long – and eight inches,' Alfie informed her. 'She has a beam of fifty-seven feet and two inches.'

Kate had no idea what a beam was. She had never been particularly interested in the town's shipbuilding industry.

'And a depth of thirty-five feet and nine inches.'

Kate looked at Alfie. She liked his accuracy. It was something she prided herself on.

'And she'll be propelled by a triple-expansion steam engine.'

Kate smiled.

This time it was genuine.

When *W.F. Vint* arrived at the north ferry landing, Kate and Alfie were the first off, Alfie being a true gentleman and allowing his charge to go before him.

When they reached the timekeeper's cabin, Alfie waved up to the old man.

'Won't be long, Herbert,' he shouted out, taking Kate's arm and guiding her to the admin building. When they were safely inside the main entrance, Kate turned to her escort.

'Thank you, Alfie. I appreciate you coming to get me. I hope they won't have docked your wages?'

Alfie shook his head, although he wouldn't have cared if they'd docked an entire day.

'I'll take you back when you're done?' Alfie crossed his fingers.

'Are you sure that wouldn't be too much trouble?' Kate tried to disguise her relief.

Alfie's face lit up.

'No trouble at all! Just you come 'n get me when yer ready.'

Alfie disappeared back out into the yard and Kate made her way up the stairs.

Pushing the door open at the top, she was greeted by Bel's smiling face.

'Kate, you're here!'

She bustled over.

'Let me take your coat. Oh, and your lovely hat.'

She looked down at Kate's hands.

'And your gloves.'

Bel looked at Kate. She was as white as a sheet and she looked frozen to the bone. Still, she'd made it. She'd been warned that there was a chance Kate might back out at the last minute.

'Polly's going to be over the moon,' she said, carefully placing Kate's black funnel-neck coat across her arm. 'I've just seen her go into the canteen. The girls'll be telling her now.'

'Kate!'

Helen came bustling out of her office.

'You made it!'

Unlike Bel, Helen knew next to nothing about Kate's background and had no idea what an achievement it was for her to have made it here. All Helen knew about Kate was that she was a dressmaker sent from heaven.

'Gosh, you look freezing.' Helen looked across at Bel and Marie-Anne. They were the only workers left in the office, the rest of her staff having made a beeline for the door within minutes of the lunchtime klaxon sounding out.

'Marie-Anne, would you be so kind as to bring in a tea tray for two, please?'

'Of course,' Marie-Anne said. She had never known Helen be so polite.

Marie-Anne had just gone to make the tea when Polly came bursting through the door.

'Polly!' Bel hurried over to her sister-in-law and gave her a hug.

'Isn't this amazing?' Polly's face was flushed. 'Rosie told me about you all donating your clothing coupons and paying for the dress. I can't quite believe it.'

'I don't think any of us could bear to see you going down the aisle in some drab, second-hand dress.' Bel laughed. 'I think we've done this as much for ourselves as for you.'

Polly laughed. 'That's what Dorothy and Gloria just said!'

Helen reappeared. 'Kate's all ready for you. Come on. I've only been able to wangle half an hour. I've sent Harold on some bogus errand so there's no chance he'll find out we've converted my office into a makeshift seamstress's shop.'

Polly started to make her way over to the office, which had all its blinds pulled down for privacy.

'Oh, and Polly,' Bel said, a cheeky smile on her face, 'I'll be wanting a blow-by-blow account later on of exactly what happened last night.'

Polly blushed and headed into the office.

'Thank you so much for doing this.' Polly looked at Helen and Kate.

'Well, it's not very often you get married, is it?' Helen joked. 'Anyway, I won't chatter. You've got half an hour.' And with that she was gone, shutting the door firmly behind her.

'And you don't have to thank me either,' Kate said. 'Because Rosie has told me I'm getting paid whether I want to or not.' She looked at Polly in her overalls and steel-capped boots. 'Right, first of all I need you out of this.' She waved a hand at Polly, making no effort to disguise what she felt about her present attire.

As soon as Polly was stripped down to her underwear, Kate got to work.

Sensing her need to concentrate, Polly kept quiet as Kate measured and remeasured, jotting figures down in her little notebook.

As she did so, Polly looked about the office, careful not to move.

It was the first time she had seen the inside of Helen's workplace. It was lovely and warm thanks to a three-bar electric fire in the corner. Winston was curled up in his basket next to it. In her mind the ginger tom would always be synonymous with the night of the air raid.

Had it really only been six weeks?

So much had happened since then.

And now she and Tommy were just three weeks away from getting married and spending the rest of their lives together.

After a little while, Kate stepped back and wrapped up her tape.

'I think we're done with the measuring,' she said. 'Which leaves us fifteen minutes to talk about *the dress*. What're your thoughts? Ideas?'

Polly put on her clothes.

'You know, Kate,' she said, pulling on her overalls, 'I've never been very good with clothes, as Bel has always been at pains to point out.'

Polly bent down to put her boots back on.

'I said to Rosie that I think I'd quite like you to just do what you think is best.'

She looked up to see that Kate's face had lit up.

'Well, if you're *sure*.'

Helen shut the door and walked back into the main office. She had given her staff an extra half an hour's lunch break, telling them that she needed the place empty until then.

'Do you fancy a cup of tea?' Marie-Anne asked.

'No, thank you,' Helen said, pulling out her packet of Pall Malls from her skirt pocket. She perched herself on the side of the window sill and cracked open the window. She was hit by a blast of wind and shut it again.

She took a cigarette out, not offering Bel or Marie-Anne one as she knew neither of them smoked.

'Polly's a lucky girl.' She looked at Marie-Anne and Bel, who were sitting at their desk, drinking tea.

'Because she's marrying Tommy?' Marie-Anne asked, immediately wanting to snatch back her words.

'Well, there is that,' Helen said, catching the look of embarrassment on Marie-Anne's face and realising she must have heard that she and Polly had been love rivals.

'Tommy's a good catch, for sure. But I actually meant Polly's lucky to have Kate designing her wedding dress.'

'Do you know Kate?' Bel asked. Kate had certainly never mentioned knowing Helen.

'Oh, yes,' Helen said, blowing out a plume of smoke. 'I discovered her about a year ago.' She hesitated. 'Well, to be more exact, it was my dear mother who found her first.'

'Really?' Bel felt her brain snap to attention at the mention of Miriam. Her half-sister. Her *secret* half-sister.

'So how did your mother hear about Kate?' Bel asked, trying to sound casual.

'I believe it was word of mouth,' Helen said. 'I think it must have been quite soon after the Maison Nouvelle opened. One of my mother's friends had been there and was expounding Kate's virtues.' Helen took another drag of her cigarette. 'After our first visit we realised why.'

Helen looked round for an ashtray. Seeing one on top of one of the typists' desks, she walked over and picked it up.

'I get Kate to make most of my clothes now.' She perched herself back on the window sill and tapped ash into the cut crystal. 'She knocked this skirt up in days.' Helen looked down at the deep red skirt with oversized pockets that was nipped in at the waist and flared over her hips.

As they chatted, it occurred to Bel that this was the first occasion she had talked to Helen for any length of time. They had exchanged a few words at Tatham Street when Helen had been looking after Hope following the bombing, but they had just been pleasantries or practicalities regarding Hope's childcare.

She wanted to get to know Helen better. They did, after all, share the same blood. And, bizarre though it still felt, Helen *was* her niece.

'So, Bel, what are you going to wear for the wedding?' Marie-Anne said.

'Oh, well, it sounds odd,' Bel sat up straight, 'but I'm going to be wearing my wedding dress.'

Helen and Marie-Anne looked at her as though she was barking mad.

Bel laughed.

'Don't worry, I won't be turning up in a flowing white gown, looking like Miss Havisham.'

Helen chuckled. *So, Bel wasn't totally uneducated.* She'd always just seen Bel as Polly's sister-in-law, but lately she'd realised there was more to her. She had a mixed-race sister, for starters. *And that awful mother of hers.* And no father to speak of.

'Who's Miss Havisham?' Marie-Anne asked.

'She's a character in a book,' Helen explained, 'who gets jilted at the altar and spends the rest of her days moaning about it, taking it out on others – and wearing her wedding dress.'

Helen stubbed out her cigarette.

'Silly woman. Should have realised she was better off without him and got on with her life.'

Bel thought she heard a bitterness in Helen's voice. A resentment not dissimilar to Miss Havisham's.

'So, come on, Bel, tell us about this wedding dress you're going to wear?' Helen asked, curious.

'Well, it's not really a *wedding* dress, more of the dress I got married in.'

'Mmm,' Helen said.

'Because my marriage to Joe was my second marriage,' Bel said, 'I didn't want to wear white. Also, neither of us wanted to get married in church. Joe's not a believer, and I'm pretty half-hearted about the whole thing, so Kate made me a gorgeous pastel pink dress. She also made me the most incredible fascinator. We always said if the dress was worn on its own, it could pass as a party dress.'

Helen sat up straight.

'Not the dress Kate's got displayed in the window?'

'Yes, that's the one,' Bel smiled. 'It was one of the first dresses she made after she started up. I said it was pointless sitting in my wardrobe if it could be used as a window display.'

'Oh, I love that dress!' Helen said. 'Every time I go there, I look at it and admire it. The detail's incredible.'

'I know,' Bel said. 'I often stand outside the shop and listen to people saying how gorgeous it is.'

As they chatted on, Helen looked at Bel. She was very pretty. Very English, with her pale complexion and naturally blonde hair. She would almost go as far as to say she was refined. If it wasn't for her slight accent and clothes, you wouldn't have thought she belonged in the east end.

God, she reminded her of someone.

She just couldn't figure out who it was.

It'd come to her in time.

She was sure of it.

'Come in!' Dr Parker barked at the door of his office.

He looked up from a report he was writing to the British Medical Council arguing the case for more research into the development of prosthetics.

'Hello, Tommy!' He stood up and put his hand out.

The two men shook hands.

'Sit down.' Dr Parker pointed towards a chair that had a stack of files on it. 'Just bang them on the floor. One of these days I'll get organised.'

Tommy put the files in a neat pile at the side of the desk and sat down.

'Thanks for seeing me, Doc. I wanted to pick yer brains. Maybe ask yer a bit of a favour.'

Chapter Thirty-Eight

A week later

Saturday 5 December

'Nice to meet yer at long last,' Pearl said as she pulled a pint of bitter and put it on the bar. She grabbed a cloth from under the counter and quickly dried her hands of overspill.

'I've heard a lot about yer,' she said, her voice gravelly. She coughed to clear her throat. 'Glad yer made it back in one piece.' She stuck her hand out. Tommy noticed her fingers were stained yellow with tar.

'Nice to meet yer too, Pearl,' Tommy said, shaking her hand. Bel's errant ma was exactly as he had imagined. Polly had described her well. He smiled. For some reason he felt sorry for her.

'Bet yer glad this place was left standing,' Tommy said, looking around the pub.

Since being discharged from hospital he had walked past the bomb site at the end of the street on a number of occasions. Seeing it with his own eyes had made him realise, even more than he already had, just how incredibly lucky Polly and Arthur and the rest of the Elliot household had been to escape unscathed.

It had strengthened his resolve.

'Yer right there, pet. Could just be a pile of bricks here now.' Pearl's face was unusually serious for a moment. She would never admit to the sheer panic she'd felt that night, fearing the worst for her daughter and granddaughter. 'Good job it's still here. I'd 'ave been out of a job otherwise.' She forced out a bark of laughter.

'Welcome back, lad!'

Pearl turned to see Bill, who had come back up from the cellar, where he'd been changing a barrel. He stretched out a large hand that was as rough as sandpaper.

'Pleased to meet you,' he said, shaking Tommy's hand vigorously. 'I'm Bill – the landlord of this revered establishment. For my sins.' He smiled. He'd been eager to meet Tommy, not just because he was Polly's fiancé, but because, in his books, anyone who put their life on the line to win this war was a hero.

Polly felt someone nudge her and turned to see that Ronald had sidled up and was stretching out a bare, tattooed arm along the bar.

'Ronald.' A fag was dangling from his mouth as he spoke. He grabbed Tommy's hand. 'Honour to meet yer, lad. Pearl here's told me all about yer 'n what yer've been deeing 'oot there.'

Polly sensed Tommy's unease.

'Oh, look!' She took her port and lemon off the bar. 'There's a free table. Best grab it.'

Tommy paid for the round, in spite of Bill's objections.

'Nice to meet yer all,' Tommy said. 'And thanks, Bill, for allowing us to take over half yer pub after the wedding.'

'Our pleasure, pet,' Pearl said, edging in front of Bill. 'Least we could do, isn't it?' She looked up at Bill, who was nodding his agreement.

'Blimey,' Polly said as they made their way over to the free table, 'I think that's the most civil I've ever heard Pearl. And I mean *ever*.'

Tommy laughed.

'I think that might be due to the large glass of whisky I noticed she had stashed by the pumps.'

Tommy took a swig of his Vaux bitter, wiping away the creamy froth from his upper lip.

'So, Ronald's your neighbour out back?' Tommy said.

'And Pearl's suitor.' Polly rolled her eyes.

'And what about Bill?'

'Another suitor.' Polly took a sip of her drink.

Tommy cast a look over at the bar to see Bill and Pearl serving customers and Ronald sitting there, a pint and a whisky chaser in front of him.

'So, it sounds like Bel's getting on better with her ma these days,' Tommy said. He had always liked Bel from first meeting her at the Elliots'.

'She is.' Polly thought for a moment. 'They still enjoy sniping at each other, but I think that's just how they communicate.'

She took another sip of her port.

'Having said that, Bel doesn't seem as angry towards her ma as she used to be.'

'Oh, aye?' Tommy asked.

'Well,' Polly dropped her voice, 'I think Pearl's told her about her real dad, but Bel's not said anything to me.'

'That surprises me.' Tommy knew Polly and Bel were close. Always had been.

'I know,' Polly said. 'Bel can be a closed book at times. I'm sure she'll tell me when she's ready.'

Tommy took another sup of beer.

'So, is there anything else I need to know about the wedding? Or anything I need to do? I don't feel like I'm being much help.'

Polly chuckled. 'That's because there's nothing much to do, really. The joys of having a simple wedding. The church is booked. The banns are being read – which reminds me, we should go tomorrow. Just to show our faces.'

Tommy nodded.

'Kate's making my dress. I don't even have to be involved in the design. She's doing it all.'

Tommy smiled. He was so glad that Polly was at least going to have a special dress to wear.

'Ma's doing a spread,' Polly continued, 'but that won't need to be done until the night before. And Arthur's getting me some flowers from the allotment on the actual morning and Bel will be making them into a bouquet. So really, it's all sorted.' Polly paused. 'Oh, and Rina and Vera are going to see what they can do about making us a cake. I've told them anything will do, and to use one of those cardboard toppers I've seen in the shops instead of icing. With the way rationing's getting, I'm just thankful we're to have a cake at all.'

Tommy looked at Polly's face and listened to the tone of her voice, but could not pick up any regret that their wedding day was going to be a very modest one. She didn't seem to harbour any regrets about spending the gratuity money.

He didn't care how they got married – whether it be in rags at the local registry office or some grand affair like the one Lily and George had planned. As long as Polly married him, everything else was incidental.

The pair chatted away, oblivious to those around them and unaware that they were gradually having to raise their voices to be heard as the pub became full to bursting. When Tommy went to the bar for another round, he was stopped by those he didn't know, slapped on the back and offered a drink. Word had got round that Tommy, who most knew as either 'Arthur's lad' or 'the dock diver', was back.

Polly watched Tommy as he refused all offers of a drink. Saw his discomfort at being the centre of so much attention. And the relief when he'd made it back to their table.

'So, anyway,' Tommy said, 'I went to see the doc the other day.' It had actually been an entire week, but Tommy had been putting off telling Polly.

'Really?' Polly was surprised he hadn't mentioned he'd had an appointment.

'We had a good chat.' Tommy took a breath. 'And the doc thinks I'm well enough to do what's called a "medically supervised" dive.'

Polly felt herself stiffen.

'Really? That surprises me.' She looked at Tommy. 'But what about your ruptured spleen? Wasn't there a question mark over whether or not it would be safe for you to dive again?'

Tommy shuffled on his chair.

'Ah, well, I asked the doc to look into that fer me ...' His voice trailed off.

'And?' Polly could feel her heart starting to beat faster.

'He says there's nothing to say I will come to any harm—'

'—and nothing to say that you won't,' Polly finished his sentence.

Tommy leant forward and took hold of Polly's hand.

'Please, Polly. I need yer support in this.' His eyes pleaded. 'I love you more than I've ever loved anyone ever before in my life. Or ever will.'

Polly saw the love in Tommy's eyes. Heard it in his voice.

'But you know my other love is diving. I can't imagine life without being able to dive. I need to know if I can still do it.'

Polly looked at Tommy.

'I know, Tommy, I know.'

'And,' he added, 'I really *need* to know that I can keep on being of some use to the war effort.'

Polly looked at Tommy.

'By going back to work at the yard?'

There was the tiniest of hesitations.

'Aye,' he said simply.

Polly looked at him. 'I know I'm being soft, I just feel terrified that something will happen to you.' She hesitated, unsure whether to carry on. 'I sometimes feel so happy that I worry it's all going to be whipped away.'

She felt her throat tighten.

'That night after the air raid, when Helen told me you were in the Ryhope, I wouldn't allow myself to believe it until I'd seen you with my own eyes.'

She took a deep breath.

'I just couldn't believe that you'd come back to me. That you were alive. I have never been so thankful, so incredibly relieved, and so, *so* happy. I can't even put into words how I felt. I think I've spent every day since pinching myself to make sure I'm not dreaming.'

Tommy looked at the woman he loved. It brought him such pleasure but also such pain to hear her words.

'I'll be fine. Honestly, if there was any serious danger, I know the doc wouldn't allow it. Come on,' he said, looking at their empty glasses, 'let me walk you home and you can ask me in for a cup of tea.'

Polly smiled.

'Walk me home?' she repeated. 'All of ten yards across the road?'

'Exactly,' he said with a mischievous smile, 'which leaves us more time to drink lots of tea.'

Polly laughed.

They stood up and Tommy grabbed her hand as they made their way through the packed pub and out the front door. Once outside, Tommy put his arm around Polly's waist and pulled her close.

'You know I've never done – and will *never* do – anything to cause you unhappiness?'

'I know,' Polly said. 'I know.'

Later on, as Tommy made his way back to the Major's flat, he argued with himself about whether or not he should have been more honest with Polly.

If he'd told her the whole truth, though, she'd have worried and he'd already brought enough anxiety and upset into her life without doing it again. Especially if it was unnecessary.

No, he'd done right.

He'd tell her only when he was certain he was able to do what he wanted to do.

Chapter Thirty-Nine

One week later

Saturday 12 December

'Bet yer glad to see yer Tommy back?' Stan the ferryman asked Arthur as he made his unsteady way onto the old paddle steamer.

'Aye, I am that.'

The two men went through their usual ritual of Arthur trying to pay the penny fare and Stan refusing to let him. The old man had, in Stan's opinion, more than earned his free pass after a life of working on the Wear.

'Polly said he's doing a dive today?' Stan asked as the ferry churned water and moved away from the landing.

'Aye.' Arthur said, looking up at skies, clear but for the overbearing grey barrage balloons. He grabbed the railings as the paddle steamer hit wash.

He looked up at the squawking gulls tailing a fishing trawler back to the south quay. Today's dive would be a success, he was sure. That wasn't his concern. What did worry him, though, was what the lad was really up to.

He could read Tommy like a bloody book. Had seen his face when they'd been listening to the latest news reports about the Allied offensive in Tunisia having met with only minimum success, but he'd held his tongue. Tommy was his own man. He had to do what was right for him.

As the ferry reached North Sands, Arthur tipped his flat cap to Stan by way of thanks and made his way up to J.L. Thompson's.

'I can't believe you've sanctioned this, John!'

Helen was fuming. She was standing, hands on hips, glowering across her office at Dr Parker. Even Winston the cat had forsaken his spot by the electric fire and had slunk out to the main office.

'Helen, there's nothing I can do to stop him. He's a very determined bloke. If I'd said no, I know he'd simply have got some other doctor. He's been my patient from the off. The least I can do is try and make sure he's all right. Or as all right as can be.'

'Have you made sure the St John's ambulance is on hand?'

'Of course I have.'

'And they've got a half-decent driver, not some old fogey with cataracts who drives about as fast as I can run – and that's in my high heels?'

'Yes, I've got a full and competent crew, all sharp as a button, all on standby at the quayside – as we speak.'

Dr Parker felt his anger rising to the surface.

Was Helen doubting his competence?

Or was she worried sick about the man she clearly still loved?

'Well, I'm not going down to watch. I'm staying here!' she said, folding her arms. 'Let's just pray to God nothing goes wrong. If not for the yard's reputation, then for Polly's sake.'

Dr Parker looked at Helen.

Her concern for Polly surprised him.

Still, it took all his willpower not to slam the office door behind him.

*

'Eee,' Dorothy said, 'reminds me of when we all first started.'

The women were all sitting on palettes by the quayside. Near enough to have a good view, but not so near as to cause a nuisance and get in the way of Ralph, the two divers and linesmen. And Tommy, of course.

Arthur was sitting further down the quayside on one of the huge metal cleats. Polly could tell he wanted to be on his own so hadn't tried to persuade him to join them.

Gloria took hold of Polly's hand and squeezed it. 'You feeling nervous?'

Polly forced a smile.

'A little,' she admitted.

Gloria looked at Rosie. 'I thought Charlotte was desperate to come?'

Rosie sighed heavily, as she was wont to do whenever she talked about her little sister.

'She was. I've sent her up to the office to watch with Helen, Bel and Marie-Anne. She pulled a face, but I said it was either that or not at all.'

'Look, they're getting Tommy ready!' Dorothy pointed ahead.

Polly didn't need telling. Her eyes had been fixed on Tommy from the moment he'd given her a kiss, told her not to worry and walked over to where Ralph and the rest of the diving team were.

'They're off!' Dorothy shouted out.

'They're not doing a bleedin' race, Dor!' Angie rolled her eyes at the rest of the women.

They all watched as one by one the men of the diving team made it to a large, flat-bottomed wooden boat bobbing gently by the side of the dock.

Polly caught movement in her peripheral vision and turned to see Dr Parker walking over to the St John's ambulance just fifty yards or so away. He looked serious. If she didn't know better, she'd have said he also looked a little angry. He nodded over in her direction. She returned the gesture with a nervous smile.

'Remember how we used to call them "monster men"?' Martha said.

'Yes,' Hannah said. 'I thought they were rather scary.' She looked at Olly, who was sitting next to her, and gave him a self-deprecating chuckle. 'Then again, I think I found most things scary at that time.'

'Seems like another time, doesn't it?' Polly said, her eyes still glued to Tommy. He was wearing his old canvas suit and weighted boots. Two divers stood on either side of him and were carefully placing a huge twelve-bolt copper helmet over his head.

The women all murmured their agreement. All quietly thinking of the changes the past two years had brought to their own lives.

Polly's leg started bouncing nervously as the divers screwed the helmet onto the metal corselet and the linesmen attached his air tube and started feeding ropes through the metal rings attached to Tommy's suit.

The women fell silent as the men stood back, their work done. Ralph stood in front of Tommy and raised his thumb in the air. Tommy mirrored his actions before manoeuvring himself around a hundred and eighty degrees. He stepped back and made his slow descent down the iron rungs of the ladder at the side of the boat.

Gloria put her arm around Polly and gave her a hug. 'He's going to be just fine. You'll see. And just think, if he gets over this hurdle it means he can come back to work. When he's fully recovered, that is. It'll be like he's never been away. And better still, you'll be man and wife.'

Polly looked at Gloria, her eyes sparkling. 'I know. I've been thinking that ever since he told me. Well, once I got over the shock of him wanting to do this.'

'How long will he be down there for?' Martha asked.

'About ten – possibly fifteen – minutes,' Rosie said.

Both Polly's legs were now jigging up and down.

'He'll be fine, Polly. Honestly.' They were words Rosie repeated to herself every day whenever she started to worry about Peter.

She'd found that if you said something enough times, you actually started to believe it.

'So, what now?' Charlotte asked.

'We wait!' Helen snapped, lighting up another cigarette.

Charlotte found herself inching towards Bel and Marie-Anne.

'Are you sure you won't have a cuppa, Charlie?' Bel asked.

Charlotte shook her head vehemently.

'God, why couldn't Tommy simply have waited a bit longer?' Helen said, blowing out a billow of smoke.

Charlotte had to suppress a cough. She wasn't used to people smoking around her.

'So,' Marie-Anne said, 'if it goes all right today, when do you think he'll be coming back to work?'

'Knowing Tommy, tomorrow if he's given half a chance.' Helen blew out more smoke. *Not that she thought Tommy's intention was to return to work.* She looked around for the ashtray. 'Dr Parker has to pass him, though. Medically, that is.' Helen took one more look out of the window before turning and marching back to her office. 'Shout if anything happens. God forbid!'

'Why's Miss Crawford in such a mardy?' Charlie whispered.

'She's always like that,' Marie-Anne said.

'Mmm,' Bel said, thoughtfully. 'She's mellowed a bit of late. Something's got her goat, I reckon.'

'How long's it been now?' Polly looked at Olly, who was holding out a stopwatch.

'Fifteen minutes ...' He paused, waiting a few seconds. 'Exactly.'

Just then, there was sudden movement on the pontoon. One of the linesmen shouted something across to Ralph, who shouted something back, but Polly couldn't make it out.

The women all froze.

Ralph started barking orders at all the men.

He seemed panicked, or rather, as panicked as Ralph got.

'Oh my God, something's happened.' Polly's voice was barely a whisper.

She caught sight of movement and turned to see Dr Parker running across to the quayside.

A second later Polly was hot on his heels.

'What's wrong?!' she shouted. She looked to her left to see Arthur on his feet, almost balancing on the edge of the quay and looking down at the river.

'It's all right, pet.' Ralph looked up at Polly. 'Drama over.'

Polly looked to see the two linesmen were holding a length of rope and the ventilation tube in their hands.

'Slight hiccup with the air valve. It's fine now.' He looked at Polly. 'Get yourself back to yer pew.' He winked. 'He'll be coming up in a minute.'

Polly looked across at Arthur, who had stepped back. She could see the relief on his face as he sat back down.

Dr Parker stayed where he was.

'Bloody hell. I think I stopped breathing then,' Angie said.

'Me and you both,' Dor said.

Polly sat back down next to Gloria, who took hold of her hand and patted it.

'Nearly over with,' she said.

The linesmen, distinctive in their dungarees, were pulling hard on thick ropes slung around a huge pulley. There was a glint of metal as Tommy's helmet appeared, water pouring around its three small portholes.

Polly gripped Gloria's hand hard as Tommy slowly clomped his way up the metal ladders, before his big steel-capped boots thudded onto the pontoon's decking. The two divers started to unscrew the helmet. They were working as fast as they could, but it still felt like an age.

Finally, they lifted the helmet off, revealing Tommy's flushed and sweaty face.

'Thank God!' Polly let out a gasp of air.

She looked at Tommy, who immediately sought her out. Spotting her, he waved over, giving her a wink and mouthing, 'I love you.'

'Ahh,' Dorothy and Angie said in unison.

'Děkuji Bože,' Hannah muttered under her breath. She didn't feel like she could handle any more bad news.

They all watched as Tommy was slowly stripped of his outer armour.

As soon as his helmet was off, Dr Parker jumped onto the barge.

No one could hear what they were saying, but it was clear from Tommy's nods and shakes of the head that Dr Parker was hearing what he needed to hear.

Climbing back up onto the quayside, Dr Parker nodded over to Polly, showing her that all was well.

Polly forced a smile, although she thought his face still looked strained.

'I think a celebration's in order when we all leave here?' Gloria suggested. 'I think we're all in need of a stiff drink, eh?' She smiled at Polly.

'I should say so!' Polly's voice was rasping.

'You can really start to enjoy the run-up to married life now,' Gloria added.

'Ha!' Dor said. 'More like enjoy your last week of freedom!'

They all chuckled.

'Right you lot,' Rosie said, picking up her boxed-up gas mask and overall. 'I'll leave you all to it. Have a drink for me.'

Polly watched as Arthur slowly climbed down onto the pontoon. He shook hands with divers and linesmen and then did something that surprised her. He took Tommy's head in both hands and kissed him on the forehead. She had never seen Arthur do anything like that before.

He turned and Ralph helped him back up onto the quayside as Tommy sat and went through the slightly laborious process of taking off his diving gear and lead-weighted boots.

'I'll see yer back home, pet!' Arthur shouted to Polly as he started his way back across the yard to the main gates.

'Come on, then,' Martha said, standing up and stretching her back. 'If we go now, we might be able to get a table.'

'The Admiral?' Olly asked.

'Where else?' Dorothy laughed.

'I'll wait for Tommy. I'll catch you all up,' Polly said.

'Well, dinnit hang about,' Angie said. 'I wanna meet Tommy. Proper.'

Angie had only become friends with Dorothy and the rest of the women after Tommy had left for the war.

Polly smiled.

'All right. See you all there.'

Polly sat and enjoyed the quiet of the yard, which had now more or less shut up shop for the day. Her thoughts wandered to their wedding and what would happen afterwards. She hoped they would be able to afford their own little place for their own little family.

She watched Tommy walk over, his clothes dry as a bone thanks to his waterproof suit.

She wondered if their first child would be a boy or a girl.

'See?' Tommy said, grabbing hold of Polly and kissing her. 'I told you. Nothing to worry about.'

Polly kissed him back, putting her arms around his waist.

'I feel like we've just been given a pass,' she said.

Tommy looked at her, a question on his face.

'You know,' she explained. 'Like we really are at the start of the rest of our lives. You're going to be all right. And you can still dive. It's amazing really, isn't it?'

All those dreams she thought had been smashed to smithereens just two months ago were back. And best of all, those dreams were becoming a reality.

Tommy pulled away.

'Give me five minutes,' he said. 'The doc's waiting to give me the once-over.'

Tommy kissed Polly quickly and jogged over to the St John's ambulance, where Dr Parker was waiting.

'So, I've kept my side of the bargain,' Tommy said. He was taking deep breaths while Dr Parker listened to his chest.

'Quiet!' Dr Parker commanded. He was in no mood for niceties. 'Another deep breath.'

Tommy did as he was told.

Dr Parker stood back.

'Turn around.'

He pressed his stethoscope against Tommy's broad back. He could see the scars from when Tommy had been caught in the original blast and hadn't quite got the distance he'd needed between himself and the ensuing explosion.

'Right, you can put your shirt on now.'

Tommy again did as he was told.

'So, you'll pass me. Give me the thumbs up,' Tommy said.

Dr Parker expelled air.

'I'm not happy about this. Not happy at all. I'd feel a lot happier, to be honest, if I was sanctioning your medical discharge. It would be much better for your health if you stayed put. Did your bit for the war here, repairing these ships.' He threw his arm out towards the open doors of the ambulance.

God, most blokes would be thanking their lucky stars that they were still alive.

Dr Parker took another breath.

'You heard Ralph. He's cock-a-hoop thinking you're coming back to work. The two young lads he's got under him barely look out of short pants. You're needed *here*. Helen's always telling me about the pressure to get the ships built and repaired as quickly as possible. All the yards up and down the country are struggling.'

Tommy looked round to see where the two medics and the driver were.

Seeing Tommy's concern that their conversation might be overheard, Dr Parker stuck his head out of the back of the van and told the three men to take a ten-minute break.

'I know what you're saying,' Tommy said. 'I understand. I know I'm needed here, but the thing is, I'm needed more over there. *Really*. The Italians might not be anything special on land, but they have the advantage at sea. Their divers are a pain in our backside. Have you heard about the raid on Algiers in today's papers?'

Dr Parker nodded. He had read the reports about the Italian Royal Navy sinking two Allied ships and damaging two more in the harbour of the Algerian capital.

'We're so behind,' Tommy said, his voice full of frustration. 'What you just saw me wearing is prehistoric compared to what they've got. We're catching them up, but we need experienced divers out there.'

He took a deep breath.

'I've *got* to get back out there.'

He looked at Dr Parker's face. The doctor's expression had changed. Tommy knew what he was thinking.

'I know,' he sighed. 'It's going to break Polly's heart. I know. Imagine how it makes me feel.'

He rubbed his face.

'I'm just praying she'll understand.'

Dr Parker looked at Tommy.

'She's going to hate you,' he said simply.

As Helen will hate me.

And with that Dr Parker started filling out the form that would send Tommy back to the war.

Back to Gibraltar.

Chapter Forty

'So, you up for a quick drink at the Admiral?' Polly asked as they both walked across the yard. 'Everyone's dying to see you.'

She chuckled.

'Angie is particularly desperate to meet you. I think she's feeling like the odd one out.'

'Of course,' Tommy said, turning to look at Polly. Her face was vibrant. So full of joy. If he could put off this moment, he would, but he knew he couldn't.

'Do you mind if we go for a walk first?' Tommy slid his arm around Polly's waist and pulled her gently towards him. 'Give us a chance to chat on our own.'

'Course.'

Polly looked at Tommy.

'You know what?'

'What?' He smiled down at her upturned face.

'I don't think it's possible to be any happier than I am now. Although,' she added, a twinkle in her eyes, 'I think that I might well be even happier this time next week.'

If he had had even the slightest inclination to put off this conversation until another day, then the mention of the wedding – and the fact it was now just seven days away – meant that he had to have this chat now, before Polly agreed to be his wife.

Tommy felt his shoulders sag.

'Come on, let's go down to the wharf,' he said, letting Polly break free and hand in her time card.

They turned left out of the main gates and headed towards the edge of the river.

'You know, we'll have to start thinking about getting our own place,' Polly said.

Tommy didn't say anything. Instead he wrapped his arm around her shoulders and pulled her close.

'Obviously, we'll have to live with my ma for a while, but I was thinking we might be able to rent one of the cottages on Laura Street.'

Tommy remained silent.

'Or the Diver's House?' Polly asked as they reached the metal railings by the river's edge. Secretly, she was hoping that Tommy would dismiss the idea, as she didn't want to be quite that far away from her ma and Bel. Especially when they started their family.

Tommy took her in his arms and kissed her.

'Pol,' he said, moving a thick strand of hair away from her face. 'I need to tell you something.'

Polly heard the seriousness in his voice.

'It's something I know you're not going to like.'

'You're worrying me,' she said. 'What is it? What am I not going to like?'

Tommy cupped her face in his hands. There was no other way round this.

'I'm going back out there.'

Polly stared at Tommy.

'What?'

'I'm going back to Gibraltar.'

Polly continued to stare at Tommy in disbelief, his words not quite sinking in.

'You're going back to Gibraltar?'

Tommy nodded.

'I'm so sorry, Polly. I have to. They need me.'

Polly grabbed his hands and pulled them away from her face.

'No,' she said, shaking her head. 'You don't *have to*. You're needed here.'

She stepped away from him.

'I don't understand. You've just done a dive. You're going to start work back here.'

'Exactly,' Tommy said. He stepped forward and tried to take her back into his arms. 'I'm well enough to work here, which means I'm well enough to go back.'

Polly dodged his embrace.

'No, no, no. That's not true. You're *not* well enough to go back. You're not strong enough. You've been terribly ill. For God's sake, you nearly died. It's a miracle you're still here.' Polly could hear her voice getting louder.

'I'm so sorry, Polly.'

Again, he reached forward to take her in his arms to reassure her.

Again, she moved away.

'I need to go back there,' he implored. 'Look at me.' He splayed his arms out wide. 'I'm fit and healthy.'

'No, you're not! You're not *fit and healthy*. You're far from it. You're not half as strong as you used to be. Any fool can see that.'

Polly stopped. A thought suddenly slammed into her mind. Tommy *couldn't* go back – even if he wanted to.

'You won't pass the medical,' she said, as much to herself as to Tommy. She knew what Dr Parker had said. Tommy's body would always be at risk from infection. No spleen equalled greater risk. 'There's no way they'll allow you to go back.'

Polly could feel a rush of relief and almost laughed with joy.

'Tommy,' she said, her voice softening. 'It's incredibly courageous of you to want to go back out there, but there's no way they'll let you. Your body's just not up to it.'

There was a moment's silence.

'I've been passed,' Tommy said quietly.

'What?' Polly was genuinely perplexed.

'I've been passed – medically.' Tommy hesitated. 'By the doc.'

'What? Dr Parker's passed you?' Polly said, her eyes glued to Tommy. 'I don't understand.' Her mind was whirring. Was this really happening? All of sudden everything seemed unreal.

'Please, Polly, I know this is hard on you,' Tommy pleaded. 'But I need you to understand.' He didn't like the blank look on Polly's face.

'My love for you is everything,' he said, stepping towards her and gently taking both her hands in his own. 'Everything,' he repeated. 'You are my world. I've never wanted anyone as much as I've wanted you.'

He took a deep breath.

'But this war is all-consuming. It's not about me. Or you. Or us. It's about winning. We *have* to win this war. There's no other way. If we don't, we mightn't even *have* a future together.'

Tommy freed one hand and touched the side of her face.

'You've got to understand, Pol. I've got to go back. I'm needed more there than I am here. It's really that simple.'

Polly looked at Tommy. The reality of what she was hearing suddenly overwhelmed her. Tears started to well up. Her chest filled with the most unbearable sorrow and she started to cry. Great heaving sobs.

'Please, Tommy, don't do this.'

Tears were already streaming down her face and dripping from her lips.

'Please. I can't lose you again. I can't. *Please* do this for me.'

Polly knew she was begging but she didn't care. She would get on her knees if she thought it might make Tommy change his mind. She reached out and wrapped her arms around his neck and held him tight.

Tommy held her tight too.

'I'm sorry ... I'm so sorry, Pol,' he murmured into her ears. He could smell her skin and hair. Her scent.

He felt his heart breaking and realised it was his own hands that were ripping it apart.

They stayed like that until Polly was unable to cry any more.

There was nothing left.

She pulled herself away and looked Tommy in the eyes. She knew it didn't matter what she said or did. He was resolute.

Tommy was going and there was nothing she could do about it.

And with this realisation, the sorrow dragging her under was pushed aside by the anger that was now rising up.

A terrible, vitriolic anger, and its target was right here in front of her.

The love that she felt for Tommy – had felt for him over the past two and a half years – was congealing into hatred.

Polly wiped her eyes with the sleeve of her overalls.

'After everything that has happened. After everything you have put me through.'

She grabbed the railings and looked up at the outline of the barrage balloons floating high in the night sky.

'You made me fall in love with you and then you left me. Told me you had to go to war. And I understood. It broke my heart, but I understood. I waited and waited. Worried every single day that something terrible might happen to you. Feasted on your letters when they arrived, beyond relieved that you were still alive.'

She brought her attention back from the sky and turned to face Tommy.

'When I thought you were dead, I wanted to die myself. Sometimes I didn't feel like I could breathe, imagining a life without you.'

Tears of sadness had now turned into tears of resentment, born of the remembrance of the grief she had endured.

'So don't think for one moment that I will marry you now. I have no intention of wearing white only to end up shrouded in black for the rest of my life.'

She glared at him.

'I hate you, Tommy Watts. I hate you as much as I loved you. I wish I had never clapped eyes on you. I wish Helen *had* seduced you. Had taken you off me. Spared me all the hell you've put me through.'

Adrenaline was making her feel nauseous and she took a deep breath.

'We have the chance of a life. A happy, loving life.'

Tears were once again spilling down her face.

'And you're choosing to give it all up. Sacrifice the life we could have. For what? Do you think that one person might change the course of this war? You've done your bit, Tommy. More than your bit. And you could keep doing your bit here.'

Polly let out a bitter laugh.

'But, no. You've got to play the hero. Go back out there. Have another game of Russian roulette – why not?'

She cast Tommy a look that could only be described as demonic.

'The more I think about it, the more I think you've really got a death wish, Tommy Watts. You've always said to me how much you're not like your mam. But I think you're *exactly* like her.'

Polly paused.

'I think you *want* to die.'

Her words cut deep.

Polly pushed Tommy away with both hands.

'Just go!'

She pushed him again.

'Leave me alone. I never want to see you again. Ever.'

Chapter Forty-One

After sending the St John's ambulance away, Dr Parker walked over to the admin building.

Walking up the stairs and opening the door to the main office, he was struck by an eerie quietness. There was no one else about. Everyone had gone home.

He headed for Helen's office. The door was open.

He stood in the entrance and looked at Helen sitting at her desk. Her head was bent over a pile of order forms. Sensing someone was there, she looked up.

'Well, thank goodness that all went off all right,' Helen said, grabbing her packet of Pall Malls on her desk and reaching for her ashtray. 'I'm guessing Tommy passed his medical?' She sat back in her chair.

'He did,' Dr Parker said, not making any effort to come into the room.

He heard purring and looked down at the floor to see Winston cleaning himself in front of the electric fire.

How he wished for such an uncomplicated life.

'I've got to tell you something,' he said simply.

Helen looked at him. Her beautiful emerald eyes were ice-cold.

'He's going back, isn't he?' It was a question to which she knew the answer.

Dr Parker nodded.

'You've just sanctioned him as being medically fit for service, haven't you?'

Her words were accusatory.

Dr Parker nodded again.

There was no use trying to explain to her that there was nothing he could do. Tommy was going back out to Gibraltar regardless.

'I don't know who I'm more furious with – you or him!' She tried to keep her voice at an acceptable level. '*You* for allowing it, or *him* for wanting it.'

Dr Parker looked at Helen and once again saw the fierce love he firmly believed she still held for Tommy.

She would never stop loving him. He knew that. Had known it from the moment Tommy had woken up in his hospital bed.

'Well, my dear,' Dr Parker said, finding it difficult to hide the hurt in his voice. 'You're just going to have to be furious – with us both.'

And with that, he turned on his heel and left.

Helen pushed herself out of her chair and stood for a moment, taken aback. She picked up Winston, who started purring even more loudly. The cat nuzzled her neck.

Realising she wasn't going to get any more work done, she put Winston down and picked up her bag and gas mask. Leaving the admin building, she scrabbled around for her torch.

'Bloody blackouts!' she cursed under her breath.

Passing through the main gates and walking up the start of the embankment, she heard a woman crying.

She flashed her light around and that's when she saw her. Crouched down by the side of the Admiral, her knees up to her chest, her head in her hands.

Helen hurried over.

'Polly! Oh my God! Polly!' She bobbed down the best she could in her tailored dress, dropping her torch, which rolled to the side. 'Look at me!' She grabbed hold of Polly's hand.

Polly looked up.

Her eyes spoke of her deep, deep heartache.

Helen would not want to be in Polly's shoes now. Not for all the tea in China.

Here was a woman ripped apart by love.

'Oh, Polly, I'm sorry. I'm so sorry. John told me.' She coaxed Polly up. 'Come here.' She gently pulled her to standing. 'Where's Tommy now?'

Polly's eyes flashed at Helen. A new target for her anger.

'If I knew I'd tell you! You could go to him! Have him! Have him all to yourself!'

Polly started crying angry tears again.

'Oh Polly, that's all in the past now. That was a lifetime ago.' Helen's voice was almost weary. She surveyed Polly. 'I'm just surprised he's left you here, like this?'

Polly looked at her. The anger had short-circuited and sorrow reconnected.

'I told him to go. I never want to see him again.'

Her words felt as though they were choking her. Her hand went to her throat.

Polly swallowed hard.

Hand still at her throat, she inhaled air.

'I told him the wedding's off.'

And with that, Polly broke down into uncontrollable tears once again.

Helen held Polly as her body juddered.

They stayed like that for a few minutes, until a couple of shipyard workers came out of the pub. The brief show of light before the door banged shut drew their attention to the two women.

Helen glowered at them.

They walked on.

'We were meant to be meeting everyone here.' Polly cocked her head over to the main entrance.

'Are they in there now?' Helen asked, half dreading the answer. She'd never ventured into the Admiral before.

Polly nodded.

'Do you want to go in and see them?' Helen crossed her fingers the answer would be no.

'Yes, I best go and tell them what's happened.'

Helen took a deep breath.

'Come on, then.'

When they walked into the smoky pub it took a moment for Helen's eyes to adjust to the light.

'There they are,' Polly said. 'Over there.'

Helen looked over to where Polly was pointing. At the same time, the women spotted them.

Their faces dropped.

Helen guided Polly over to their table.

'Oh my God, what's happened?' Dorothy had grabbed Angie's hand in shock at the state of their friend. She had seemed the happiest person on the planet the last time they'd seen her.

'Is Tommy all right?' Gloria asked, looking up at Helen.

'Oh, Tommy's just fine.' Polly spat out the words.

Gloria, Dorothy, Angie, Martha, Hannah, Olly, Bel and Marie-Anne were all staring at Polly, agog.

'What's happened?' Bel was sitting on the far side of the table. She tried to reach Polly's hand but couldn't.

Polly looked around at all the women, her eyes red and puffy.

Her words were clipped and seething with anger.

'He's going back to war.'

There was silence.

In the end, it was Helen who spoke.

'Let me get you a drink, Polly. Brandy?'

'Please,' Polly said.

Helen looked around the table. Most of the glasses were just about empty.

'Why don't I get another round in?'

Martha stood up.

'I'll give you a hand. I know what everyone's drinking.'

'You've called off the wedding!' Dorothy couldn't contain herself.

Everyone was staring at Polly in disbelief.

It was shocking that Tommy was going back to war, but for Polly to then call off the wedding was something none of them would have foreseen in a million years.

The women's attention was diverted to Helen and Martha making their way back over to the table. Helen had what looked like a very large brandy in one hand and a gin and tonic in the other. Martha was carrying a tray with the rest of the drinks.

'Here you are.' Helen gave Polly her drink.

'Thanks.' Polly looked up. 'Sorry for being a total cow out there.'

Gloria pulled a stool out for Helen next to where she was sitting.

'Don't be daft,' Helen said, sitting down, grateful to be next to Gloria.

For the next hour all the women sat and gently coaxed information out of Polly.

The large brandy had the calming effect she needed, but it was also causing sporadic outbursts of tears and anger.

In fragments, the whole scene that had taken place in the yard was relayed.

'I think what makes this all harder is knowing that nothing I will ever say will get him to change his mind,' she said, finishing her double brandy.

She looked worn out.

Bel knew to take the reins and told Polly that they best be getting home. Agnes would need to be told the news. And Arthur. Poor Arthur. He was going to be devastated.

'I'll see you all in the morning,' Polly said.

'See ya, then,' Angie said.

'Sleep on it.' Hannah stood up and made her way round the table to give Polly a hug.

'Please don't make a decision on the wedding this evening. See how you feel in the morning. Everything always looks different in the light of day.'

Polly hugged Hannah back, but her eyes looked dead.

'It won't,' she said simply.

The women saw the hardening of Polly's heart.

'I'll never marry Tommy.'

Chapter Forty-Two

After a cold and windy ferry crossing, followed by a fifteen-minute walk through the east end, which seemed to be full of children and courting couples, Bel and Polly arrived at St Ignatius Church.

'Please, Polly, sleep on it,' Bel implored. 'There's no rush. You can tell the vicar tomorrow. Like Hannah said, you might feel differently tomorrow.'

Polly looked at her sister-in-law.

'I won't.' Polly's voice was steely. 'Just as I know that Tommy won't change his mind tomorrow, neither will I change mine.'

Bel followed Polly round the side of the church. It was a building they knew well. It had been a mainstay of their childhood and where they'd gone to Sunday school. It was where Bel had married Teddy and Lucille had been christened. Whatever the occasion, though, she and Polly had always been there together.

Just like they were now.

'Do you want me to come in with you?' Bel asked.

'No,' Polly said, knocking on the door of the rectory. 'It won't take long.'

Polly was true to her word. Bel had only been shuffling about trying to keep warm for a matter of minutes when she reappeared.

'It's done.'

Bel could have cried. Would cry later, no doubt, when she told the whole sorry story to Joe.

As they passed the ruins at the start of Tatham Street, neither uttered a word.

It was here Polly had learnt that Tommy had been returned to her.

Now, just two months on, he was being snatched away.

When Polly and Bel walked through the front door at Tatham Street, it was like walking into a morgue.

Agnes heard them open the door but chose to wait in the kitchen.

As soon as Polly saw her ma, she burst into tears.

Agnes looked at Bel as she took her daughter in her arms. She could see the terrible sadness – also mixed with anger – in Bel's eyes. The ripples of Tommy's decision to go back to war would spread as far as they would go deep.

'He's going back, Ma. He's going back.' Polly's voice was muffled against her mother's chest as she held her tight.

Agnes held her daughter for a good while, until she had exhausted herself and the sobs had finally died down.

'Come on,' she said. 'Come and sit down. Bel's made us a nice pot of tea.'

Agnes gave Bel a weary smile.

The three women sat around the table as Bel poured the tea.

'How did you know?' Bel asked Agnes, adding extra sugar to Polly's cup and handing it to her.

Agnes looked at Polly. She was deathly pale.

'Tommy,' she said. 'He came around here straight after.'

Polly suddenly started fishing around in the top pocket of her overalls, agitated.

She pulled out her engagement ring and slammed it on the table.

'He can have this back as well.'

She may have exhausted the tears, but not the anger.

They all looked at the pretty ruby and diamond engagement ring oscillating on the top of the kitchen table.

Bel worked hard at holding back her tears. It was all so sad. So terribly sad.

Realising how quiet it was, she looked at Agnes.

'Is Lucille next door?'

Agnes nodded. She had not wanted the little girl to see Polly in the state she was in now.

'And Arthur?'

'He left with Tommy. They've gone for a drink.'

'Do you think he'll be able to talk some sense into him?' Bel asked.

'You never know,' Agnes lied. When Tommy had sat her down and told her what his intentions were, Agnes had seen that his mind was made up.

They drank their tea in silence. Words seemed futile.

After Polly finished, she rebuffed her mother's urge to eat something. Instead, she took herself off to bed, praying that sleep would give her some respite from the living hell she had just been plunged back into.

'Her mind's made up,' Tommy said. 'I can tell. She's had enough, and to be honest, I don't blame her. She's right, I've put her through enough. If I was her, I'd probably do exactly the same. Why put yourself through the wringer for the second time?'

Arthur took a sip of his whisky. He nodded, but didn't say anything.

'You understand why I'm doing what I'm doing, don't yer, Grandda?'

Tommy knew that the old man would be gutted he was going back.

'Aye, I do,' Arthur conceded. 'But that's not to say I'm happy about it.'

'Did yer know?'

'I had an inkling,' Arthur said. 'Guessed yer would if yer could.'

Tommy took a gulp of his beer.

'I just wish I could make Polly understand,' he mumbled.

Comparing him to his mother had hurt, but Polly was wrong if that's what she really thought. He did not have a death wish. Anything but. Since falling for Polly, he had never wanted to live more. *Couldn't she realise that?*

'I can't stay here if I feel I could still be of more use over there.' Tommy looked around the crowded bar. The air was thick with smoke. There were mainly shipyard workers here, enjoying a quick pint before heading home.

'I still think about the nurse,' he admitted.

Arthur nodded his understanding.

'I keep thinking that I might not have been able to save her, but I can save others.'

He paused and took a sip of his drink.

'For every limpet mine I get off the bottom of a boat, there'll be at least a dozen lives saved.'

Arthur nodded. It was so like his grandson to be thinking about saving lives rather than killing.

The two men sat in silence for a while, both immersed in their own thoughts.

'Give her time,' Arthur said eventually. 'She'll come around.'

Unfortunately, thought Tommy, time was not on his side.

When Arthur returned home shortly before ten, Agnes was still up.

She had made a fresh pot of tea and had got the whisky out in anticipation.

'Tea?' she said.

'Do yer mind if I just have it straight?' Arthur took a tumbler from the sideboard, sat down at the kitchen table and poured himself a drink.

Agnes put a splash of Scotch into her cup and added tea and a touch of milk.

They chatted for a little while.

Arthur confirmed what Agnes had surmised when she had seen Tommy.

The lad was adamant.

Agnes told Arthur that Polly had already been to see the vicar and had cancelled the wedding.

The pair agreed that a truce in the near future seemed unlikely.

Polly and Tommy's love had become another casualty of this damned war.

Chapter Forty-Three

The next day

Sunday 13 December

'Polly's called off the wedding?' Rosie asked, shocked.

Charlotte looked from Gloria to her sister and then back to Gloria. They were all in the front lounge. Gloria was sitting on the sofa while Rosie poured the tea. Charlotte was keeping Hope amused whilst trying not to miss a single word of the conversation.

'Yes,' Gloria said, taking her cup and saucer off Rosie. 'Her mind seemed pretty much made up.'

She took a sip and looked at Rosie.

'You don't seem all that surprised that Tommy's going back out there, though?'

'I'm not, really,' Rosie said. 'I had a feeling there was more to this dive than simply getting the thumbs up to go back to work.'

Gloria was quiet for a moment while she blew on her tea.

'Well,' she said finally. 'It certainly was a bolt out of the blue for Polly. She clearly had no idea. It was like she was in shock. Shaking. Horrible vacant look in her eyes.'

'Perhaps she didn't want to see the signs,' Rosie mused.

'So, you don't think they'll get back together?' Charlotte asked. She sounded desolate.

Gloria shook her head.

'Well, not for the foreseeable anyway. Polly can be incredibly stubborn. And she's hurt ... And young.'

Rosie nodded sadly.

'Do you think there's anything we can do?' Rosie took a biscuit from the plate on the coffee table and gave it to Hope, who immediately dropped it on the carpet.

'You've got to do something,' Charlotte demanded as she picked up the biscuit, pretended to eat it and then handed it back to Hope.

'I reckon we play it by ear,' Gloria said. 'See what she's like on Monday. Try and get her to see sense.'

'Mmm,' Rosie said. 'Or perhaps Polly's actually making the right decision?'

Gloria and Charlotte looked at Rosie, more than a little surprised.

'Perhaps,' Rosie said thoughtfully, 'she's protecting herself. I mean, just imagine if they got married as planned. Then Tommy leaves. There's a good chance Polly will find herself pregnant, and if the worst, but not exactly unexpected, happens and Tommy doesn't come back – well, then Polly's stuck at home, bringing a child up on her own.'

She paused.

'Just like her own mother did. With barely two pennies to rub together. And it's not as if she'll be able to keep working if she has a baby.'

Another pause.

'And let's face it, she's unlikely to find a decent bloke to take her and a child on.'

Gloria and Charlotte looked at Rosie, slightly horrified.

'What about true love?' Charlotte argued. 'And even if she did have a child, at least it will have had a mam and dad who loved each other. And the child would grow up knowing her father was a hero.'

Rosie didn't say anything. Instead, she bent down and picked up Hope.

'Look at the state of you,' she said gently. 'I think we need to clean you up.'

Gloria watched Rosie with her little girl. She had often thought it unusual that Rosie hadn't fallen pregnant with Peter.

Was that because she too hadn't wanted to be left on her own with a baby to bring up?

Or was it something else?

'So, come on then, Ange, spit it out.' Dorothy looked at her best friend as they walked down Fawcett Street.

'Wot do yer mean "spit it out"?'

The two women were walking back from Meng's Restaurant. It was meant to be a treat after they'd both fulfilled their Sunday obligations of visiting their respective families – as well as an attempt at cheering themselves up after yesterday's bombshell. It hadn't hit the mark on either score.

'Well,' Dorothy said, with more than a hint of exasperation, 'you've hardly uttered a word about the Polly and Tommy debacle.' They came to a stop to let an old couple walk past, before turning left onto Borough Road. 'I've been wittering on about poor Polly and—'

'And about Tommy,' Angie butted in. 'And how awful he is to do something like this ... Polly's been through enough ... he should have thought about her feelings ...' Angie let her voice trail off.

They both shielded their faces as a gust of ice-cold wind blew dust at them.

'Well,' Angie said, 'I personally feel like shaking Polly.'

Dorothy looked at her friend, aghast.

'But she's our friend,' she said. 'And that means we all stick together.'

'But it doesn't mean we have to agree with each other, does it?'

They walked along Borough Road.

'I think Polly's mad not to marry Tommy.'

'But he's broken her heart – *again*,' Dorothy argued.

'It's not as if he meant to,' Angie hit back.

She took a deep breath.

'He's gannin back to war. *Not off with another woman.*'

'That may well be,' Dorothy countered, 'but he's already done his bit. Like Polly said, he's not exactly in the best of health. He's obviously twisted Dr Parker's arm to give him the go-ahead. He doesn't *have* to go. He's already done this once before with Polly when he could have stayed on as reserved occupation. God, Ange, think about it. There's a good chance he won't come back this time.'

They both looked to their left as they passed Gloria's flat.

'She's gone to Rosie's,' Dorothy said, reading her friend's mind. 'Gone to tell her the news.'

The two turned left up Foyle Street.

Suddenly Angie quickened her pace.

'Who's that gannin into our flat?' She flashed a look of concern at Dorothy. 'Mrs Lavender never has visitors.'

Dorothy saw the back of a man trying the front door to the flats.

'Better not be anyone trying to rob us!' Angie barked.

Dorothy hurried to keep up. She'd never known Angie to be in such a mood. God help the bloke if he *was* a burglar.

'Oi!' Angie shouted out.

A young man with short strawberry-blond hair turned round.

As he did so, the main door to the flats opened and Mrs Lavender appeared in the doorway.

'Wot yer deeing?' Angie demanded, having reached the bottom of the steps.

'Oh … umm …' stuttered the young man. He looked at Mrs Lavender and gave her a quick smile, before turning his attention back to the woman on the street. She looked as though she wanted to lynch him.

'I'm—' he started to explain.

Mrs Lavender shuffled forward.

'This is Quentin, girls.' She gestured to Angie and Dorothy to come up. 'Our neighbour,' she said. 'You know, the one I told you about.'

'Oh, *Quentin*!' Dorothy walked past Angie, throwing her a thunderous look. 'How lovely to meet you at long last.' She hurried up the stairs and stuck her hand out.

Mrs Lavender turned and hobbled back into the main hallway, holding open the large black oak door.

'Come in. Get out of the cold.'

Quentin and Dorothy followed Mrs Lavender's orders and stepped into the tiled hallway. Mrs Lavender's flat door was open and the smell of fresh bread told them the old woman had been baking.

'Come on, Angela,' Mrs Lavender beckoned with a bony hand that still had traces of flour on it.

The look on Angie's face still showed signs of suspicion.

'He won't bite,' the old woman laughed.

'Hello there.' Quentin stuck out his hand. 'Quentin Foxton-Clarke. Pleased to meet you.'

Angie took hold of it with a slight reticence.

'Thought yer were robbing the place,' she said.

Quentin laughed a little self-consciously.

'My fault,' he said. 'Always forgetting my keys. Thank goodness for my – or rather *our* – lovely neighbour here.' He turned briefly to Mrs Lavender before diverting his attention back to Angie. 'Otherwise I might well *have* to break into my own home.'

Dorothy looked at her friend and their new neighbour. They were both blushing a little. Either that or there had been a sudden change in temperature.

There was a moment's awkward silence.

'I'll get your keys, Quentin,' Mrs Lavender said. 'Will you be about for Christmas?'

'Yes, I will indeed, Mrs Kwiatkowski,' Quentin told the back of the old woman as she shuffled off into her flat.

She smiled. He was the only person she knew now who could say her name, never mind pronounce it properly.

'Well, we can't stand about yakking,' Angie said, making a move for the stairs.

'No, no, of course not. Well, lovely to meet you,' he said, eyes still trained on Angie. 'Both of you,' he added quickly, throwing Dorothy a slightly apologetic look.

'Oh, and good to know Mrs Kwiatkowski has someone looking out for her.'

Dorothy watched as her friend forced a smile and Quentin half raised a hand hesitantly in the air to bid them farewell.

'I just don't understand why Polly won't marry him,' Martha said, spooning out the roast potatoes.

She was at the kitchen table with her mam and dad. They'd just sat down to eat their Sunday dinner.

'I think she should support Tommy,' Martha said, sitting back while her mother piled peas onto her plate.

Mrs Perkins looked at their daughter. She knew why Martha felt so strongly about Polly's reaction to Tommy's news. Since the air raid at Tatham Street she'd had quite a few heated discussions about Martha continuing to work as an ARP warden – with both her husband and with Martha herself.

'I'm inclined to agree with our daughter,' Mr Perkins said. He was standing, carving the rather meagre joint of pork that had been placed in the middle of the table. 'The lad obviously wants to do his bit and we should all support him in that – especially his future wife.'

Mrs Perkins looked at her husband. She took a spoonful of mash and dumped it on his plate.

'Yes, but his future wife is clearly worried sick about the person she loves and doesn't want to see him come to any harm. Especially when he has already had a close brush with death.'

'That may well be,' Mr Perkins countered, 'but you can't stop someone when their heart's set on something.'

'I agree,' Martha said as her father shared out the slices of pork. 'You've got to support someone if they really want to do something.'

Mrs Perkins looked at her daughter. Her incredibly brave and strong daughter. And then at her husband, who adored Martha – and had done from the day she had been handed to them.

Like Polly, Mrs Perkins also knew that she was not going to get her own way.

Martha may have escaped death by a hair's breadth, but it had not deterred her from doing her ARP work.

She was just thankful that, these past two months, the town had been given a reprieve from any more air raid attacks, which meant Martha had been given a rest from risking her own life trying to save the lives of others.

Chapter Forty-Four

Monday 14 December

The mood on Monday morning could only be described as maudlin.

No one even tried to pretend to be happy.

During their short mid-morning tea break, none of them had said much. The conversation had been forced. They'd all had a communal moan about the bitterly cold weather and looked up at the grey clouds hanging heavy and low.

At lunchtime they'd all made their way to the canteen. Standing in the queue, they had not indulged in their usual discussion about what to eat. Even Muriel had forced herself to keep shtum, refraining from asking any probing questions about the ill-fated lovers.

It wasn't until they'd all finished their lunch that there was an attempt at conversation.

It was hard not to talk about the elephant in the room.

It was hard to know exactly *what* to talk about.

Lily and George's wedding was clearly out of bounds. Even any mention of Christmas seemed inappropriate.

This was the first time since they had all become friends that there'd been an awkwardness between them.

Gloria struggled to hold her tongue. She desperately wanted to take Polly aside and tell her that she thought she was making a terrible mistake, but instinct told her to hold back.

It was Angie, surprisingly, who took the plunge into uncharted waters and, much to Dorothy's horror, started talking about what a great job 'our boys' were doing out in North Africa. Martha had been quick to agree.

Dorothy just as quickly changed the subject. There was no doubting *her* alliance.

On the way back to *Brutus*, Rosie spoke quietly to Polly and told her that if she wanted time off, she just had to ask.

It was clear; the squad was split.

Later that evening when Helen went to see Hope, as she did most Monday evenings, she and Gloria talked about what – if anything – they could do to resolve what they believed amounted to a stand-off between Polly and Tommy.

'Perhaps a meeting between the two could be orchestrated,' Helen suggested as she got Hope ready for bed. She'd bought her little sister the cutest nightie from Risdon's.

'That's not such a bad idea,' Gloria shouted through from the little kitchenette. 'Worth a try. Any port in a storm 'n all that.'

'Arms up,' Helen said as she slipped the thick floral cotton nightie over Hope's head and tucked her into her cot.

As she read Hope her bedtime story, her mind started to stray.

She wondered what had happened to the lovely lemon-coloured romper suit she'd bought for her unborn baby. The one that had been left in the café during the panic to get her to the hospital when she was having her miscarriage.

Again, her mind wandered unchecked to that awful day and she wondered whether or not her instinct had been right. Was the baby she had been carrying a girl?

Chapter Forty-Five

Tuesday 15 December

Tuesday's shift was grey and grinding. The skies were the colour of gunmetal and there were sporadic rumblings of thunder throughout the afternoon.

The poets of the Romantic movement Charlotte was studying for her end-of-term exams would have claimed that nature was merely reflecting the sombre mood of Polly's mindset, for it was clear that she had pulled up the drawbridge to her heart and surrounded it with impenetrable defences.

As the day progressed, a tiny thread of hope started to weave its way around the squad as Gloria quietly mentioned Helen's idea to each of the women whenever they were on their own.

As soon as Polly had left at the end of the shift, Dorothy gathered everyone together. She was just about to speak when suddenly it started to hail.

'Admiral?' she shouted out, grabbing her bag and boxed gas mask and holding them above her head.

The women's scrunched-up faces showed their acquiescence as bullets of ice bounced off them.

En route, Martha dropped by the drawing office to get Hannah and Olly.

Rosie went to the admin offices to fetch Bel and Marie-Anne. Her intention had been to invite Helen as well – after all, the idea they were about to discuss was hers – but when she got there, Helen was holed up in her office with Mr Havelock and Harold. Rosie could just about see Helen's expression through the haze of her grandfather's cigar smoke. She did not look happy.

Within fifteen minutes of the klaxon sounding out, the troops had been rallied and were sitting round the table in the far corner of the pub.

'So, the basic plan is to get Polly and Tommy together and hope to God they manage to sort themselves out,' Dorothy summarised. She took a sip of her port and lemonade, happy that the squad's differences in opinion were being overshadowed by their joint desire to reunite the star-crossed lovers.

'Hopefully, in time for them to get married,' Bel said. She still couldn't, or perhaps wouldn't, accept that the wedding wasn't going ahead. She'd heard from Maud and Mavis, who ran the sweet shop, that the final banns had still been read, despite Polly's visit to the vicar on Saturday night.

'Let's hope so,' Marie-Anne chipped in. She, too, had been gutted at the sudden turn of events.

'Yes, fingers crossed,' Gloria said.

Hannah clapped her hands and looked at Olly.

'*Doufejme,*' he said in Czech.

'"Hopefully",' Hannah translated, smiling at Olly.

'We're going to have to work quickly, though,' Rosie stressed.

'Yes,' Martha agreed. 'We've only got three days.'

'It's cutting it fine, but it's not impossible,' Dorothy said with confidence.

'So, how we ganna make it happen?' Angie looked round the table, the question etched onto her face.

It took an hour and another round of drinks, but they got there in the end.

*

328

'Thanks for helping out with my unit,' Major Black said as Tommy pushed the wheelchair up the ramp to the top of the steps and let them both into the flat.

'I think it's more the other way round,' Tommy said. 'They're helping me.'

He went into the lounge and put on the fire.

'I feel so much fitter already.'

The Major looked at Tommy and wasn't totally convinced he was ready to go back to Gibraltar. Tommy had been teaching his men and training alongside them for the past few days and every night had more or less collapsed exhausted into bed within an hour of getting back to the flat.

'Aye,' the Major said, wheeling himself over to the sideboard. 'There's benefits both ways.'

He held the decanter up at Tommy, but he shook his head.

'What you're teaching my lads is invaluable,' said the Major, pouring himself a Scotch. 'And at the same time, you're getting your levels of fitness up before you go back out there.'

He turned and looked at Tommy.

'Which they need to be.'

He swallowed a mouthful of single malt.

'You'll be no good to anyone if you're not up to it and get ill.'

The Major thought Tommy was rushing things and had told him so. He had also told Tommy that if he'd been in his shoes, he would have married his sweetheart first, and only then told her he was going back.

Tommy went into the kitchen and switched on the oven. He got the steak and kidney pie that Agnes had sent round yesterday and put it on the top shelf. Beryl had brought it round and told him that they were 'all hoping Polly came to her senses'.

Tommy appreciated that others cared and supported him in his decision. But he also knew chances were that Polly would rail against any interference. It might even make her dig her heels in more.

Tommy made himself a cup of tea and went back into the lounge while the pie heated up.

'I've got another favour to ask,' Tommy said, taking a sip of his tea and looking over to the Major. 'I promise this'll be the last one.' He gave a slightly apologetic half-smile.

'Ask away, lad,' the Major said.

'Can you make contact with Commander Bridgman? See if I can have a chat with him about heading back out there?'

The Major took a sip of whisky. He was quiet for a moment while he savoured the burn trickling down his throat.

'You're not jumping the gun a bit? At least wait until the New Year. That's only a fortnight away. Give yourself more time to get back on your feet properly?'

'Nah,' Tommy said. 'After I speak to him and he sanctions my return, it'll take a good few weeks to organise getting me back over there. By that time, I'll be as fit as a fiddle.'

The Major looked at Tommy and pulled a cigar out of his top pocket.

He took his time lighting it.

Commander Bridgman was not known for his procrastination.

He'd wager he'd have Tommy back as quick as a flash.

Certainly quicker than Tommy anticipated.

Chapter Forty-Six

Wednesday 16 December

The first part of the women's plan was put into action shortly after seven o'clock on Wednesday morning.

Gloria had dropped Hope off a little earlier to ensure she and Polly left for work together.

'How are you feeling today?'

Polly and Gloria were standing shivering on the ferry as it see-sawed its way across the Wear. Today the waters looked a murky green. The skies above a mud-grey.

'Awful,' Polly admitted. 'Just awful.'

'Still angry?'

Polly nodded.

'Angry and all muddled up,' Polly said, her face reflecting the veracity of her words.

'Muddled in what way?'

They both grabbed the railing as the paddle steamer hit wash.

'I just don't understand how I can love Tommy *so* much.' Polly paused. 'And yet feel so *angry* towards him.' She looked at Gloria, unsure whether to be completely candid.

Seeing her uncertainty, Gloria encouraged her. 'Go on,' she said, her voice gentle.

'I know what everyone's saying.' Polly looked at Gloria for her reaction.

Seeing that her face was neutral, she continued.

'You all think that I should be proud of him. That he's doing what he's doing for his country.'

Again, she looked at Gloria.

'Carry on.' Gloria gave Polly's arm a gentle squeeze.

'I understand that all up here.' Polly tapped her head with a gloved hand. 'But that doesn't stop me feeling so angry.'

She let out a short gasp of frustration.

'It's the opposite of what people say. "Don't let the head rule the heart." But there's a big part of me that *wants* my head to rule my heart. For my head to tell my heart that I should love Tommy regardless. That I should cast aside this awful anger and deep resentment.' Polly took in a scoop of sea air. The seagulls squawked as they soared above.

'But my heart's not listening. It's like it's gone stone deaf.'

Gloria put her arm around Polly's shoulder and gave her a hug.

'You mightn't be able to let go of the anger at the moment,' Gloria said. 'But you will. It'll burn itself out. I promise you.'

Polly looked at Gloria and knew she was speaking from experience.

As they made their way off the ferry, Gloria decided to simply take the bull by the horns.

'We're all going to the Admiral on Thursday night. And yer coming. I'm not taking no for an answer.'

She gave Polly a gentle nudge.

Polly's face was sad, but she attempted a smile.

'Looks like I don't have a choice.'

At lunchtime, Gloria chinked the side of her teacup with a stainless-steel teaspoon as though she was about to make a toast.

The women fell silent and looked at Gloria, who was sitting at the top of the table.

'You'll be pleased to know that Polly is accompanying us to the Admiral tomorrow after work.'

'Yeah!' Dorothy declared.

Everyone else voiced their enthusiasm.

Polly forced a smile that didn't quite reach her eyes, but it was a smile, nevertheless.

Gloria looked down the table at everyone as they started chattering away to each other.

The ice had been broken.

If their plan didn't come to fruition, then this, at least, would be the runners-up prize.

After finishing her lunch, Rosie told her squad she needed to chat to Ralph and his team about a ship that might need bringing into the dry basin for some welding work to be done on her hull.

Gloria herded everyone back to the ways. *Brutus* was just about ready to take centre stage. She just needed a bit of a manicure before her big day.

When Rosie returned twenty minutes later, she gave Gloria a nod.

The second part of their plan had been put into action.

At the end of the shift, Rosie timed it so that she caught Bel and Marie-Anne coming out of the admin block.

'Did you get the thumbs up?' Bel asked as the three of them were jostled about in the usual end-of-shift bottleneck at the main gates.

Rosie nodded. Ralph and his team had been in a particularly good mood as they'd just caught a news bulletin on their little wireless announcing that the Russians had beaten back the Italian Eighth Army along the Don River, north-west of Stalingrad. Rosie crossed her fingers that the

Red Army would stay strong. They all knew so much hung on the outcome of the war on the Eastern Front.

When Bel got home, she told Arthur that Ralph had asked if Tommy would meet him and the rest of his team for a drink in the Admiral after work tomorrow. They wanted to buy him a pint before he left, as well as to 'wet the baby's head' – yard-speak for christening *Brutus* in anticipation of her launch the following day. If Arthur suspected something was afoot, he didn't let on, but dutifully walked round to John Street and relayed the invitation.

Bel kept herself busy until Arthur's return. She tried to act nonchalant when Arthur told her that Tommy was chuffed he'd been asked and to tell Ralph he would see them all there. Arthur had thought Tommy's keenness to be within spitting distance of Thompson's at the end of the day shift might have more to do with catching a glimpse of Polly, or better still, bumping into her.

It was now the fourth day since the falling-out. Arthur had hoped that Polly's ire might have cooled down, but it would seem not. Whenever she was about, you could cut the atmosphere with a knife. Not that she'd been about much. She'd come in late, force down whatever food her ma put in front of her, then go to her room, shut the door and not come out until the next morning.

Whether or not she was sleeping was a different matter.

The dark circles under her eyes suggested not.

When Polly walked into the Maison Nouvelle, she was surprised to see Helen there.

She had a clothes bag over her arm and was saying her thanks and farewell to Kate.

Helen looked at Polly and then at her wedding dress, on show in the middle of the shop.

It was quite simply beautiful.

'If it was me,' said Helen, 'I'd get married just so I could wear that dress.'

Polly looked at Helen and had to let out a short burst of laughter. She believed her.

'Are you coming for a drink tomorrow night at the Admiral? After work?' Polly asked.

Helen shook her head.

'I've got too much to do before the launch.'

Polly caught the excitement in Helen's voice and guessed that whatever was in the canvas clothes bag was her outfit for her long-awaited date with *Brutus*.

Helen's love, Polly realised, was her job.

'You enjoy, though,' Helen said, heading out the door. 'I've got Harold to put some money behind the bar as a way of saying thank you for everyone's hard work.'

After Helen left, Kate made them both a cup of tea out the back.

When Polly apologised to Kate for wasting her time, Kate dismissed her words with the wave of a delicate hand. Polly offered to pay for all the work that had gone into the dress, but Kate told her not to worry – the dress would be sold.

'I've already had interest,' she told Polly as they both supped their tea.

Leaving the shop, Polly couldn't help but turn to take a final look at her wedding dress.

It hurt.

But what pained her the most was that the hurt was, in part, self-inflicted.

Chapter Forty-Seven

Thursday 17 December

On Thursday morning Rosie nipped up to the admin offices on some bogus errand and spoke briefly to an excited-looking Bel.

Returning to her squad, who were scattered about *Brutus*'s deck, welding areas that had been marked out with large white chalk crosses, Rosie went to see Gloria, and then Dorothy and Angie, and finally Martha. Pretending to check their workmanship, she gave each of her squad a thumbs up. Their faces could not be seen due to their metal masks, but their eyes, visible behind their protective tinted glass, showed their glee.

Polly was totally unaware of what was happening around her, so determined was she to lose herself in her world of spitting and glittering metal.

During the lunch break, Dorothy had to work hard to keep her excitement under wraps, although they were able to pass off the buzz of anticipation as their joy at having finished *Brutus* ahead of schedule.

At the end of the shift, they all packed up quickly and headed to the Admiral, determined to get a table. They did not want Polly and Tommy's reconciliation to be conducted whilst squashed up at the bar.

Dorothy and Angie made a point of dragging Polly off to the toilets to get her to give her face a quick wash.

'This is meant to be a night out,' Dorothy cajoled.

'Even if we're still in our dirty overalls – ' Angie chipped in.

'It doesn't mean our faces have to look grubby as well,' Dorothy finished off.

Polly, however, drew the line at wearing lipstick.

When Ralph and his diving squad came in, Rosie waved over to them and Bel smiled at them as they got a table near the women welders.

'So, a toast to *Brutus*,' Martha said, raising her half-pint of shandy.

'To *Brutus*!' the women all chimed in as they chinked glasses.

'May she stay strong 'n help us beat bloody Jerry,' Angie said.

'Hear! Hear!' Dorothy said, her eyes darting to the pub's entrance.

'And comes back in one piece,' Gloria went on.

'And sooner rather than later,' Marie-Anne added.

They all took a sip of their drinks.

For the next half an hour they all chatted away.

Polly tried not to think about Tommy or what he was doing now.

After her second port and lemonade, she started to feel a little light-headed. Although she was listening to her friends' banter, her mind kept slipping back to Tommy.

The anger was still there, but she could feel something else. Another feeling that was starting to nudge its way past her defences.

Was it doubt?

Tommy looked at his watch and felt his heart sink.

The Major had told him to expect a call from Commander Bridgman at around five o'clock. Tommy had reckoned he would be able to have the necessary conversation, which wouldn't take long as neither he nor his commander were men of many words, and still make it across the river and down to North Sands by half five.

In time to possibly see Polly leave Thompson's at the end of the shift.

He looked again at his watch and at the clock on the mantelpiece.

It was now half-past five.

The klaxon would be sounding out and Ralph and his team would be making their way to the Admiral.

Polly and her pals would be making their way to the main gates.

Tommy made himself a cup of tea, keeping the kitchen door wide open so he could hear the phone when it rang. Not that he could fail to hear it even if all the doors were shut. The ringer had been set to loud.

Walking back into the lounge, Tommy set the cup and saucer down next to the black Bakelite phone.

He waited.

And waited.

Six o'clock came and went.

Half six.

Seven.

Ralph and his unit would have had their usual two pints by now.

They might have pushed the boat out and had a third, just in case he'd got held up.

Half seven.

Even if the commander rang now, and even if they were only on the phone for a few minutes, he still wouldn't make it to the Admiral until eight.

Tommy sat back resignedly.

The women kept up their cheery banter until seven.

They managed to keep Polly there until half past, when she declared she was 'shattered'.

She left for home with Bel and Gloria.

The brief respite brought by the alcohol had been replaced by tiredness.

And now depression seemed to be nestling up alongside the anger.

Bel struggled to hide her disappointment at Tommy's no-show, and Gloria her sense of defeat.

It was now Thursday evening. Neither of the women could see Polly and Tommy sorting out their differences in the next twenty-four hours, then making a mad dash down the aisle on Saturday morning.

When Agnes answered the door and saw Polly, Bel and Gloria – minus Tommy – she knew the women's well-meaning plan had failed. Bel had told her what they intended to do. She hadn't said much. Her feeling being that whether her daughter got back with Tommy or not, the prognosis was still not good. Perhaps it would be marginally better if Polly and Tommy made up and even got married ... She wasn't sure.

'What will be, will be,' she said quietly to Gloria as she handed over a sleepy Hope.

Gloria nodded her agreement, carefully putting her daughter into the pram before taking her leave.

Pushing Hope up Tatham Street, Gloria speculated whether they had all really been wanting a happy-ever-after ending for themselves as much as for Polly, when there was actually no such thing. Other than in the movies Dorothy dragged them all to see.

'Oh, Jack,' she said to the open skies. 'What I'd give to be coming back home to you this evening.'

*

'My jaw's actually aching from having to pretend I'm happy,' Angie said as they all trudged up the embankment to catch the tram back over to the other side.

'What can we do now?' Martha said as they reached Dame Dorothy Street.

'I don't think there's anything more we can do,' Rosie said, looking at her watch. She had promised to bring some fish and chips in for supper seeing as she wasn't working at Lily's this evening.

'I just hate to give up,' Dorothy said, her voice oozing despondency.

'But we can't force them to make up,' Marie-Anne rationalised as they reached the bus stop.

'Perhaps it's for the best,' Rosie said, putting her hand out as the bus approached. 'Sometimes things happen for a reason,' she added as the bus's brakes screeched to a halt.

Dorothy, Angie, Anne-Marie and Martha all looked at Rosie.

It was not a good look.

It was a look that said that they were neither convinced nor comforted by their boss's words.

Chapter Forty-Eight

Gibraltar

'Watts!' The commander's brash voice was even more animated than usual.

'Sorry I couldn't call earlier. Having some problems with a few "hogs", if you get my meaning.'

The commander knew that Tommy would understand. 'Hogs', or maiali as they were known in Italian, were slow-speed manned torpedoes, the rounded front a detachable warhead containing three hundred kilos of explosives and a time fuse. Having just been used in the raid on Algiers, they were a pain in the Allies' backside. A deadly pain.

'Thank God you're alive.' The commander spoke through a swirl of smoke. 'Of course, I was one of the last to know. You know what communication's like out here. Anyway, you all right?'

He paused.

'All in one piece? Sorry, hate to put it so bluntly, old chap.'

Commander Bridgman listened.

'Brilliant news. Brilliant news.' He stood up before sitting down again and yanking open the top drawer of his desk.

'What was that, lad? You want to come back?'

A wide smile spread across the commander's face. He pulled out a half-bottle of Scotch.

'You've just made my day. No, make that my week!' He poured a good measure of whisky into a cup on his desk.

'Not to put any pressure on yer, lad, but when do yer think you'll be wanting to come back to the Rock?'

Commander Bridgman took a mouthful of Scotch.

'What? Seriously? Yer right as rain?'

He took a deep drag on his rollie. Spat out loose tobacco.

'You've got medical clearance?'

'You sure?'

'This just keeps on getting better. Hang on there.' Commander Bridgman got up and shouted through the open doorway to Able Seaman Grantham, who was in the next room.

'Grantham. Get me a list of all scheduled flights leaving our green and pleasant land!'

Two minutes later, Able Seaman Grantham was placing the requested timetable in front of the commander.

'Here we are. RAF Usworth … Next available flight out …'

There was a pause.

'Aye. Should be able to get you on this one … Saturday the twenty-sixth … Boxing Day.' The commander sat back in his seat.

'Do you think you'll be right for that?'

A smile appeared on his face.

'Fantastic. See yer then, laddie. I can fill yer in on everything that's been happening.'

He was just about to hang up when he added, 'Bloody glad to have you back on board. Bloody glad.'

342

Chapter Forty-Nine

'Cheer up! It might never happen!' one of the platers' apprentices shouted over to the women welders as they all trudged across to the ways to see *Brutus* baptised. He whooped with laughter when six dark, scowling faces turned on him.

'Yer wanna be careful,' Angie bellowed over. 'It might *just* happen to you!'

Dorothy tugged her friend away from further confrontation.

In normal circumstances, the women would have all been cock-a-hoop. The launch of any ship was a cause for celebration. And today even more so, as not only had they beaten their deadline in getting *Brutus* into the water by a good few weeks, it also looked as though they were going to hit a new production record. The highest in thirty-six years.

'Bloomin' heck,' Angie said, staring up at the main stage where Helen was standing with the mayor, Myers Wayman, as well as Mr Havelock, Miriam and half a dozen other local bigwigs and dignitaries for the traditional smashing of the champagne bottle.

'Blimey,' Dorothy said, 'she certainly looks the part, doesn't she?'

Polly looked at Helen in her stunning navy-blue dress, but all she could think about was her own stunning ivory wedding dress.

A dress that she should have been wearing tomorrow.

A dress that was now for sale.

The women tried to stay together as they were pushed from all sides and hundreds of workers crowded around the quayside to get a view.

'Can you hear what they're saying?' Martha asked.

They all shook their heads.

Mr Havelock was speaking into a microphone, but his words were unintelligible.

'I'm surprised Charlotte didn't want to see the launch?' Gloria asked Rosie.

'Oh, believe you me, she did,' Rosie said. 'She pleaded. Begged. Even offered to clean the house from top to bottom.'

Gloria laughed out loud. 'I know what I would have said!'

Rosie chuckled.

'To be honest, I would probably have let her come, but the school's red-hot on absenteeism. The head teacher made a point of telling me pupils have to have a very good excuse if they want even half a day off school. I didn't think she'd be too impressed if Charlie wanted time off to watch a launch. Especially as she's only just started at the school.'

Rosie and Gloria looked down at the slipway as half a dozen shipwrights pulled away the blocks, and then up to see a mechanical arm of steel flinging a bottle of champagne against the bow.

A huge roar sounded out around the yard.

'There she goes!' Gloria shouted out as *Brutus* slowly eased her girth down the ways, gaining momentum at a leisurely pace. She looked at Helen, the epitome of professionalism, talking to Mr Thompson. Jack would be so proud of his daughter if he could see her now.

Polly watched as the waters of the Wear parted and *Brutus* ploughed her way into the river. White foam rose up, mirroring the effervescence of the exploding bottle of champagne.

Polly did her maths.

It was exactly two years and one week since they had watched their first launch. She recalled it so vividly, not because of how proud she'd felt, but because, just a few weeks previously, she had said a heart-rending goodbye to Tommy at the train station.

Like now, she had watched the tugboats gently guide the newly launched ship along the river to the engine works.

Back then, she had made a wish for Tommy's safe return.

How much had changed.

Looking back, she realised how young and naïve she'd been. Now she felt older. Her heart more worn and battered.

'What're you thinking about?' Rosie asked, breaking her reverie.

Letting out a laugh that was wholly without mirth, Polly rolled her eyes.

'Tommy,' she said. 'What else?'

'How are you feeling about everything?' Rosie asked tentatively, knowing that tomorrow must be playing heavily on Polly's mind. As it was for them all.

Polly avoided the question.

'I don't know how you do it,' she said instead.

'With Peter?' Rosie asked.

Polly nodded.

Rosie sighed a little sadly.

'Ours is a very different relationship to yours,' she tried to explain. 'I don't know if I'd feel like I do if I was in your shoes.'

Polly looked at Rosie before focusing back on the afternoon's main attraction.

'Thank you,' Polly said.

'For what?' Rosie asked, curious.

'For not judging me,' Polly said simply.

She looked at Rosie.

'I just don't feel I know myself any more. Does that sound stupid?'

Rosie shook her head, showing she understood.

'I don't understand how I can feel like this,' Polly said. 'I used to think I was a good person, but I'm not.' She took a breath. 'I actually think I'm an awful person.'

A pause.

'But knowing it doesn't mean I'm able to switch back to the person I was.'

Rosie could see tears beginning to pool in Polly's eyes.

'I feel like I'm the most unpatriotic person ever.'

Rosie let out a short burst of laughter and put her arm around Polly.

'How do you figure that one? Look what you just helped build.' She nodded her head over to *Brutus*'s back end.

'Because I should be waving Tommy off with my whole-hearted blessing,' Polly argued. 'I should be bursting with pride that he is going off to war. Serving his country. *Saving* his country.'

Polly exhaled.

'I really wish I could, but I can't … It's like something inside of me won't let me.'

As Helen waited patiently for the start of the afternoon's show, she thought of how well the whole yard had done to have completed *Brutus* a month ahead of schedule. The launch had originally been scheduled in the New Year – ironically the same time as her due date.

Helen pushed the thought from her mind.

Today was about her life now – not the life that could have been.

She watched as the men prepared for the launch. Two more rows of blocks had been built on either side of the row that held the centre keel, like a wide pair of wooden railway tracks on which another pair of tracks called sliding ways had been rested. Thick yellow grease had been melted and poured between them. Helen's eyes fell on the launching triggers placed at both ends of the tracks, ready to be released, allowing *Brutus* to start her maiden voyage.

Her grandfather had started to speak. His voice was strong and confident, belying his advancing years and fragile physique.

Down by the side of the slipway lay heavy coils of rusty chains, like an oversized pile of guts, ready to act as breaks to ensure *Brutus* didn't hit the riverbank opposite.

Listening to her grandfather's speech and exclamation of 'May God bless her and all who sail in her!' Helen thought of the day when she would be the one to speak. The one to press the button that would smash the bottle. The one to launch the ship.

She was determined that day would not be far off.

Helen watched as *Brutus* moved slowly, majestically forward, before plunging into the water. The blocks of the sliding ways gathered around her wide hull, floating like debris.

The ship had been born.

The wooden blocks a sort of afterbirth.

The tugs, like midwives, taking her away to the engineering works further down the river, where she would get her engine.

And her first feed of oil.

Helen felt a mix of pride and power. She had been at the helm, metaphorically speaking, when it came to building this ship.

Her intention was to be there for many more.

'*Well done, Papa, dear.*'

347

Helen looked to see her mother, done up to the nines, ingratiating herself with her father. She must want something. Money probably.

Helen felt the urge to slap her – and her grandfather for that matter.

They were as bad as each other.

She would never forgive them for the way they had behaved towards her when she had been expecting her child. Or for their undisguised glee when she'd had her miscarriage.

Just as she would never forgive her mother for sending her father over the border and forbidding his return, so terrified was she of people finding out that her marriage was a sham.

If it wasn't for her mother, her father would be here now, revelling in her success.

Looking again at her mother, Helen thought how outwardly she appeared to be the ideal of a doting daughter. A loving wife and mother. With her perfectly bobbed blonde hair, make-up, French-polished nails and olive-green dress, she was the envy of those who were not privy to the truth.

I will never be like you, so help me God, Helen vowed to herself.

Seeing Mr Thompson, Helen put out her hand and smiled graciously as the owner of J.L. Thompson & Sons took her gloved hand and expressed his gratitude for all her hard work.

'Thank you, Mr Thompson.' Helen spoke clearly and confidently. The cheering of the workers below had died down now that *Brutus* was being settled in her new, albeit temporary, home.

'I was hoping to chat to you about the future,' she said. She held his hand for a second longer than normal before releasing it.

'*My* future, to be exact,' she said.

'Talk to my secretary,' Mr Thompson said. 'And set up a meeting.'

Mr Thompson looked at Mr Havelock's granddaughter. Jack Crawford's daughter. She might well have her father's looks, but it was clear she had her grandfather's drive and ambition.

'And congratulations,' he added as he made to leave.

Helen raised her perfectly shaped eyebrows questioningly.

'It's official,' Mr Thompson said with a genuine smile. 'The yard's hit a new tonnage record.'

'That's wonderful news,' Helen said, a wide smile spreading across her face.

She watched as Mr Thompson made his way back down to the yard, shaking hands and saying the odd word here and there.

She felt so excited she could burst.

Her immediate thought was that she couldn't wait to tell John, until she remembered they weren't speaking.

On the south side of the river, there was the usual large crowd of proud Sunderland folk who had braved the cold weather to see their town's latest creation. Amongst the swell was Joe, Lucille perched on his shoulders. He rarely missed a launch, especially one from the shipyard where both his sister and his wife now worked.

Agnes and Beryl were standing in front of him. They had brought Hope and were taking turns carrying her. They had both agreed it was important the little girl saw the fruits of her mam's labour.

Tommy and Arthur were positioned further along the south docks, just a few yards in front of their old home, the Diver's House. It hurt Tommy to recall Polly's enthusiasm about where they might live once they got married. He thought about tomorrow – what should have been their wedding day – and felt awash with sadness.

Tommy knew it was pointless to scrutinise the hundreds of workers gathered on the north side in an effort to get a glimpse of Polly, but he did anyway.

Arthur, meanwhile, was contemplating how this might well be his last launch and felt fortunate to be watching it with his grandson. He only wished that Tommy and Polly had patched up their differences. He had thought and thought about possible ways to persuade the pair to make up and enjoy the short time they had together, but he had drawn a blank.

He had been hoping the women's plan that Agnes had told him about might be a success, and that once the pair were in the same room as each other, they'd sort themselves out. But that had failed.

And, of course, he'd asked Flo for her advice, but even she had not given him any clues.

Chapter Fifty

By the time the launch was all done and dusted, it was nearly half-past five. Spotting Hannah walking towards the main gates with Olly, Polly grabbed her haversack and gas mask, said a quick goodbye to the women and broke into a trot.

'Hannah!' she shouted out.

Hannah and Olly both turned. Their movements synchronised.

'Are you two off anywhere in particular?' Polly asked as she reached them and came to an abrupt halt.

Hannah shook her head.

'No, why?'

Polly sighed.

'Ma says I should go and see your aunty Rina and Vera at the café. Thank them for their offer of making the wedding cake ...' Polly blinked back a sudden welling of tears that seemed to come from nowhere ' ... and apologise for not going to see them personally when I called the wedding off.'

'You don't need to apologise. Aunty Rina and Vera were just sad when I told them.' Hannah tried to sound sincere, but she was really telling a half-truth. Vera had been sad. Much as the old woman revelled in her reputation of being unsentimental, with a skin thicker than a rhinoceros, she had failed to hide her disappointment that Polly and Tommy had split up.

Her aunt's reaction to the news, on the other hand, had been a bit shocking. Normally Rina was a very empathetic woman. But on hearing the news, she'd bashed the tray down on the counter and given anyone who would listen a mini sermon on why humanity as a whole needed people like Tommy to do whatever they could to win this war.

'Honestly, you don't have to,' Hannah said as they all handed over their boards to Alfie.

'No, I do,' Polly said. 'Even if it's just to appease my ma. She'll give me an earbashing if I don't.'

'All right, then,' Hannah said, throwing Olly a concerned look. 'We'll come with you.'

Twenty minutes later, after a squashed ferry journey back over the river and an equally squashed walk back up to High Street East, they'd reached Vera's.

Walking into the café, they were hit immediately by warmth mixed with the comforting smell of freshly made bread.

Looking over to the main counter at the far end of the tea shop, Polly could see the top halves of Rina and Vera, who were standing side by side behind the counter.

Seeing Hannah, Olly and Polly, they both waved.

Vera pointed over to a spare table by the window. Her face looked serious. Polly could have sworn she gave Rina a slightly apprehensive look.

A few minutes later, Vera brought over a pot of tea and three cups and saucers on a tray, before hurrying over to the front door and changing the sign to 'Closed'.

She shuffled back again.

'You all right, pet?'

Polly was taken aback by Vera's tone. It lacked its usual bite. She nodded and once again swallowed hard.

'I just wanted to say thank you for offering to make the cake.' Polly couldn't bring herself to use the word 'wedding'. 'And that I'm sorry I didn't come and tell you myself. Personally.'

'Yer ma sent yer round?' Vera said.

Polly nodded, a little shamefaced.

'Dinnit worry, pet,' Vera said. 'Nothing's spoilt.' She unloaded the contents of the tray onto the table. Seeing Rina drying her hands on her pinny as she made her way over, Vera picked up the tray again.

'Just shout if yer want owt to eat,' she said, before turning to clear the table next to theirs, even though a couple were still sitting there.

'Polly, this is a surprise,' Rina said as she reached them. She smiled briefly at Hannah and Olly, before focusing back on Polly.

'How are you, my dear?' There was no trace of her Czech-oslovakian roots. Her pronounciation was perfect BBC.

Polly forced a smile.

'I'm all right.' She took a deep breath. 'I just wanted to apologise for not coming in person to tell you that the wedding was off.' Another swallow. 'And to thank you for the offer of baking the cake.' There, she had said it. Hopefully she could drink her tea down relatively quickly, make her excuses and go.

Go home and bury herself under her bedcover.

Rina pulled a chair from the table that was just being vacated by the couple, who had taken Vera's not so subtle hint that it was closing time. She sat down and looked at Polly. Seeing the despair on the young girl's face softened her heart. She looked terrible. She might be as pretty as a picture, but it went no way towards camouflaging the mental hell she was clearly languishing in.

'How are you?' she asked. 'Honestly?'

Polly looked at Rina. There was something about her demeanour that demanded a truthful answer.

'Awful,' Polly said.

Rina looked at her.

'I want to show you something,' she said, getting up and going back to the other side of the counter. Her head disappeared for a moment. When she reappeared, she was carrying her handbag. She manoeuvred her way back to the table, sat down and plonked the bag onto her lap.

Polly, Hannah, and Olly watched with interest as she flicked the clasp. Unzipping the inside pocket, she pulled out a worn and rather dirty piece of paper.

She handed it to Polly.

Everyone looked at the paper.

Out of the corner of her eye, Polly saw Hannah sit back in her chair.

'What is it?' Polly asked.

'That, my dear, is what is known as a *Kindertransport* number.' Rina's voice was sad.

Polly looked at her, puzzled.

'*Kinder* is the German word for "children",' Rina explained, glancing across at Hannah. 'And *transport* is self-explanatory.'

She paused.

'It was Hannah's number when she was sent over here.'

Polly was listening intently. This was not what she had expected. Hannah had never talked much about the practicalities of how she had been brought here.

'I won't go into all the details as I know it still upsets my niece.' Rina glanced quickly at Hannah. 'But when my sister and brother-in-law made the decision to send their only child over to me – to this country – it was the hardest decision they had ever made. I know the pain they went through because I spoke to my sister at the time.'

She looked across at Hannah again. Olly had taken hold of her hand.

'Do you know why I carry this tatty and worn piece of paper with me wherever I go?' Rina was working hard to keep the grief out of her voice.

Polly shook her head.

'I keep it as a reminder of what love is,' she said, looking at Polly.

'My sister and her husband loved Hannah so much that they let her go. They sent her away. To somewhere safe. Somewhere she stood a chance of living. My sister told me that she felt her heart had been ripped from her chest. It was as though she was missing a part of her very being when she sent Hannah away. But I told her that what she had done was the greatest act of love I had ever seen. She had sacrificed her own feelings and her own needs to ensure the safety of her child.'

Rina looked at Polly.

Tears appeared in the eyes of both women.

'People do not yet know of the terrible evil that is happening overseas. The atrocities that are being committed on innocent people as we sit here drinking our tea.'

Another look at Hannah. She hadn't wanted to say this in front of her.

'So, we need people like your Tommy to try and do what they can to stop it. Sometimes in life, love has to be sacrificed for a greater love.

'What your Tommy is doing is a huge act of love. He is not only prepared to sacrifice his love for you, but he is prepared to sacrifice his own life to save those he doesn't even know.'

She paused.

'There is no greater act of love, in my opinion.'

355

And with that, Rina put her hands on top of Polly's and squeezed them.

'I've got to go now,' she said simply, looking over to Vera, who was busy tidying up. 'Otherwise, I will be subjected to a full half-hour of moans and groans.'

She smiled, her eyes looking deeply into Polly's.

Then she got up and left.

As Polly walked home, Rina's words kept going round and round in her head.

The feeling of doubt she'd had last night was back.

She felt a shiver of panic.

Had she made the most terrible of mistakes?

She walked on.

Sometimes in life, love has to be sacrificed for a greater love.

Chapter Fifty-One

Like every morning for the past seven days, Polly woke with a sense that something was amiss.

It took all of two seconds this morning for her brain to fully engage, and with it came the awful awareness of her present reality.

What made it a hundred times worse this morning was that today would have been her wedding day.

As Polly got up and pulled on her work clothes and then her overalls, she felt sick to the pit of her stomach.

'Try and eat something,' Agnes said when Polly came into the kitchen.

'Honestly, Ma, I can't.' Polly poured herself half a cup of tea, splashed some milk in it and took a slurp.

Agnes simply stood and watched her daughter, unsure what to say.

Polly was out the door within minutes.

Walking to work, she wrapped her scarf tightly around her neck. It was bitterly cold. There was frost on the ground, making the whole of the east end look prettier and less grey.

The perfect day for a winter wedding.

By the time she'd reached Thompson's, she knew what she had to do to get through this day.

Work.

Work until she dropped.

357

'You all right?' Rosie asked as soon as Polly reached their workstation.

Polly looked at Rosie, and then at Gloria, Martha, Dorothy and Angie, who were standing round the five-gallon barrel fire, warming their hands and stamping their feet. She was surprised to see that they had beaten her to work.

'Please don't say anything,' Polly said, forcing back the tears that had started to well up on seeing the concern in their faces.

'Here, get this down yer.' Angie handed her a cup of steaming-hot tea before going back to her place next to Dorothy.

'Yer know we're here for yer all day,' Gloria said. 'We won't fuss over yer.' She looked around at the women. 'Will we?'

They all nodded in agreement.

'But you just say if yer want to talk, or cry, or scream and shout.'

'Or if you have a change of mind,' Martha said.

Her words elicited scowls from the rest of the women.

Polly looked at Martha. She could never be angry with their gentle giant. She was just saying what they all thought deep down.

'Oh, Martha.' Polly let out a slightly strangled laugh. 'Even if I did, it's too late now.'

The women all looked at Polly. It was the first chink they had seen in the armour of anger she had been encased in this past week.

Tommy killed the engine of his black BSA. He'd been able to get it out of storage after being given a petrol allowance for his work with Major Black and his Home Guard unit.

He didn't dismount, though. Just sat with one hand on the throttle, the other over the warm engine. He knew in his heart of hearts that it was pointless being here. But all the same, he had to come. Just in case.

He let out a bitter laugh.

Who was he kidding? No one but himself. That was for sure.

He looked at the entrance of St Ignatius. The door was open, but it was quiet. There were no signs that another couple had filled the gap they had left.

Tommy couldn't fail to notice what a beautiful day it was. Crisp, fresh and frosty white.

He gave it until a quarter past; when it came, he was going to go, but couldn't.

He waited until half past.

It wasn't until midday that he turned on the ignition, kick-started the engine and rode away.

He only had himself to blame.

This had been his choice.

Helen came out of her office and walked over to Bel's desk.

'Is she all right?'

There was no need to specify whom she was asking about.

'I think so.' Bel looked at Helen. She looked stunning today. The glow of yesterday's launch was still very much present, though there was sadness in her emerald eyes, and concern.

'She's not had a break.' Bel looked across to Marie-Anne. 'Has she?'

Marie-Anne shook her head. She personally thought that Polly was mad. She had no sympathy for someone who would purposely destroy something they would all have given their right arm for: true love.

The klaxon sounded out and Helen walked over to the window. She watched Rosie take off her helmet, followed by the rest of the women.

Bel and Marie-Anne joined her at the window and looked down at the yard. The frost had gone, allowing the slightly depressing grey of the shipyard to return.

'Has anyone heard from Tommy?' Helen asked.

Bel shook her head.

Helen thought of John. They too had not spoken since the day of the dive, when she had returned home after leaving Polly at the Admiral and called the Ryhope.

She had been angry. Had told John in a polite, civilised manner that Polly and Tommy had split up and that Polly was distraught. That the wedding was off. And that this time Tommy would be lucky if he came back home in anything but a box.

Then she'd hung up.

She thought he might have called her back, but it had been a week now and he hadn't.

She hated to admit it, but she missed him.

Chapter Fifty-Two

Tommy rode carefully. As he always did when he had the old man riding pillion.

Arthur had asked if he would take him to the cemetery and Tommy had agreed.

It was ironic that on the day he should be getting married, he was going to visit a grave instead.

It wasn't often that Arthur asked him for anything, though, so when his grandda suggested going to see Flo this afternoon, there had been no hesitation.

When they pulled up outside the cemetery on the Ryhope Road, Arthur carefully got off, removed his helmet, unbuttoned his winter coat and took out the bunch of flowers that had survived the journey relatively unscathed.

Tommy hung both helmets on the handlebars and unzipped his jacket.

As they passed through the open wrought-iron gates, Tommy looked at Arthur.

'I don't know what to do. About Polly,' he admitted.

Arthur nodded but didn't say anything. He had no idea what to say. He'd never been particularly good when it came to talking about feelings, never mind affairs of the heart.

Flo, he begged silently, *help me out here, pet.*

'It's strange,' Tommy said, casting a sidelong look at Arthur. He slowed his pace. The old man looked exhausted. 'I knew exactly what I had to do when I started to get better. When I thought there was a chance I might be able to go back to the Rock.'

They made their way up the wide gravel path.

'When I'm diving, I always know what to do, even when things go wrong. It's like an instinct.' He pushed his hair away from his face in frustration. 'But with Polly I honestly have no idea what to do for the best.' He blew out air. 'It's like I'm floundering around at sea, not knowing whether to go north, south, east or west.'

As they neared the part of the cemetery where Flo was buried, Arthur handed Tommy the bunch of wild flowers he had picked that morning. Tommy took them and watched as his grandfather adjusted his tie. He had on his best suit.

'When it comes to Polly, I've always been unsure what's right and what's not. Should I just go and see her and beg her to have me back? Even if it is just for a week?' His departure date was playing heavily on his mind. 'Or should I just leave her be and let her get on with her life without me?'

They turned left off the main pathway and started walking on grass still crisp with frost due to the shade of the large, overhanging oaks.

'Is it cruel to try and win her over and then leave her again?' Tommy asked.

They came to a stop, having reached Flo's headstone.

It was a simple, well-kempt plot with a basic headstone stating that Florence Elizabeth Watts was a much-loved wife, mother and grandmother. Underneath were the dates of her birth and her death.

Tommy looked at Arthur.

'Aye, lad,' he said, 'put them on there.'

Tommy crouched down and carefully laid out the wild flowers. His grandfather never put them in a vase with water, saying he preferred them to have a natural life and end up back in the soil where they'd come from.

They both stood in silence for a short while.

As they walked away, Arthur gave the grave one last look.

They had started back towards the main gates when Arthur came to a sudden stop, as though struck by an idea.

'If yer nana were here now,' he said with great certainty, 'I know exactly what she'd say.'

Tommy looked at Arthur.

'Go on,' he encouraged.

Arthur laughed to himself as if seeing the whole scene being played out in front of him.

He looked at Tommy with a smile on his face.

'She would come stomping out the kitchen – because, of course, she was always in the kitchen. She would stand there, hands on her hips, looking at the two of us as though we were simpletons, and she'd say in that way of hers, "Tommy, lad, if yer want something, you've just gotta go 'n get it. No one else is gonna get it and stick it on a plate in front of yer. Life doesn't work like that."'

Tommy smiled.

Even though he had been small at the time, he could remember his grandmother saying just those words. They were words of advice he had taken to heart as a child. Words he had acted upon as he'd grown up and become a man – when it had come to doing the job he wanted, at least.

They walked on a little further.

Suddenly Tommy stopped.

He looked at Arthur.

'Will you be all right getting the bus back to Tatham Street?'

Arthur looked at his grandson.

'Of course I will, lad.'

By the time the words were out of Arthur's mouth, his grandson had broken into a jog.

Arthur watched as Tommy reached the main gates and disappeared from sight.

Seconds later, he heard the revving of the motorbike.

Chapter Fifty-Three

Tommy jammed on his helmet, then hooked his arm through the spare helmet that Arthur had worn on the journey there. Turning the ignition key, he kick-started the engine, dropped the clutch and twisted the throttle.

There was only one thought in his mind.

He rode along the Commercial Road and continued onto Hendon Road before veering left on West Wear Street, slowing down as he turned right into Bridge Street. Seeing that his way was clear, he accelerated and blasted across the Wearmouth Bridge. He took the corner onto Dame Dorothy Street, the foot pedal almost scraping the surface of the road.

Again, he twisted the throttle and sped down the quarter-mile stretch before jamming on the brakes. The back end skidded out a fraction as the bike came to a halt. Fierce impatience suddenly raged. Not just at the passing traffic but at himself. For leaving this too long. Turning right and going carefully over the bumpy cobbles, he descended the steep embankment to the gates of Thompson's.

A few workers either arriving or leaving the yard turned their heads on hearing the bike's low, thumping engine. An uncommon sound these days and one that could just about be heard despite the clanking and clamouring of the shipyard.

Tommy turned left and came to a halt at the timekeeper's cabin.

He pulled off his helmet, his hair ruffled and his face full of determination.

Alfie looked down, saw who it was and instantly knew why he was there.

'Polly Elliot!' Tommy shouted up. It wasn't a request. He rested his helmet on the tank and slowly released the clutch.

The bike very slowly thudded its way across the yard. Barely faster than walking pace.

Workers stopped what they were doing, fascinated by the sight. Cars, vans and ambulances were unusual but not entirely uncommon sights in the town's second-largest shipyard – but a motorbike? That was an anomaly. Riveters stopped riveting, caulkers stopped caulking, crane drivers left metal plates dangling in mid-air. The little tea boy downed his see-saw of tin cans and started running behind Tommy's bike, his face full of gleeful fascination.

Tommy was unaware of the attention he was attracting. He was focused on one thing and one thing only. His vision fixed on the quayside where he knew Polly and her squad would be.

He spotted Martha first. She was turning around, pushing up her mask, looking at whatever it was that was catching the attention of those around her.

His eyes desperately seeking out Polly, Tommy finally saw the rest of the women welders, their backs to him.

He could see the amber glow of their welds bringing a rare splash of colour to their drab surroundings.

Rosie's familiar face, her blonde curls in disarray, appeared next to Martha as she too pushed up her metal mask. She looked small next to her.

A hundred yards away, he saw Dorothy rise from her haunches and turn around. Her mouth fell open at the same time as her hand tapped the back of the woman next to her.

A flurry of sparks died instantly as Angie upended her mask.

Martha looked down at the two remaining welders.

Both were sitting, both had one leg straight out, the other at a right angle.

Both backs were hunched over flat welds.

One of the women looked up at Martha and put down her rod before twisting round.

She took off her mask.

It was Gloria.

Polly was oblivious to all around her. Engrossed in her weld, the hypnotic shower of molten metal allowing her to escape the darkness that had consumed her these past seven days.

Rosie stepped towards her, switched off her machine and dropped down onto her haunches.

She pointed ahead.

Polly pulled off her mask and turned just in time to see Tommy bring the bike to a halt.

Kicking out the bike stand, he switched off the engine. Leaning forward, he quickly placed both helmets on the ground and swung his leg over the back of the bike.

Tommy strode over to Polly, his eyes not leaving her once. The noise of the yard made any kind of speech pointless.

He saw the look in her eyes and his heart lifted.

Polly's world of sparkling metal suddenly died, replaced by Rosie, who had bobbed down directly opposite her. Just inches away.

She mouthed something that Polly couldn't work out and then Polly saw her point to something behind her.

Something was happening in the yard.

Pulling off her mask and banging it down on the ground, Polly twisted herself around.

Tommy!

Pulling herself to her feet, she turned to see him striding over.

She felt her heart hammering against her chest as she stepped forward, her body moving of its own accord.

She needed to feel his body against hers.

She loved this man. Regardless of what the future might hold.

It was a fight she would never win.

That she no longer wanted to win.

And then she saw him mouth the words.

I love you.

Tears welled up as he reached her.

Through the blur, she saw his face bend down to hers.

She felt his lips on her own. Gentle at first. Then more urgent.

She felt his lips on her neck and on her ear.

And then she heard his voice.

'I love you, Polly Elliot.'

She flung her arms around his neck, breathing in his scent.

'I love you too, Tommy Watts.'

Rosie, Martha, Gloria, Dorothy and Angie stood rooted to the spot. Their eyes not once leaving their friend. They watched with tears stinging as Polly and Tommy kissed.

When Polly put her arms around Tommy's neck and he lifted her off the ground, Dorothy couldn't contain herself any longer.

'Yes! Yes! Yes!' she exclaimed. Not that anyone could hear her words.

Her arm punched the air in victory. Ecstatic that love had won.

Angie jumped up and down, her own exuberance uncontained. Her helmet fell from the back of her head and clattered to the ground.

She grabbed Dorothy's hand in excitement and they both raised their arms to celebrate love's victory.

Martha was standing arms akimbo. She looked at Dorothy and Angie and then back at Polly and Tommy. A huge gap-toothed smile plastered across her face.

'Thank God for that,' Gloria said aloud. Whatever happened now, at least Polly's future would not be blighted by regret. She knew what that was like, had lived it, and would not wish it on anyone.

Rosie put her hand to her forehead, shielding her eyes from the glint of sunlight that had appeared a little earlier and had stayed to shine its light on this real life theatre.

Brushing away a tear, she thought of Peter.

The women watched, along with most of the workforce, as Tommy kissed Polly one final time before grabbing one of the helmets. He pulled the bottom chinstraps wide. Raising the helmet above her head, he gently pulled it down. He stepped closer so that their bodies were just about touching and fastened the straps.

Quickly putting on his own helmet in one sweeping motion, he turned, climbed on the bike and kicked back the stand with his left foot.

Putting her hands on Tommy's shoulders to balance herself, Polly climbed on the back. With her feet just about touching the ground, she slid her arms around Tommy's waist. Their bodies were now meshed together as Tommy carefully manoeuvred round in a half-circle, before turning the ignition and starting the bike.

It spluttered into life, the engine thumping over.

The women watched as the bike slowly weaved its way across the yard.

Tommy slowed to a halt to nod his thanks to Alfie, who had also been watching the whole drama, enthralled.

And then they disappeared from view.

Chapter Fifty-Four

When Tommy pulled the bike up outside the Major's flat, there was no hesitation from either Polly or himself.

Neither of them needed to say anything.

Instead, they both dismounted, took off their helmets and walked up the ramp.

Polly waited until Tommy fished out his key from his trouser pocket and opened the door. He pushed it wide, before turning to Polly. This time when he picked her up, it was to take her over the threshold of what for the next few hours would be their temporary home.

This moment was not about the past or the future, but about the present. The here and now.

When Tommy carried Polly into his bedroom, he said a silent prayer of thanks that the Major had gone with Joe to a unit based in Houghton-le-Spring. He wouldn't be back until much later.

Putting Polly down on the bed, he kissed her and she kissed him back with equal ardour.

As they became more passionate, their desire fired by the knowledge that this time there would be no holding back, Polly suddenly started to chuckle.

'Wait,' she said, her eyes dancing with a mixture of desire and laughter.

She sat up and undid the laces on her boots.

Kicking them off, she gently pushed Tommy back down on the bed and let her long brown hair fall like a curtain around his face, so that their vision was of each other and nothing else.

Polly dropped her head to the side and kissed his neck. She could hear the sound of his breathing become heavy as she kissed his neck and his ear before returning to his lips.

Between kisses and caresses, they undressed one another. The start of their lovemaking was speckled with more laughter as Polly struggled out of her overalls and the layers of clothes she had on underneath.

Neither needed to say that this time there would be no pulling back, no waiting until there was a gold band on Polly's left hand. They did not have the luxury of time or the security of a future together that they could plan.

The time they had together was short – too short.

They didn't need to say the words. They had said enough.

Instead, they showed each other their love with the touch of their hands and their lips, the feel of their skin and the movement of their bodies together.

After they had made love, they remained lying on the bed, holding each other close, still needing to feel their bodies touching.

Polly looked at Tommy.

'I'm sorry,' she said simply.

Tommy angled his face so that he could see hers. Her eyes.

'For what?' he asked.

'For all those awful things I said to you.' She suddenly felt ashamed at her behaviour. 'About your ma—'

Before Polly could say any more, Tommy put a finger across her lips.

'Shh,' he said. 'You don't need to apologise. I know you didn't mean those things. I know where they came from. You were angry. And you were angry because you love me.'

He kissed her, seeing that she was going to say more.

'I should have been more honest with you too, about what I wanted to do ...' he said, touching her cheek gently. Tracing it with his finger.

Polly shuffled round in the bed so that she was on her side, looking at Tommy's profile.

She drew in a deep breath.

'Have they given you a date?' She exhaled as she spoke. Needing but not wanting to hear the answer.

Tommy turned his face to look at Polly. His eyes now filled with apprehension.

'Next Saturday,' he said simply.

'Boxing Day?' Polly felt a moment's panic.

Tommy nodded.

Be brave!

Rina's words came back to her.

She thought of Hannah's parents.

Tommy put his arms around her and they cuddled.

They stayed like that for a while. Tommy felt Polly's tears on his chest and he pulled her closer.

They were quiet for a moment before Polly pitched herself up on her elbow.

'Tommy Watts,' she said, drying her eyes and looking down at her lover.

'Yes?' He looked up at her. Her cheeks were rosy, although there were still smudges of dirt from the yard on her forehead. He didn't think she had ever looked more beautiful.

'I want to ask you something,' she said. Her eyes were serious.

'Yes?' Tommy asked, mirroring Polly's position and hitching himself up on his elbow. He touched her face with his free hand.

'I want you to know that you can say no.'

Tommy nodded, his look reflecting the earnestness of his lover.

She looked into Tommy's hazel eyes, knowing that she would see his answer there.

'Tommy Watts,' she repeated.

She paused.

'Will you marry me?'

Tommy's eyes lit up and sparkled with sheer delight, a huge smile immediately spreading across his face.

'I would *love* to marry you, Polly Elliot!' He could hardly get the words out quick enough. 'I would drag you down that aisle now, this very moment, if I could.'

He kissed her.

Then kissed her again.

And for the second time that afternoon they made love.

Chapter Fifty-Five

When Major Black arrived back at the flat it had gone nine o'clock. He found Polly and Tommy in the kitchen making a big pot of tea. Polly was in her overalls, looking as though she had only recently come back from work.

'I was just on my way home,' Polly said. 'There's a fresh pot of tea if you want a cup?'

'No time, my dear,' the Major said, bringing his wheelchair to an abrupt stop at the entrance to the kitchen. 'I'm needed elsewhere for the next week or so.'

He pushed both wheels forward towards his room.

'Glad to see you two have sorted out your differences!' His voice trailed behind him.

The sound of a wardrobe door swinging open could be heard.

A few moments later he bellowed out, 'Give us a hand, Tommy lad!'

When Tommy arrived at the bedroom doorway, he saw the Major had already got out an overnight bag, flung it on the bed, and was now pulling clothes from the drawers of his dresser and plonking them in his lap.

'Listen, laddie,' the Major said as he did a 180-degree turn back to the bed. 'The flat's yours from now on until you go,' he said, transferring the clothes into his holdall.

He zipped up the bag.

'Which means, if you want your fiancée to stay here until you fly out, then that's more than all right with me.'

Tommy's face lit up.

'That's very kind of yer, Major. Are yer sure?'

'Never been more sure.'

The Major heaved the bag onto his lap. Tommy knew not to help. He followed the Major as he wheeled himself to the front door.

'If you need me,' he opened the front door, 'I'll be at the Grand.'

Tommy looked out into the darkness and saw the outline of a military car parked up on the cobbles.

Seeing the look of confusion on Tommy's face, the Major explained.

'Big powwow going on there. Army and navy. Putting our heads together. They reckon it's easier to have me there. On tap, as it were.'

The Major carefully eased his wheelchair down the ramp.

Tommy heard him chuckle.

'Who am I to complain, eh?'

'Really?' Polly said, holding her tea. 'He says I can stay here until you go?'

Tommy nodded.

'Like man and wife?'

Tommy nodded again.

'Which we will be soon,' he added. They had agreed to go to the registrar on Monday to see how quickly they could get married.

'What do you say?' Tommy asked, a little unsure.

'Yes.' Polly put her tea down.

'Yes, yes, yes.'

She put her arms around Tommy's neck and kissed him. Tommy kissed her back.

'But ...' he hesitated ' ... what about yer ma?'

Chapter Fifty-Six

'What?' Agnes's face could only be described as thunderous. It was bad enough knowing that her daughter had just spent several hours alone with Tommy at the flat, but this? This was something else entirely.

'I'm going to stay with Tommy at the Major's flat,' Polly repeated, her voice steady. She was doing just what the Major had been doing an hour ago. Only her clothes were not being packed quite so neatly.

'And the Major's not going to be there? At all?'

Agnes was thrown by this. The Major had popped in for a quick cuppa when he'd come back with Joe. He hadn't mentioned anything about going away for the week.

'That's right, Ma, he's not going to be there,' Polly said simply.

'So, the two of yer are going to be living in mortal sin?' Agnes tried to keep her voice low, although why she was doing so, she wasn't sure. The whole of the east end would know by the morning, the way gossip travelled around these parts.

Polly pulled the toggles on the bag and tied them into a tight bow.

'Ma, we'll be married in the next few days.'

'That's not the point.' Agnes threw both arms up to the ceiling in exasperation.

Polly heaved the bag onto her shoulder and faced her mother. She'd known this would be her ma's reaction. She'd come prepared.

'You're right, Ma. That's not the point.' Polly's voice held no anger. 'The point is that Tommy and I have exactly seven nights left together. Six and a half days.'

Tommy was leaving at thirteen hundred hours on Boxing Day.

'And as this might be the last time I see him for a very long time, if not for ever ...' Polly forced back the tears. Forced herself to stay strong. 'Then I want to enjoy every moment we have left.'

In the next room, Arthur and Bel were sitting quietly. Neither pretended they were doing anything other than eavesdropping.

Hearing Polly's last words, Bel went over and gave Arthur a big hug.

'Eee, I don't know what I would have done if they hadn't made up.' She was half laughing, half crying.

'Better late than never,' Arthur said. 'Each as stubborn as the other.'

Bel laughed. She'd been on cloud nine after watching Tommy and Polly in the middle of the yard.

'Bloody brave as well. Facing the wrath of Agnes.'

'She'll come around,' Arthur said, patting Tramp and Pup, who, having sensed the anger in Agnes's voice, had trotted back into the kitchen.

'I don't think she's got a choice,' Bel said.

Chapter Fifty-Seven

Sunday 20 December

'Apologies for my tardiness,' George said as Dorothy let him into the flat.

'He means "lateness",' Dorothy told Angie, who was standing in the doorway of the kitchen.

'I'm hoping you two didn't both spend your rent money at the Ritz last night?'

'Nah,' Angie said, going back into the kitchen and pouring George a cup of tea, adding just a little milk, which was the way he liked it.

'But it was hard not to. We had a lot to celebrate.' She put the teapot down on the kitchen table before getting the bourbons out of the cupboard and putting them on a plate.

'Yer favourites,' Angie said, sitting down and giving George her full attention.

George smiled. They went through the same ritual every week when he came to collect the rent.

'I'm guessing the reason for your celebration was the rekindling of Polly and Tommy's love affair?' George smiled. Rosie had relayed the whole scene to them last night, along with how ecstatic Charlotte had been on hearing that Polly and Tommy were back together.

'I think it was more than a "rekindling",' Dorothy chuckled. 'An inferno more like!'

George suppressed a smile and took a big sip of his tea. He liked Dorothy's dramatic take on life.

'Has Rosie told yer?' Angie said, pouring herself a cup.

'About?' George asked.

'Have you seen Rosie today?' Dorothy asked, pulling out a chair and sitting down.

George looked at Dorothy and then at Angie.

'No, I've been out most of the afternoon.'

'They're living in sin!' Angie couldn't contain herself.

George looked confused.

'Tommy and Polly!' Dorothy and Angie said in unison.

'Really?' George was genuinely surprised.

'Yes!' Dorothy was bursting with excitement. 'Polly's moved in with Tommy.'

All the women had nearly choked on their tea and biscuits when Polly had told them at work this morning.

'At the Major's?' George asked. Now this was quite a turn-up for the books.

Both women nodded.

'The Major's at the Grand,' Angie informed.

'Apparently there's some big meeting of military minds going on there this week.' Dorothy tapped her nose as though it were all top secret.

George thought it odd he'd not heard about it.

'Said the flat's Tommy's to do with as he pleases. And if it pleases him to have Polly living there until he has to leave, then that's fine with him,' Dorothy improvised.

'Really?' Now George was intrigued. 'That's very kind of him.'

'Very liberal,' Dorothy said, eyes widening to stress her point.

'Mmm,' George agreed. 'But what do you mean by "until he has to leave"?'

Dorothy and Angie's enthusiasm seemed to deflate instantly.

'That's the downside to all this,' Dorothy explained.

'Tommy's flying back out there on Boxing Day,' Angie said.

'Gosh.' George felt his own heart go heavy. God only knew how Polly felt. Poor girl.

'That's jolly quick, isn't it?'

'It is,' Angie said. 'Jolly quick.'

Dorothy looked at her friend. She had never heard her use the word 'jolly' before.

'They're still going to get married, though,' Dorothy said, grabbing a bourbon and biting into it.

'Registry office,' Angie said, pulling a face.

Dorothy looked at her friend again. She could be a number-one snob at times.

'Bloody shame they didn't kiss and make up before – then they'd at least have had a nice wedding,' George mused, more to himself than to his tenants.

'I know,' Angie said. 'Polly says she doesn't mind.'

'She's not got much choice, by the sounds of it.' George drank the rest of his tea. 'Have they set a date next week?'

'Nah,' Angie said. 'They're just gonna grab whatever slot they can.'

'They're going tomorrow,' Dorothy butted in. 'To see when the registrar can fit them in.'

'Dear me,' George said, 'it really is going to be a rather rushed affair.'

'I knar, but if he's gannin on Boxing Day they dinnit have much choice, do they?' Angie said, finally taking a sip of her tea.

Dorothy noticed that whenever George visited, Angie drank her tea with her little finger sticking out as though she were lady of the manor. She'd have to rib her about it later.

'Well, my dears,' George said, pushing himself out of his chair with his stick. 'This has been a most illuminating visit.'

'Here's the rent,' Dorothy said, handing him an envelope with the money. 'Best not forget it as Angie here is developing expensive tastes and I doubt very much there'd be *owt* left, as she'd say, by next week.'

George chuckled, stuffed the envelope into his inside pocket and bade the pair farewell.

Chapter Fifty-Eight

George's mind was working at full speed from the moment he walked out of the flat. Turning right at the bottom of Foyle Street, he made his way to the bus stop at the end of Toward Road.

On the corner of Borough Road there was the *Echo* boy, standing blowing into his hands.

George went to get a paper but stopped when he saw the headlines. The names of men from the town who were in the 125th Anti-Tank Regiment of the Royal Artillery, who had been captured in the fall of Singapore and were being held in Japanese prisoner-of-war camps, were beginning to filter through. It explained the early print run.

'God help them,' George muttered to himself as he crossed over the road, sticking his hand into his inside pocket and pulling out the envelope containing the rent.

Reaching the young lad, George looked down and saw the state of the boy's footwear. His oversized boots were being held together by string.

George took the proffered newspaper, then pulled out a couple of notes and pushed them into the boy's cold hand.

The little lad's eyes nearly popped out of his head.

'Cor, thanks, mister!' There was no containing his delight.

George hobbled on. Hearing the bus behind him, he hurried to the stop.

Boarding the bus, George paid his fare and sat down. It wasn't busy. It was a dark and cold winter's night. Any-

one in their right mind would be at home or indoors somewhere warm.

George had never been a great lover of public transport,
preferring the freedom and independence of having one's
own car – this evening, though, he was glad of the time to
think.

And the more he thought, the more he was sure about
what he wanted to do.

Looking through the paper, he spotted an article on
the young girl from the Suffolk Street air raid. The report
said she was back home, having been fitted with her new
hands. She was soon to be back at work in her old job at the
Post Office.

His decision was now cast in cement.

He just hoped Lily didn't put up too much of a fight.

'I'm back!' he shouted as he stepped through the front door.

He felt a sense of urgency.

Having made up his mind, he had to get everything
sorted. And pronto.

'Ah, *mon amour*,' Lily said, as she swished her way out
of the back parlour. Tonight she was in her favourite red
taffeta dress that accentuated her ample bosom and nipped
her waist in so tightly that George was surprised she could
still draw breath.

'My dear,' George said, hobbling down the polished
wooden floor to greet her. He gave her a kiss and then
kissed her again.

'You all right, George? You look a little flushed. Has
anything happened?'

'No, no,' George said, taking off his hat and coat and
hooking them onto the stand in the hallway. 'Well, nothing
bad, anyway.' He went to Rosie's office and rapped on the
door.

'She's not in yet,' Lily said. 'Shouldn't be long, though. What did you want to see her about?'

George opened the door.

'It's not Rosie I want to see,' he said, throwing his arm in the direction of the room. 'It's you.'

Lily glanced at George as she walked into Rosie's office. He had that look on his face. Whatever it was, he meant business.

'So …' Lily walked straight over to Rosie's desk and took out her Gauloises from the top drawer, wasting no time in lighting one. 'You have my rapt attention, George.' She blew out smoke. 'Fire ahead.' She grabbed an ashtray and sat down on the chaise longue.

'I've just come back from the flat—' he began.

'Still standing? The terrible two haven't turned it into a den of iniquity?' Lily suppressed a smile. She knew it wound George up.

'Yes, yes, my dear.' He was never quite sure if Lily was aware of the irony of her comments.

'I was offered a bourbon today – of the biscuit variety. That's about as decadent as they get in the flat, from what I can gather. I think they save their partying for the Ritz. That's if they've got any energy left. They looked shattered. Which isn't surprising by the sounds of the overtime Rosie says they've been doing.'

'Oh George, honestly, you'd bring tears to a glass eye.' She crossed her legs. 'They've got more than enough energy to party and work around the clock. They have youth on their side.'

'Anyway,' George said, impatient to get to his point. 'They were telling me that Polly and Tommy are both living at the Major's house.'

'Really?' Lily was clearly shocked. 'As in living *together*?' George nodded.

'Yes, my dear. Together as in *man and wife* together.'

'Blimey.' Lily leant forward and tapped cigarette ash into the ashtray. 'Agnes won't approve. In fact, I would have thought she'd be mortified. Especially about Polly. She's about the last girl on the planet I'd have thought would live in sin with a man.'

'Well, it would seem this war makes people do things they wouldn't normally do,' George said, walking over to the decanter of cognac and sloshing a good measure into one of the thick-cut crystal glasses.

Lily frowned.

'I'm a little surprised, though. I would have thought they would have waited.'

'Well, that's the point,' George said. 'Tommy's going back on Boxing Day, of all days. They obviously want to make the most of every minute they've got left.'

George took a large gulp and made his way over to Lily. He eased himself down next to her.

'Poor Agnes,' Lily said again.

Her comment surprised George. He frowned questioningly.

'Well, her daughter's going to get a bit of a name for herself, isn't she? And Agnes, I know, is the type of woman – mother – who might not have much, but she has her pride. To have a daughter so obviously *not* waiting until she is married. Well – ' she puffed air ' – in Agnes's eyes, it will bring shame on the family.'

'I think it's too late for that,' George said. 'But it's not too late for them to get married.'

'Oh, so they're getting married?' Lily was now looking lost. 'Honestly, George, so much information to be taking in. And from you, of all people.'

She took his cognac and took a swig.

'Sorry, darling, I should have got you one.'

George got up and poured Lily a drink.

'They're going to the registrar tomorrow,' George said, handing Lily her glass and sitting back down. 'To see when they can be squashed in.'

'What a shame,' Lily said. 'If only they'd kissed and made up earlier, they could have had their wedding at St Ignatius.'

'My words exactly!' George said. 'Which got me thinking,' he said.

'About?' Lily eyed him suspiciously.

'About the fact that if anyone should have a proper wedding, it should be Tommy and Polly.'

'Darling, we're getting married in a registry office and ours is still a proper wedding,' Lily said, her curiosity now growing.

'You know what I mean,' George said.

He looked at Lily.

Took a deep breath.

'I kept thinking on the way back here,' he began, 'about Polly giving away what amounted to her wedding money.' He looked around and realised he had left the *Sunderland Echo* on the bus. 'You know that poor girl she gave the money to? The one who was going to get fitted with artificial hands?'

Lily nodded.

'She was in the paper. She's got her new hands and is starting back at work soon.'

Lily took a sip of her drink. Her face was unusually serious.

'I know,' George said, reading her thoughts. 'Brave. So much bravery. So much sacrifice. So much selflessness.'

He took another sip of brandy.

'And there's Tommy. He's done more than his bit for the war. Bloody miracle he came back alive – never mind in

387

one piece. And there he is, chomping at the bit to get back out there. Twisting every arm that needs twisting to get the green light to go back and start ripping mines off the bottoms of boats. Without any thought for his own safety.'

He took a breath.

'And also leaving behind the woman he is clearly desperately in love with.'

'When he could have easily stayed at home,' Lily interjected. 'Gone back to the Wear rather than the mines of the Mediterranean.'

'I couldn't have put it better myself,' George said.

Lily took George's free hand.

'I'm in agreement with you, *mon cher*,' she said, 'but I'm not sure where this is going?'

George pushed himself up and hobbled over to the cherry-wood desk to pour himself another cognac.

He took a breath, turned around and looked at Lily.

'I want to give them our wedding,' he said simply.

Lily had just taken a sip of her brandy and she spluttered a little before taking a huge breath and coughing.

'Is my hearing going as well as everything else?' she said, her voice rasping.

'No, darling, your hearing isn't going and neither is any other part of you. You are just perfect in my eyes.'

'George, you should know me now.' Lily coughed again. 'Flattery will get you nowhere.'

She sat back on her sofa, put her hand on her bosom and took a deep breath.

George was bolstered by the fact she hadn't said no straight away – not that it would have mattered if she had.

'The pair deserve it,' George said. 'I can't think of a couple who are *more* deserving, to be honest.'

Lily eyed George. She cleared her throat and took a sip of brandy.

'Is this because you never got to marry your sweetheart before you were commissioned?'

It was a topic they rarely discussed, but Lily knew it had been one of the few regrets that George had had in his life. The poor girl had contracted TB while he was away and had died before he returned.

'No,' he said, sadly. 'I can see why you'd say that. But no, this really is purely because I feel it's the right thing to do. They could have a wonderful wedding. A honeymoon at the Grand before he left. They could invite everyone they wanted without worrying about how many they could get through the door at Tatham Street. It would be our way of giving something to two people who are giving so much themselves.'

Lily stood up and walked over to George.

'You know I'm right,' he said.

She kissed him, then picked up her packet of Gauloises and the lighter.

'I just need to powder my nose,' she told him, before walking out of the office.

When she stepped into the hallway, the front door opened and Rosie appeared.

'You looking for me?' she asked, seeing Lily.

'No, *ma chérie*,' Lily said. 'But I need to borrow your office for a short while. Do you mind waiting in the kitchen?'

'Of course,' Rosie said. 'I wanted to see Kate anyway.'

'Ah,' Lily gasped in despair. 'You'll have to drag her kicking and screaming from her room – she's working on something *très* intricate.'

As Rosie made her way up to the third floor, she noticed Lily head for the back door, which meant she needed either to think or to kill time.

Five minutes later Rosie and Kate were heading down the stairs, followed by Vivian and Maisie. They were about to start work at the Gentlemen's Club, but having seen Rosie and Kate had decided to join them for a cuppa in the kitchen.

They all converged with Lily as she came in from the backyard.

'George and I will see you all in the kitchen in five minutes,' she said.

'So, *mon cher*,' Lily said, sashaying over to George, who was now leaning on the mantelpiece looking into the fire he'd just lit.

He looked around at Lily. He could tell by the flush in her cheeks and the slight reddening of her nose that she had been out the back and had not gone to powder her nose as she'd claimed.

'First of all,' she said, 'I just need to check that this isn't some elaborate ploy to get out of marrying me?'

George just laughed, not bothering to answer her question.

'I thought not.' Lily picked up her glass of cognac.

'Well, it has to be said, this is a big "ask", George.' She paused. 'I would even go as far as to say, the biggest you have ever asked me.'

George considered for a moment before agreeing with a sombre nod of the head.

Lily had known from the moment George had said that he wanted to give their wedding to Polly and Tommy that this was exactly what they would be doing. Even if she hadn't wanted to, she knew that she didn't really have a choice. Their wedding day had to be a joyful one and it wouldn't be if George was resentful.

She knew George.

She knew when he had his mind set on something.

And there was no doubt that he had his mind set on this.

It was against her nature, though, to simply hand him what he wanted without a little negotiating.

'George, darling,' she began. 'You are the kindest, loveliest man I think I have ever met. And I know you don't like to even hear it said, but you are also the bravest man I know.'

She walked over to the fire and kissed him sensuously. She then picked up the poker and stabbed the coals.

'I have thought about what you want.' She walked back over to the chaise longue and sat down, crossing her legs, not once taking her eyes off her future husband. 'And I will, indeed, give you my consent.'

She paused.

'On one condition.' She continued to eye him. 'And I will not waver on this point.'

Another pause.

'I will agree to give our wedding to the young ones, if you will accompany me to their wedding in your uniform.'

There was a moment's silence.

George looked at Lily. She was a born businesswoman. Opportunistic to the last and always determined to get what she wanted, no matter how long it took.

Just as Lily knew that George would not back down, he knew that Lily would not relent until he had agreed to the deal.

'I often wonder if I love you because you're so shrewd – or in spite of it,' he said.

Lily smiled.

'I'll take that as a yes, then?'

'Good. You're all here.'

Lily looked around the kitchen table at the four expectant faces.

'Woe betide us if we weren't,' Vivian whispered to Maisie.

Lily scowled.

'I've told you before, Vivian, it's rude to whisper!'

Lily took a deep breath. Her bosom lifted as she did so and Kate thought that the dress might need a little altering. Lily had put on a few pounds these past few months. The Chinese herbs might have helped her hot flushes, but not the slight weight gain.

Lily looked at George and smiled before directing her attention back to the women.

'George and I have something to tell you.'

She paused for dramatic effect.

'We have decided to call off the wedding,' she said, poker-faced.

Lily looked at the four upturned faces. Pleased by the display of shock and disappointment she observed, she continued.

'But not because we don't *want* to get married.'

Again, she looked at George and smiled.

'I still want to become Mrs Macalister – just as much as George wants to make an honest woman out of me.' Lily allowed herself the slightest of smiles. 'But we have decided – in the spirit of Christmas – that we're going to give our wedding at the Grand as a present to Polly and Tommy.'

Again, Lily examined the second lot of looks of shock and surprise in as many minutes and felt a wave of satisfaction.

'Polly and Tommy, of course, don't know that yet, as George and I have just agreed that this is what we'd like to do, but we wanted you all – as our nearest and dearest – to be the first to know.'

'And also,' George added, 'we wanted you to hold the fort while we nipped to Tatham Street.'

Before anyone had a chance to say anything, George had opened the kitchen door and the pair had disappeared into the hallway.

Rosie, Kate, Maisie and Vivian were still sitting, speechless, when they heard the front door shut.

Chapter Fifty-Nine

'Gawd, what an awful building,' Lily muttered as George helped her out of the MG. She had thrown on her full-length fur coat for their impromptu trip out. It was keeping the cold out but there were still flashes of red taffeta visible. Lily's fleshy bosom was also very conspicuous, despite the gold silk scarf she had flung round her neck.

'Many would argue the point that this Early English-style church is actually architecturally stunning,' George said. 'Graduated Lakeland slate. Stone gable coping. Spire. Stunning stained glass. And all together rather magnificent in its grandness.'

Lily scowled at George.

'This is a time when you simply agree with me, George. It's called humouring. Now come on, let's see this bleedin' vicar.'

Walking through the main door at the side of the large red-brick church, they were greeted by the smell of snuffed-out candles and a slight change of temperature, although it still couldn't be classed as warm. Evening service had just ended.

Lily scanned the church. There was an old woman in a pew on her knees, hands clasped in prayer. Despite the dim lighting, the tall, grey-haired vicar could be seen tidying up.

George coughed, but the sound was lost in the vastness of the building.

'Hello there!' Lily shouted out, waving a hand. Her coat fell open, showing the full splendour of her theatrical dress.

George cringed inwardly. This might have been better coming from him. But Lily had taken the reins and was clearly determined to be in charge.

'Sorry to bother you, Reverend.' Lily's heels clacked loudly as she walked down the aisle. George followed her. The praying woman was still kneeling, but now looking up.

'Good evening.' The vicar stepped down from the raised altar just in time to stop Lily from joining him on hallowed ground.

'Can I help you?' he asked.

'Yes,' Lily said, holding out her hand, 'you most certainly can. My name is Lily.'

Lily never gave her surname.

'And this is my future husband, George Macalister. Former captain in the Ninth Battalion Durham Light Infantry. Awarded the Distinguished Service Order for "gallant and distinguished services".'

George felt like stepping back into the dark recesses of the nave. The deal he had just struck, he realised, went beyond simply the wearing of a uniform.

The vicar shook their hands, giving them both his well-rehearsed smile. His face was impartial. Not giving away even the slightest hint of astonishment at the sight of this outlandish, orange-haired woman whose coat alone would keep the church running for at least a year. There was something familiar about her, though. It was that hair. Rang a distant bell.

Lily looked around and saw that the praying woman was now sitting in the pew, watching them with open-mouthed fascination.

'Can we go somewhere private, please?'

'Of course,' the vicar said, following Lily's gaze. 'Follow me.'

A few minutes later, Lily, George and the vicar were seated in a rather unkempt but slightly warmer room that appeared to be an office of sorts.

The orange hair came back to the vicar and he realised that the woman and her fiancé had been at a christening he'd conducted. Must have been a year or so ago now.

Goodness, how could he have forgotten that baptism?

'I'll get straight to the point,' Lily said, eyeing the empty whisky glass on the window sill. 'George and I need you to marry someone on Christmas Day.'

The vicar clasped both hands in front of him and smiled benignly. He felt the slightest irritation that this odd couple thought they could simply march into his church and demand he marry someone. And on Christmas Day of all days. Following the Christmas Eve midnight Mass and then the morning service, he fully intended to do what everyone else would be doing. Eating, drinking and enjoying well-deserved time off.

'I'm afraid that's not going to be possible,' he said. 'First of all, as a rule I don't conduct marriage ceremonies on the day that celebrates the birth of our Lord Jesus. And secondly, I'm afraid I have a legal obligation to read out the banns of marriage on three consecutive Sundays before the wedding itself.'

'Ah, well, luckily for us,' Lily said, smiling across at George, who was sitting ramrod straight in his high-backed armchair, 'I believe that you have already read the banns for the couple in question.'

'Thomas Watts and Polly Elliot,' George said.

The vicar looked at Lily and then at George and could not think of any reason why the two seated opposite him would be in any way associated with the Watts boy and the Elliot girl.

'Well, yes, you're right. I have indeed read out their banns,' the vicar said, trying to keep the surprise out of his voice. 'But it was my understanding that the couple, who I believe broke up for a short while, have now decided not to follow the traditional route of marriage and have instead decided to ... well ... cohabitate ...'

The vicar let out a nervous cough. The gossip had spread like wildfire and most people in the parish had heard by the end of the morning's service that the town's dock diver and the woman welder were now living in sin somewhere on John Street.

'Without getting into the whys and wherefores of the choices they have made,' George said, leaning forward with both hands on the ornately carved head of his walking stick, 'the couple in question have decided that they would like to be married before Petty Officer Watts returns to his unit in Gibraltar, where he will be carrying on his work removing explosives from the hulls of Allied ships.'

The vicar heard the steel in the former captain's voice. Subconsciously he flicked a look over at his empty whisky glass.

It was something that did not escape Lily's notice.

'Well, Reverend Winsey, I don't know about you, but it's a bit nippy in here. I think we could all do with a little something to warm our cockles?'

The vicar, suddenly aware he was in unfamiliar territory, welcomed the crutch of a drink, which – he thought a little resentfully – he would already have been enjoying had the pair not turned up.

He stood up.

'Yes, of course.' He rummaged around in his oak cabinet and pulled out two glasses, holding them up to the light to ensure they were clean before pouring a good measure into each of the tumblers, as well as into his own.

'Cheers,' Lily said, raising her glass.

They all took a sip.

'So,' Lily continued the thread of conversation, 'to summarise, the necessary banns have been read out, the young couple we've discussed want to get married, and it sounds as though, apart from the Lord Jesus's birthday celebrations, the church is otherwise free to bind the betrothed in holy matrimony.'

The vicar took a deep breath.

'I'm sorry. It's just not going to be possible.' He was damned if he was sacrificing his Christmas Day at the insistence of a couple who, it was plain to see, were more heathen than holy.

'At a push,' he said, pulling out the top drawer of his desk and fishing out a battered hardback appointments book, 'I can overlook their present living arrangements and put a date in the diary for the New Year.' He opened the book and put on a pair of wire-rimmed spectacles. He licked his thumb and finger and flicked over a page.

'It looks like the following Saturday is free.'

'No, I'm afraid that's not an option.' Lily tried to keep the impatience out of her voice. 'Like my future husband just mentioned, Petty Officer Tommy Watts will be yanking mines off the bottoms of boats by then – in an effort to save all our bacon.'

She paused to make her point.

'So, I'm afraid it's got to be this Friday. Christmas Day.'

'Officer Watts leaves Boxing Day,' George added.

The vicar took another sip of his whisky.

Lily looked at the vicar. She knew men like Reverend Winsey. They were going to be sitting here all evening arguing their case, but if he were being asked the same favour by a monied, outwardly respectable middle-to-upper-class couple whose young girl had got herself in the family way, he'd be falling over his oversized frock to accommodate them.

The thought angered her.

'When I came into the church,' she said, her tone clipped, 'I couldn't help but notice that you had a poster outside asking for donations to repair the church roof.'

The vicar looked at Lily and nodded.

'My future husband,' Lily looked at George, 'informs me it is of Early English design, and since it is, from what I can see, quite frankly huge, you're going to need a lot of people delving into very deep pockets before you get anywhere near the amount you need.' She paused. 'By which time you might be giving open-air sermons to the kindly but poor folk of the east end.'

The vicar looked at Lily. He had said more or less the same thing earlier today to the bishop, although obviously the wording he had used was much more sugar-coated and, loath though he was to admit it, cloying.

The vicar took another sip of whisky. The woman opposite him might look like she'd just stepped off the stage, but underneath the garish make-up and costume was a hard-nosed, no-nonsense businesswoman.

For the first time he wondered exactly what kind of business she was in.

'So why don't we treat this like a mutually beneficial transaction?' she suggested. 'You marry Polly and Tommy on Christmas Day and when the couple are being showered in confetti, you will find a sizeable wad in your donation box.'

Lily's voice was affable. Her words spoken with a smile, but no one was under the illusion that there was to be any further bartering.

The vicar looked at Lily and then at George.

He swigged the rest of his whisky and picked up his pen.

Finding the page for the twenty-fifth of December, he wrote: *1 p.m. Wedding. Thomas Watts and Polly Elliot.*

He swivelled the book around to show Lily and George the inscription.

Lily smiled and George downed his drink.

'It's a pleasure doing business with you,' Lily said as they stood up.

George didn't say anything, but instead gave the vicar a firm handshake.

'Now,' Lily said, her tone all sweetness and light. 'We'd better get off and tell the happy couple the good news.'

Chapter Sixty

Driving slowly along Suffolk Street, there was no ignoring the bomb site that had once been terraced houses.

Crossing under the bridge that heralded the start of Tatham Street, George and Lily could just make out the outlines of mounds of debris and bricks from the air raid in October.

Neither said anything; they were determined this was to be a happy occasion.

George managed to pull up and park outside number 34 without too much hullabaloo.

He had been here before on Bel and Joe's wedding day, when he had acted as chauffeur, and on a few occasions since then when Maisie had needed dropping off or picking up. Each time the car had been mobbed by youngsters all in awe of his red MG.

This evening, thankfully, the street was quiet. A peace gifted by the darkness and cold of a winter's evening and the fact it was a Sunday.

George opened the passenger door for Lily and helped her out.

Standing on the doorstep, Lily looked around. Whenever she was here, which was infrequent, the place never failed to remind her of home. Her real home in the capital's East End. It gave her mixed feelings.

George rapped the front door with the head of his walking stick.

A few moments later Joe answered.

Glancing down, George noticed Joe was leaning heavily on his own walking stick and could tell he was still suffering.

'Well, hello there!' Joe didn't try to hide his surprise. 'Come in! Come in!' He opened the door wide and stood back to allow them in.

'Nothing wrong, I hope?' he asked, keeping his voice low. These days anything unexpected tended to herald unwanted news.

'No, not at all, old chap,' George reassured, giving Joe a pat on the back.

Joe gave a relieved smile. 'Thank God.' He looked at George and then at Lily and dropped his voice. 'Ma's only just stopped behaving like a bear with a sore head. You've come at the right time. A Sunday-dinner truce has just been consumed.'

Joe gave them a cheeky smile.

'Go on in,' he gestured.

When Lily and George walked into the kitchen, they were greeted with a genuine welcome by the whole Elliot clan. The two dogs also appeared from under the table, where they had been waiting in anticipation for any titbits. Lily surreptitiously pushed them away with the side of her foot.

Bel jumped up and offered to take Lily's fur coat, as much out of politeness as to feel such a luxurious garment with her own hands.

'No, thank you, Bel, we're not staying long.' Lily smiled at Maisie's half-sister. It still amazed her that the pair were related.

Looking down, she saw Lucille half hidden behind her mammy, staring up in wonder.

Lily bent down and cupped the little girl's pale face with her heavily jewelled hand.

'You all right, sweet pea?'

Lucille nodded energetically and offered up a dazzling smile.

'Is Rosie all right?' Polly asked, her face full of concern.

'Yes, yes,' Lily said, looking at Polly and then at Tommy, who was sitting next to her. It was the first time she had clapped eyes on him. She could see instantly why Polly – and probably a number of other women too – had fallen for him. He had rugged good looks, but without the ego. She smiled at him. He smiled back but his eyes were wary. She would bet money he was a bit of a loner.

'We've come bearing good news,' Lily said, looking at them all. 'It being nearly Christmas and all.'

She looked at Agnes, who was pointing at the big ceramic pot in the middle of the table. Lily shook her head. There was barely enough room to swing a cat, never mind squash her and George around the table to drink tea.

'No, thank you, Agnes. I was hoping we might drag you all to the pub for what we hope is a celebratory drink.'

George looked over to Arthur, who was sitting in the far corner next to Agnes.

'George and I,' Lily began, her attention now focused solely on Polly and Tommy, 'would like to give the soon-to-be Mr and Mrs Watts a joint wedding and Christmas present.'

Lily looked at George and then back at Polly and Tommy.

'That gift being our wedding. At the Grand. On Christmas Day. Which, of course, includes the overnight stay in the honeymoon suite.'

Everyone in the room simply stared.

'And before you try and object,' George broke the silence, 'I'd like to add that this is one gift that can't be rejected or returned.'

He smiled at Polly, who was now looking at Tommy, her eyes wide and her mouth slightly open.

'Oh ...' Lily looked at Agnes ' ... and we've just paid a visit to your parish vicar. The Reverend Winsey has also kindly agreed to marry your daughter and future son-in-law.'

It was the first time Agnes had smiled in twenty-four hours.

Polly stood up.

'Lily ... George,' she stuttered. 'I don't think I've ever known such kindness. But really,' she looked down at Tommy, 'we can't accept. No way. It's just too much.'

Tommy stood up.

'I'm bowled over,' he said. 'Really I am. But Polly's right. We just can't accept. You can't just *give* us your wedding.'

Lily let out a laugh.

'But we can. And we have. Like George's just said, *it's a done deal*. Whether you like it or not, I'm afraid you're going to have to accept. Even if you don't want to.' Lily heaved in air. 'Because we've cancelled our slot at the registry office,' she lied. 'So, I'm afraid there's no going back now.'

Polly looked at Tommy and then at her ma and then back at Lily and George.

'Honestly,' Polly said, tears starting to prick her eyes, 'I really don't know what to say. I really don't.' She swallowed hard and suddenly felt like bursting into tears. Happy tears. She half laughed and half cried at the same time, manoeuvring her way around the table and taking two strides towards Lily and George.

Lily opened her arms and gave Polly a hug.

'Thank you,' Polly said. 'Thank you so much. This is so incredible. I can't quite believe it.' Her voice was choked with emotion.

Lily squeezed her tightly and Polly breathed in Chanel N° 5.

Tommy went over to George and shook his hand, gripping it with both his own, wanting to show just how thankful he was.

'Thank you,' he said. 'Thank you ... I'm taken aback. Totally.'

George knew Tommy's joy was not because of his own wishes to have a fancy wedding or to get married in a house of God, but because he knew how much it would mean to Polly. This was the wedding she deserved.

'Come on, then!' George said. 'A drink to celebrate the impending nuptials!'

No one needed telling twice. Within a few minutes, they'd all piled out of number 34, walked across the road and bustled into the Tatham.

Agnes nipped next door to get Beryl and her two daughters, Iris and Audrey.

Seeing Lily and George walk into the pub, followed by the whole of the Elliot clan, Bill and Pearl gave each other a curious look. Bill quickly put the tray of dirty pint glasses he was holding down on the bar and shook hands with George, who had arrived first, asking if he could purchase a bottle of 'the good stuff'.

'Eee, we dinnit normally see the likes of you in these parts,' Pearl said. She was genuinely surprised. The only time she'd seen Lily and George here had been for Bel's wedding reception.

Pearl started polishing glasses and checking them before putting them on a clean tray.

'Am I right in thinking Maisie keeps a bottle of cognac behind the bar?' Lily asked.

Pearl nodded, reached under the counter and pulled out a bottle of Rémy that was still three-quarters full.

'For the women?' Pearl asked.

Lily nodded.

'My girl all right?' Pearl said.

'Right as rain,' Lily said. 'She's got a day off tomorrow. I believe she's coming into town to do her Christmas shopping.'

Lily knew that Pearl and Maisie shared an unusual bond.

'Tell her to pop in here for a quick chinwag when she's done,' Pearl said.

'Sit yourselves down,' Bill said. 'I'll bring the drinks over.'

Once everyone was seated and had a drink in their hand, including Bill and Pearl, George pushed himself to his feet and raised his glass.

'It's not me and Lily that need the thanks this evening, but these two young ones. They are both a credit to their generation.'

He looked at Agnes and then at Arthur.

'If they were my "bairns", as we say in these parts, I'd be proud as punch.'

He looked at Tommy and Polly.

'Proud as punch,' he repeated.

George looked at Lily.

'My future wife and I think what you are doing, Polly, is amazing.'

He chuckled.

'Actually, that's a lie. I think it's amazing. Lily thinks you're as mad as a hatter.'

Everyone laughed.

George looked at Agnes before returning his attention to Polly.

'And I know your decision to work at Thompson's was not greeted with the utmost of joy. Understandably, of course.'

Another look to Agnes, who was sitting next to Lily – polar opposites.

'I would have felt the same had you been my daughter. But you're doing an invaluable job, Polly. And a bloody hard one. If it weren't for women like you, building and repairing ships we desperately need to win this damn war, then I dread to think what would happen.'

George was quiet for a moment, wanting – needing – to choose his next words carefully.

'And you, Tommy.'

He paused.

He looked at Arthur, who was looking at his grandson with unadulterated pride.

'You are a very brave man and we are all in your debt.'

George raised his glass.

'So, a toast.'

'A toast,' everyone repeated.

'To Tommy and Polly.'

'To Tommy and Polly.'

Chapter Sixty-One

Monday 21 December

'Oh. My. God.' Dorothy stood and stared at Polly.

'Bloody Nora, Pol!' Angie had to practically scoop her chin off the floor.

'That is some wedding present!' Martha said, gawping.

'Well, it couldn't have happened to a nicer couple.' Gloria had her hands on her hips. A look of disbelief on her face.

Rosie looked at her squad, all standing around their makeshift fire. She smiled at everyone's reactions. She too was delighted for Polly.

As the women fired questions at Polly, wanting to know every minute detail of Lily and George's impromptu visit last night, Rosie thought about Peter. She couldn't help it. Any mention of the war or weddings brought him to mind. She had accepted that now.

She looked at Gloria, who she knew worried about her boys out in the Arctic. Luckily for her, Bobby and Gordon wrote regularly. Hopefully, Tommy would too. If only Peter were also able to write to her.

The women's excitement and interrogation ended with the klaxon blaring out the start of the shift, but their questions immediately started up again when the horn sounded out the beginning of the lunch break.

They were joined in the canteen by Hannah and Olly. On hearing the news, Hannah clapped her hands and hugged Polly, all the while making a series of exclamations in Czech, which Olly translated.

A little while later Bel arrived with Marie-Anne. Polly had given Bel the go-ahead to tell Helen and Marie-Anne the wonderful news and that, naturally, they were invited if they were able to come. It being Christmas Day and all.

Polly told Dorothy, Angie and Marie-Anne to each bring a date, if they wanted. Not one of the trio seemed particularly enamoured with any potential beaux they had met at the Ritz. What followed, therefore, was much discussion as to whether or not it would be preferable to go as a girlie threesome, with the hope of meeting their own Mr Rights at the wedding. Everyone knew weddings were fertile ground for meeting one's future husband, although, as Dorothy pointed out, that might have been the case before the war, but not necessarily now.

Rosie made everyone chuckle when she told them how Charlotte had actually jumped up and down on her bed on hearing the news last night. Secretly Rosie had been slightly dismayed that Charlotte's enthusiasm for what she saw as the equivalent of a Hollywood wedding had been equalled by her adoration of Lily for making such a 'sacrifice' and being so 'kind and generous'.

Polly told Rosie to tell Maisie and Vivian to bring whoever they wanted, and that it went without saying that Lily and George should invite as many people as they wished.

None of the women said anything, but they all knew Gloria would have given anything to be able to go to the wedding with Jack.

After Rosie had eaten her lunch, she told everyone she had to nip in and see Helen.

When she returned ten minutes later, everyone looked at her, curious as to what they had needed to chat about.

'We're going to be a man down – or I should say a woman down,' she told them, her face serious as she poured herself a lukewarm cup of tea. 'As Polly here,' she continued, the beginnings of a smile forming, 'has just been given paid leave of absence as of end of shift today. It's just been sanctioned by Helen.'

Polly's eyes lit up.

'So,' said Gloria, who had been in on the plan, 'this will be your equivalent to a honeymoon. Only before the wedding, not after.'

'Really?' Polly's face lit up.

Rosie reassured her with a smile.

'Oh my goodness! That's wonderful! Thank you, thank you, Rosie!'

Polly jumped up and flung her arms around her friend.

'Wait till I tell Tommy!'

At the end of the shift, Polly said her goodbyes and hurried over to see Ralph and the diving team to invite them to the wedding.

Ralph declared himself 'chuffed to pieces fer yer both'. The other two divers and the two linesmen all beamed at her and agreed that they were too. They all had a soft spot for Polly. When the younger diver asked about what to wear, Polly found herself being stared at by all five men and realised that they were worried about the Grand being so posh. When she left them, she'd hoped she'd done a good enough job of reassuring them that it did not matter one iota.

By the time she reached the admin building, everyone had gone home. She was banking on Helen working late and was right. When she walked into the main office, she saw the light on in Helen's office. She knocked on the open door and was immediately waved in.

'Polly, I'm overjoyed to hear the news!' Helen got up out of her chair, wanting to go and give Polly a hug, but holding back.

'Thanks,' Polly said, walking into the office. 'And thank you so much for giving me paid leave.' Polly, too, felt an unexpected awkwardness. She hadn't seen much of Helen since the night of her falling-out with Tommy. She still felt awful about what she'd said, and also a bit embarrassed about the state she'd been in.

Helen dismissed Polly's gratitude with a flick of her hand.

'I know Bel's already invited you,' Polly said, 'but I wanted to invite you personally. There's no time to send invites out.' Polly looked down and saw Winston curled up in his basket, his two large green eyes staring up at her. It was the first time Polly realised that Mrs Crabtree's cat and Helen had the same startling, emerald-coloured eyes.

'You will be able to come, won't you?' Polly asked. 'Obviously, I'd really like you to come, but I know the girls would too.' This was a little white lie. They hadn't said as much, but this was probably because they were far too preoccupied with more pressing matters, like what they were going to wear.

'And I know Tommy would love you to come.'

Polly paused.

'He's asked me if you could invite Dr Parker as well? He's not sure he's going to be able to get up to the Ryhope to ask him personally.'

Polly saw Helen hesitate and misread it.

'Of course, you both probably have something else planned. It *is* Christmas Day, after all.'

'No, God, no,' Helen laughed. 'Far from it! I'd love to come. I really appreciate you asking me. And Tommy. I'd

411

have totally understood if I was the last person either of you wanted there.'

Polly shook her head. 'After everything that's happened these past few months,' she said, 'and more so this past week, I've realised that life really is too short to hold resentments.'

Helen thought she heard sadness in Polly's voice, which wasn't surprising, but also acceptance.

'Honestly,' Polly said, 'everything that happened before – when I first started at the yard – that's in the past now.'

Helen looked at Polly. She was pretty sure she didn't know about her declaration of love to Tommy. If she had, she wasn't sure Polly would have been quite so forgiving.

'So, you'll come?' Polly asked.

'Of course. Wild horses wouldn't stop me,' Helen said. This would be the perfect excuse to bail out of the usual Christmas celebrations with her mother. With her father in Scotland, she had not the slightest desire to spend the day at home.

'And you'll ask Dr Parker? I know it would mean a lot to Tommy.'

'Yes, of course.'

Polly looked at Helen.

There it was again.

The hesitation.

Helen suddenly sat back down in her chair, defeated. She took a cigarette out of her packet of Pall Malls and sparked it up.

'We've had a bit of a falling-out,' she confessed.

Polly stepped forward and sat down on the chair in front of Helen's desk.

'Why?'

Helen looked at Polly.

'We haven't spoken since you and Tommy had *your* huge falling-out.'

'Really?'

Polly thought Helen looked a little guilty.

'Why?'

'I was annoyed after the dive,' Helen said. 'Blamed him for Tommy going back out there.'

Polly leant forward.

'Oh, Helen, Dr Parker couldn't have stopped him.'

Polly looked at her and realised her falling-out with Dr Parker had upset Helen more than she was letting on. More than she was probably admitting to herself.

'The poor bloke's done nothing but try and help Tommy. And – I know this for a fact – Tommy said if 'the doc', as he calls him, hadn't sanctioned the dive or signed his medical certificate, he would have found someone who would. Even if he'd had to pay him.'

Helen looked at Polly.

She knew she was speaking the truth.

She took a deep breath.

'God!' she declared. 'I hate apologising!'

Polly laughed out loud.

'Now, why doesn't that surprise me?'

When Polly left, hurrying off to her next port of call, the Maison Nouvelle for a last-minute dress fitting, Helen dialled the operator.

'Ryhope Hospital.'

She listened.

Then sighed.

'Yes, I'll hold.'

After her dress fitting, Polly practically ran the half-mile from the boutique to John Street.

413

Hearing her coming through the main front entrance, Tommy opened the door to the flat.

'I've got the rest of the week off!' she said breathlessly, stepping over the threshold to the flat. 'Rosie asked Helen and Helen's given me paid leave of absence!'

Tommy pulled Polly close.

'That's brilliant!' he said, taking her in his arms.

Kissing her passionately, he pushed the door shut with his foot.

Neither of them had to say it, but they were now on a countdown.

Four more days to their wedding.

But also, only five more days before they would be parted. Again.

They didn't need to say it, but they intended to make the most of every minute of those remaining five days.

Chapter Sixty-Two

Tuesday 22 December

'So, this is what it feels like to be on honeymoon,' Polly whispered into Tommy's ear when she woke up the next morning.

Tommy smiled, his eyes not yet open.

'So, this is what it feels like to be married,' he whispered back, pulling his soon-to-be wife close and kissing her.

Pushing a strand of hair away from her eyes and kissing her again, this time chastely on the nose, he looked at the woman he loved more than anything in the entire world. This was the image he would take away with him to war. He resolved there and then that if he were to lose his life out in the middle of the Mediterranean Sea or at the bottom of the Atlantic Ocean – if he had time before death claimed him – then he would imagine Polly's face just as it was now, and in doing so he would die with love in his heart instead of hate.

He brushed aside another wisp of Polly's hair.

'Would Mrs Watts like a cup of tea to start off her John Street honeymoon?' he asked, a smile playing on his lips.

Polly kissed the smile. Taking hold of her soon-to-be husband's hand, she placed it on the small of her back and pressed herself against him.

'Mrs Watts would love a cup of tea.' She paused, kissing lips that were now becoming more serious.

'But not quite yet.'

*

The first two days of their honeymoon were spent in a blur of making love, chatting and drinking tea. They managed a quick and rather blustery walk around Mowbray Park, stopping to kiss under the outstretched but now rather bare arms of their favourite old oak tree. They had a cup of weak tea and a scone in the museum's little cafeteria, followed by a stroll around their favourite exhibition room, which was filled with scaled-down models of ships – those made from metal and those from wood – all built on the banks of the Wear. They had an even windier walk along the south docks, passing the Diver's House, and reminisced about the evening just over two years ago when Tommy had proposed.

They never talked about the future, however.

This honeymoon was about basking in their love. Past and present.

Along with most of the Elliot household, they'd gone to see Reverend Winsey and had the required rehearsal in a bitterly cold St Ignatius Church.

Lucille, as the only bridesmaid, loved being the centre of attention. The anticipation of a visit from Father Christmas – on the same day as her aunty's wedding – was sending her into a fever of excitement. And to top it all, Bing Crosby's crooning about a white Christmas had the knock-on effect of making Lucille and all her little friends obsessed with a need for it to snow on Christmas Day.

Agnes had managed to put her concerns about 'mortal sin' to one side after she had gone to see Beryl. Agnes had stomped next door, spitting nails, the night Polly had left for her new temporary home. Her fury had practically rocketed through the roof when her best friend had not been equally incensed by Polly's shameful behaviour. Instead, Beryl had told Iris and Audrey to go to their rooms, before shutting the door to the kitchen and letting rip at Agnes, telling her that if there was a God up there, he would not give two hoots if Polly and Tommy were living together – especially when it was just a matter of days before they officially became man and wife. Beryl had gone red in the face trying to keep her voice down. Her own worries about her husband and sons had flicked to anger and that anger had turned itself on her best friend.

'I think the good Lord – ' Beryl had sucked in air ' – will just be counting his lucky stars that Tommy, and men like him, are risking life and limb to do battle with the Devil himself.' She'd glared at Agnes. 'Never mind that your daughter is working herself to the bone building bloody ships day in, day out.'

Agnes had been shocked by her friend's reaction. They had always – *always* – agreed with one another. Been there for each other through thick and thin.

She'd left Beryl's house feeling like she had been physically shaken.

The next day she had got up and told Bel to go to the Major's flat to tell Polly and Tommy that they were expected round for Sunday dinner.

When her daughter and her live-in lover had arrived, Agnes had been relieved that Polly didn't seem to be holding a grudge.

Agnes could see that her daughter, for now at least, was blissfully happy.

Before they'd sat down to eat, Agnes had taken Tommy aside.

Knowing that they would not be able to afford one gold band – never mind two – she had given him Harry's wedding ring.

'Well, will yer look at that!' she'd exclaimed when Tommy had tried it on. 'Talk about made to fit.'

417

Realising the reasons for Agnes's actions were more fiscal than sentimental, Arthur had gone into his room and returned with Flo's wedding ring, knowing that, like the engagement ring, it too would be a perfect fit.

Agnes's mood had also been lifted no end by Lily and George's gift of a wedding. Lily might not be most people's idea of a fairy godmother, but she had granted Agnes her lifelong wish for her daughter to have a proper wedding.

It also meant that neither she nor Beryl would have to worry themselves silly over how they would put a decent dinner on the table on Christmas Day.

Instead, the mother of the bride dragged Beryl into town and they each bought themselves a new outfit – complete with hat. They were the first new items of clothing either woman had bought themselves for many, many years.

The women welders, naturally, talked about nothing else apart from Polly and Tommy's Christmas wedding.

Or rather, Dorothy and Angie talked about nothing else. Rosie, Gloria, Martha, Hannah and Olly hardly managed to get a word in edgewise.

The pair's excitement doubled, if that were possible, when Rosie asked them if they wouldn't mind bringing George's uniform round to Lily's on Christmas Eve.

Dorothy and Angie somehow managed to keep their near-on hysteria under wraps until they were walking home from work.

'"Would you mind"!' Dorothy bellowed out.

'Yeah,' Angie laughed out loud, sounding more than a little deranged. 'As if we're gonna "*mind*"!'

'This is going to be the *best* Christmas *ever*,' Dorothy declared, grabbing her best friend's arm and squeezing it until Angie shouted out in pain.

'Sorry, just a bit excited,' Dorothy apologised, trying unsuccessfully to rein in her exuberance as they turned into Foyle Street.

'Cor,' Angie said, rubbing her arm, 'just think, we're going to see inside – ' she dropped her voice as they neared their flat ' – a *bordello*.'

'I *knoooow*,' Dorothy said, again reaching for her friend's arm.

Bel was easily as excited as the squad's 'terrible two', but, unlike Dorothy and Angie, was managing to keep a veneer of decorum in place.

She was, after all, the matron of honour.

Bel felt akin to the swans she had seen during a rare trip to Barnes Park, who had seemed to glide serenely on the lake while all the time paddling manically under the water. She had a hundred and one things to do to make her sister-in-law's wedding the best ever.

There was no doubting the reception at the Grand would beat any other wedding hands down, but she needed everything else to be equally wonderful.

When Marie-Anne dared to suggest that Polly should perhaps 'pitch in a little', Bel had gasped – that everyone knew a bride is '*never* to be disturbed on her honeymoon, unless *absolutely* necessary'. Marie-Anne thought that, deep down, Bel was quite happy Polly was out of the way so that she could be the bride by proxy right up to the morning of the wedding.

Bel had gone through the wedding list so many times she reckoned she could probably recite it in her sleep. The list consisted of quite an eclectic mix of guests: Maud and Mavis the sweet-shop owners, shipyard bigwig Harold and his wife, Jimmy the head riveter and his motley crew, along with their significant others. The men's wives, Polly had told Bel, were apparently getting a little tetchy about their husbands' friendship with the women welders. Polly had thought it would be the perfect occasion for everyone to meet. Bel personally wondered about the wisdom of this, but followed instructions all the same.

Polly had also asked Bel to invite Alfie, and to tell him to bring his aged grandmother.

Rosie had asked if she could invite her next-door neighbour Mrs Jenkins and her husband, Kenneth. Polly thought it was because Rosie felt guilty about her lack of neighbourliness. Bel thought it was because Rosie felt sorry for the woman as she seemed rather lonely, had no children and rarely went out.

Polly had said 'of course', although Bel thought that her sister-in-law would have said 'of course' to inviting the whole of the east end, which she wasn't far off doing already.

During it all, Pearl had sidled up to Bel and pointed out that as Bill had been prepared to give up half the pub for Polly and Tommy's 'first wedding', it would be rude not to invite him to this one. Bel knew Polly would agree, but when her ma suggested that it would also be rude not to invite Ronald as he was their neighbour and had provided them with a fair few bottles of whisky over the past couple of years, Bel had hesitated. Her ma was, as usual pushing boundaries. She'd have to ask Polly.

Bel had given her ma strict instructions to stay as sober as possible on the day. She was also to find herself a dress to wear that was appropriate for her age. Pearl had muttered something about going to see Kate, at which point Bel had told her that Kate was probably up to her ears in wedding dresses and party frocks and not to bother her. She knew, though, that her ma wouldn't take a blind bit of notice. She also knew that Kate, for some unknown reason, had a soft spot for her ma and would sort her out.

In addition to her many duties, Bel had also had to convince Mr Clement, the photographer, to give up a few hours of his Christmas Day. He had said he would if he could bring his wife and three children to the Grand.

Bel had acquiesced, but only if Mr Clement, in turn, agreed to defy ration regulations and use every bit of photographic paper he possessed. She knew from her own wedding that the government had stipulated only two photographs could be taken per wedding. She was determined this was not going to be the case for her sister-in-law.

'I don't care how you do it,' Bel had told the wiry, grey-haired photographer, 'but there's going to be lots of photos. And at least one photograph has to be ready the next morning.' Tommy was going to return to war with more than just a picture of Polly in his head.

'And there's the whole wearing something old, something new, something borrowed and something blue,' Bel had lamented to Marie-Anne. As Polly had seemed totally unconcerned about this particular wedding tradition, Bel had made the decision on Polly's behalf that the dress would be 'new', the ring 'old', and Polly would borrow her ma's gold cross and chain.

'Blue' would be the garter, once, that was, she'd had the chance to get one.

'Everyone's asking me what presents they should get the bride and groom,' Bel had gasped in exasperation to Marie-Anne, who had made the fatal mistake herself and been curtly told to ask her mother for ideas.

Bel had not been able to tell Helen to do the same when she had started badgering her as to what to buy Polly and

Tommy. Not only because Helen was her boss, but because she couldn't imagine Helen's mother giving up a second of her precious time to think up a present for a woman welder – never mind one who was close friends with her husband's lover.

The problem was solved during a chat in their lunch break about Hope's 'totally adorable' flower-girl outfit that Helen had bought for her. Bel already knew from Gloria all about the 'adorable' and also *very* expensive dress. The chatter, however, had led to Helen asking Bel about Polly's wedding bouquet and if there were going to be any flowers in the church.

When Bel had told Helen that Arthur was going to get what he could from the allotment, Helen had not even tried to hide her disdain.

But then her face had lit up.

'That's it! Flowers! John and I will gift the wedding flowers.'

Bel had made a mental note to tell Polly that it would seem Helen had apologised to the good doctor, and it would also seem that she had been forgiven.

During the conversation Helen had told Bel, between puffs of her cigarette, 'You really remind me of someone. I just can't think who it is.'

Helen had scrutinised her and Bel had got paranoid that she might somehow work it out, but she'd dismissed the idea.

It was preposterous.

Helen would never guess in a million years.

The only part of the wedding that Polly had told Bel she wanted to take an active part in was the cake.

So, on Wednesday morning Polly and Tommy collected Arthur from Tatham Street and the three walked to the café in High Street East, sank a pot of tea and devoured three huge bacon butties.

Arthur reminisced about days gone by when Tommy had been just a lad, and the two of them would meet Jack at the café before work for a bacon bap breakfast.

They talked briefly about the latest war news. The newspapers were full of reports coming back from Stalingrad that Germany's Sixth Army was trapped.

The trip also gave Polly the chance to apologise to Arthur for being such a nightmare during what she called her 'week of madness', and to ask if the old man was still willing to give her away.

'Dinnit be daft, pet,' Arthur told her. 'Like I said to yer afore, yer making an old man very happy.' He reached out and patted Polly's hand. 'I don't think there'll be a prouder man on this planet, come Friday.'

His words made Polly want to cry, but she stopped herself. This was not the time for tears.

Spotting Rina in the kitchen on her own, Polly went to see her.

She gave her a hug.

'Thank you, Rina.'

Once again, she pushed back tears.

Polly didn't have to say why she was offering her thanks, nor did Rina have to ask.

Just before they all left, Polly caught Vera and told her to do whatever she wanted with regards to the wedding cake. The old woman muttered something under her breath about having to make all the decisions herself, but she wasn't kidding anyone. She was pleased as punch that she and Rina had been given carte blanche to do exactly what they wanted. And, moreover, that the Grand were providing the ingredients.

*

Despite all the running around and never-ending chores, Bel had to admit to herself and to Joe that she was loving every frantic second of organising her best friend's wedding.

'It's so exciting, isn't it?'

'Yes, it is. Very,' he said, deadpan.

Joe had been tasked with making sure that Arthur's suit was clean and pressed, as well as his own 7th Armoured Division uniform. He'd also been told to go out and find a Christmas tree, which was easier said than done, as, like everything these days, they were in scant supply. It was imperative, though, Bel had said. Christmas wasn't Christmas without the decorating of the tree. She was determined her daughter's Christmas was to be as magical as possible.

Neither of them said anything, but they both crossed their fingers that Jerry would want the same for their children and that there would be an unofficial Christmas Day amnesty.

Or, at the very least, no air raids.

Realising that Bel was run ragged, although trying her hardest not to show it, Rosie had offered Charlotte's services as she had now broken up from school.

'To be honest,' Rosie said, 'you'll be doing me a favour if you give her something to do. She's bouncing around the house like a rubber ball. She's already done all her homework for the whole of the Christmas break and she's been to see Marjorie in Newcastle. I'm struggling to keep her occupied. I was hoping she might have made some friends at school – that she'd want to go around to their houses and do things girls her age normally do.' Rosie sighed. 'But it would seem not.'

Bel reassured Rosie she would happily keep her busy.

It was why she was now heading into town, having got the afternoon off work to meet Charlotte and give her a list of last-minute presents and bits and bobs to buy for the wedding.

If Charlotte wasn't able to get them all today, there was always tomorrow – Christmas Eve.

As Bel hurried to catch the tram, she looked up at the pewter-grey clouds.

They looked heavy.

Bel kept her fingers crossed they forecasted snow.

It would make her daughter's Christmas even more special and it would be the cherry on the cake for a perfect Christmas wedding.

Chapter Sixty-Three

Christmas Eve

Thursday 24 December

'This is what I'm going to miss,' Tommy said as he put his arm around Polly's shoulders and pulled her close. 'Just lying here with you, in this bed, warm as toast, feeling your skin next to mine.'

Polly put her arm across his chest, pulling herself closer still so she could rest her head on her lover's chest.

'Me too,' she said simply, tracing the raised scar that ran down the middle of his torso.

'I keep wanting to say things,' she said, 'and then stopping myself.'

'Say them.' Tommy kissed the top of her head. 'You can say anything to me, you know that.'

'I know,' she said, 'but they're stupid things like, "You will take care, won't you?" It's pointless to say that because I know you'll be careful, as careful as you can be.'

Polly looked up and Tommy kissed her.

'You know that I *will* be careful.' He moved a little so that he could see her properly. Look into her eyes. 'You know I don't have a death wish, don't you?'

Polly felt herself colour.

'I know. I know,' she said. 'I should never have said that.'

'If anything were to happen to me out there – which it won't – but if it did, it won't be because I have some strange inherent desire to end it all.' He paused. 'Like my mam.'

Polly nodded.

Tommy shuffled round so that he was now lying on his side, facing Polly.

'But while we're on the subject, I need to know that if anything were to happen to me, then *you* will carry on living?'

Polly knew what he was saying. It was far more likely that, if he didn't come back, she would be the one who might be tempted to follow in his mam's footsteps.

'I will,' she said. 'I won't do anything stupid.'

'And that you won't spend the rest of your life in mourning? That you'll make the most of your life?'

Polly nodded.

'It's just,' Tommy looked serious, 'if there's one thing this war has taught me, it's that life is precious.'

'I know,' Polly said. 'And I promise you, I'll treasure it, regardless of what happens.'

Tommy kissed Polly.

He knew she meant what she'd said.

'Now,' he said, looking over to the clock on the bedside cabinet and seeing it was already eight, 'we've got a wedding to sort.'

'A cup of tea first, though,' Polly said.

'Definitely a cup of tea,' Tommy agreed as they both snuggled back under the covers.

'Where yer off to?' Pearl was still in her salmon-coloured polyester dressing gown but had put her thick winter coat on top to brave the cold and have her morning fag in the backyard.

'Church,' Bel said, looking around for her bag and boxed-up gas mask. 'Are you all right looking after Lucille this morning? Beryl's gone into town Christmas shopping with Agnes.'

Pearl nodded as she went over to her granddaughter and ruffled her hair. Lucille didn't look up as she was engrossed in drawing a picture of Santa Claus. The kitchen table was strewn with cut-up cereal packets and crayons.

'Why yer gannin to church? Yer've not got God, have yer?' Pearl laughed, then started coughing.

'No, Ma.' Bel rolled her eyes to the ceiling. 'I'm meeting Helen there to sort out the flowers for the wedding. You know, the one tomorrow?'

Ignoring her daughter's sarcasm, Pearl narrowed her eyes.

'So, it's "Helen" now, is it? You two getting pally with each other?'

The mother–daughter banter had been dropped.

Bel ignored her mother's question, instead going over to Lucille and giving her a quick kiss on the forehead.

'You be good for your nana now,' she instructed. Lucille nodded quickly before hunching herself back over her masterpiece.

'Just be careful, Isabelle.' Pearl followed Bel out into the hallway. 'That family's no good. There's bad blood runs in their veins.'

Bel turned and glared at her ma.

'Does that include me as well?' she said, before slamming the door behind her.

Five minutes later Bel had arrived at St Ignatius. It had only been a short walk along Tatham Street and then Suffolk Street, but long enough for Bel to push her ma's words of warning firmly out of the way.

This was not the time for doom and gloom; it was Christmas and there was a wedding to organise.

Bel smiled as she looked around the normally grey urban surroundings. Everything was starting to glitter with the frost and ice that had appeared overnight. The trees that normally looked eerie and skeletal had been transformed by what looked like a light sprinkling of icing sugar.

'Hi, Bel!' Helen waved as she strode out of the church's side entrance.

A young lad in a light brown overall coat was tailing her.

'The church looks amazing,' she beamed. 'Even if I say so myself.'

Sensing the young lad behind her, she swung round.

'Be gone! Your work here is done!'

The boy looked disappointed and turned to make his way back to the little blue van that Bel had just noticed was parked on the corner with its rear doors open. There was a trail of what looked like green fir leading from the van to the church entrance.

'Oh, blast! Wait there!' she shouted to the boy's back.

Helen hurried into the church, returning seconds later with her purse. She took out a note and pushed it into the boy's hand.

His face lit up.

'Thank you, ma'am. Thank you.' He tipped his over-sized tweed flat cap at Helen.

'Tell Beatrice she's done a wonderful job,' Helen said, ignoring the boy's words of gratitude. 'And that I can rest assured the bridal bouquet will be delivered as arranged?'

The boy nodded vigorously before shutting the rear doors and climbing into the driver's seat. Bel was surprised he could see over the wheel, never mind drive the thing.

'Come on,' Helen beckoned to Bel. 'Come and see!'

Bel could hear the same excitement in Helen's voice that she herself felt about Polly's wedding.

Walking through the thick wooden doors and into the dusky interior of St Ignatius Church, it took Bel's eyes a few seconds to adapt to the change in light.

When they did, she took a sharp intake of breath.

'Oh my goodness!' Bel stood rooted to the spot, staring.

There, on either side of the altar, were two magnificent floral displays made up of ivory roses and cream-coloured freesias, a few sprigs of holly and a scattering of mistletoe.

But what had taken Bel's breath away – and was something she had not expected – was the sight of the most perfect, luscious Christmas tree she had ever seen.

And it had been beautifully and very tastefully decorated with a smattering of silver baubles. Strips of glittering tinsel had been hung from its branches like sparkling icicles and a large silver star had been placed on the top.

'This is amazing,' Bel said. 'I really am stuck for words.'

Helen looked at Bel, then back at the two magnificent floral displays and the picture-perfect Christmas tree. *Her mother was going to go mad when she realised what she'd done.*

'I'm rather pleased, even if I say so myself,' Helen said, starting to walk down the aisle.

'How on earth did you manage to get all those flowers? You must have raided every florist in town?' Bel said.

'Not far off,' Helen laughed. 'But when you've got money – and when people realise that you're Mr Havelock's granddaughter – then just about anything's possible.'

Bel picked up the slightest hint of bitterness.

'Anyway,' she turned to Bel, 'I best go and tell the vicar the wedding flowers are all in place – and break it to him that I've also added a Christmas tree to the display.'

Helen chuckled.

'Do you think he'll mind?' Bel asked, genuinely concerned. She had been amazed he had agreed to have the wedding on Christmas Day in the first place, never mind now having a fir tree within spitting distance of the altar.

'Well,' Helen said, dropping her voice, concerned that the church's acoustics might make her voice travel, 'he should be cock-a-hoop his parishioners will have something interesting to look at during midnight Mass rather than his ugly mug. Although I'll bet my boots he has a good moan about it belittling the true meaning of Christmas – before mentioning the fact they need donations for the repair of the roof.'

Helen turned and went to fetch her handbag and gas mask from a pew.

'I'll see you tomorrow,' she said. 'And good luck with everything. Polly's lucky to have you.'

Helen let out a guttural laugh.

'If I ever get married, I'll be sure to ask you to organise it all.'

Bel watched as Helen sashayed down the aisle.

Something told Bel that Helen had no expectations of getting married.

Or perhaps no desire to.

As Bel hurried back home, she felt so excited.

Was it because it was Christmas?

Was it because she was well on her way to making Polly's wedding the best ever?

Or was it because she was getting to know her 'other' family?

Her ma was wrong.

Mr Havelock might have bad blood coursing through his entire body, but that wasn't to say it had infected the rest of the family.

Chapter Sixty-Four

Charlotte heaved her shopping bag into the Maison Nouvelle.

'Do you mind if I leave this here for a little while?'

'Of course not,' Kate said. She was sitting at her workbench stitching pale blue glass beads onto what Charlotte thought looked like a headband.

'I've just got one more thing to get,' she said, hurrying back out of the door.

Kate smiled to herself. Rosie could be pretty conniving when she wanted. Not only was she keeping Charlotte out of mischief, as well as out of her hair, she was also ensuring that she was helping Bel with the wedding. It wasn't a case of killing two birds with one stone but three.

Leaving the boutique, Charlotte hurried down Holmeside, turned left into Waterloo Place, then crossed over onto Athenaeum Street, before taking another left onto a very busy Fawcett Street.

Dodging shoppers, she finally reached Bridge Street, where she stopped and tried to find the shop she'd been told was around here somewhere.

The town was packed. Everyone seemed to have left their Christmas shopping until the last minute. Either that or they were out enjoying themselves, partaking in the Christmas spirit.

Charlotte spotted two Admiralty officers who looked as though they were doing just that. They weren't drunk, but they did look a little unsteady on their feet. If it wasn't for their age, she might have described them as dashing.

Suddenly she caught sight of two women walking down the street.

Was that ...?

Charlotte stood and looked hard.

Her vision was temporarily blocked by a tram slowly gaining momentum as it headed for the Wearmouth Bridge.

Charlotte squinted a little. It was freezing cold, but the sun was shining. Dazzling. She put her hand to her forehead to stop herself being blinded.

Yes, it was.

It was Maisie and Vivian.

Mind you, they didn't look like they'd been shopping. They weren't carrying any bags or parcels.

Charlotte lifted her hand to wave and catch their attention.

She was just about to try and cross the road when she saw one of the Admiralty turn around and say something to Maisie. She laughed as he folded her in his arms and kissed her, before taking her hand.

Charlotte dropped her own hand.

The other naval officer was now speaking with Vivian and was offering her his arm.

They were clearly out on a double date.

Charlotte stayed where she was.

The officers seemed a little old for Maisie and Vivian. Must have been at least twice their age.

Charlotte stumbled a little as she felt someone bump into her.

'Sorry, pet!'

Charlotte smiled and looked back to see where Maisie and Vivian and the two white-suited officers were going.

She caught them just as they disappeared through the main doors of the Grand.

*

433

When Charlotte got back to the Maison Nouvelle, she knocked on the door as she always did nowadays to stop Kate having kittens every time she entered the shop. She had noticed her sister always shouted out straight away whenever she came to the boutique and Charlotte had decided to do something similar.

Kate came out of the back room.

'You done all your chores then?'

'I have.' She let out air dramatically. 'It's like a bull bait out there, though.'

Kate chuckled.

'I know, anyone would think it was Christmas.'

Charlotte heard a rustling to her side and looked round to see Bel appearing through the divide in the curtain that provided the backdrop to the front window display.

She was holding her wedding dress.

'Thank you so much, Charlie, for doing everything. You are a real star. I don't know what I would have done without you.'

Bel gave Charlotte a hug while holding her dress out so as not to get it creased.

'Now come and show me what you've got.'

Charlotte picked up the bag she had left earlier and the confetti she had bought from the bridal shop on Bridge Street and took them into the back room.

While the three of them drank tea and oohed and aahed over the things Charlotte had bought, Charlotte kept thinking about Bel's sister and Vivian.

There were a few times she'd thought about mentioning that she'd seen them – after all, Maisie was Bel's sister and the pair lodged with Kate at Lily's – but each time something had stopped her.

Chapter Sixty-Five

Just after six o'clock there was a knock on the front door of number 7 Cairo Street. Martha had just returned from the yard and was helping her mam get the tea ready.

Not long before that Mr Perkins had staggered in with a rather emaciated Christmas tree, but it was a tree all the same. He had then gone up into the attic to bring down the decorations.

'Who's that at the door?' Mrs Perkins said, drying her hands on her pinny. 'We're not expecting any visitors, are we?' She looked at Martha, who shook her head.

'Who's that?' Mr Perkins stuck his head out of the square opening in the landing ceiling.

He watched, his vision upside down, as his wife answered the door. Martha was behind her. Forever protective.

'Oh, goodness me,' Mrs Perkins said. 'Well, this is a surprise.'

She looked at the delivery boy who had somehow managed to cycle with the wicker picnic hamper balancing on the basket on the front of his bicycle. He had put the bike on its stand and was now standing, knees bent and arms outstretched, holding the hamper that had a huge red bow tied around it.

'Are you sure you've got the right address?' Mrs Perkins asked.

She felt herself being nudged aside as Martha squashed past and took the delivery from the skinny young lad before he collapsed under its weight.

Martha looked at the tag dangling from one of the leather straps that were holding the hamper intact.

'"Mr and Mrs Perkins",' she read.

'Well, this is a surprise,' Mrs Perkins said, flattening herself against the wall of the hallway to allow Martha and the hamper to get past.

'Wait there, young man,' she said, grabbing her handbag by the front door.

She took out a coin and pressed it into the lad's cold hands.

'Merry Christmas.'

The boy looked down at the shiny coin and gave Mrs Perkins a big smile.

'Merry Christmas to you too!' A stream of smoky cold air accompanied his words.

Shutting the front door, Mrs Perkins hurried into the back parlour.

'William, get yourself down here,' she shouted.

Mr Perkins was already doing just that and was halfway down the ladder. He picked up the bag of decorations he had dropped down onto the landing and hurried down the stairs.

He found his wife and Martha standing around the table, looking down at the hamper.

'Well, it's not going to open itself,' Mr Perkins laughed. 'Go on, open it!'

Mrs Perkins carefully unbuckled the straps and slowly lifted the lid off the basket.

She gasped when she saw what was inside.

It was a hamper like no other she had ever seen. Certainly not since the start of war.

Partially hidden by straw, she could see a tin of fruit, a jar of marmalade, another jar of chutney and an oblong packet of biscuits – but it was what had been placed in the middle of the picnic basket that had her eyes out on stalks.

A massive gammon joint.

'Look,' Martha said, picking out an envelope that was lying next to what would most certainly be their Boxing Day meal. She read out the inscription on the front: '"Mr and Mrs Perkins". Nice handwriting.'

'You open it, William,' Mrs Perkins said, anxiously.

Mr Perkins did as he was told and carefully opened the envelope.

He read the few lines that had been written in blue ink on thick, good-quality writing paper.

Then he handed it to his wife.

Mrs Perkins took longer to read the note.

When she put it down, she had tears in her eyes.

'Come here,' she said to Martha and gave her a big hug.

Later on, after they'd all decorated the tree and Martha had gone to bed with a big mug of hot chocolate and a couple of biscuits from the hamper, Mrs Perkins settled herself in the old rocking chair that had once belonged to her father.

She picked up the note she had put on the mantelpiece and read it once more.

Dear Mr and Mrs Perkins,

If it wasn't for your brave daughter Martha, I would not be here now, nor would a mother and her little girl be celebrating this Yuletide.

You must be very proud parents.

Wishing you all a very Happy Christmas,

Kind regards,

Helen Crawford (Miss)

Chapter Sixty-Six

'Are yer ready?' Angie banged on Dorothy's bedroom door.

'Nearly!'

A few seconds later the door swung open.

'Ta-da!' Dorothy flung her arms out theatrically.

'Yeah, Dor, yer look fine. Now let's get going or we'll never get there,' Angie said.

Dorothy screwed her eyes up and glared at Angie.

'Why, Angela Boulter, I do believe you're nervous.' Dorothy was doing a very good impression of an accent from the Deep South.

'Am not!'

Dorothy threw her head back and roared with laughter.

'Well, *you* mightn't be, but Ahh sure as hell ahhm!'

'Dor, stop sounding like you've just stepped off the set of *Gone with the Wind*. Act normal.'

Dorothy gasped. 'How can I act *normal* when we're about to visit a house of ill repute?'

'That's exactly why I'm nervous,' Angie bit back.

'Aha, so you *are* nervous.'

'Bloody Nora, Dor.' Angie shoved past Dorothy and opened up the wardrobe. She carefully took out George's uniform still in its dry-cleaning bag.

'Better not forget the real reason we're going there,' Dorothy hooted, although by the high state of excitement she was in, there was a good possibility she would.

'Come on, Dor.' Angie marched down the hallway and opened the front door. 'I'm going whether you're ready or not.'

Dorothy watched Angie walk out in her lovely canary-yellow dress. It showed her curves off and went surprisingly well with her blonde hair.

'I think you've forgotten something,' she shouted after her as she grabbed both their winter coats from the tallboy. 'Blue and yellow isn't a good look.'

Quickly grabbing both their gas masks and locking the door behind her, she hurried down the stairs and caught up with Angie as she opened the main front door.

'Ah Angela, how are you?'

Dorothy couldn't see the face, but recognised the voice.

'I'm fine thanks, Quentin. How are you?' Angie said.

'Hi Quentin!' Dorothy squashed herself next to Angie, who had the clothes bag draped over her arm and was looking down at their neighbour standing at the top of the steps that led down to the basement.

'Gosh, you both look very ...' Quentin hesitated.

'Gorgeous? Stunning? Glamorous?' Dorothy suggested.

'Well, yes, all of the above,' Quentin said, although his response was directed at Angie.

'So, are you doing anything special for Christmas Day?' Quentin asked, his eyes nervously flitting from the ground and then back up to Angie.

'We are indeed, Quentin,' Dorothy answered for her friend. 'We are going to a Christmas wedding, and the reception is to be held at the Grand.'

Angie looked at her friend, who was now speaking as if she was on a visit to Buckingham Palace.

'Howay, Dor,' she said, making her way down the steps to the pavement. 'And fling me my coat, I'm bloomin' freezing here.'

Quentin smiled.

'You up to owt?' Angie asked as she handed over George's uniform in exchange for her thick olive-green woollen coat.

'Gosh,' Quentin said, brushing back a mop of hair that was the same colour as Angie's. 'Nothing quite so exciting.'

'So, what yer deein'?' Angie persisted.

'Well,' Quentin shuffled on the spot, 'just staying in. Listening to the King's speech. That sort of thing. Chicken sandwich ...'

'Yer jokin'?' Angie seemed intrigued. *Didn't posh people with names like Quentin have five-course nosh-ups on Christmas Day?*

'Right, best get a move on,' Dorothy said, handing Angie the uniform back so she could put on her own coat and stop herself from turning blue. Red and blue also did not go.

'Good evening, Quentin,' Dorothy said, again in a voice of aristocracy-cum-royalty.

'See yer,' Angie said. 'And happy Christmas!'

Her Yuletide cheer was met by a smile that spread across the entire width of Quentin's pale but not unhandsome face.

'Yes, I'll say ... Merry, *merry* Christmas!' he shouted back.

He was still standing on the same spot when Angie and Dorothy turned the corner at the bottom of their street.

It took the pair twenty minutes to get to Lily's.

They were both trembling with cold and nerves by the time they reached the front door.

Dorothy's shaking had been exacerbated by nearly going head over heels on black ice a few times.

'You knock!' Dor said.

'No, you knock!' Angie said.

Dorothy took a deep breath and raised the brass knocker.

They both jumped back when the door opened on the second knock.

Lily had been waiting.

'Mes chers!' Lily opened the door wide. *'Entrez! Entrez!* Come in, come in!'

She gestured for them to enter the house.

Dorothy took a deep breath and stepped over the threshold.

Angie followed, her arm now aching from carrying the uniform, which was heavier than it looked.

Both Dorothy and Angie stood stock-still and gazed in awe at the huge Christmas tree in the hallway, at the magnificent chandelier, the polished parquet flooring and the wide, sweeping staircase.

As soon as Angie was in and the door shut behind her, Lily reached over and took the uniform from her.

'Ahh, *merci, merci beaucoup!'* she said, unzipping the front of the clothes bag and having a quick look.

'I'll just go and put this somewhere safe,' she said. 'Go into the office and see Rosie. She was just about to leave. It being Christmas Eve and all that.'

'Dorothy ... Angie,' Rosie welcomed them both as she opened the door to her office. 'Come in! Thanks so much for bringing the uniform over. It's been crazy today. I've got to get off in a minute and see Charlotte. Not fair to leave her on her own on Christmas Eve.'

Dorothy smiled as she walked into the office, trying her hardest to appear as though this was the most normal thing ever – popping into *a bordello* to drop something off for a friend!

Angie followed Dorothy, openly gawping at the sheer opulence of Rosie's 'other' workplace. The floor-to-ceiling velvet curtains, the beautiful desk, the roaring fire, the chaise longue, the oriental rug ... Everything. It was amazing. Beautiful and so stylish.

Just then, the doorbell went.

Rosie sighed and looked at her watch.

'The clients should know to use the back.'

By the time she had walked across the office, Lily had already reached the front door.

'You should be using the back entrance!' Lily reprimanded, looking down at the suited man standing on the doorstep. 'Sorry, but I'm going to have to insist you go around the back.' She looked nervously at her neighbours to her left and right.

'No, honestly—' the man started to say.

'Oh, all right then, come on in.' Lily waved her hand impatiently. 'Chop-chop!'

As soon as he was over the threshold, he too stared about the hallway in disbelief.

It was even more impressive than Peter had told him.

'The girls are in the back.' Lily turned around to see George coming out of the parlour. The sound of Bing Crosby's 'White Christmas', along with a stream of cigar smoke and perfume, escaped into the hallway.

'George will introduce you.' Lily's impatience was undisguised.

'Sorry, I think there's been a misunderstanding,' the man said.

He looked at Dorothy and Angie standing in the front room.

And then at Rosie.

She was exactly as Peter had described.

He'd been too late to catch her at the yard and knew by this time she'd be at the bordello.

'I've actually come to see Rosie,' he said, walking into the office.

'Well, she doesn't *work* here as such,' Lily said, following him. 'Not any longer.'

Toby looked at Dorothy and Angie and then back again at Rosie.

He stepped forward and put his hand out.

'Mrs Miller, I'm Toby, Peter's friend.'

Everyone fell silent, all thinking the same thoughts.

No, please, God. No.

Not Peter. Not now.

'Oh God!' Dorothy couldn't help herself.

Toby looked at her, then back at Rosie, who was standing there, mute. Her face full of fear.

'No,' he said, his face full of apologies. 'No, it's not bad news. Not at all.'

Rosie looked about her. All of a sudden, she felt faint.

She walked back to her desk and sat down.

'That's good to hear,' she heard herself say.

Lily hurried over to the decanter of brandy, sloshed a good measure into a glass, took a quick slug herself and then handed it to Rosie.

'George, can you get everyone a drink, please? I think we all need one.'

Lily turned to Toby.

'Why didn't you say who you were in the first place?' She moved to the side of the desk and pulled out the top drawer to retrieve her Gauloises.

Toby opened his mouth to speak.

'So, Peter's all right?' Lily asked, casting a look at Rosie, who had gone as white as a sheet.

Toby stuck his hand in the inside pocket of his suit and pulled out an envelope.

'Peter's well,' he said. 'He knew I was going to be in the area and asked me to pop in and see his wife.'

He looked over at Rosie, who was now listening intently.

As were the two young women.

'He asked me to give you this.'

He held out the envelope.

Lily snatched it off him and handed it to Rosie.

443

She looked at it, but didn't open it.

'I'll read it later,' she said, sliding it into the pocket of the cream slacks she was wearing.

'I'm afraid you'll see it's not Peter's handwriting. It's mine. It came over the wires.'

That was all Toby could divulge.

'Here we are!' George came into the room with a tray of drinks.

'I'm afraid it's a choice of brandy or brandy.'

George looked over at Rosie, then to Lily, who gave him a tight nod that all was well.

'Here, let me take that,' Dorothy said, seeing that George was standing somewhat lopsidedly as he'd had to hook his walking stick over his arm in order to carry the tray.

Like an experienced hostess, she took the tray to Toby first.

'Thank you,' Toby said, taking a large bulbous glass containing an equally generous measure of Rémy.

'You're welcome,' Dorothy said.

The pair smiled at each other.

Dorothy then took the tray to Lily, to George and finally to Angie, before taking her own drink and putting the tray down on the coffee table.

George raised his glass.

'A toast.' He looked at Rosie and gave her a wink.

She smiled back but still looked a little dazed.

'To Peter!' he said.

Rosie raised her glass.

'To Peter,' she mouthed.

'And a very merry Christmas to all,' George added.

There was no doubt in his mind that this was the best Christmas present Rosie could wish for.

Rosie had a sip of her brandy and stood up.

She felt a little steadier on her feet.

She felt for the letter in her pocket, reassuring herself it was safely tucked away.

'Thank you, Toby, for coming here.' She moved around the desk and shook his hand again. This time with more vigour. 'Peter always talked about you fondly.' She looked at him and smiled.

'I'm guessing that you didn't just drop by because you were in the area, though – you've probably had quite a journey to get here?'

Rosie knew that Toby was based mainly in Scotland when he wasn't over enemy lines.

Toby chuckled. Peter was right. She was smart as well as a damn good-looking woman.

'Some things are worth making the journey for,' he said simply.

'Well, if that's the case,' Lily chirped up, 'why don't you stay and enjoy yourself? Unless you've got to get back somewhere straight away?'

Toby caught Dorothy's eye.

'No, I'm here until Boxing Day,' he said.

'Well then,' Lily said, forever the businesswoman. She had spotted the cut of his suit and it said in no uncertain terms that he was well heeled. *Very* well heeled. 'You might want to enjoy the company of one of my girls to tide you over the Christmas festivities?'

Dorothy and Angie both took large gulps of their brandies. Never in a million years had they expected to see Lily in her role as madam. All they needed now was to have a peek in the back parlour where they could hear 'the girls'.

'Well, that might not be such a bad idea,' Toby said.

He looked at Dorothy in her stunning red dress. It had taken all his concentration to stay focused on the job in hand.

'Well,' Lily said, turning to lead the way to the back parlour, 'let me introduce you to the girls.'

'Oh, I don't think there's any need for that,' Toby said, smiling at Dorothy. 'I'd be very happy if this young woman would be my companion during my short stay. I'm sorry, I don't even know your name?'

Everyone was now looking at Dorothy.

Angie had gone bright red and was desperately trying to stop herself from having the screaming heebie-jeebies. They were going to be in stitches when they left.

'It's Dorothy, but everyone calls me Dor.'

Dorothy was suppressing a smile.

Lily was just about to say something when Dorothy beat her to it.

'I'm afraid, though, Toby,' she allowed herself a half-smile, 'that I don't work here. I'm not one of Lily's girls.'

Dorothy forced herself not to look at Angie, otherwise she knew she'd have a fit of the giggles.

'Gosh, I'm so sorry.' Toby looked mortified.

Everyone chuckled.

'I can introduce you to some of the girls who do in fact work here, though,' Lily said. She took a good slug of her brandy. This Christmas Eve was turning into one she would remember for a variety of reasons.

'No … no thank you …' Toby stammered. 'I was only really interested in Dorothy here.' He shook his head at his own stupidity. 'I'm so sorry.'

He looked at Angie.

'I'm guessing you two are friends?'

They both nodded.

'We work with Rosie. At the yard,' Dorothy explained.

'Ahh, you're welders,' Toby said. 'How fascinating. I'd love to know more.'

He paused.

'Would it be rude of me to ask, having made such a huge faux pas, if you would go out for a drink with me?'

Everyone was now watching with interest.

'Well – ' Dorothy looked at Angie and knew she would hate her for what she was about to suggest ' – there's a rather spectacular wedding happening tomorrow.'

Toby showed his surprise.

'Yes, I know, on Christmas Day of all days,' Dorothy said. 'And as it happens, my "plus one" has just been called away on important business, which means there's a vacancy there, if you'd like to take it.'

Dorothy saw Angie's face change out of the corner of her eye.

'I most certainly would like that,' Toby said. 'Very much indeed.'

After they all finished their drinks, Toby offered to drop Rosie off at Brookside Gardens and then Dorothy and Angie at Foyle Street, before heading back to his 'digs'.

Pulling up outside the flat, it was agreed he should pick Dorothy and Angie up at half past twelve in time for the wedding at one.

After Toby drove away, Angie rounded on Dorothy, but before she had a chance to get her words out, Dorothy jumped in.

'You're going to ask Quentin,' she said simply. It wasn't a suggestion or an order, just a basic statement of fact.

She looked at her watch.

'It's not too late and look, his light's still on. Probably up reading Chaucer or something.'

'But—' Angie started to say.

'This is not a time for "buts", Angie dear. You heard the poor bloke. He's going to be sat at home on his lonesome, eating chicken sandwiches and listening to the King's speech. You'll be doing him a massive favour, and in return he can teach you lots of things you've been wanting to learn about being posh.'

Angie opened her mouth to object but stopped.

She did want to learn more about being 'posh'. More about everything, really.

'He can show you which knives and forks to use,' Dorothy said, now spurred on by Angie's lack of objection. 'He can even teach you how to waltz properly. All that kind of stuff.'

Deciding to take the bull by the horns, Dorothy quickly went down the steps to the basement flat, knocked on the door and hurried back up again.

'Go on then,' she said, gently pushing her friend into action. 'Go and tell him he's your plus one.'

Chapter Sixty-Seven

'So, are you all set? Everything organised?' Tommy pulled Polly towards him before she had time to take off her coat. He felt the need to have her next to him for every moment possible before he had to leave.

Polly kissed him.

'Well, according to the best sister-in-law anyone could ever hope to have – yes, I am.'

Polly had spent the last couple of hours with Bel, going over everything she needed to know about her big day with military precision. If anyone had asked who was the most nervous, Polly would have told them Bel. Hands down.

'I will thank her profusely tomorrow,' Tommy said. 'She's given me the best wedding present ever – time with you.'

Tommy reluctantly let Polly free.

She shrugged off her coat.

'Is that supper I can smell?' she said.

'It certainly is.' Tommy followed Polly into the kitchen, where he had set the table and even found a candle in one of the cupboards that he'd already lit. 'Courtesy of the fish shop.'

'Perfect,' Polly said, sitting down at the table while Tommy jokingly put a tea towel across his arm and took out two plates with a fish lot on each.

They both chatted away, telling each other about what had occurred during their few hours apart.

Polly told Tommy how excited Lucille was about Santa's arrival and how it would seem that Father Christmas had a great helper in the form of Charlotte, who had managed to get everything Bel had asked for. Even confetti – a rarity in these times of rationing.

'The house was in utter chaos,' Polly said. 'Oh, and you should have seen Lucille's little face when Joe hauled the Christmas tree through the front door. God knows how he managed to do it. I'll bet you he's suffering now.'

Tommy felt for Joe. He had not heard him complain once about what he called his 'gammy' leg, but he knew from his time on the ward that shrapnel injuries could leave a man in lifelong pain.

'And yer ma?'

'She seems really happy,' Polly said. 'Actually, the most relaxed I've ever seen her at Christmas. She keeps going on about how strange it's going to be not to have to cook.'

'What? Like she's going to miss it?'

'No, quite the reverse. More like she's over the moon that she's not.'

Polly had a drink of water from her tumbler as they both ate their fish and chips.

'Arthur said you'd had a nice time. He looked shattered, though,' she said.

'We did. Went down by the docks. Saw some old faces there, which was nice. Just chatted really. He seems happy. Tired, but happy.'

Tommy had also met up with the Major in town to make arrangements about leaving on Boxing Day. A car had been ordered to pick him up from the Grand at midday. This was something Polly didn't need to know this evening. He'd also asked the Major how the big powwow was going at the Grand, but he'd seemed a little evasive and was instead keen to hear about the wedding and to sort out a time to come to the flat in the morning to put on what he called his 'clobber'. It had been decided that all the military men going to the wedding would wear their uniforms. Joe had told them about George's reluctance to wear his regalia and had suggested that they all do the same as a show of solidarity.

'So,' Tommy asked, 'has the very-soon-to-be Mrs Watts decided on her whereabouts this evening?'

They had chatted about whether or not they should keep with tradition and spend the night apart, which would, of course, also keep Agnes happy. It had been a difficult call, though, as they both felt resentful about having to give up their second-from-last night together.

'Mmm,' Polly said. 'Well, I was chatting to Bel and she suggested that I sort of do both.'

Tommy raised his eyebrows.

'She suggested I spend most of the night here, but come back home in the early hours and have another couple of hours' sleep before I get up and, in her words, "begin the most memorable day of my life".'

'That sounds like a perfect solution to the dilemma,' Tommy said. That was something else he must remember to thank Bel for.

Rosie was sitting up in bed.

In her hand was Peter's note.

She read it over and over again until finally her eyelids got too heavy and sleep claimed her.

She slept all night with her husband's words of love pressed to her chest.

Kate was sitting in the back pew at St John's Church in Ashbrooke.

She was well wrapped up, with a thick woollen coat on, hat, scarf and gloves, but even so she was still cold.

Tonight, though, it was worth it. She loved midnight Mass. Loved hearing the Nativity readings.

She listened as the vicar read the words from the Gospel of Luke:

'And she brought forth her firstborn, and wrapped him in swaddling clothes and laid him in a manger; because there was no room for them in the inn.'

But she knew she was going to enjoy the vicar's sermon the most when he began with the words:

'Hope. Faith. Peace. Joy. And Love.' His voice loud and clear, but also soft and sincere. 'These words,' he said, 'encapsulate the message of the Advent. They are the true meaning of Christmas. The story of the birth of our Lord Jesus Christ is really a story about these five wonders of the world.'

Kate nestled back in her pew, no longer feeling the cold.

At about one o'clock in the morning, when everyone was tucked up in bed fast asleep, or trying to stay awake for a sneak look at Santa, the first flurry of snow started to descend on the town.

It looked like Lucille's and Bel's wishes for a white Christmas and a white Christmas wedding were about to come true.

Chapter Sixty-Eight

The Wedding Day

Christmas Day

Friday 25 December

When Polly woke up, she automatically felt for Tommy.

Of course, he wasn't there.

She was back home in her room at Tatham Street.

Two feelings collided with one another as she sat up in bed.

This was her wedding day!

The rush of excitement mixed with adrenaline made her feel a little nauseous. This, she knew, was going to be a day like no other. The church, her amazing dress and the reception at the Grand ...

But the other, conflicting feeling was one of panic.

This was her last day with Tommy.

Might even be her last ever.

Stop it!

She thought of Rina's words. She had spoken about love and sacrifice, but Polly had also heard a story of bravery.

Like Hannah's parents, she wanted to be brave.

She was *going* to be brave.

She was going to fight back any worries about Tommy and his imminent departure and instead enjoy every minute of this incredible day.

*

Getting out of bed, Polly pulled on her dressing gown, wrapping it tightly around her.

Quietly opening her bedroom door, she tiptoed down the cold tiled hallway. She wanted to greet the start of this special day on her own. To think her own thoughts undisturbed, if only for a few minutes.

Pulling on her boots, which she had left in the passageway just a few hours earlier, Polly slowly opened the front door.

As she did so, she let out a quiet gasp of disbelief.

It was as though she had opened the door into another world.

A beautiful, surreal world covered in a thick glistening pure white shroud.

The shock of ice-cold air, coupled with the surprise at seeing this idyllic winter wonderland, gave Polly another surge of adrenaline.

She walked out of the house and onto the road.

Slowly turning, she looked around at the empty street and the virgin snow, speckled with just a few trails of small paw prints from the neighbours' cats.

Polly looked up to the still-dark sky, and she felt the tickle of snowflakes on her lips and eyelids.

She closed her eyes and stood silently in the snow.

This street had been her home her entire life.

She had been born here, grown up here with Teddy and Joe.

How she would have loved to have had Teddy here today.

'Be with us today, won't you?' she said, a stream of cold air billowing out of her mouth.

Turning and looking down at the bomb site that now marked the start of Tatham Street, she realised just how much had changed.

Since the start of this war she had lost one brother and had had another return injured.

She had fallen in love, got engaged and waved her love off to war. Believed him dead, rejoiced in his return, and was now getting married on the day before he left her for the second time.

'Aunty Polly! Aunty Polly! It's snowing!'

Polly's reverie was broken by the sound of her niece's joyful exclamation.

'LuLu!' Polly put both her hands out.

Lucille, still dressed in her nightie, dressing gown and slippers, charged at her and allowed herself to be scooped up and swung in the air.

'My, you're getting too big to be hauled about!' Polly laughed as Lucille looked up to the skies and stuck her tongue out to catch the snowflakes fluttering around them.

Polly put her niece down.

Lucille danced in a circle, then grabbed her aunty's hand. 'Santa's been!' she beamed, dragging Polly back indoors.

From the moment Polly and Lucille stepped back over the threshold, the madness brought on by it being both Christmas and her wedding day was soon under way.

Lucille showed Polly her presents from Santa. She had already tipped out the contents of her stocking and the prize orange that had been put in the bottom had rolled next to Tramp and Pup's basket. They were sniffing it but seemed unimpressed. There was a handful of nuts by the range and an assortment of toys, most of which were second-hand or had been made by Joe, laying amidst scrunched-up wrapping paper, or rather newspaper.

Lucille's most revered present had, not surprisingly, come from Maisie.

Polly smiled as Lucille raised her new dolly in the air as though it was a trophy.

455

It was the first coloured doll that Polly had ever seen. According to the box, which had been flung under the kitchen table, it had been made by a British doll-maker called Norah Wellings and was called 'South Sea Islander'. The doll was made from dark brown velvet and was wearing a grass skirt and a smile.

Polly chuckled to herself. Only Maisie could have found such an unusual – and clearly very expensive – doll.

Hearing her daughter's voice resounding through the house, Bel came padding downstairs, looking wide awake and in full wedding mode.

Polly was made to eat a bowl of porridge to give her the energy to get through the day. In the middle of the table was placed a big pot of tea that was to be regularly topped up as the morning wore on.

Joe took Lucille – and her new dolly – out to play in the snow and to build her first-ever snowman.

The front door was left ajar to allow Beryl to pop in and out, sometimes with Iris and Audrey, who were being permitted to wear make-up for the first time.

The delivery boy from the florist arrived with a beautiful bride's bouquet simply made up of red roses, as well as the buttonholes and corsages, each an ivory rose encased in a single green leaf.

Polly, Bel, Agnes, Beryl and Pearl stood and gawped.

'Wait until you see the display in the church!' Bel said.

On hearing the wedding flowers were Helen Crawford's wedding gift, Pearl muttered, 'More money than sense.' But only so her daughter could hear.

Vivian showed up mid-morning, looking more like Mae West than Mae West herself in a red fishtail dress with a plunging neckline. She refused a cup of tea for fear it would spoil her make-up and got to work on Polly's hair straight away.

Polly had given Vivian more or less full rein over what to do with her hair. She knew that anything would look better than the only two styles she knew – loose or tied up in a turban. Vivian had told her that she was going to do an 'up *and* down do', which made no sense to Polly.

Positioned in the middle of the kitchen on a hard-backed chair, Polly was ordered to stay there until Bel had done her make-up and Vivian her coiffure.

Arthur had a quick shave, put on his newly pressed suit and tie and made his escape to the John Street flat. Not before, however, Bel had put in his buttonhole and given him a once-over.

Joe, now wearing the uniform of his old regiment, left shortly afterwards, having been officially released from doing any more chores, although he was called back within seconds of leaving by a slightly demented Bel waving Tommy's buttonhole, which Arthur had forgotten to take.

At eleven o'clock everyone stopped what they were doing to listen to the church bells. It was only the second time the Ministry of Home Security had allowed them to be rung since the war had started. The first time being just over five weeks ago in celebration of the British victory at El Alamein in Egypt.

They had just stopped ringing out across the town when Kate turned up with the dress.

She had been transported to the house in George's MG and her arrival was treated as though the King himself had turned up for a visit.

The whole household came to a standstill as Kate's diminutive form, dressed in a simple, classy black dress she had designed herself, her arms outstretched, carefully carried the wedding dress down the hall.

The kitchen door was shut, leaving just the women in the room, the dogs having been ushered into the scullery.

Twenty minutes later Polly was standing in the middle of the kitchen. All the chairs had been pushed back to create as much space as possible

Kate, Bel and Vivian stood back.

They all gasped in unison.

None of them needed to say a word. The looks on their faces said it all.

The dress was stunning.

The ivory chiffon dress had been embroidered throughout with intricate patterns. A scattering of crystals had been sown into the fabric, giving off a subtle sparkle. The sweetheart neckline was sensual but still classy, and the perfectly tailored bodice accentuated Polly's nipped-in waist.

The long sleeves and flowing train completed a perfect silhouette of femininity.

When Agnes came back from Beryl's, she took one look at Polly and her eyes filled with tears – the first, but certainly not the last, that she would have to force back on her daughter's wedding day.

Bel went up to her and Joe's room and put on her dress. Her thoughts went to her own wedding day just over a year ago. Then her hand went to her flat stomach. She pushed away thoughts of the child she'd love to have but which showed no signs of showing up.

Just after midday, Gloria turned up and there were more gasps of delight on seeing Hope looking adorable in her exquisite flower-girl dress.

Lucille immediately took command of her charge, grabbed her little hand and took her to see what Santa had brought.

Gloria looked at Polly.

'Eee. You're a sight for sore eyes,' she said, before leaving for the church.

When Polly was finally allowed to go into her bedroom and look at herself in the full-length mirror, she too gasped.

'Oh, my goodness,' she laughed. 'Who's that?' She pointed at herself in the mirror.

She turned to look at her dressmaker, make-up artist and hairstylist who were all standing in the doorway watching her reaction.

Polly looked back at herself again.

This time she simply stood and stared.

She turned, blinking back tears of gratitude.

'Don't you dare cry!' Bel ordered.

'And don't touch your hair,' Vivian said.

Polly looked at Kate, who was inspecting the dress from top to bottom.

'Thank you, Kate,' she said. 'Thank you so much. I really am stuck for words. It's gorgeous.'

She turned back to look at herself again.

'Oh, I forgot!' Kate suddenly said, backing out of the room and returning a minute later with a small box.

She handed it to Polly.

'It's your "something blue". And my wedding present to you.'

Polly opened the small box and took out a garter that was more a work of art than a piece of hosiery.

'Oh my goodness! That's incredible.' Polly marvelled at the sky-blue beading, embroidery and lace that had been sown onto the fabric. 'I think it should be put in a display case – not worn where no one can see it!' she said.

'Wrong, hon.' Vivian walked over to Polly and took the garter. '*Someone* is going to see it.' She winked at Polly before carefully crouching down – no mean feat in her figure-hugging dress – and putting the garter on Polly, adjusting it expertly in the middle of her thigh.

'And, finally ...' Kate said.

She disappeared once again and returned moments later.

' ... the veil.'

She handed it to Vivian.

'It's amazing, isn't it?' Bel said as she watched Vivian take the six-foot-long tulle. It too had a scattering of twinkling crystals embedded in it to complement the dress.

Vivian slid the comb into place, careful not to spoil the fruits of her morning's labour.

Again, everyone simply stood still and looked, momentarily entranced by the vision before them.

'Right.' Bel broke the spell.

She looked at her watch.

'It's nearly half past. We need to get everyone to the church.'

On cue, they heard the honk of George's horn as he pulled up outside the house. It was followed by cries of excitement as just about every child who lived on Tatham Street ditched their presents from Santa to see a life-sized bright red toy crunch its way slowly down the street through the snow. Its arrival was made all the more spectacular by the long ivory ribbon decorating the bonnet – while the driver was dressed in full military regalia, the medals adorning his chest glinting in the bright midday sun.

Amidst shouts of 'Don't be nervous!' and 'Just enjoy it!' the house slowly emptied itself.

Agnes, wearing a rather glamorous black dress and matching hat, was the last to say goodbye to her daughter.

She gave Polly a hug and then stood back and simply looked at her.

'Beautiful.'

Feeling the tears coming again, she stopped herself from saying anything else.

Taking Hope's little hand, they walked out the front door and climbed into the front passenger seat.

Bel, Kate, and Vivian had already concertinaed themselves in the back along with Lucille, who was wearing her new yellow dress and was sitting on her mother's lap, gazing out at the growing swell of spectators.

Chapter Sixty-Nine

Over the river at 1 Park Avenue, Roker, Helen was also just getting ready to leave.

She had dithered as to whether or not to wear the new blue dress that Kate had made for the launch. John hadn't seen her in it as they had been in the middle of their falling-out.

She was glad they were friends again.

She'd missed him; not that she'd tell him that.

Checking herself in the hallway mirror, she was glad she'd opted for her favourite black rayon crepe dress instead. She'd had to pour herself into it, but seeing how it accentuated her hourglass figure, it was worth it.

Helen looked at her watch. It was half twelve.

She went over to the window at the side of the house.

This was one day she wasn't going to use public transport.

One of the pluses of having a grandfather who was rich and powerful was that he also had a chauffeur-driven car that he had been permitted to use in spite of fuel rationing.

She walked to the bottom of the stairs.

'Right, Mother, I'm off now!' she shouted up in the direction of her mother's bedroom.

'Oh, darling!'

Miriam came out of her room and walked to the top of the stairs.

Helen could tell instantly that she had already started on the gin and tonic.

'I'm guessing by the lack of activity and the absence of Mrs Westley that you're not having your usual Christmas Day soirée?' Helen asked.

Miriam let out a light laugh. She had been in particularly good spirits since Helen's miscarriage. Her daughter's heartbreak had been her reprieve from what she saw as the ruination of her life.

'Darling,' Miriam squinted, inspecting her daughter as she always did before she left for any kind of a do, 'as you have chosen to go to some welder's wedding today rather than enjoy a Yuletide at home, I have not been left with much of a choice.'

She started to make her way down the stairs.

'On top of which, I have not even got a husband by my side. I'm hardly going to entertain a load of happily-marrieds when I'm sitting at the table with just your grandfather for company.'

Helen bit her tongue as she always had to when it came to any kind of conversation regarding her father.

Miriam suddenly stopped mid-step.

'And especially as I haven't even got a Christmas tree to show off! How could I have a Christmas dinner party with no Christmas tree?'

She continued to walk down the last few carpeted steps.

'It's still a total mystery where the bloody thing went. Sounds to me as though the delivery firm took it to the wrong address. There'll be hell to pay when I get to the bottom of this.'

Helen gave her mother a smile that for once was genuine.

Miriam reached the bottom step.

'No, my dear, I'm doing what everyone else seems to be doing these days.' She took a breath. 'I'm going to do what *I* want to do. I'm sick of trying to please everyone else.'

Helen gasped.

'Mother, I've never known you to do anything *but* please yourself.'

Miriam ignored her daughter's barbed comment.

'So, what *are* you doing then?' Helen walked back over to the window. She looked out and saw her grandfather's shiny black Jaguar pull up.

'Sorry, Mother, must dash!'

She hurried to the front door.

Slamming it shut behind her, she made her way to the car, taking care not to slip in the snow.

Chapter Seventy

When everyone had gone, Polly stood in the middle of the kitchen. It looked as though it had been ransacked.

Bel, who had thought of just about everything, had left a little nip of brandy in a sherry glass on the table, along with a mint next to it.

Polly knocked it back in one go, before popping the mint imperial into her mouth.

She took a deep breath.

It was finally happening.

She was marrying Tommy.

She was marrying the man she loved.

A man whose love had taken her completely by surprise that day in the yard two and a half years ago.

Feeling a little dizzy and short of breath, she sat down on the kitchen chair. She jumped on hearing the blare of George's horn. His arrival was followed by the shouts and jubilant cries of the neighbours' children.

She stood up.

She didn't think she had ever been this excited, nervous and happy all at once.

Picking up her bouquet, she walked to the front door and stepped out into the brilliant sunlight that had appeared late morning. Its rays seemed to reflect the white of the snow that was clearly determined to stay put.

George was standing ramrod straight. He had the passenger door open and was looking every bit the high-ranking and highly decorated army officer that Lily had wanted to show the world.

Arthur was sitting in the back, the window down, chatting to the rosy-faced children who had gathered round.

Polly took a deep breath, hooked the length of her veil over her arm, hitched up her wedding dress and carefully walked the few yards to her carriage.

Before driving off, George adhered to the age-old custom of throwing pennies from the car as they made to leave.

Only, George, being George, was throwing silver rather than copper.

His argument being that it was Christmas, after all.

Chapter Seventy-One

'Hi, Gloria!'

Rosie clapped her gloved hands together as she and Charlotte approached the church. The sun might be glorious, but it was still icy cold.

Half the congregation was loitering outside, chatting and moving from one foot to the other on the pavement that had been shovelled clear of snow for the wedding entourage.

The air of excitement and anticipation was as crisp and clear as this Christmas Day.

A cursory scan of the crowd showed Marie-Anne was chatting to Rina, Hannah and Olly. Vera was with them and looked to be either squinting because of the sun or scowling at whatever Marie-Anne was saying.

Martha could be seen towering above her mam and dad, and just about everyone else, for that matter. She looked self-conscious. Rosie knew she felt uncomfortable in anything other than a pair of overalls.

Dorothy and Toby were chatting away. Angie was standing a little awkwardly with a slim, blond-haired chap who was wearing what looked like a very expensive suit.

Pearl was with Bill and Ronald, puffing away on a cigarette. She had a flimsy winter coat wrapped around her, the occasional breeze causing the bottom half to flap open. Rosie thought the violet-coloured dress she had on looked unusually classy. Certainly not her normal style.

Joe was standing with his friends from the Home Guard. Major Black, of course, was the centre of attention, chortling away and filling the air with the distinctive oaky aroma of cigar smoke. Rosie thought they all looked incredibly smart and handsome in their khaki uniforms.

'Everyone's just going in,' Gloria said, smiling at Charlotte, who, she thought, was looking very grown up in her new red dress. 'I swear Bel's missed her vocation as a drill sergeant. She's in there now, organising, or should I say *ordering* everyone about. Even Lucille and Hope are behaving themselves.'

As everyone slowly made their way into the church, Rosie spotted Helen and Dr Parker. They looked like a Hollywood couple. There was no denying Helen resembled Vivien Leigh, only taller and curvier, and Dr Parker was not unlike James Stewart, only younger and with lighter hair.

'Wow!' Charlotte said on walking into the church and seeing the Christmas tree, which now had carefully placed candles on its branches. They had just been lit, their flickering yellow glow adding to the rather magical ambience.

'Hi, you two.' Bel came hurrying up the aisle. Charlotte stared at her in the pretty pink dress she had only ever seen the shop mannequin wear.

'Can I put you here?' Bel gently herded Charlotte, Rosie and Gloria into one of the pews near the front. She had purposely put Gloria in the seat by the aisle so she could have a good view of Hope as she walked with Lucille behind the bride.

Rosie looked around and saw Jimmy and his squad, their significant others in the pew further back. Alfie and his grandmother were in the pew behind them, along with Harold and his wife. Maud and Mavis were sitting in the pew behind them with Mrs Jenkins and her husband. Rosie thought her neighbour looked as happy as Larry. She was glad.

She felt pretty happy herself.

She thought back to her own wedding at Guildford registry office and smiled. She put her hand in her coat pocket and felt the corner of Peter's letter. Having it near to her made her feel as though a part of him was with her now.

'So,' Charlotte said, keeping her voice low, 'you were going to tell me how you and Peter met.'

'Well, it's a long story.' Rosie looked at her sister. She'd told Charlotte that she'd heard from Peter and it would seem that this – and the romance of the wedding – had triggered the morning's inquisition.

'Oh, look, there's Lily,' Rosie said.

Charlotte knew her sister was purposely changing the subject but looked anyway. She'd quiz her later.

At the end of the pew, second from the front, Lily's vibrant auburn-coloured hair was clearly visible. They could also see the back of her fur coat. There was a space next to her ready for when George had completed his chauffeuring duties.

Kate was on her other side.

And next to Kate were Maisie and Vivian.

All of a sudden, the church seemed to go quiet.

There was a general rustling sound as people started to shuffle around in their seats.

'I think she's just about to arrive,' Rosie whispered to Charlotte.

They both craned their necks, as did everyone else now seated in the church.

There were audible gasps when the sunlight from one of the stained-glass windows fell on Polly as she came through the main entrance, followed by Arthur and George.

George broke away and hobbled down the side of the church to take his place next to Lily, who was watching his approach with a proud smile on her face. Rosie thought George looked self-conscious in his uniform.

Bel, who had been perched on the back pew, her eyes trained on the entrance, hurried over to Polly and made her stand still as she circled her, arranging her veil from behind, and then from the front.

Next to Polly, in the partial sunlight, was Arthur, nervously pulling at his cuffs, looking very dapper and also very proud.

Rosie caught Polly smiling nervously at her matron of honour, before Bel moved aside and allowed Arthur to step forward and offer the bride his arm.

Bel quickly returned to her pew and ushered Lucille and Hope into position behind the bride, giving them both a quick kiss and a reassuring smile as she took her own position at the rear.

A few moments later the first notes of the organ vibrated through the church, and the sound of Wagner's 'Bridal Chorus' filled the air.

Tommy was staring at Polly.

She looked unbelievably gorgeous. Radiant.

Her hair loosely piled high reminded him of a Greek goddess.

Her long, flowing ivory dress was like something you saw in the movies. Even her veil seemed to sparkle.

Tommy felt spellbound as he watched Polly walk slowly down the aisle.

Dragging his gaze away from his bride, Tommy looked at Arthur. He had been like a father to him, and to Polly too.

Here were the two people he loved most in this world.

Watching Polly moving towards him, the words of Mrs Reid suddenly came to mind.

If anything were to happen to you, she'll need a part of you to keep her going.

He hoped there might soon be three people he loved more than anything in this world.

Tommy smiled at Polly as she finally reached him.

'Gorgeous,' he said, shaking his head, still mesmerised.

The vicar cleared his throat, looked out at the packed pews and began the ceremony. A wedding that had ended up being rather beneficial for all parties involved. He glanced briefly up to the wooden beams of the ceiling, smiled and began.

'Dearly Beloved, we are gathered here today to witness the marriage of Thomas Watts and Pollyanna Henrietta Elliot.'

As Polly stood next to Tommy, she took hold of his hand. She couldn't remember what had been said in the rehearsal and if they were 'allowed' to do so, but feeling the tightness of Tommy's grip, it was clear he was not going to let go.

They stood and listened to the vicar as he made his address to them as a couple and to the congregation, talking about the gift of marriage and how this day was a celebration of their love.

Polly tried to focus on everything that was being said, so determined was she to remember every moment of this day, but all she could think about was the feel of Tommy's hand on her own and the beating of her heart as she occasionally took a sidelong glance at her future husband, who looked incredibly handsome in his Royal Navy uniform.

When the first hymn was announced and the whole congregation started singing 'Make me a Channel of Your Peace', she felt Tommy squeeze her hand. She had told him it had been her favourite as a child; now, as an adult, it was the words she loved as much, if not more, than the music.

After the hymn, Reverend Winsey waited until everyone had sat down before he asked, 'First, I am required to ask anyone present who knows a reason why these persons may not lawfully marry, to declare it now.'

There were the usual smiles, chuckles and coughs before he looked at Polly and Tommy and asked if either of them knew of a reason they might not lawfully marry.

'If so, you must declare it now,' the vicar demanded.

Polly and Tommy smiled and shook their heads.

There was a dramatic pause before the reverend turned to Tommy.

'Thomas Watts, will you take Pollyanna Henrietta Elliot to be your wife? Will you love her, comfort her, honour and protect her, and, forsaking all others, be faithful to her as long as you both shall live?'

You could hear a pin drop.

'I will.' Tommy's voice was loud and clear and very certain.

The vicar cleared his throat again and turned his attention to Polly.

'Pollyanna Henrietta Elliot, will you take Thomas Watts to be your husband? Will you love him, comfort him, honour and protect him, and forsaking all others, be faithful to him as long as you both shall live?'

'I will,' she said with a smile.

Turning to his audience, the vicar raised his voice and asked the congregation if they, as family and friends, would support the couple now, and in the years to come.

There was a resounding *'We will.'*

The prayers, Bible reading and, thankfully, the relatively short sermon seemed to pass in a blur before it was time for the vows to be made.

As instructed by the vicar, Polly and Tommy turned and faced each other.

Their eyes locked as Tommy took Polly's right hand and he repeated the words of the vicar.

'I, Tommy Watts, take you Pollyanna Henrietta Elliot, to be my wife, to have and to hold, from this day forward; for better, for worse, for richer, for poorer, in sickness and in health, to love and to cherish, till death do us part.'

As he spoke the words, he realised that Polly had already done all these things.

He knew she didn't care about money, and she had already shown him that she loved him whether he was fighting fit or at death's door.

Seeing that Tommy had forgotten to release Polly's hand, the vicar gently loosened it before guiding Polly to take Tommy's right hand again.

With a slightly trembling voice, Polly repeated the same vows, trying to keep the tears at bay when she said the words 'to love and to cherish till death us do part', for she knew that she would keep her vows even if Tommy was taken from her.

When the vicar announced that it was now time for the 'Giving of Rings', Joe stepped forward and handed the two gold bands to the reverend, who then blessed them, explaining that they symbolised their unending love and faithfulness. That they were a reminder of the vows they had made today.

Neither Tommy nor Polly thought they would need reminding. Ever.

Tommy gently slid the gold band onto Polly's finger.

Feeling it shake, he kissed it.

A few 'ahs' could be heard coming from the pews.

Tommy looked into Polly's eyes and said the time-honoured words:

'All that I am, I give to you, and all that I have I share with you.'

When it was Polly's turn to put the ring on Tommy's finger, she suddenly felt the enormity of the occasion.

She took a deep breath.

'Tommy Watts, I give you this ring as a sign of our marriage. With my body I honour you.' Polly's voice trembled a little. You could feel the emotion in the air. 'All that I am I give to you, and all that I have I share with you.'

If Polly had looked to her left, she would have seen that her ma had tears running down her face, and that Beryl was pushing a hanky into her hand, all the while dabbing at her own tear-stained face.

The vicar then turned to his audience.

'Thomas Watts and Pollyanna Henrietta Elliot have given their consent and made their marriage vows to each other.

'They have declared their marriage by the joining of hands and by the giving and receiving of rings.'

He paused. Took a deep breath.

'I therefore proclaim that they are husband and wife.'

He then took Polly and Tommy's right hands and joined them together.

And in a booming voice declared:

'Those whom God has joined together let no one put asunder.'

Polly added her own prayer that this included the war.

As the vicar ended his speech, Lucille started to clap, followed by Hope.

There were a few chuckles and what sounded like a few choked cry-laughs.

Polly looked up at Tommy and they smiled and kissed each other. Both a little self-conscious about being so public with their affection.

The congregation started to shuffle and murmur. This was always the high point of any wedding and Polly and Tommy had not disappointed.

After everyone settled back into their pews, the organ once again struck up.

Everyone was directed to a sheet that had been placed in the hymn book, and asked to sing 'Ding Dong Merrily on High' while the signing of the Register took place.

Polly and Tommy, with Agnes and Arthur as their witnesses, signed the thick hard-backed green ledger laid out on a table behind the altar, while the church was filled with the enthusiastic warbling of their guests. All were clearly enjoying singing the carol, even if they couldn't quite reach the high notes.

Afterwards, the Lord's Prayer was recited before the vicar brought the ceremony to an end with the words:

'God the Holy Trinity make you strong in faith and love, defend you on every side, and guide you in truth and peace; and the blessing of God almighty, the Father, the Son and the Holy Spirit, be among you and remain with you always.'

Everyone chorused an enthusiastic 'Amen.'

As the organ struck up Mendelssohn's 'Wedding March', Tommy and Polly thanked the vicar and made their way, now husband and wife, down the aisle.

They were holding hands, both smiling from ear to ear, radiating pure joy and happiness.

Once outside, everyone gathered round, congratulating the happy couple.

Mr Clement, aided by Bel, organised a group shot. He thanked his lucky stars the sun was out and the snow had not melted. He couldn't have wished for better conditions. It wasn't even windy.

Lily slipped off back into the church to stuff a bulging brown envelope into the donation box for the repair of the church roof, while George nipped off to get the car.

When he pulled up outside the church, he honked his horn, signalling it was time for the new Mr and Mrs Watts to make their way to the Grand. Everyone cheered and tossed confetti over the couple, as they ducked and clambered into the back of the MG.

They drove off to a cacophony of clanking cans, a 'Just Married' sign hanging rather precariously from the boot.

Chapter Seventy-Two

Toby had kindly agreed to get Bel to the Grand as speedily as possible so she could begin overseeing phase two of the wedding celebrations.

True to his word, as soon as George had pulled away, Toby had pulled up in his Austin 8 and Bel, Dorothy, Angie and Quentin had all crammed in.

Toby had driven down the stretch of Suffolk Street and Tatham Street as fast as the snow would allow him, overtaking George's MG and blaring his horn.

Dorothy's beau for the day was clearly enjoying the challenge of the adverse weather conditions and by the look on Dorothy's face, she was too.

Turning left onto Borough Road, the back end of the grey Austin slid out and they all cried out. Partly through fear and partly with excitement.

When they swung right onto Fawcett Street, Bel automatically grabbed Angie's hand.

'I think Toby must have been a professional racing driver before the war,' Bel said into Angie's ear.

Bel looked at Quentin, who looked a little pale around the gills.

'This your new fella?' she asked as they drove up the main shopping street, which looked so festive with Christmas trees or decorations displayed in almost every window.

'No!' Angie seemed outraged by the suggestion. 'Quentin is our neighbour! He's only been invited so he can teach me how to be posh.'

'Ahh,' Bel nodded, as though this made complete sense.

Arriving at the Grand, Bel sprang into action, making sure the five-piece band was in place, the champagne was chilling ready for the toast, and the buffet was being prepared. Polly had asked if, instead of a sit-down meal, they could have a spread so that everyone could simply relax, chat, dance, and eat and drink what they wanted, when they wanted.

Once Bel had been assured that everything was in hand, she started organising the guests, getting them ready for the newly-weds' arrival.

George had taken a detour to allow them more time to get to the hotel. Bel had told him to go down by the south docks so they could look out across the river to Thompson's, the place Tommy and Polly had first met and fallen in love, and then along the quayside, where they had become engaged.

When the MG finally pulled up, Bel was waiting with Mr Clement. He had been told to take a photo of Polly and Tommy on the steps of the hotel, which had two magnificent fir trees decorated with silver baubles on either side of the entrance.

Just before the flash of the light bulb, Tommy turned and kissed Polly. It was to be the photograph that Tommy would take with him, and which he'd keep with him at all times.

When Polly and Tommy walked into the Grand a huge cheer rang out.

Although most of the ground floor of the hotel had been cordoned off for the wedding reception, there was still a smattering of guests as well as a handful of Admiralty.

Everyone in the vicinity stared at Polly in her beautiful ivory wedding dress, her hair piled up high in swirls, apart from a few perfectly curled and positioned strands that gave her a look that was both elegant and wanton. Next to her, Tommy, his fair hair cropped short, standing tall in his immaculate navy-blue uniform, also looked incredibly handsome.

But it was the way the two kept looking at each other that captivated people's attention the most.

And so, the wedding celebration began.

A couple of waitresses came from the kitchen, making their way around the guests, offering a selection of hors d'oeuvres from huge silver trays.

Although Polly and Tommy had begged everyone not to give them presents, there was still a sizeable mound forming on a table around a large vase that had been filled with an elaborate display of red berries, sprayed pine, sprigs of fir and, of course, some holly and ivy.

The quintet started up with 'The Lady's in Love with You', followed by a lively version of 'Jingle Bells'.

Bel gave everyone twenty minutes to settle in before giving the hotel manager the nod.

Stepping forward, he rang a little brass bell to catch everyone's attention.

'The bride and groom will now have the first dance,' he announced, as the band started playing Johann Strauss.

Tommy looked a little nervously at Polly. They had practised the waltz in the flat, but it was a different matter doing it in front of so many people.

'Just think we're on our own by the river,' Polly whispered into her husband's ear.

'Remember?' she said.

Tommy closed his eyes.

'I'll never forget.'

He slid his right hand down the perfectly fitted wedding dress to the small of his wife's back. Polly took hold of his left hand, which he then raised in the air.

'Here goes, Mrs Watts,' Tommy whispered.

Everyone watched the lovers as they waltzed, perfectly in tune with each other.

Rosie put her hands on her sister's shoulders.

'Are you going to teach me how to waltz?' she asked Charlotte. 'I'm hoping that education of yours has stretched to ballroom dancing.'

Charlotte turned her head to look at her sister.

'I dunno about ballroom dancing, but I know how to waltz. It's easy.'

Rosie chuckled.

'Easy when you know how.'

Rosie looked across at Lily, who was wearing her green dress. She had told everyone she would wear it today as it would mean she would have to get another one made for when she and George finally did get married.

George still looked a little tense in his military wear, with his row of medals on display. The DSO, a silver-gilt, curved-edged cross, white enamelled with a gold crown in the middle, was particularly prominent, even from a distance.

When the music changed, the manager made a gesture to show that the floor was now open to all.

Tommy kissed Polly.

'Thank goodness for that.' He let out a sigh of pure relief.

Polly rested her head on Tommy's shoulder as they continued to slow dance even though the tempo was more upbeat.

She smiled as she looked about her.

Hannah and Olly were dancing close together.

Rosie was laughing as Charlotte was trying to show her how to waltz and failing miserably.

Dorothy looked very at ease with her potential new beau. According to Vivian, who had not stopped talking the entire time she had been doing her hair, Dorothy had met the very good-looking Toby last night at Lily's.

Angie, on the other hand, did not look at all at ease with her partner, Quentin. He also appeared to be giving her a dancing lesson, which looked almost as unsuccessful as Charlotte's.

As Tommy slowly moved around, Polly saw Pearl at the bar drinking whisky with Bill and Ronald. She wondered which one Bel's ma would choose. She hoped Bill.

And then she spotted Helen and Dr Parker. Polly watched them. They intrigued her. Helen had made it clear they were simply friends. As had Dr Parker to Tommy. But their body language as they danced said quite the opposite.

After a little while the band took a short break and the manager made a show of opening up the double doors to a smaller room, which was taken up with an oblong table that had been filled with the wedding buffet.

Everyone stood and stared for a moment. It was a feast fit for a king. There was smoked salmon, slices of goose, gammon, slabs of pâté, baskets of freshly baked buns, trays of sandwiches and other delicacies that most of the guests had not seen, never mind tasted, in a long time.

The manager beckoned to Tommy and Polly to be the first to sample the magnificent spread.

It didn't take long for everyone else to follow.

As Polly chatted, ate and looked around her she felt humbled that this most wonderful and also most extravagant of days was happening because of the kindness and thoughtfulness of others.

How apt, she thought, that such generosity and unselfishness was happening at this special time of the year.

As the afternoon wore on, Polly introduced Tommy to Jimmy and his squad of riveters, who had all brought their significant others. The women made a point of saying how wonderful it was to finally meet 'the women welders'. Polly knew their worries had been put to rest.

Maud and Mavis regaled Tommy with stories of when Polly was a little girl, and Mr Clement introduced his wife and daughters and told them he was sure he'd got some 'smashing shots'.

Polly had gone to find Kate, who was chatting to Alfie and his grandmother. Polly didn't think she looked as decrepit as they'd all been led to believe.

'I'm so glad you didn't sell the dress,' Polly said to Kate, looking down and touching some of the embroidery on the bodice.

'You don't think I was really going to sell it, do you?' Kate laughed.

After being introduced to Mrs Jenkins and her husband, Tommy introduced Polly to the Home Guard unit he'd helped to train. When the Major wheeled himself over to where they were all sitting, Polly leant over and gave him a kiss on the cheek.

'I know what you did,' she whispered in his ear. She smiled and mouthed, *Thank you*.

Tommy, she knew, still had no idea. She'd tell him later.

As the afternoon turned into early evening, Vera and Rina brought out the wedding cake.

Everyone gasped at their ability to produce something so exorbitant and grand during these times of rationing. Both women batted away the compliments, with Rina explaining that it was Vera who had created the very beautiful and extremely intricate decorative roses.

As no one was at all keen on making speeches, George did the honour of making the toast to the newly-weds.

Everyone gave a boisterous three cheers before sipping their drinks. Polly looked over to see Lily looking as proud as punch of her future husband. She had hardly left his side all day.

Tommy was introduced to Toby and was intrigued to find out that he was a friend of Peter's. They were joined by George. Being surrounded by others in military outfits was making George feel so much better about fulfilling his side of his bargain with Lily – helped along by the hotel's very nice selection of whiskies.

Naturally they ended up talking about the war. Whether it was because of the wedding, or the fact that it was Christmas, there seemed to be a feeling of hope that as the year was drawing to a close the future was looking much brighter for the Allies. Certainly better than it had a few months previously. As Toby pointed out, Rommel was trapped in Tunisia, the Germans had failed to take Stalingrad, and the Japanese looked ready to abandon Guadalcanal.

They all made a toast to victory.

And a speedy one at that.

While Tommy chatted with Ralph and the rest of the diving team, Polly found herself gravitating back to her squad, whom she'd hardly seen since Monday – the longest time she had been parted from them in two and a half years. They all gassed away as though it had been months rather than days.

A little later Polly saw that Dorothy and Toby were slow dancing to the band's rendition of 'White Christmas', and Angie and Quentin were playing with Lucille and Hope. Bel had told Polly of Angie's rather bizarre comment in the car on the way to the Grand that Quentin had only been invited so he could teach her how to be posh. Polly didn't see much evidence of that. They both seemed to be having far too much fun.

When her feet started to ache and her voice began to go hoarse, Polly went to sit with her ma and Beryl, who was keeping a particularly beady eye on Iris and Audrey. They seemed to be spending rather a lot of time chatting and dancing with two of Joe's younger Home Guard pals.

The three women sat in a contented silence for a while, watching the guests, smiling at some of the high-spirited antics, and raising eyebrows as Maisie and Vivian danced together.

None of them, however, noticed two naval officers hurrying in from the cold.

Charlotte was standing next to Rosie, who was chatting to Harold and his wife, when she spotted the pair.

She watched them for a while.

Yes, they were definitely the same ones she'd seen yesterday.

She looked across to Maisie and Vivian, who were having a break from the dance floor and were chatting at the bar with Lily and George.

It didn't take them long before they too spotted their dates from yesterday.

Charlotte watched as the two men, dressed in their smart white uniforms, stopped at the bottom of the wide staircase and looked on at the wedding party.

She caught their surprise at seeing Maisie and Vivian standing by the bar.

Charlotte expected them to walk over, greet each other, embrace and kiss as they had done yesterday.

But they didn't.

They didn't even wave.

Or mouth *hello*.

All four simply looked at each other and then looked away.

How odd.

484

Charlotte looked at Maisie, then at Vivian.

At Lily and George.

And then at her sister.

Dr Parker and Helen were chatting on one of the small leather chesterfields set back a little from the rest of the party.

Dr Parker didn't think he'd had such a lovely day in a long time.

Thank goodness they'd put their falling-out well and truly behind them. Their friendship was back on firm footing. He was thankful that Polly had nudged Helen into apologising.

'That's a nice dress Charlotte's got on,' Dr Parker said, seeing her looking bored as Rosie chatted to Harold and his wife. 'You know,' he glanced at Helen, 'I think I recognise it.'

Helen laughed.

'Kate said she had an idea what to do with it. As always, she's worked wonders.'

'So,' Dr Parker changed the subject, 'what's your mother up to today? Seeing as she's not throwing her usual Christmas extravaganza.'

'Good question,' Helen said. 'I have no idea. I'm just so pleased I'm not having to spend it with her and all her old cronies.'

Dr Parker took a sup of his bitter.

'Well, I for one am so glad Tommy and Polly decided to get married on Christmas Day. It's been rather special, all in all, hasn't it?'

Helen smiled and nodded.

They were quiet for a moment.

They both knew they'd been a tad antisocial. They'd chatted with Polly and Tommy, of course. Tommy had thanked John for all that he had done for him and John had dismissed it, saying it was his job and wishing him luck when he got out there. Polly had thanked Helen for the gorgeous floral displays and her beautiful bouquet. Like John, Helen had dismissed it and said she was just glad that Bel had unwittingly given her the idea.

Helen had briefly chatted with the women welders, but most of the day had been spent with John, or with Gloria and Hope. She had enjoyed being able to socialise with them openly, rather than having to be all clandestine for fear of her mother finding out. Helen and Gloria had both said how much they would have loved Jack to have been there with them and they both agreed that Hope was growing up fast. She needed to know her father.

'John?' Helen suddenly sounded very serious.

'I have to know something. I've been wanting to ask you for a while, but I keep putting it off. Trying to tell myself that it's not important. Or rather, that it would be best not to know.'

Dr Parker took a swig of his pint of bitter.

Was it that obvious?

Did Helen realise that he was in love with her?

'Go on,' he said, even though he didn't want her to do any such thing.

'It's probably totally the wrong place to ask you.'

She looked around.

Everyone seemed so happy. So festive and jolly.

'But I'm just going to say it.'

She paused.

Dr Parker braced himself for humiliation.

'Was ...' Helen hesitated.

She took a deep breath.

'John ... was my baby a girl? Like I'd thought all along?'

Dr Parker stared at Helen.

This was the last question he would have imagined Helen asking him.

He immediately felt guilty for being relieved.

Looking at Helen's face he could see that the heartache of her miscarriage was still very raw.

He took hold of her hand, looked into her startling emerald eyes and nodded.

'Yes, your baby was a girl,' he said.

Helen kept hold of his hand tightly, as she had done in the hospital after her miscarriage.

'Are you all right?' Dr Parker looked at her.

God, how he wanted to hold her. Comfort her. Kiss her.

'Yes, I'll be fine.' Helen took a deep, juddering breath. 'Just don't be too nice to me otherwise I'll cry. And I don't want to cry.'

She looked at John.

She had an insane urge to kiss him.

She laughed.

'Can't possibly cry,' she said. 'Not with the amount of mascara I've got on. I'll end up looking like a panda.'

'Well,' Dr Parker said, glad to see a smile on her face, 'you'd still be a very beautiful panda.'

Helen nudged him playfully.

A part of her felt relief that she'd asked. She knew now, and she had not fallen apart.

Perhaps she could finally start to move on.

'Well, look who's here.' Dr Parker's voice had changed from jovial to serious.

Helen looked up and followed John's gaze.

'Talk of the devil,' she said.

'At least we now know what she's up to today,' Helen said. 'I should have guessed she would end up here.'

Helen stared at her mother, who was chatting to the doorman and giving him a Christmas tip. She was clearly well on her way. Amelia was behind her.

'Helen.'

Suddenly Helen's view of her mother was blotted out by a vision of pastel pink.

It was Bel.

'Hi, I hope you two are enjoying yourselves?'

'Wonderful wedding,' Dr Parker said. 'And Helen tells me it was mainly your doing.'

'Hardly,' Bel chuckled. 'All of this is down to Lily and George.' She looked around and saw they were both sitting at the bar. Lily was roaring with laughter at something George had said.

'Actually, I just wanted to come and thank you for the flowers,' Bel said.

She thought Helen looked a little distracted by something happening behind Bel.

'Oh, you're welcome, Bel,' Helen said.

Bloody hell! Her mother had spotted her and was coming over.

Bel felt someone behind her. Instinctively she turned around and came face to face with Miriam.

It was the closest she had ever been to her half-sister.

'Darling,' Miriam glanced at Bel before focusing on Helen, 'you didn't say the wedding was at the Grand!'

Miriam looked at Dr Parker and forced a smile.

Dr Parker forced one back.

Miriam turned and looked at Bel again. She then stared back at Helen.

'Well, aren't you going to introduce me to your friend?'

Helen glanced at her mother.

Then at Bel.

She hesitated for a moment.

'Yes, Mother, this is Mrs Isabelle Elliot.'

Helen turned to Bel.

'And this, as I'm sure you've gathered already, Bel, is my mother. Mrs Miriam Crawford.'

Miriam and Bel looked at each other and tentatively shook hands.

'Well, darling,' Miriam turned her attention back to Helen, 'mustn't keep Amelia floundering around on her own over there.' She turned to see Amelia chatting to the manager. 'So, toodle-oo. Enjoy the rest of your wedding.'

Bel watched Miriam worm her way through the throng of guests to her friend.

She turned back to Helen and Dr Parker.

'Well, I'd better get back to the other guests.' Bel paused. 'Thanks again, Helen.'

She looked at Dr Parker. 'And lovely to see you.'

When Bel had gone, Helen sat up on the sofa and looked at John.

'Please tell me I'm going mad? That I'm seeing things?'

Dr Parker didn't say anything. He had been equally taken aback.

Helen took in a deep gulp of air and slowly breathed out.

'Same hair. Same mouth. Same lips.'

She paused.

'Same eyes.'

Another pause.

'If it weren't for the age gap, they could be twins.'

Dr Parker watched Helen and saw the proverbial penny drop.

She had mentioned a few times to him of late that Bel reminded her of someone.

Now she knew.

Bel was the absolute spit of her mother.

When nine o'clock struck, Tommy looked at Polly, who nodded.

They had agreed beforehand that this was the time they'd leave the party.

489

Determined that everyone else should stay for as long as they wanted, they went around all the guests, saying their thank-yous and goodbyes.

They looked for Lily but couldn't find her.

Seeing George, they both squeezed their way through the melee.

'We're going now, George, but we really wanted to see Lily as well, to say one final thank you.'

'Lily's just had to nip to the ladies' room,' George said. 'But don't worry, I'll tell her. You've both thanked us at least two dozen times already, so get yourselves off.'

Tommy shook his hand.

'Thank you,' he said, his tone and handshake showing just how much his words were meant.

'You just take care of yourself out there,' George said, his face serious.

'I fully intend to,' Tommy said.

Polly flung her arms around George and hugged him tightly.

'Thank you. Thank you both. This has meant so much to us. It's been truly magical.'

George felt himself becoming unusually sentimental.

'Go on now. You're wasting precious time.'

It took Polly a few minutes to locate her ma and Bel. They were sitting with Arthur in the reception area. They looked happily exhausted.

'Thanks, Ma,' she said, bending down and giving her a hug. 'For being so understanding.'

Neither of them needed to acknowledge what Polly was referring to.

Agnes cupped her daughter's face in her hands.

'You're just like your father, stubborn as a mule.'

She paused, then smiled.

'But I wouldn't have yer any different.'

Bel stood up.

'I think I've got the best sister-in-law in the whole wide world,' Polly said.

'No, I think I have,' Bel said. And she meant it. She would be forever indebted to Polly. She had rescued her when she was a child, taking her to Agnes after she'd been abandoned by her ma. Polly had not only saved her life that day but given her a new one.

The two lifelong friends hugged each other hard.

'Thanks. For everything,' Polly whispered in her ear.

'I've enjoyed every minute!' Bel laughed. 'Now go and enjoy your honeymoon. Your *proper* honeymoon.'

Arthur pushed himself out of his chair.

'Congratulations, pet,' he said, holding her hand firmly.

'And don't worry about this one,' he said, nodding over to Tommy, who was chatting to his new mother- and sister-in-law.

'He's going to be just fine.'

He paused.

'My grandson is a very lucky lad. You've brought such light into his life. And into my life too.'

Polly thought it was one of the loveliest things anyone had ever said to her.

When Tommy gave his grandda a hug, Polly saw tears in the old man's eyes.

'I'm so proud of yer, Tom. I don't think you realise how much. I've always been proud of yer.'

Arthur grabbed his grandson and gave him another hug, holding on to him for just a few extra seconds, loath to let him go but knowing he had to.

'Go on, now!' he said, his pale blue eyes looking watery. 'Get yerself off 'n enjoy yer honeymoon.'

*

When they reached the top landing, Polly held her rose bouquet out so everyone could see.

There was a ripple of excitement.

'I hope whoever catches my beautiful bouquet ...' Polly shouted out.

She quickly scanned the room but couldn't see Helen.

' ... I hope that they are as lucky as me.'

And with that she turned around and threw the bouquet high into the air.

When she turned back, she was just in time to see it almost hit Angie in the face.

Quentin had caught it just in time.

Everyone laughed.

Quentin went almost as red as the roses.

He handed the bouquet to Angie, who accepted, albeit a little reluctantly.

'*Merry Christmas everyone!*' Polly and Tommy shouted out to the guests gathered below. To all the people they loved and cared for, and with whom they had shared this amazingly special day.

'*Merry Christmas!*' everyone chorused back.

Chapter Seventy-Three

When Tommy and Polly walked into their honeymoon suite, they were speechless.

Tommy whistled.

'We're one very lucky couple,' he said, turning a full three hundred and sixty degrees, taking in the room's carved wooden panelling, tapestry curtains, huge oil paintings – and, of course, the most amazing four-poster bed.

'I think that's about triple the size of our bed in John Street.' Tommy laughed.

Polly pulled back the covers to see that the women welders had sprinkled the sheets with confetti.

Bel had also made sure that room service had left a tray of nibbles should they get hungry during the night. She was under no illusion the pair would be wasting their last night together sleeping.

There was also a little bottle of Scotch, which she knew was Tommy's preferred tipple, and another of port, which was Polly's.

Polly and Tommy looked at each other. There was a tinge of sadness in their eyes.

This was to be their first night as a married couple – and their last.

At least for the foreseeable future.

Until this war was won.

And it would be won, Polly had decided.

After what she had experienced this last week there was just too much goodness in the world.

And because of that, she was sure good would triumph in the end.

It *had* to.

She'd realised they were all playing their part in making sure that happened.

'There's something that you haven't seen yet.' Polly turned to Tommy.

He was taking off his uniform, all the while continuing to take in the extravagance of the room.

He had never seen anything like it in his life.

'Oh, yes? And what's that?' he asked, bringing his attention back to his gorgeous wife in her beautiful dress.

'It's something I have been wearing the entire day, yet no one has seen it. Nor will anyone else see it,' Polly said with a cheeky smile. 'It's for your eyes only.'

As she spoke, she lifted her dress to just above her knee.

Her garter had dropped down a little during the course of the day.

Tommy stared.

'Well, that's lovely!' He threw Polly a cheeky smile. 'The garter too.'

He dropped down on one knee and gently pulled the unique handmade hosiery down his wife's leg.

Polly lifted her foot off the ground as Tommy took the garter off.

He held it, inspecting its intricate design.

'It's lovely,' he said simply. 'Kate?'

Polly nodded.

'Of course.'

Tommy handed Polly the garter and she too admired it.

Her eyes narrowed.

Something on the inside had caught her interest.

Holding it up close, she inspected what looked like swirls of pale blue stitching.

'Kate's sewn some words on the inside ...' She squinted some more.

Tommy saw tears form in her eyes.

'What does it say?'

Polly looked up at her husband.

'It's five words,' she said.

Tommy raised his eyebrows questioningly.

Polly smiled.

A single tear escaped and ran down her face.

'Hope ... Faith ... Peace ... Joy ...

'And ... Love.'

Epilogue

Arthur checked his suit was hanging in the wardrobe and that his room was tidy. He ran a comb through his thin grey hair and then climbed into bed.

'Now, wasn't that just the most perfect of days, Flo?'

Arthur took the framed photograph he had of his wife from the bedside table.

'Our Tom looked so handsome. So happy.'

He got himself comfortable.

'I worry about what'll happen over there, but yer right. It's out of my hands now. It's time to let go.'

Arthur wiped the glass front of the photograph with the sleeve of his pyjamas and then rested it on his chest as he lay on his back, looking up at the ceiling.

'We did right by our boy, though – didn't we?'

Arthur's eyes started to flutter.

He was struggling to keep them open.

He felt so tired.

It's time, Arthur.

'Ahh, Flo.'

The relief in the old man's voice was clear.

'I thought you'd never let me.'

Arthur felt himself sinking. His whole body was infused with the most amazing feeling of well-being.

Contentedness.

Peace.

'Yer look lovely, Flo. Yer always were a bonny lass.

'What's that? I'll like it over there?'

Arthur smiled.

'Ah, pet, yer know me. I'll like it anywhere as long as you're there. *Anywhere.*'

Arthur took a deep breath and slowly exhaled.

It was the last breath he would take in this world.

And as one soul left the front room of 34 Tatham Street, another soul came into the world in another part of town, although it wouldn't make itself known for at least a few months.

Welcome to

Penny Street

where your favourite authors and stories live.

Meet casts of characters you'll never forget,
create memories you'll treasure forever,
and discover places that will stay with
you long after the last page.

Turn the page to step into the home of

Nancy Revell

and discover more about

The Shipyard Girls...

Dear Reader,

Christmas is such a magical time of year, and so it felt really important for me to capture and reflect that in this seventh instalment of the *Shipyard Girls* series. I hope you feel I have succeeded.

Christmas with the Shipyard Girls is also a particularly poignant book for me personally as I was going through a difficult time when I wrote it.

Because of that, the themes of the book – the Christmas message of love, faith, hope and charity – are especially heartfelt.

I'm sure there have been times when you, like me, have felt as though you're hanging in there by the very tips of your fingers. Or perhaps you're doing so right now. If you are, please, keep a tight hold. You *will* get through it.

And so, as Christmas approaches, I'd like to wish you, dear reader, Love, Faith, Hope and Charity – not just this Yuletide – but the whole year through.

Merry Christmas and a very Happy New Year!

With Love,

Nancy
x

HISTORICAL NOTES

I found this wonderful, and very appropriate Christmas card, while I was researching *Christmas with the Shipyard Girls*. It's a character called 'Rosie the Riveter'. She was a WW2 cultural icon, representing women who worked in the shipyards and factories.

It made me smile.

I hope it does you too!

Merry Christmas!

Turn the page for a sneak
peek into my new novel

Triumph of the
Shipyard Girls

J.L. Thompson & Sons, North Sands, Sunderland

Boxing Day 1942

'Thank goodness you've come!'

Helen heaved a dramatic sigh of relief.

Manoeuvring herself around her desk, she strode across the office and gave Dr Parker a hug.

'I was worried you might be called into theatre on some kind of emergency at the last moment, leaving me to deal with my dear mama and all her old cronies on my lonesome.'

Dr Parker wrapped his arms around Helen, returning her embrace. She smelled of expensive perfume. As always, he had to force himself to let her go.

'I wouldn't have missed one of your mother's infamous soirées for all the tea in China,' he said, a smile playing on his lips.

'Come in and take your coat off.' Helen walked over to the tray that had been left on top of one of the filing cabinets.

'Talking of tea?' She took hold of the ceramic pot.

Dr Parker hung his jacket up on the coat stand by the door and rubbed his hands.

'Yes, please, I'm parched.'

He watched as Helen poured carefully, adding a touch of milk, just the way he liked it.

'How are you feeling after yesterday?' He scrutinised Helen's face as she turned and handed him his cuppa.

'Still in shock,' she admitted, exhaling.

She walked back to the cabinet and poured herself a cup.

'The thing is, John, I'm at a loss as to what to do. I can't just forget it – and I'm not the type of person who can just shove it under the carpet.'

'That's true,' he agreed, eyeing her.

'I have to know,' she said, picking up a pile of papers, shuffling them together and tapping them on the desktop. 'Otherwise, I'll always be wondering.'

She paused, papers still in hand.

'Either way. Even if it *is* just some fluke that my mother and Bel look alike ... that they look practically *identical* ... God, if it wasn't for the age gap, I'd say they were twins.'

Another pause.

She put the papers in the top drawer and slammed it shut.

'*Either way*, I need to know.'

She walked over to the large windows that divided her office from the open-plan work area that made up the rest of the administration department and yanked the wooden venetian blinds free, lowering them ready for tomorrow morning when everyone would be back from their two-day Christmas break.

As she did so, her gaze was naturally drawn to Bel's desk, which had, as always, been left neat and tidy.

'I mean, it's not as if I can just ask Bel, can I?' She turned back to look at Dr Parker drinking his tea. 'I can't just casually say when she gets in tomorrow, "Lovely wedding, Bel, wasn't it? Oh, and by the way, I couldn't help but notice that you are the absolute spit of my mother. You wouldn't know if you're related by any chance, would you?"'

Dr Parker allowed himself the slightest of smiles. Helen's dry sense of humour always amused him.

He looked across at her; her sparkling emerald eyes never failed to captivate him. 'The thing is, Bel's probably totally unaware of the fact that she *has* a doppelgänger. She didn't seem particularly shocked when she was introduced to your mother at the wedding yesterday.'

'Mmm.' Helen took a sip of her tea and put the cup and saucer back on the tray. 'That's true. But then again, that could be because she's *well aware* of the fact that she looks like a younger replica of my mother.'

Helen was quiet for a moment.

'Really, John, when Bel was introduced to my mum at the Grand, it must have been like looking into a mirror – a mirror that shows you an image of your future self.'

Still feeling the need to play devil's advocate, Dr Parker argued, 'Bel was run ragged yesterday organising Polly and Tommy's wedding. She probably barely even *registered* Miriam.'

'Possibly,' Helen said.

She put her hands on her hips and stared down at her desk, lost in thought.

'It could also be that she didn't react to seeing my mother because she *knows* fine well that she looks like her.' Her face became animated. She looked up at Dr Parker with wide eyes. '*Knows* that they are ...' she waited a beat '... *related*.'

Dr Parker took a final slurp of his tea and stood up.

'I think you had one too many gin and tonics yesterday and your imagination has gone into overdrive. This is simply a case of two women who look alike.'

He went over to the stand and slipped his coat back on.

'Now, come on, get yourself ready. I feel like you're procrastinating because you don't want to go to your mother's Boxing Day extravaganza.'

Helen let out an exasperated sigh.

'Oh, John, *don't*. It's going to be hideous. And even more of an "extravaganza" as Mother has made it quite plain that she feels she was deprived of a proper Christmas Day celebration because I deserted her to go to *some welder's wedding*.'

As John helped Helen into her winter coat, he had to force himself not to wrap his arms around her, hold her tightly, then turn her around and kiss her.

God! Perhaps *he* was the one with the overactive imagination.

As they walked out into the stillness of the shipyard, Helen looked around and took in the metal and concrete landscape she loved so much.

It was a rarity to see it so tranquil.

'I don't think I've ever been here when it's so quiet,' Dr Parker said as he buttoned up his overcoat against the icy-cold air and plummeting temperatures of the late afternoon.

As if in defiance of the peace, the clanking of steel suddenly sounded out from the platers' shed.

Dr Parker looked askance at Helen.

'We've still got a skeleton staff keeping things ticking over,' she explained.

Five minutes later they had left the confines of the yard and were scrunching through thick snow along the promenade. Daylight was just beginning to fade, although there was still enough light to see the dark blue-green waters of the North Sea and the outline of the lighthouse on the North Pier.

'So ...' Dr Parker looked up at the darkening skies. The clouds looked heavy with yet more snow. 'I'm guessing that Tommy will be somewhere over the Atlantic by now?'

He tried to sound casual when really he was desperate to know how Helen was feeling about the departure of the man he knew she had loved all her life.

The man who had just married another woman.

'I'd say so,' Helen said, pulling up the cuff of her coat sleeve and looking at her watch. 'It's gone half four. I know his flight was at one – so, allowing for delays, and the time difference, he should be there by now.'

A worried look fell across her face.

'God willing.'

Dr Parker saw the flash of anxiety and felt the familiar stab of jealousy whenever Helen showed any kind of emotion towards Tommy.

They walked for a while in silence. The snow was glinting with a sparkling topcoat – the result of the morning's fall.

Eventually it was Dr Parker who spoke.

'So, how are you *feeling* about everything?' he ventured, his mind still on Tommy – or rather, on Helen's thoughts about Tommy leaving.

Helen sighed.

'Well, a little confused, to be honest.'

Dr Parker's heart sank. They had not talked openly about Tommy since the day Helen had declared her love for him at the hospital. That had been over two months ago, and Helen had barely mentioned it since.

'Well,' Helen said, 'I was thinking last night when I was trying – *unsuccessfully* – to sleep ...'

Dr Parker felt the familiar ache in his chest. His heart.

'I was thinking,' she said. 'Trying to work out that *if* Bel *is* related to my mother – and to me for that matter – then what are the possible options?'

Dr Parker was momentarily confused. Had Helen deliberately avoided talking about Tommy and her feelings for him, or was she genuinely obsessing about Bel?

Sometimes he thought he could read Helen like a book; other times she was a complete and utter mystery.

'Options?'

'Well ...' Helen said as they crossed the road. There was no need to check for any traffic. The roads were empty.

'There's the possibility that Bel could be my mother's illegitimate love child, before she met Dad. I mean, they *do* look like mother and daughter. And the age gap is about right. I've worked it out. Mum would have been about sixteen. Possibly seventeen.'

'True,' Dr Parker conceded.

They continued walking.

'Actually, I wouldn't mind having another sister.' Helen laughed. 'I always wanted a sister when I was growing up. I might now have an *older* sister – as well as a *little* sister.' Helen smiled as she thought of Hope. She'd looked particularly gorgeous in her ivory flower-girl dress yesterday.

'What about your aunty?' Dr Parker knew that Miriam had a sister who was very similar in looks, but the complete opposite in nature.

'Mmm,' Helen mused. 'I did think about Aunty Margaret – that Bel could possibly be her child, but I just can't see her having a child out of wedlock. Besides, she was never able to have children with Uncle Angus – could never carry them to full term ...' Her voice trailed off.

Dr Parker knew Helen would be thinking of her own miscarriage earlier on in the year.

Stepping aside, he let Helen pass through the wrought-iron gate to the park. The place had been turned into a winter wonderland. Bushes and trees were draped in thick white shrouds. The model boating lake was a sheet of ice. The bowling green no longer green.

'The other spanner in the works,' Dr Parker said, 'is, even if your mother or your aunty Margaret had had an illegitimate child, why would Bel's mother – what's her name again?'

'Pearl.'

'Why would Pearl claim that Bel was *her* daughter? From what I've seen of her, she doesn't strike me as your typical adoptive parent.'

'That's putting it politely,' Helen said. 'The only reason someone like Pearl would take on a child would be if she was being paid handsomely for it. And the woman clearly hasn't got two pennies to rub together.'

By now they had reached the other side of the park.

'Which,' Helen continued, 'brings us to the men in the family.'

'Your grandfather?' Dr Parker said, pulling open the gate.

Helen burst out laughing.

'Hardly, John!' She walked out and onto Roker Park Road. 'Do the maths. Bel's roughly the same age as me. She's more likely to be his granddaughter.'

Helen's face suddenly lit up.

'Unless it was my grandmother's secret love child? She was much younger than Grandfather. And I get the impression she was a bit of a dark horse.'

They crossed the road and started walking the short distance to the corner of Park Avenue.

Helen looked at Dr Parker.

Her excitement waned.

'But that still brings us back to the problem of Pearl, doesn't it?'

Dr Parker nodded.

Helen could feel herself getting exasperated.

'There's just far too many ifs and buts and maybes and maybe nots. It'll end up driving me mad.'

She took Dr Parker's arm as they crossed Side Cliff Road to her front gate. It was the only house in the vicinity that had managed to keep its Arts and Crafts ironwork.

'To be continued,' Helen said.

Dr Parker smiled and shook his head.

'I still think that imagination of yours is running riot.'

Secretly, though, he wondered if Helen's current obsession with Bel was her way of avoiding thinking about Tommy.

They walked up the short pathway and up the stone steps. Putting her key into the front door, Helen turned to Dr Parker.

'I'm thanking you in advance,' she said with a grimace. 'I'm sure this is probably the last place you fancy being today. On Boxing Day of all days. And one of your rare afternoons off.'

Dr Parker dismissed her words with a shake of his head.

If only Helen knew. He didn't give two hoots where he was right now – as long as he was with the woman he loved.

When Helen opened the front door, they saw Miriam walking into the lounge, her hand clutching a glass of what could only be a large gin and tonic.

Their arrival caught her eye and she turned to welcome them with outstretched arms.

'Darlings!' she said, air-kissing her daughter and then Dr Parker. 'I thought you'd deserted your dear mama – again.'

Neither Helen nor Dr Parker said anything.

Miriam inspected her daughter.

'Go and get yourself spruced up.' Miriam tilted her head up towards the landing. 'I've put out a lovely dress for you to wear.

'And John,' Miriam purred, 'come and meet the rest of the guests. They're all *dying* to meet you.'

She suddenly burst out laughing.

'*Dying*. Well, I hope not.'

She leant towards Dr Parker.

'But at least if they are, we've got our very own doctor on hand to save the day!'

She chuckled again at her own joke.

Not for the first time, Dr Parker was reminded of his own mother. She too had a tendency to laugh at her own jokes.

As Miriam took Dr Parker's arm, more to steady herself than in affection, Helen shook off her coat and hung it up.

She didn't go upstairs, though, but instead headed through to the back kitchen.

Dr Parker knew she was on her way to see the cook, Mrs Westley.

As he walked into the lounge with Miriam by his side, Dr Parker stole a sidelong glance at Helen's mother.

There was no doubting it, she really was the double of Bel.

**WANT TO KNOW
WHAT HAPPENS NEXT?**

Triumph of the
Shipyard Girls
Nancy Revell

ORDER YOUR COPY NOW

HAVE YOU READ

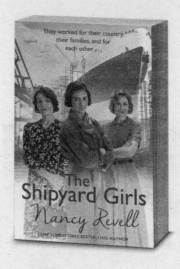

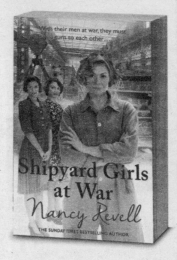

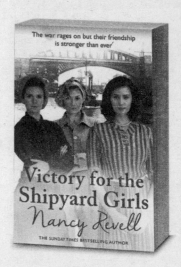

Join the Shipyard Girls

THEM ALL?

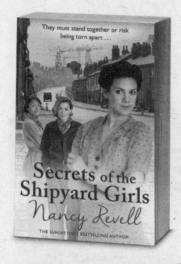

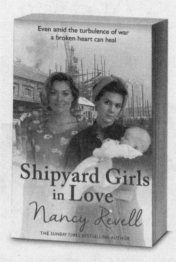

through love, life and war…